MAYA & NATASHA

MAYA
&
NATASHA

A NOVEL

Elyse Durham

MARINER BOOKS
New York Boston

This is a work of fiction. Names, characters, places, and incidents are products of the author's imagination or are used fictitiously and are not to be construed as real. Any resemblance to actual events, locales, organizations, or persons, living or dead, is entirely coincidental.

HarperCollins books may be purchased for educational, business, or sales promotional use. For information, please email the Special Markets Department at SPsales@harpercollins.com.

FIRST EDITION

Designed by Chloe Foster

Library of Congress Cataloging-in-Publication Data has been applied for.

ISBN 978-0-06-339361-5

24 25 26 27 28 LBC 5 4 3 2 1

To my love—

I made this for you.

PROLOGUE

LENINGRAD, AUGUST 1941

On a Friday, on a cheap street near the Neva, on an unmade bed in a colorless communal apartment, a very young woman rocked in pain. The midwife, sitting in the corner with her chin in her hand, waited to catch the babies—two babies, with the Germans knocking on the door of the city. The midwife had lived through the loss of two husbands and five children and had already witnessed two wars. She'd delivered babies in ditches and whorehouses and prisons. And yet she could not imagine a worse entry into motherhood than this particular day, in this particular room, and she pitied the little blond woman writhing on the bed, whose name was Elizaveta.

Elizaveta was a dancer, and she was no stranger to pain. Once, while performing with the Kirov Ballet, she'd sprained a ligament near her right ankle and still finished her solo, and Stalin himself gave her a standing ovation as she hobbled off the stage. But it seemed to the midwife that the closer Elizaveta got to bringing her children into the world, the more she faded from it. She bucked and strained as if she wanted to fly out of her body and leave everything—and everyone—behind. Her eyes darted from one wall to the other. She looked as though she'd lost her very soul somewhere in the room and it would be hers again, if she could only find it. Her faded blue nightgown, borrowed from a sympathetic neighbor down the hall when Elizaveta's belly swelled too much to wear her own, was too big and hung off one shoulder.

Just as the midwife commanded Elizaveta to push, a tank rumbled down the street and shook the bed. The men and women of Leningrad, who'd spent the summer digging ditches and building fortifications around the city, had been warned two days before to prepare to fight or flee. While Elizaveta labored, everyone else in the city was packing or preparing or running at full steam between the two. The air smelled of hot ash and panic.

And this is why no one congratulated Elizaveta when the last pangs came and her daughters were delivered into the midwife's bony hands. They were beautiful babies—good and strong, with loud, lusty cries, the kinds of babies who could weather anything. The midwife had seen enough bad births to know to be thankful for the good ones, but she had no well-wishes to offer. She glanced at the red-faced new mother and again felt pity for her, stuck with two babies, and alone, with an invasion breathing down their necks. She laid the babies in their mother's arms and tried to think of something suitable to say. But when the afterbirth was delivered and the midwife bent to cut the babies' cords, an old injury in her back began to twinge, and the sharpness of this sensation flattened her pity into annoyance. She muttered only that now the linens needed washing, and where was she supposed to find soap in a time like this?

Elizaveta's neighbors, who heard the entire birth through the thin walls of the communal apartment, weren't much better. They all shook their heads at Elizaveta's fate. To have one child in these times was a misfortune; to have two felt like negligence. The building supervisor, an old man in the apartment three doors down, had a soft spot in his heart for the little dancer. When he heard the babies' first cries, he went to cross himself in response, but a plane buzzed low overhead and his fingers froze over his collarbone and he dove under his bed in fear—and that was the closest thing Elizaveta got to a blessing that day.

The midwife, anxious for her own family and eager to get away from Elizaveta's hollow eyes, packed up her things in a hurry. Later, when she unpacked at home, she would realize that she'd left a sharp pair of scissors behind. The babies still lay where the midwife had placed them, rooting around for their first meal, and Elizaveta made no motion to help them. She stared straight ahead as if the birth had made her blind. The midwife stood to go, and just before she closed the door, Elizaveta gave her a look that curdled her stomach.

The midwife should have stayed longer. It wasn't good to leave new mothers alone; you never knew what they would do. She should have offered some comfort. But what comfort can be offered to a woman on the eve of war? The midwife knew no happy fate awaited this mother or her children, and she wanted to stay and help, but her own family waited at home. To give herself the strength to leave, she hardened her heart and said, "If only you'd kept out of trouble," and then turned and slammed the door.

Elizaveta was nineteen years old, and she had no family. Her parents, like so many, had been killed in the Year of '37, dragged off to the Gulag under false accusations of inciting insurrection; her grandparents were lost to stray gunfire during the Revolution. She was an only child, and now she was alone, with two children of her own.

The closest thing she had to siblings were her fellow dancers at the Kirov Ballet, and even these substitutes were absent. That morning, at the company's first class of the day, it had been announced that the entire company—dancers, seamstresses, orchestra, and all—would be evacuated to Molotov that evening, along with all the students and teachers at the Vaganova Ballet Academy, the Kirov's school of ballet. As Elizaveta's daughters cried in concert with the sirens outside, all of her fellow dancers stuffed the essentials of their lives into duffel bags and suitcases and prepared for the evacuation, along with all the government officials the state had deemed too important to die.

The Kirov was the pride of the Soviets, the premier ballet company in the world, and Elizaveta had once been its most promising dancer. While even talented ballerinas excel in a single specialty—some bodies are built for leaping, or for quick pirouettes, or for long, sinuous arabesques—Elizaveta, who had sacrificed her childhood at the Vaganova, seemed poised to take them all. The speed of her allegro was as breathtaking as the majesty of her adagio, both underlined by a magnetism that was impossible to define or ignore. She seduced entire audiences with a single glance.

But when she became pregnant, Elizaveta's body, which she'd known so well, became foreign to her. Her spins slowed, her attack softened, and her balance—thrown off by her stomach, which, in the eyes of the other dancers, grew much faster than a pregnant stomach should—ebbed away by the week. Her name appeared on the company's casting lists less and less and then disappeared altogether. During Elizaveta's fifth month, the company physician took her aside and warned her to stop attending classes—not because he thought she was in danger but because the ballet master, who preferred absolute uniformity in his dancers' appearances, instructed him to do so. "You don't want to hurt yourself," the physician said. "Or your child." Elizaveta said nothing in response, and she did not come to class again—and because of this, she did not hear the announcement that the company was being evacuated.

Katusha, Elizaveta's closest friend, realized this an hour before the train was supposed to leave for Molotov. She arrived at Elizaveta's door at four that afternoon. In one hand, she carried a suitcase containing everything she owned; with the other, she carried a basket of food, an assortment that took her all day to find in the few unshuttered shops across town.

She was too late. Katusha heard the babies crying, knocked hard, called Elizaveta's name and knocked harder. No voice came in reply. The building supervisor, who had gone out in search of some sort of present for the babies and came up empty, arrived at that moment and, hearing the babies' wail and seeing the alarm on Katusha's face, pulled his keys out of his pocket and hurried to the door without being asked.

The door swung open and rattled on its hinges. Katusha and the building manager rushed in and, seeing Elizaveta, stopped short. The little dancer, the one for whom Stalin applauded, the one for whom everyone had such hopes, the one who, until nine months ago, was poised to become the prima of the Kirov and perhaps all Russia, perhaps the entire world, lay with slit wrists on the bed, the sun streaming into her open eyes. Even in death, she was graceful: her arms were splayed out as if in a final port de bras, her hands open, her feet wide apart. She was naked, and her body bore both the marks of her pregnancy and the art to which she'd dedicated her life: her toes were gnarled and calloused, her limbs winnowed away to nothing but muscle and bone, and the great flap of her belly lay empty. In her first and only act of love as a mother, she had taken off her faded blue nightgown and wrapped her daughters in it. Her daughters, pink and wailing, lay between her feet on the bed.

If Katusha had come an hour earlier, if she had not spent the afternoon searching shop after shop for bread and sausage and sweets to tempt her friend's waning appetite, if the invasion had started a week later, if Hitler had not grown greedy for the wide reaches of Russian land and the ripe wheat fields of Ukraine, if Elizaveta's lover had not made false promises and then abandoned her, if the ballet master had not taken offense at the variations of the female form, Elizaveta might have lived. If she had lived, she would have been evacuated with her babies to a safe haven on the sea, and the babies might have grown up as ordinary sisters living ordinary lives.

But that is not the story that there is to tell.

The world turns by hands as selfless as Katusha's. The oldest of a family of seven, she'd nursed her family through illnesses that claimed several of her siblings and cared for an infant sister after her mother died in childbirth. She was a very practical person, one who knew when and how to put herself aside, to do what needed to be done.

But it wasn't a sense of duty that made Katusha step toward Elizaveta's cooling body. Oh, how she had longed to fold that body into her own, to kiss her hair, to give her the love and care she'd needed and deserved. Katusha had stood by for years and watched Elizaveta hung out to dry by a chain of thoughtless lovers, had listened to her weep over them, had consoled her however little she could. None of these men saw Elizaveta as Katusha did: the kind of woman you could spend a lifetime loving, the kind of woman worthy of devotion. The kind of woman whose love could move you to give everything away. Katusha had never told Elizaveta of her love, and now death had carried her too far away to hear.

But love is as strong as death. Katusha understood what she must do. She closed Elizaveta's eyes and took Elizaveta's daughters in her arms, and they became hers from that moment.

There was no time for a funeral. The first evacuation train was leaving at six, and there was no guarantee that the second would make it past the Germans. Katusha wrapped the infants in sheets from their mother's deathbed and left Elizaveta with the building manager, who promised to have the undertaker carry her away. In the end, he would bury her with his own hands, just a day before the blockade began in earnest, and three weeks before he died himself, the building's first victim of starvation.

Katusha made it to the train station just as the conductor gave the call to board. Several hundred people crowded the platform—dancers, set painters, musicians, teachers, propmen, choreographers, seamstresses, husbands, children, wives, along with several dozen government officials and their families. As they boarded the train, everyone told themselves that they were leaving only for a day or two, that this trip would be like every other trip they'd taken to the country. In truth, they would return three years later, after Leningrad had been shelled and starved to its very limits.

But the dancers did not yet know any of this, and they settled first in Molotov and then Tashkent, performing for bands of weary soldiers, and heard very little of what went on at the front. Every now and again there would be a letter telling them that another part of the Kirov had been destroyed by artillery fire. But for months, and then a year, there was silence, and only the knowledge that everyone they knew back home was suffering more than could be understood, that Leningrad was filled with things too horrific to be spoken. The Germans cut off all food supply to the city, in hopes of starving the entire city to death, and waited for it to fall.

Yet the city did not fall. The siege kept on, and the city population dwindled from two million to one million, and still, it did not fall. Shostakovich penned his hymn to Leningrad, and all the musicians of the Leningrad Radio Orchestra who had not starved were called to assemble. In August 1942, a year after the siege began, on the same day that Hitler had planned to have a victory banquet at the Leningrad Astoria, the orchestra—skeletons in baggy tuxedos—performed Shostakovich's symphony in the Grand Philharmonia. Loudspeakers, flown in by helicopter, broadcast the symphony out over the entire city, over the living and the dead, and over the Germans, who had been shelled that morning to ensure their silence, and who, hearing the symphony, began to despair of finding victory.

As the dancers waited for the war to end, they lived in dachas in Tashkent and did their best to keep up their strength. They shivered through classes in a drafty warehouse. Though far better fed than those left behind, they, too, struggled to find food. They performed *Swan Lake* in flimsy costumes that hung like rags from their bodies, for crowds of people in quilted hats and jackets who'd driven for hours to see them, and everyone dreamed of the day when they would return home and perform at the Kirov again.

And there, by the bright blue ribbon of the Tashkent Sea, Katusha raised her babies. The Kirov ballet master, who felt somewhat culpable for Elizaveta's death, gave Katusha a paid leave of absence from the company and fought for her to have a little room of her own in the settlement, while most of the dancers were packed six or seven to a bedroom. The accompanist, who missed her nieces and nephews back in Leningrad—all of whom, she would later discover, had died—borrowed a crib from someone in the village and placed it next to her piano in the rehearsal room so Katusha could still come to company class if she wanted, a kindness for which Katusha was very grateful. She named the babies Maya and Natasha.

The men and women of the company, in need of distraction both from the suffering back home and the austerity of their own lives, adopted Maya and Natasha as their own. Everyone wondered if they would grow up to be great dancers. How could they not, as Elizaveta's daughters? (Nobody knew who their father was, not even Katusha—though some had their theories—and this didn't seem to matter much one way or the other.) Between rehearsals, the dancers amused themselves by staging tiny races between Maya and Natasha and seeing who would toddle over to them first. As the girls grew, everyone began to notice differences between them—many differences, as if their existence was an exercise in opposites. Maya was shy, Natasha was outgoing. Maya had brown eyes, Natasha, blue. Maya was slow and contemplative, Natasha quick and impulsive. And the dancers loved both equally.

In 1944, word came that the siege had ended and the Kirov had been repaired, and the company boarded the train in June at the same station where they'd arrived three years prior. Everyone held their breath, prepared for the worst—after all, Moscow had once burned to the ground, and hadn't it risen again?—and wept when the train pulled into the station. There it was, the ancient city they had loved and left—pockmarked and shelled and scarred, but free, and theirs again.

In September, the company performed at the Kirov for the first time since the siege—Petipa's *Sleeping Beauty*—and when this performance was announced, so many people swarmed around the outside of the theater, eager for tickets, that the dancers barely made it inside for rehearsals. Many of the performers pitched in with last-minute repairs to the theater: prima ballerinas swirled around with mops instead of partners, and the men climbed high on rickety ladders and washed windows.

Katusha, who left the company and joined its costume shop in order to raise the girls, brought Maya and Natasha to opening night, though they were still too little to sit through an entire ballet. She took the twins by the hand and marched them up Glinka Street, past demolished houses whose original shapes she still remembered and past palaces reduced to rubble. Despite all the destruction, the city retained much of its beauty. The palace of Catherine the Great gleamed as brightly as it had when royals ascended its stairs. Nevsky Prospect stretched long and wide and proud as in the days of Gogol. And the Kirov Theatre was restored to its former glory.

Ah, the Kirov, the Kirov, the richest and grandest venue in Russia, every surface covered with gilding and scrollwork and crests. An enormous chandelier hung from the ceiling, big enough to squash four men flat if it fell. Four tiers, dotted with candelabras, encircled the stage like diamond bracelets on a woman's wrist. Katusha winced when she saw the great stage. Elizaveta had wanted nothing more from life than to dance on that stage until she died.

Perhaps Elizaveta haunted it still. Perhaps she watched Katusha and Maya and Natasha take their seats in the very top ring, just against the lip of the balcony. Maya, who had become a quiet and pensive little girl, started when the orchestra began to play. The swell of music held her in awe, and she listened with rapt attention, so pleased that it frightened her. Natasha, eager as ever, sat with one hand gripping the balcony, leaning toward the stage as if she wanted to fly into it. Though they were too little to have such thoughts, both of them would look back on that evening as the moment when they found what they wanted from this life.

And who wouldn't want it, when being a professional dancer meant you were a cut above, meant that you were given better food and warmer clothing, maybe even a more beautiful apartment—that when you or your family were sick, you went to the special hospital for Party members, the one with private rooms, instead of the filthy public hospitals that packed fifty patients to a ward? And maybe, as long as you kept your wits about you and didn't go out of your way to be stupid, you wouldn't be arrested, and you would be spared the random interrogations and knocking on doors and cartings-away in the dead of night that had haunted everybody for as long as they could remember.

Years later, when the girls grew and Katusha told them the story of their rescue, she did not cast herself as the hero; she told them that the state itself had saved them, that it had whisked them away to shelter with the other artists and dancers and Party officials and their families. Katusha's words sank into their marrow. Like a mother, the state had nurtured and cared for them since the day of their birth, and someday, it would be their duty to give back in kind.

And this, in those postwar days, when the United States was emerging as an enemy, was what the state wanted for a gift: it wanted ballerinas—ballerinas it could send out all over the world as proof of the superiority of its people. Male dancers were impressive—they communicated the muscle and the determination of the Soviet people, strong calves and arms a fleshly shorthand for artillery and armaments—but ballerinas even more so. The ballerina, with her sweetness and her secret strength, could convey all that had to be said to the West and the rest of the world. You could fall in love with her and not know you were falling in love with Russia; you could appreciate the graceful reach of her port de bras and not know that you were appreciating the distillation of a thousand years of history into a single sweep of the arms. You could admire the sculptured elegance of her body as a work of art, not considering what it really was—the work of an athlete who had trained for her entire life in Soviet gyms, supported by the Soviet state, fed on Soviet crops, and dressed in fabrics made by Soviet factories. A male dancer could impress, but a ballerina could dance out and disarm the world, could leave the audience asking what sort of philosophy had produced something so beautiful.

That first night at the Kirov, Maya and Natasha were too young to understand all this. They fussed after the first intermission and fell asleep during the prince and princess's pas de deux, which even Katusha felt dragged on. But when the curtain first rose from the stage and their eyes were still dazzled by the grandeur of the dancers, by the precise placement of their feet and hands, by their jeweled tiaras and painted eyes, both girls were so awed that they reached for each other's hands in the dark.

PART I

CHAPTER ONE

LENINGRAD, SEPTEMBER 1958

Maya and Natasha sat in the back of a cramped red trolleybus, trying not to look at their watches. They were seventeen years old, and they were very, very late—which, as usual, was Natasha's fault.

It was the first day of their last year at the Vaganova Ballet Academy. Half an hour before, they'd left Katusha's apartment with plenty of time to catch the 4:30 trolleybus, which would have put them at the Vaganova early enough to claim their favorite room in the dormitory, which would have settled the nerves that had cost Maya sleep since June. But Natasha turned back at the last minute to repack her suitcase for the third time. Though the bus trip was only twenty minutes long, Natasha was convinced it would permanently wrinkle everything she owned.

The bus was crowded, and the two girls shared a seat, both to save room and because closeness was their usual attitude. When they were little, they'd pushed their beds close enough together that they could sleep holding hands. Katusha had reminded them that morning to stick together and care for each other during this last year of school, but her words were unnecessary. For Maya and Natasha, being close was less a preference and more a biological necessity, as if each held some source of energy the other couldn't live without.

"Pinky," Natasha said. "His name was Pinky."

"It was not!" Maya said. "I never would have fallen in love with someone named Pinky."

"You were six!"

"That didn't make me an idiot."

They were constructing an oral history of Maya's unrequited loves, a list so long that its beginning was apocryphal. Neither of them could remember the name of Maya's first love, a freckled boy from their first year at the Vaganova. He'd dropped out after a semester, at which point Maya fell for him. (Maya specialized in falling for unattainable people.)

"What is it with you and names that start with *P*?" Natasha said. "Pinky, Petrov, Pyotr . . ."

Maya shushed her. "Don't be so loud!" Pyotr, their quietest and slenderest classmate, was her latest obsession. But he lived in his own little world, one that did not include Maya, and her infatuation served no purpose except to give Natasha something to rib her about.

Every time the trolleybus accelerated, it pressed Maya into the hard vinyl seat. On an ordinary day, the bus's mechanical rocking calmed and soothed her, but today all she could think about was keeping her hair in place. Though they wouldn't have any classes until tomorrow, she'd twisted her hair into its usual position—a high bun that must, no matter what, remain aloft and intact—in an effort to feel more like herself. That is, more like the self she longed to be. That is, more like a dancer.

Natasha put her suitcase on her lap and peeked inside as if it carried kittens instead of clothes.

"I will never understand," Maya said, leaning forward so as to spare her bun from smooshing, "how you can care so much about such ugly clothes."

Despite Khrushchev's mania for material goods—"Every American has a toaster and refrigerator," he'd complained in a recent speech, "and why not us?"—everyone still wore the same shapeless, lifeless garments they had under Stalin, the same stiff shirts and itchy wool trousers, the same dresses of various unflattering shapes and prints. For all the attempts at modernization, fashion had not improved, and no amount of repacking would have kept Natasha's wardrobe from looking shabby.

"It's important to take good care of our things," Natasha said. She handled her worn cardigans like they were precious imported goods purchased from Passage, the grand department store on Nevsky Prospect that they sometimes glanced into but never patronized. "Because someday, we'll have nice things. Maybe even someday soon." She was convinced that when they joined the Kirov company next year—for her, this was always a "when," not an "if"—they'd suddenly have every luxury they could imagine, and that, more than anything, was what Natasha wanted.

Maya and Natasha did not look much alike. None of the other passengers, tied up in their own troubles, had even realized the two slender girls were sisters, let alone twins. Natasha had her mother's face—the full, round cheeks and lips, the blue eyes that were as quick to clear as to cloud over. Maya's long face and slightly beaky nose looked nothing like her mother's or sister's. But both girls had the same dark hair, the same clear skin, the same wide, eager smile. They looked like cousins—both pretty, both young, but only distantly related.

Their life together was a dense construction of secrets—like Pinky and Pyotr—and shared preferences—summer over spring, pirozhki over pelmeni—and inside jokes, like their penchant for referring to themselves in the plural as "Matasha" after an elderly teacher jumbled up their names. Chief among their pastimes was a nameless, wordless game, the sort of game you could only play with someone you'd known before words were necessary. The game consisted of putting your foot on top of the other person's foot without their noticing and pinning their toes to the ground. The key was to do it sneakily, when the other person's attention was elsewhere. They'd been playing it for so long that they did it without thinking.

Natasha was easily distracted, which meant Maya almost always won this game. She'd snuck her foot on top of Natasha's nearly as soon as they sat down and left it there, a sensation so familiar it was comforting to them both. But when the bus rolled to its next stop, Natasha gasped. "Look!" she said. "Pyotr's getting on!"

"Where?" Maya leaned toward the window. "I don't see him."

Natasha freed her toes from underneath her sister's and clamped down on Maya's foot. "My mistake," she said, shaking her head. "Maybe it was actually Pinky."

"You cheated," Maya said. "And his name wasn't Pinky."

"It was too. And sometimes you have to cheat to win." Natasha pointed out the window again, this time with genuine enthusiasm. "Look!"

The bus had stopped beside the Kirov Theatre. Though Maya and Natasha had seen the Kirov in every light and every season, they'd never seen it quite like this—a majestic layer cake in aquamarine and white, the early autumn sun shining on it just so.

"Soon, we'll dance there every day," Natasha said, "Just like Elizaveta."

"Like Elizaveta," Maya repeated, the corner of her mouth tugging down.

They'd always referred to their mother by her first name. They picked this habit up from Katusha, who loved to tell them of their mother's grace, her immense talent, her dream of becoming one of the Kirov's brightest stars. When they were old enough to ask, she'd told them Elizaveta had died in childbirth, which, in Katusha's mind, was less a falsehood and more a necessary slimming down of the truth. Being motherless was bad enough—why burden the girls with the facts of their existence?

But their mother's name carried a new significance now. Last New Year's Eve, the truth came out. Food and alcohol being much more plentiful than they were during the war, everyone overindulged themselves out of relief and rejoicing and a bit of fear that this new prosperity wouldn't last. Katusha, who had a weakness for sweet spirits, emptied half a bottle of plum brandy and, growing weepy, told the girls that their mother had killed herself. "When the Kirov doctor sent her home, he took away the only thing she loved," Katusha said. "She belonged at the Kirov. She was too beautiful to die." And then she praised Elizaveta's beauty, describing every feature in surprising detail—her eyes, blue and calm, like the Neva; her small and slender hands; her eyebrows' startled arch—and fell asleep.

Maya and Natasha tucked a blanket around their godmother and went to bed. Through some unspoken pact—perhaps a sense of honor toward Katusha, or horror at their mother's suicide—they never mentioned Elizaveta's story again, to Katusha or each other. But it curdled inside of them. Natasha, lying awake that night, decided Elizaveta's thwarted desire had been her undoing. Surely life was bearable if you got what you wanted. Maya, however, could invent no comforting aphorisms for herself. It was one thing for your birth to cause your mother's death (weren't mothers always dying of childbirth in fairy tales?) and another for your mother to look at you, newly born, and choose death instead. Maya wondered what had been wanting in her.

As the bus pulled away from the Kirov, Natasha thought of the glory awaiting her inside, as it had for Elizaveta. Sailors lingered outside the theater with bouquets of red carnations in hopes of catching their favorite dancers. (For Natasha, one of the chief draws of being a ballerina was being admired.) But seeing the Kirov made Maya think of the spring recital last June, which was the last time she'd been inside and the first time she'd realized she and her sister might have different futures.

The spring recital was the Vaganova Ballet Academy's annual showcase, an evening when Leningrad's cultural elite packed the Kirov to hunt for future stars. Maya and Natasha, along with several of their classmates, danced an excerpt from *The Nutcracker* in identical pink tutus and with identical choreography: two piqué turns and an arabesque, something even the children at the Vaganova could do with ease. Natasha executed hers flawlessly, but just as Maya rose en pointe to make her first turn, the shank in her pointe shoe snapped, and she wobbled and fell to the floor.

That the shank had snapped at that particular moment was an extraordinarily bad stroke of luck. That it had snapped at all was, regrettably, a little bit Maya's fault: she'd known it needed to be replaced for weeks. Though she could have gone to the Vaganova's cavernous shoe storeroom and asked for another pair, she knew that her arches looked better in these worn-out shoes, so she wore them anyway. She was lucky, her teachers told her afterward, that she hadn't been hurt.

But Maya didn't think of herself as lucky. She would have been lucky if the shank hadn't snapped at all, or if it had snapped after she finished her solo. To fall onstage felt like a terrible omen. Maya wondered if the ghosts who haunted the Kirov—Petipa, perhaps, or Anna Pavlova—had decided that she was not destined to be a dancer.

Maya knew better than to believe in ghosts: to believe in ghosts, or saints, or souls, was to be backward, to cling to the foolish superstitions that had once stupefied the masses. But some Russians still prayed for the souls of those they loved; some Russians sought help from the saints though forbidden from acknowledging their existence—and Maya, every now and again, thought she felt her mother's presence, always unexpected, and often unwelcome, as if her mother wanted something from her that she could not give. Maybe Elizaveta's ghost lingered in the Kirov too. Maybe she'd reached out and snapped the shank in Maya's shoe, jealous that Maya might live the life that she had not.

In the split second after Maya fell—even now, the thought of that cold stage floor on her back made her shudder—she looked up and saw Natasha, who, ever the performer, continued dancing with the others, did not offer her a hand up, did not break her smile, did not even look down at her. She danced as if nothing had happened. She danced as though Maya did not exist.

This was the first time Maya noticed something known to every teacher at the Vaganova: Natasha, unlike her sister, knew how to seduce an audience. The teachers, who had long stopped looking for any sign of Elizaveta's talents in Maya, often had to remind themselves that Natasha was not their old friend reborn.

Though this was a frequent subject of conversation in the Vaganova teachers' lounge, Alexei, the school director, forbade the teachers to speak of it in front of the girls. "What would be the point?" Alexei would say. "Natasha has a presence: you can't teach it; you can't create it. You either have it or you don't, and Maya doesn't. She'll join the corps at the Kirov when she graduates, dance until she ages out, and then perhaps she'll join Katusha in the costume shop."

In reality, Maya was capable of much more than her teachers or even she was aware: she was just as strong as her sister, but, out of an unconscious desire to avoid anything that could jeopardize her most precious relationship, Maya held herself back. That, and every now and again she got distracted by her fellow dancers during class. She'd become mesmerized by the formations of bodies around her and fall a step behind.

But Maya had no idea that she did either of these things: sometimes she thought that her timidity was hereditary, as if the muse that blessed her and Natasha possessed a finite number of gifts to distribute, and her sister's excessive grace left her with a deficit. Other times, Maya blamed herself for her middling talent. Her teachers encouraged this view: they told her that she thought too hard about every little movement she made instead of letting go. This advice only worsened Maya's self-consciousness, and after the disaster at the gala, she was kept awake all that summer by thoughts of her deficiencies, imagined or real.

These thoughts weren't the only thing that kept Maya awake. Early that summer, Natasha had fallen in love with Ivan, a fellow member of the senior class. Ivan had watched Natasha dance since they were children, but as he stood in the wings at the spring concert, sweaty from his own variation, he found himself transfixed. He fell in love with her not because she was beautiful—though that was certainly the first thing that got his attention, and who wouldn't fall in love with Natasha, sixteen, with jewels in her hair?—but because she, out of all the other dancers crowding the stage, looked like she was enjoying herself the most. Ivan had suffered a great loss as a child, and he was not sure life could be enjoyed. But perhaps life would be easier alongside someone who appeared to enjoy it—and this was why, the moment the curtain fell, Ivan began to woo Natasha, whose vanity made her an easy conquest. For the rest of the summer, they were each other's shadows.

Katusha tried her best to fill the hole Natasha left behind—playing checkers with Maya, asking about her hopes for the school year, taking long walks with her by the Neva River—but she was a poor substitute, and Maya made no secret of this, and soon Katusha left her to her own devices. Maya sat by the window, missing the nearness of her sister's body, picking at the paint on the windowsill and waiting for Natasha to come home. To her, being without Natasha was like missing a lung—who could live without it?

Now, squeezed in beside Natasha on the cramped little trolleybus, Maya was able to pretend that her sister was only hers. She leaned her head on Natasha's shoulder and pressed her foot onto hers and watched the city whirl by. As long as she had Natasha, as long as the two of them kept close, they'd have love enough to survive anything.

The Vaganova Ballet Academy sat on a narrow street with a park on one end and the Fontanka River just beyond. It was a quiet street in a quiet neighborhood, stuffed with theaters and somnolent cafés that livened up only in the evenings, like nocturnal dollhouses. The school was long and narrow and yellow and faced a building of its exact make, a twin, creating a canyon effect that could feel, depending on the mood of the passerby, confining or comforting, a prison or cocoon.

Early that morning, the school acquired a steady hum, like a beehive taken up by a new colony after long lying dormant. The worker bees, left alone all summer and weary of the quiet, applied themselves to their tasks with renewed vigor. The administrators piled fresh paperwork onto their desks, admiring the tidiness of their stacks, lamenting streaks and blots in their copying. The teachers compared their student rosters and envied and consoled one another for their lots. The academic tutors freshened up their chalkboards and then stood by the window, smoking one last cigarette before the stampede arrived. The physical therapist rolled up all her clean towels and recounted her supplies, fretting over how little of everything she had. The laundress put fresh sheets on every mattress and put extra sheets on mattresses that were stained or yellowed. And the janitor, armed with his ancient push broom, swept through all of the classrooms one last time, even though he'd dusted all of them the day before and knew they were spotless.

Maya and Natasha arrived at the school so late that everyone was already at dinner. But fate appeared to smile on them: their favorite room in the dormitory was unclaimed. It was unclaimed because it was, in fact, a converted broom closet, but that had never bothered Maya and Natasha. Though they lived with Katusha in the summers, they rarely had time to visit her during the school year. This little room was the place they thought of as home, a place to sleep between the classes and rehearsals that kept them busy six days a week, a place to rest on the seventh. They'd lived in it since they were eight years old.

Home would not, to the outside observer, have appeared remarkable, or even suitable for two growing dancers. The floorboards were creaky and splintery, but dancers' feet are used to hardships, and loose floorboards proved a boon for sneaking contraband past the dorm mothers—cigarettes, perfume, spare condoms (which everyone called by their official name, Rubber Product #2). The room was very small: between the two beds, the dresser, and the girls themselves, there was barely room to move around. Neither girl minded this: until this year, all either of them needed was a world just big enough for themselves.

Maya breathed a little easier now that they were here. She loved this little room—loved the way it had sheltered and nurtured them since they were too small to stretch out to the foot of the bed. This was the place where they'd taught themselves to sew ribbons onto their pointe shoes, Natasha bloodying her fingertips in the process. It was the place where they'd lain awake the night before every single recital and performance, too excited to sleep. It was the place where they'd hidden tiny bottles of vodka last spring, when they'd passed their examinations and been promoted to their final year. All Maya wanted was to spend the night here with Natasha, pretending like everything wasn't about to change.

The girls tossed their worn suitcases on their beds, snapped them open, and began their yearly ritual: placing their few prized possessions on their respective sides of the room. Natasha: a couple dog-eared photos of Ivanka Plisetskaya, the flame-haired dancer she adored; a cake of pink soap a friend smuggled back from Paris; a tattered little bear of unknown origin. Maya: a picture of Katusha at the lake; a leaf-green hair ribbon Natasha bought her last year; a tarnished silver watch that the ballet master had given her on her eleventh birthday. The girls arranged their possessions in corner shelves above their beds, shrines to the things they loved.

This was the last time they would perform this ritual. Maya rubbed a smudge from the watch face and returned it to its resting place. Where would this watch rest a year from now? Maya closed her eyes and tried to imagine a hotel room someplace far away and wonderful, maybe Paris, with ruffly drapes on the window. She tried to imagine her body, not her now-body, but her year-from-now-body, more skillful and confident and strong. She would come home to this room in Paris late at night, after performances, with Natasha. They would be older, and happier, and—and—

"My God," Natasha said. "I'm so tired of this place."

Complaining about the Vaganova was one of Natasha's favorite pastimes. Every week, she'd find a new reason to be miserable. The soup was too hot. The classrooms, too cold. The teachers were backward or imbeciles. Everyone who was friends with Natasha had resigned themselves to hearing these refrains over and over. It was a little flaw you overlooked in order to love her, like a missing tooth or a mole. Usually, she made it a month or two into the school year before the complaining started—but on their first day? This was new.

Maya sat on her bed, which squeaked in its same old way as if in greeting, and started rerolling the little balls of tights that had freed themselves on the way over. "You'll get used to it," she said. "You always do."

She slid her foot out toward her sister's and pounced on it again, hoping to make Natasha smile, but Natasha pulled it away and sat heavily on her own bed, drawing her knees up to her chin. "I always hate it," she said. "The only good thing about being here is Ivan."

A pair of Maya's tights, which she'd just succeeded in rolling, uncoiled in her palm. "Thanks a lot," she said. She balled up the tights and beaned them toward Natasha, hoping to elicit a yelp or at least a satisfying thump, but the tights ricocheted soundlessly off Natasha's forehead and landed limp on the floor. "You sure know how to make a girl feel important."

Natasha flung the unspooled tights back at her sister. "You know I didn't mean you," she said. "Just wait—when Pyotr finally notices you, you'll feel the same way. All you'll want to do is be with him, and you'll forget I even exist."

Maya smiled at her sister's exaggeration. She could never forget Natasha—how could your right hand forget your left?—and she opened her mouth to say as much, but someone knocked on their door.

Natasha jumped up and opened the door, and there was Ivan. He picked Natasha up and spun her around, and she shrieked and laughed and made a show of trying to escape from his arms, though both Ivan and Maya knew she didn't want to escape them.

Maya turned back to her tights and rolled them tighter than was necessary. Ivan was always kind to her (and, truth be told, she even found him a little handsome), but every time he came around, she had to resist a physical impulse to shove him away—or, when she was feeling nettled, which these days was more often than not, to punch him in the face. (In her defense, Ivan did have the kinds of features that are so sculpted and perfect they're nearly offensive in their handsomeness; in other words, his face was eminently punchable.) Their room suddenly felt much too small, with him standing in it.

Ivan put Natasha down. "Want to go out for a bit?"

"God, yes," Natasha said. "Anywhere." She put on her shoes and threaded her arm through his and that was that. They left without saying goodbye, without even acknowledging that Maya existed.

Maya yanked open her dresser drawer and shoved her tights inside, where they promptly unrolled again. "See you," she said, to no one.

Maya and Natasha never set an alarm clock when they were at school. They didn't need to. At 6 a.m., footfalls thumped through the hallways. By 7 a.m., it was a stampede. One hundred girls of various ages had to fit into an oblong bathroom, with showers at the end and two rows of sinks in the middle. Fearing shoves and sharp elbows, the littlest girls woke up early and rushed in first. Maya got up at the first stampede, as was her habit, and started stretching. Natasha rolled out of bed at the last possible minute, and then only because her sister poked her in the small of her back and yanked off her blanket. Every day, Maya swore that she was never going to do this for her sister again, but she always did it anyway. Maya kept Natasha on task; Natasha kept Maya in good spirits. Both of them knew they could not function without the other. Both of them knew that, as Katusha had reminded them, they needed to take care of each other.

The two girls put on the same style of uniforms they'd worn since they were tiny—gray leotards, matching skirts, pink tights, with a thin sweater on top—and packed bags with the usual necessities—soft shoes, pointe shoes, spare needles and ribbons and thread, along with the accoutrements of studying—before joining the others in the cafeteria. Breakfast was paltry—the lunch ladies, as always, had been instructed not to overfeed the dancers—but they were used to it, and nobody wanted a stomach full of porridge on the first day of classes. There was far too much at stake, because that morning the ballet master was going to give his annual address. Ordinarily, this would have been just another boring assembly, but on this day, both Maya and Natasha anticipated it keenly. Today, the ballet master would announce the details of the spring gala, which would be their last student recital before—they hoped—moving on to the Kirov.

The entire senior class would audition for the Kirov in the spring. The number of students accepted depended on several mysterious and unpredictable factors: the quality of the graduating class, the company budget, how many Kirov dancers had injured themselves out of careers, what the Kirov ballet master had had for breakfast. Sometimes twelve students got in. Sometimes two.

Of course, the Kirov wasn't the only ballet company in the country, and anyone who didn't get in usually ended up at the Bolshoi or the state ballet in Tbilisi or one of the smaller regional companies that dotted the countryside. But the Kirov was the best, and it was what everyone wanted. Since they were children, they'd all been packed into buses and driven to Kirov performances year after year; in Leningrad—and in Russia as a whole—to be an elite dancer was to dance for the Kirov. The company was rumored to be going abroad in a year or two, which only made it more desirable—everyone wanted to see London and Paris and possibly even America, an unheard-of adventure.

Eleven students were graduating that year, and all eleven of them sat together at one long table in the cafeteria, but this was more out of a desire to avoid all the younger students than some comradely urge toward togetherness. (Everybody knew that one of the greatest privileges of making it this far was being able to look down on everyone who hadn't.)

As children, these students had all been friends. But every year, as more and more of their peers lost interest, failed examinations, or suffered injuries, the group grew smaller and smaller, and there was less room left for good will among them. The older they got, the more was at stake. They saw what had happened to their older siblings and cousins, the ones who didn't have the protection and provision that the ballet offered, the joyless lives they lived: the lucky ones wasting away at desks packed into musty rooms, and the unlucky, who crossed the government (either in accusation or reality) and ended up in prison—or worse. Each student had sworn to themselves that they, and not someone else at the table, would get into the Kirov.

And so, they'd splintered into factions, much smaller arrangements that provided the social sustenance everyone needed—but with the unspoken understanding that these, too, could someday crumble. There were Ivan and Sophrony, meaty young men, the lifters, and Anya, Kira, and Olga, the daughters of Party officials, pampered as spoiled cats and never seen without each other. Vasili and Vasilia played the role of the tragic young lovers whose constant reunifications and partings gave the entire school something to talk about. Sinewy Olaf arrived at the school years after everyone else, long after all the friendships and circles had crystallized. With curly hair and dark eyes, he was the handsomest boy in class, but in social situations his eagerness to take part gave him a perpetual hunch, as if leaning in to whisper confidences. He always hovered on the outside of groups like a gnat, annoying everyone with some new gossip in an attempt to endear himself. Pyotr, who had an elegantly pointed nose, moved half a second more slowly than everyone else, as though suspended in water. Maya and Natasha kept to themselves—or at least, they had, until Ivan upended everything.

All the seniors chewed in silence. Many of them had slept late over the summer and weren't used to the early hour, nor the din of the silverware clattering around, nor the shrill and eager voices of the younger students. Everyone's nerves were wound so tight that when Sophrony reached across the table and accidentally jostled Anya's teacup, she smacked him. "You idiot! Keep those meat-mittens to yourself, if you can help it." Nobody knew it, not even Olga or Kira, but she had a hangover—anxious about the start of school, she'd drunk herself to sleep the night before, and the clatter of the teacup bothered her much more than the loss of tea.

Sophrony's jaw clenched. "Bitch," he muttered, wiping the spilt tea with his hands, which didn't seem so large to him.

Olaf leaned toward Anya. "Why are you so irritable today?" He stood and walked over to her and sniffed suspiciously. "Are you *drunk*?"

"No," Anya said, swatting at him. "I'm just tired. And you'd make anybody irritable."

"Stop it," Ivan said. He leaned in with a napkin and helped Sophrony mop up the tea. "Let's try to get along, children." He spoke as if he were teasing, but he wasn't. His mother had disappeared when he was eight years old—she and his father had always argued, and one day she'd left Ivan at the ballet school and never returned. She left a note that said she'd run away to Germany, which cursed Ivan's father with ceaseless interrogations and Ivan with a deep need to keep the peace. "When we're all in the company, we're going to have to all be friends, you see?"

"We're not all going to be in the company," Olaf said, taking his seat again. He squashed a lemon wedge with his fist, startling Maya, who'd been staring quite shamelessly at Pyotr and his perfect nose. Had Olaf's hunch not marred his beauty, Maya would have found him attractive too, and this compounded her embarrassment.

Natasha sighed. "Says who, Olaf?"

"Karinska told me," Olaf said. He folded his arms again and surveyed his audience with obvious delight, basking in their attention.

"The ballet master has some sort of bad news to tell us today. She wouldn't tell me what. If I had to guess"—he put his hand on his chest for emphasis, signaling his worthy expertise—"I'd say they're only accepting ten students this year."

Nobody said anything. They had good reason not to believe him. Most of his rumors weren't true—or, at least, the full truth was much less interesting than what he spread around. Last year, after Natasha declared pantomime her favorite class of all—she loved to tell a story with her hands—Olaf told the entire school that Natasha planned to run away and become a movie star in America.

But this rumor was too tempting to be ignored. Everyone knew that Olaf spent a lot of time with Karinska, their partnering teacher, after class. And if any of the teachers would know the status of the company's ranks, it was Karinska—she was friends with everybody there, and she coached several of their principal dancers in roles she'd originated in her mythical youth.

Ivan took a loud gulp of tea as if to interrupt the silence. He wiped his mouth with the back of his hand. "What if they were accepting eleven? Wouldn't that be wonderful?" he said, pouring much too much milk on his porridge. "Then we could all stay together." He winked at Maya, which had the opposite of his intended effect. "I think the future's bright for everybody."

"What do you mean?" Olaf said. "Why did you wink at Maya when you said that?"

Ivan ignored this question, but Maya blushed at it anyway. She knew why Ivan had winked: he felt sorry for her because he assumed she'd be the odd one out.

Anya folded her arms and frowned at Olaf. She was the queen of her own little faction, and she didn't like the idea of a teacher favoring someone as insignificant as Olaf over her. "Even if that was true, why would Karinska have told *you*?"

Olaf shrugged. "What can I say? She likes me best." She didn't. The truth was that he was a very fragile boy, and Karinska knew it—to correct him in front of the others would crush him, so she reserved her biggest corrections for after everyone else had gone, and when Olaf shed a tear or two over his insufficiencies, Karinska slipped him a rumor to sweeten the bitter medicine. "I have a way with older women."

Pyotr threw a napkin at him. "Pig."

"Perhaps," Olaf said, removing the napkin from his head and folding it delicately into quarters, "but a knowledgeable pig."

After breakfast, Natasha disentangled herself from Ivan and hurried to her sister's side as they pushed their way down the crowded hall to the auditorium. "Ignore that idiot," she said. She took her sister's hand and squeezed it. "He doesn't know what he's talking about."

Maya took her heavy bag from her shoulder and let it fall to her feet. "Maybe. But you know my chances aren't good if they only take ten of us."

"Oh, that's nonsense, and you know it," Natasha said. "I'm so tired of hearing you talk like this. You're hardly the worst one in class."

This was true—Olga and Kira usually trailed last—but Maya was too deep in a tailspin to pull out. "I'm not the best, either," she said. "And what if I don't get in? What if I don't get in anywhere? What's going to be left for me?" She imagined herself working with Katusha in her basement costume shop, ruining her eyes over needlework done by the light of a single bulb.

Natasha slung an arm around Maya and squeezed her shoulders. "Don't fret, little goose. I still say that adagio of yours will take you far if you let it."

Maya stopped in a doorway to wipe her eyes, Natasha still by her side. Pyotr sauntered along in his usual obliviousness. Olaf walked by and then stopped when he saw Maya crying. "What is it?" he said, looking both eager and alarmed. "What did you hear?"

"Mind your own business," Natasha said.

"Is it about the Kirov? Did they tell you something already?" Olaf leaned in. To Maya, his hunch made him look like a vulture, one who fed on other people's troubles. "Are you not getting in? What did you hear?"

"For fuck's sake," Maya snapped, "leave me alone."

Olaf stepped back, surprised to have been shouted at by Maya, of all people. "I'm only trying to help." His mouth twitched, and he looked so sad that Maya almost felt bad for shouting. But then he said, "If you tell me what you heard, I can ask Karinska if it's true—"

"Goodbye, Olaf," Natasha said, pushing him toward the hallway with a finger. Olaf frowned and slunk away.

Anya, Olga, and Kira swept past, casting glares at them as they went. Natasha leaned close to her sister. "Look," she whispered, "Anya and Olga have gotten too fat. And if Kira tries to partner somebody with boobs like those, she'll knock him out cold with her first pirouette."

Maya smiled despite herself. This was how it always went: no matter how frightened or discouraged she got, Natasha always knew what to say to restore her confidence.

Triumphant, Natasha kissed her sister's head. She needed the comfort of reassuring her sister as much as her sister needed reassuring. She scooped up Maya's arm in hers. "Come on," she said. "Let's go sit behind Karinska and see if her teeth fall out when she starts snoring."

The school auditorium was packed when they arrived. As always, there weren't enough seats for everyone, and the littlest students crowded the floor in front of the stage. The room was hot, and everyone fanned themselves and chattered loudly as they waited for Alexei, the school director, to take the stage.

Alexei broke from the huddle of teachers gathered toward the front. He was very tall and thin, with streaks of gray at his temples, evidence of the difficulty of his job. Every year, those streaks grew a little wider. Everyone hushed as he ascended the short flight of steps up to the stage. He was the kind of man who never had to ask for anyone's respect, because it was just given to him: everyone who knew him admired him, and everyone who admired him felt grateful for having such a person to admire.

He looked out at them all, these children under his care. Like anyone for whom teaching is a vocation, he was happy to see them return—at least, most of them. He saw Olaf whispering in another student's ear and shook his head, knowing that Olaf would soon hover outside his office, pestering his secretary for new gossip. Alexei cleared his throat and even Olaf sat at attention.

He began by telling them the same things he always told them, the things that Nikolai, Minister of Culture, urged him to say. As dancers, but also as Russians, they must always comport themselves with dignity and integrity, etc. Alexei reminded them to tend their bodies with discipline and care, warning against the excesses of smoking and drinking and sweets. "Sweets," he said, looking down straight at Anya and Olga, "ruin dancers." Anya, not easily cowed despite her throbbing head, kept her chin raised proudly, but Olga, filled with shame, tried to shrink down into herself, which made the chocolate wrapper in her jacket pocket crinkle, which made her want to die. Kira thanked God that her mother hadn't let her eat anything but watermelon all summer.

The ballet master went on to tell them that this year's spring gala, to be performed in June, would be *Stone Flower*, a ballet that had been a hit in Moscow the previous year. Some students applauded at this; a handful of others groaned. Not everyone appreciated the story ballets about Russian mythology, with their folk-dance interludes. "Great," Maya muttered. "I'll probably get cast as the witch, and they'll make me dress up like a lizard."

"What?" Olaf whispered, turning around. "What did you say?" Maya ignored him, and when Olaf repeated his question, Natasha kicked the back of his seat.

Having given his speech, Alexei dismissed the students and exhaled. He had successfully concealed one piece of distressing news he'd learned from the Minister of Culture: the Kirov, whose dancers had done an unusually good job of avoiding career-ending injuries this year, would likely only be accepting a handful of students for their corps de ballet in the spring, which meant that most of the graduating class would have to go elsewhere. Alexei would allow fate to winnow the students; a few of them always dropped out before the end of the year, and not everyone would be a match for the Kirov's high expectations anyway.

But an additional unpleasantness remained, one he could not keep a secret. Alexei descended the stairs, his eyes sweeping the crowd in search of the two people he least wanted to see today. His heart sank when he found them. "Maya," he called. "Natasha. Please come here."

Alexei descended from the stage and leaned against it, folding his hands. He sighed. These two young women, whom he'd watched and guarded for so many years, weren't children anymore, and soon they would grow out of his protection. He knew exactly what this news would do to them, knew all too well, so he steeled himself against it, against them, and this was why his voice hardened when he told them that now, thanks to a new law, only one member of any family would be allowed abroad at a time. "The government—" He hesitated. "The government has found it is safest for everyone if other family members remain at home while one of them travels. And it's ridiculous, of course," he said, twisting his hands without realizing it, "the very idea that either of you would run away while abroad—

I can't imagine either of you doing something this foolish—but still, the Kirov has informed me that, as a result of this new law, and the tours they anticipate taking abroad in the years to come, they will not be hiring any groups of siblings until further notice." Nothing was more embarrassing to Khrushchev than a celebrity defection. In the last four years alone, they had lost two chess players, a handful of soccer stars, and even a couple KGB agents to the West.

Alexei, though relieved he'd delivered his news, braced himself for its aftermath. The girls were wilting visibly in front of him. Natasha glanced anxiously at Maya, whose eyes trailed to the floor. Alexei opened his mouth to say, "I'm sorry," but what came out was, "I'm late," and he slipped away from them and into the hallway, cursing the Minister of Culture for ever having given him this job.

CHAPTER TWO

Every pupil at the Vaganova Ballet Academy lived under the scrutiny of light—flickering green fluorescence in the hallways, sharp sunbeams through glass-paneled classroom doors, and sunlight, pure and yellow, through the half-dome windows lining the walls. In the classroom, light searched out every muscle, every limb, every damning lump of fat. Everywhere you went, the light followed. And this is what everyone worked so hard for, to be followed by a spotlight on the stage.

But Maya wanted nothing now except to shrink into darkness. After Alexei left the auditorium, Natasha tried her best to encourage her. "Your destiny is up to you," she said, rubbing her sister's arm as if the problem was poor circulation. "Not Alexei. Not all those men at the Kremlin. Don't let any other person decide the course of your life." This was Natasha's credo, and she felt proud of herself for articulating it, but to Maya, they were just words—like snowflakes on a spring afternoon, melting as soon as they'd fallen, altering nothing.

A hinge creaked. Olaf lurked in the doorway, looking guilty. He'd been eavesdropping, as he was wont to do, and Natasha hurried over to shoo him away. "Why is he always in the middle of everything?"

she grumbled when she'd returned. Maya didn't respond, and Natasha understood that there was nothing more to say. She took her sister by the hand and led her to their first class of the day.

All of the other students stretched at the barre in their usual ways. Anya, whose head throbbed, rolled her head from one clavicle to the other, trying to ignore her tendons' crackled warnings. Olga pulled her shoulder blades in and out and watched herself in the mirror under the pretense of checking her form, but really to see whether the weight she'd gained over the summer was noticeable, which it was. Kira rolled her left foot over a small rubber ball she kept in her practice bag, easing a knot out of her arch. Natasha swooped her right arm up and overhead to warm up her stiff back. Only Maya stood still, her practice sweater still buttoned up to her throat even though her underarms were damp.

When their teacher, a long-necked, heron-like woman named Madame Sofia, entered the room and nodded to the accompanist at the piano in the corner, Maya's body readied itself for the morning barre as if acting independently of her: left hand on the barre, shoulders back, head high, hips and feet splayed open. She did the same things she'd done since she was short enough to reach the half-height barre at her hip—the same pliés, tendus, dégagés, on the right side, then the left. Unlike Natasha, who was notorious for futzing through these exercises and saving her brightest self for the center floor, Maya always pleased her teachers at the barre. Its orderliness steadied her; her mind, which was as prone to worrying as her sister's was to wandering, found rest in predictability. To her, repetition was not drudgery, but a dozen opportunities for perfecting oneself, all strung together in a row. They were faithful to it, like monastics to a rule of prayer. They knew the particular ecstasy of being bodies in motion, the same way a musician understands why the word *symphony* means "agreement." It was like their bodies had all heard this music and agreed this was the only way one could move in response.

But all this sounds too exalted. As Madame Sofia guided her students through the barre, their thoughts were anything but noble: Anya was absorbed in her headache, Vasilia daydreamed about Vasili's muscled thighs, and Kira tried very hard not to fart. Even for Maya, the barre withheld its usual satisfaction. A heaviness filled her limbs, and the lump that had emerged in her throat at Alexei's words stayed there and seemed to grow. She wished she could swallow it, swallow her sorrow and absorb herself in this movement she loved more than anything.

Madame Sofia clapped her hands, and they stepped from the barre to the center of the room to begin their familiar adagio exercises. Maya took her usual place in the back, standing behind her sister. Even the accompanist, who'd been playing at the Vaganova for decades, knew what steps the girls were doing without looking up from her keys. For most of her life, Maya had understood every step that she took in the classroom as a step toward the Kirov stage, a step toward a life lived beneath spotlights. Now each movement seemed to take her closer to a bitter end.

Maya never performed as effortlessly as Natasha, even in the classroom, but the adagio, solemn and slow, was when she felt her best. To dance slowly required stamina and strength and deep inhalations that decelerated Maya's thoughts. Her eyes rested on Natasha's bare back, as they often did in class. She knew the placement of Natasha's moles as if they were a constellation, knew the exact contours of her shoulder blades and spine. Maya felt soothed by the expansion of her ribs and the slow extension of her limbs. She relished taking up space. She lifted her right leg and set the tip of her foot into its perfect little nook above her knee, and felt proud of the exactness of this movement. "Perhaps," she thought, balanced in stillness, arms reaching overhead, "it isn't over for me yet."

But then, whether through the diversion of her attention or some other weakness, when it was time to balance on her other leg, Maya lost her footing and stumbled into Natasha's shoulder blades. Natasha yelped, someone gasped, the accompanist stopped playing, and everyone stared at Maya. These stares—some pitying, some wrathful, some annoyed (Natasha's was all three at once)—revealed two new truths to Maya: she would not be accepted to the Kirov, and she would not be able to withstand the humiliation of seeing out the year at the Vaganova. For the rest of the class, Maya tried to think of when and how to quit.

The senior dancers' days were long: they went from morning workshop to partnering class, to folk dance, and then, after lunch, plunged into the dullness of all the things normal people their age had to study—history, literature, Russian. After dinner, despite their exhaustion, the students had yet another task to complete: their dreaded weekly Komsomol meeting, mandatory for the upper ranks of students. Years ago, when Khrushchev came to power and the entire country, for a moment, had exhaled, Alexei tried to get his students out of Komsomol—they are too busy, he'd pleaded with the Minister of Culture, they need time to rehearse and to rest, not to sit in a room with a hundred teenagers and hear lectures about how to serve their country. In response, the Minister of Culture stamped his cigar into his ashtray and leaned over his desk. "You teach them how to dance," he'd said. "We will teach them *why* they dance. Unless"—he picked up the cigar stub between two thick fingers and pinched it flat—"you'd rather not teach them anything at all?"

Alexei, being a prudent man who liked his house and his wife and his everyday comforts, never broached the subject again, which was why, on this bitter September day in 1958, Maya and Natasha exchanged one uniform for another, took off their leotards and put on gray wool skirt suits with jackets and shirts that must, under all circumstances and in all temperatures, be buttoned up to their throats, and they walked the three blocks to the public high school auditorium.

They were five minutes late. Maya, who feared retribution like a little child, hurried in front of her sister with long, anxious strides. "If we get in trouble, it's going to be your fault!" she hissed over her shoulder. Though she hated Komsomol, she was eager to make a good impression today. She had not decided when or how to leave the Vaganova, but her mind was made up. She would make a new life someplace else, someplace in this unfamiliar world outside the school. Even now, a hundred students her age were filling up an auditorium at the Komsomol meeting: few of them had ever hoped to dance, yet all of them had futures, maybe even enviable ones, maybe even adventurous ones. The meeting would be a preview of her future life.

Natasha fiddled with her collar and didn't look up. It was indeed her fault they were late: just as they'd headed for the door, she'd insisted on swapping out her official Komsomol blouse for one of her own, an ancient ivory thing of Katusha's. Though well-worn, the blouse had something of the memory of elegance, and it was the one article of clothing she owned that she liked. She'd recently mended a tear around the collar, which she tucked into the jacket to hide the stitches.

"Who cares if we're late?" Natasha said. "They're just going to say the same things they always say: 'Comrades, remember you exist as part of a mighty whole. Consider, comrades, that your actions affect not just your own life, but the lives of your fellow citizens.'" She recited all this in a deep mannish voice. "We've been hearing the same thing since we were in Young Pioneers. At least that was fun." This childhood indoctrination had been more to Natasha's taste: it consisted mostly of exuberant songs of peace and brotherhood and summer camps with bonfires.

Maya snorted. "The only thing you liked about Young Pioneers were the red neckerchiefs."

Natasha smiled, both at her sister's shrewdness and the memory of the smart red neckerchiefs. Satisfied that her collar was tucked out of sight, she finally looked up and saw panic in her sister's stride and, with a twinge of guilt, quickened her pace to meet her. "Honestly, what would it even matter if we never went again?" she said, trying to make light of their lateness.

A bus rattled by and interrupted their conversation, which was just as well, because neither girl knew what would happen if they stopped going to Komsomol. The tight-bunned matrons who ran the meetings could be cruel—every student knew the apocryphal story of the pig-faced boy who'd eaten an apple too loudly: one of the matrons slapped the apple right out of his hand and made him stand outside in the snow with no coat and no shoes for the rest of the class. "If you insist on eating like a pig," she said, "you will live like a pig!" He lost three toes to the cold—or so the story went. Nobody knew if it was true, and even if it was, nobody knew if the matrons would still act like this, now that Stalin was dead and Russia had been made new again—or, at least, Khrushchev claimed that it had.

Maya and Natasha reached the high school and slipped inside the auditorium—fortunately, the matrons' heads were turned—and found the Vaganova dancers in their usual row in the back. No matter what month it was, the auditorium was always too hot. At the end of a day of jumps and sweat and then a couple hours of wasting their minds on books, the last thing any of them wanted was to sit in this dusty hall and be lectured on the virtues of the Soviet Man. But they had no choice, and every week they sat in the same row, and Sophrony fell asleep, and somebody had to elbow him to keep him from snoring. Maya and Natasha nabbed the last two seats by the aisle. Natasha sat by Ivan, who looked relieved to see her.

Natasha hated Komsomol more than anyone—the dryness of the lecturers, the wasplike drone of the voices going on and on about oneness and unity and the vacuity of Western culture. She hated the coarseness of the uniform jacket and how she looked in it. "I might as well be wearing doormats," she thought, frowning at her stiff and bulky sleeves.

Even Maya, who'd walked in full of hope for the meeting, wilted as they took their seats. All the other students stretched out in rows beneath them looked so *ordinary*—all those severe parts and buns and braids exposed more dandruff than should ever be seen. Nobody looked like they were on an adventure, and Maya began to imagine dreary futures for them. Could she, who until today had hoped to spend her life on the Kirov stage, be reduced to one of them, trapped at a desk or in a factory?

Maya's resolve weakened even more when a snub-nosed man in long coveralls took the podium and began to tell them about his work in the coal mines, what a pleasure it was to toil away for his country. He spent several minutes describing in detail the assemblage of various types of drills. "So this is what my life is going to be like," Maya thought. It was so dull and so tedious that she started doubting her plan to quit school, but she didn't know what to do instead. The outside world was joyless and bleak; her own world had rejected her, and to dance anywhere but the Kirov would be a humiliation. If only there was some way she could improve. If only someone would take pity on her and offer to help. Natasha heard her sister sniffling and took her hand, as if she'd read her thoughts.

The miner continued on. "My greatest honor," he wheezed, "is to provide heat for everyone, warmth even to the sick and the old, the widows, the orphans—" He coughed for so long that the Komsomol captain, a severe-looking young woman sitting at a table beside him, offered him a glass of water, but the miner waved her off. "Imagine," he said, taking off his round glasses and wiping his eyes with an oily-looking handkerchief, "being without father or mother in this world."

"Imagine being a Maya or Natasha in this world," Anya whispered to Olga—too quietly to be heard up front, but too loudly to be intended just for Olga's ears.

Natasha sat straight up. She was immune to Anya's insults, but she worried that Maya, in her injured mood, would hear them and be hurt.

The miner was compelled, for reasons unknown but likely because he'd forgotten what he was supposed to be talking about, to keep going on about poor orphans. "Nobody to come home to in the winters—"

"No blankets," Olga whispered back to Anya, "only a Katusha to keep you warm—"

Maya stirred. Natasha leaned over and glared at the whisperers. Olaf saw her from down the row and craned his head in their direction. He raised his eyebrows at Natasha. "What?" he mouthed. Ivan, who always felt anxious at Komsomol, put a hand on Natasha's thigh, and she leaned back into her seat.

Despite having forgotten where he was going with his oration, the miner noticed a stir in the back of the room and, owing to the weakness of his glasses—he hadn't had new ones in ten years—assumed he'd struck a chord with the students and continued on with even more conviction. "With no hope for the future except the labor of your hands—"

Anya was undeterred. Her receding headache left her with a surplus of energy that could only find its outlet in unnecessary meanness. "And a footfall so heavy that only elephants will let you dance for them—"

"The fatherless—"

"The talentless—"

"—orphans."

"Mayas."

Natasha was about to take off her shoe and fling it straight at Anya's head when Ivan handed Maya a handkerchief, which she accepted gratefully. The kindness of this gesture diverted Natasha's wrath to compassion. She would do her sister much more good by being useful instead of vengeful. "Come on," she said, standing, and she took Maya by her wrist and pulled her from her seat. "Let's go."

Maya resisted. "We can't just leave!" she whispered. "We'll get in trouble!" Maya thought of the poor pig-faced boy with his missing toes. Her own toes curled in fear.

"We can go," Natasha said. "They won't even notice. Come on."

By now, the miner was ending his soporific tale with a reminder of Mother Russia, that she is mother of us all, always, that none of us are orphans as long as we stay within the warm embrace of our motherland—but Maya and Natasha were already outside in the cold.

A child who lives without parents in the city must discover many things to keep herself alive. Maya and Natasha were lucky: they never had to worry about having a place to sleep or food to eat or somewhere to get out of the rain. The school gave them all this and much more. It was, itself, nearly a parent to them.

Over the years, Maya and Natasha had found everything else they needed in the surrounding neighborhood. They'd learned to run along the river, knew which dips and clefts in the sidewalk to avoid thanks to many skinned knees. When they grew older, they found shade beneath the trees at the little round park at the end of the road, and they met there when they wanted to watch the passersby and laugh at the little families and couples strolling by, because laughing at them made their lives less enviable. And then, when they'd grown old enough to want to shave their legs and covet the makeup that had recently begun appearing in storefronts—that is, when they'd grown up enough to want to be *more* grown-up—they discovered the teahouse.

It was not a fashionable teahouse, but if Maya and Natasha were aware of this, it did not prevent them from growing especially attached to it. Once, before the Revolution, it had been a grand establishment—the sort of place where you'd see someone dressed like the tsarina and you wouldn't bat an eye, because *you* were dressed like the tsarina too—with elaborately carved chairs and imported wallpaper and pastoral etchings hung in gilt frames. On account of its grandeur, it was an ideal target for ascetic Bolsheviks, and its chandeliers and gilded frames only lasted a day into the Revolution before being tossed into smoldering woodpiles. The wallpaper, being difficult to remove, had been left alone, and it survived quite nicely until three decades later, when the Germans arrived in Leningrad. After that long year had passed, and the original owner of the teahouse was long dead of starvation, his grandson rolled up his own sleeves, stripped the smoke-stained wallpaper, and painted the walls dun gray. The chairs had somehow survived all this with carved arms unscathed—perhaps the Germans, long known for the skill of their woodcarvers, left them alone out of respect for their craftsmanship—but their cushions reeked of smoke, and the grandson put them outside on the patio, and this is where they stayed, and this is where, until frost forced them into the shabby interior, Maya and Natasha always sat and drank their tea.

Maya and Natasha were the only ones sitting outside: all the other patrons—working men and elderly women, mostly—had sought warmth either inside the teahouse or at home. It wasn't even five in the afternoon, but the sun had already begun its swift descent into the horizon, casting long shadows over everything. Maya found the growing gloom appropriate. Nothing that she saw or heard or smelled or felt seemed to have any life in it anymore. Natasha noticed the shadows, but she thought only that they meant winter was coming, and she would have to wear her old blue coat, which she hated, for the third year in a row.

Maya sighed, and Natasha put sartorial concerns aside and remembered what had brought them there, and she felt cold, even through her thick uniform. She'd spent many an afternoon cheering Maya up at this very table—over unrequited loves, injuries, cranky teachers. But this was different. This was a loss too big to be glossed over with a few glib words and some sweets. Natasha wished that someone else could sit with her sister in her grief—grieving people put her on edge, as if tragedy was catching. Natasha shivered and put her hands around her teacup, which was just warm enough to leave her fingers wanting more.

Maya sat perfectly still, gazing into her empty cup. Maybe she was trying to read her fate from the silt at the bottom, like the haggard old fortune teller who sometimes roamed this street. As well as she knew her sister, Natasha sometimes thought Maya was enigmatic on purpose. If something troubled Maya, she would never come right out and say it. Natasha would intuit its existence from Maya's weary tone, the stoop of her shoulders, a brusque word, and then she'd have to pull it out of Maya, bit by bit, like a bucket drawn up from a well.

Of course, Natasha was horrified by the ballet master's news—she'd always hoped they would get into the company together—but what could be done? She was just the better dancer. Pretending that she wasn't wouldn't help. Still, she felt sorry for Maya. To have your life's ambition thwarted—well, look where Elizaveta ended up.

Maya looked up sharply. "Stop it."

"Stop what?"

"Pitying me." She poured herself more tea and squeezed half a lemon into it and stirred and stirred—more, it seemed, for the clank of spoon against porcelain than for the tea's benefit.

"I'm not pitying you," Natasha lied, unbuttoning her jacket and admiring her blouse. "I'm trying to think of a solution."

Maya stopped stirring, and she looked up so quickly that Natasha, who knew well the limits of what could be done, shrank in her seat. "What kind of solution?"

"I don't know," Natasha stammered, regretting her words. "Maybe you could try out for a smaller company—someplace like . . . Perm."

This, unfortunately, was the wrong thing to say, and it showed on Maya's face at once. "Perm?" Maya repeated in disbelief. "*Perm*? Of all the places you could have said—"

"Why does it matter where you go, as long as you can dance? Because that's what you want, isn't it?" Natasha said, sounding like a harried parent. "You want someplace to go when we graduate. You want—"

"You don't know anything about what I want," Maya said. She threw her spoon onto the table and it bounced and landed in Natasha's teacup, splattering tea onto Natasha's beloved blouse. It was not clear whether Maya had done this on purpose.

Natasha shrieked, trying to rub the tea from her blouse but only making the stain more permanent. "Don't get mad at me, you goat," Natasha said, dabbing frantically. "None of this is my fault."

Maya stared at the table, and Natasha saw tears gathering in her sister's eyes again. "Are you saying it's *my* fault?"

Natasha should have contradicted her sister. She should have reassured her, should have tried to give her hope for a salvageable future. But Natasha was tired, and she was frightened by the appearance of a problem that she couldn't fix for Maya, and she was angry that Maya had ruined her blouse. So instead of offering the comfort that Maya needed and deserved, Natasha simply shrugged.

Maya wiped her eyes with the sleeve of her woolen jacket, which made them itch. "You don't care anyway," she said. "All you care about is fucking Ivan."

Maya knew this wasn't true, and Natasha knew this wasn't true, but when the people closest to us make us angry, the truth rarely comes into it. "At least I have somebody to fuck," Natasha muttered, and Maya, having had her fill of misery for the day, stood up and left without a word.

Later that night, while trying to fall asleep, Natasha would wince at the memory of her words and tell herself that she hadn't meant to mutter them so loudly, that she certainly hadn't meant to take her sister's self-consciousness about her virginity and use it as an instrument of pain, but in truth, that was exactly what she'd meant to do. She'd wanted to push her away.

Once, when the girls were very young, their entire class was taught to waltz. Boys being scarce, as always, the teacher paired Maya and Natasha together. "*You* lead," she said, pulling Natasha's shoulders back. "*You* follow," she instructed Maya. At first, Natasha took pride in her appointment—as pleased to be chosen as she was that Maya wasn't—but after a few minutes, she got tired of leading. The music swelled up in Natasha and she wanted to break free and spin out on her own, but Maya, frightened of making a mistake, clung to her with sweaty hands. They were bound together, an inevitable push and pull. Wherever Natasha moved, Maya followed.

Now it was always going to be like this—Natasha backing away,

Maya hounding after. Her success meant Maya's failure, and Maya's permanent dependence on her. She was never going to be free.

A few minutes later, Ivan came down the lane and took the seat that Maya had vacated. He loosened the top button of his jacket—the boys' uniforms were equally uncomfortable—and poured tea into an empty water glass. "You really shouldn't do that, you know," he said, taking a drink and wincing at its heat.

"Do what?" Natasha wasn't really listening. She was still upset, and she tried to calm herself by watching passersby. Were any of them angry with their sisters too?

"Walk out like that," Ivan said. He downed the rest of the glass and went to pour himself another. The samovar hissed out its last two swallows. "It's not good to draw their attention. You should be more respectful."

"Maya was miserable," Natasha said. "She needed to get away from those monsters." Two children, wearing jackets so small the sleeves ended at their elbows, darted out from beside their mother and returned when she scolded them. A man with sloped shoulders lumbered by, carrying a heavy-looking sack. Everyone looked weary today.

"There are much worse monsters than Anya," Ivan said. "And much worse places to be unhappy. You need to be more careful."

A dog sniffed a garbage can, then peed on it. Natasha turned to Ivan, annoyed. "Why are you lecturing me?"

"I'm just trying to look out for you," he said. "You draw a lot of attention to yourself. You can't afford to be reckless."

Natasha's mouth tightened. "Don't tell me what to do." Ivan had a habit of giving her advice as if he were a worldly old man and she his willing pupil. She was getting tired of it.

A group of young people came around the corner, making a ruckus as they went. Natasha's breath caught in her throat. All eight or nine of them wore clothes she'd only seen in American movies—big, full skirts, pinstriped suits, pants so tight they looked painful, all in glowing shades of green and pink and yellow and blue. There were more men than women, but the women's presence felt large: their skirts brushed up against their friends, they laughed loud and often, and their lips were painted a red so bright that the whole street seemed drab in comparison. The men wore their hair plastered over their heads in crested waves.

Here they came, walking down the street and singing loudly—and, judging by the laughter, badly—in English. She'd heard of them before—some alleys in the city were wallpapered with posters decrying their vices, which, if the posters were to be believed, included treachery, vanity, and avarice—but she'd never seen them, the ones called the stilyagi, who bought Western clothes on the black market and spent their days dancing to bootlegged music. Natasha looked up and down the street and felt grateful that it was deserted, that there was nobody here who would get them in trouble. What sort of trouble, Natasha wasn't exactly sure, but she was glad that she and Ivan were their only observers. She kept her eyes on them as they moved farther down the road. She felt like no one could hurt them as long as she kept them in her gaze. A yellow-haired boy in a rakish orange suit glanced over at Natasha and continued on his way, his long legs taking great strides down the sidewalk.

"They look ridiculous," Ivan said, grimacing—the tea had steeped too long and grown bitter. When Natasha didn't respond, he added anxiously, "Don't you think?" He reached for her hand.

But Natasha didn't hear him, and her hands stayed in her lap. She watched the stilyagi moving farther and farther away, and the boy with yellow hair looked back at her again from over his shoulder.

The wind whipped at Maya as she strode down the street. She wrapped her wool jacket closer around herself, and then let it fly open again. What did it matter if she were cold? Soon, she would have neither a future nor a past that did her any good, a past that built toward nothing. Natasha couldn't have suggested a worse place than Perm—the middle of nowhere, the last resort. It was not a place where promising dancers went. To dance in Perm was as good as going into exile. Natasha had no faith in her.

Maya passed a couple burrowed into each other on a bench and thought of Natasha and Ivan back at the teahouse. She'd spotted Ivan heading that way, and now they were probably burrowing too, Ivan's heavy hands patting her sister down who knows where. The thought of this on top of everything else made Maya so angry that she scowled at the next pedestrian who accidentally met her eyes, a middle-aged woman in a yellow kerchief who jumped when Maya spat at her feet as she passed. Though Maya did not know it yet, just as she did not yet know her own strength as a dancer, she had a capacity for doing very nasty things when she was angry.

Maya shuddered and hurried down the street, vivid, unwelcome imaginings of her sister and Ivan flashing through her mind. Everything had been better before he'd arrived. Before, she and her sister had been she and her sister—if someone spoke of either of them, they often spoke of both of them, "Maya and Natasha." But soon there would be only Natasha and Ivan.

She tried to outrun her dark thoughts. Her bag flapped angrily against her side, and she knew she'd have a bruise on her hip by the time she got home. Natasha wouldn't have a bruise on her hip. Ivan carried her bag around for her from class to class—it was the surest signal that somebody at the Vaganova was in love. The only part of her body in danger of bruising was her neck, with darling Ivan to nibble on it. Maya shuddered again.

She reached the school at last, throwing open the heavy double doors with the air of a returning monarch, which she instantly regretted. It was the students' free hour, and the foyer was crowded with dancers hurrying to some pastime or other; people glanced at her as they passed. "They all know," Maya thought. Surely Olaf had heard Alexei's terrible news. Surely Olaf had told everyone everything. Surely Olaf was the most irritating boy to ever haunt these halls. Thanks to him, not even Maya's misery could be private.

Maya stood in the foyer and debated where to go. She wanted to be alone—she wanted nothing of the pity being cast at her like pennies into a fountain. Going back to her room would be too sad and too lonely without Natasha—and she and Ivan would probably show up there, too.

Several deep voices echoed down the hallway—Sophrony and Ivan, possibly, or maybe even Pyotr, who was the person Maya most did not want to see. Who would fall in love with an outcast? Maya adjusted her bag on her shoulder and put her head down and headed downstairs to the library, where she hoped she'd find some peace.

The library was one of the few places in the school that was almost always empty. Every now and again, a student would venture into it to study a score in preparation for a solo, or to do research for a paper or exam. But on this first day of school, Maya was the first student to open that creaky door. The librarian, whose job left her ample time for her true passion of playing cards, looked up when she heard the creak and then pretended she was alone again.

This suited Maya. She went over to the row of old stuffed chairs and plopped into one, displacing a cloud of dust as she sat. She would bury herself in homework. Their literature teacher, whose mustache was so generous that even the other teachers were intimidated by it, had warned them to get ahead in the reading assignments if they could. "*War and Peace* is like a boulder," he'd said. "Climb to its heights, and you'll see the whole world. Let it get on top of you, and you'll be crushed." They were supposed to have read ten chapters by the end of the month, when they would go see the Americans' new movie version starring Audrey Hepburn, which was being shown as part of a cultural exchange between the two nations. (When the teacher had explained this to them, nobody asked what Russian films the Americans were getting in exchange—but whatever they were, surely they couldn't compete with Miss Hepburn.)

The book lay heavy in Maya's lap. She wondered how any book this long could possibly be interesting. She turned to a page at random, hoping to find something to prove herself wrong.

> Prince Andrei, with a radiant, rapturous face, renewed towards life, stopped before Pierre and, not noticing his sad face, smiled at him with the egoism of happiness.
>
> "Well, dear heart," he said, "I wanted to tell you yesterday, and I've come to tell you today. I've never experienced anything like it. I'm in love, my friend."
>
> Pierre suddenly sighed deeply, and dropped his heavy body onto the sofa beside Prince Andrei. "With Natasha Rostov, is it?" he said.
>
> "Yes, yes, who else?"

Maya snapped the book shut, disgusted. Her sister was preferred everywhere, even by rapturous princes in books. She sighed and rested her forehead on her palm and did not look up ten minutes later when the door creaked open for the second time that day.

Someone tapped her on the shoulder. Maya started.

"Sorry," the tapper said in a gentle voice. "I thought you'd fallen asleep."

Maya was so sleepy, and the voice was so sonorous and warm, that she thought it was Pyotr, come to console her. After all, sometimes people admire the underdog.

But when Maya turned around, she saw not Pyotr, but Olaf, looking embarrassed. "I wasn't asleep," Maya said, rubbing one eye. "I was just resting for a minute." She sighed. Of all the students in the Vaganova, of all the people to join her in the deserted library, why did it have to be Olaf? Why not one of the girls, or some little child whose fate did not include eclipsing her? Or anyone who hadn't spent the entire afternoon spreading her tale of woe?

"Oh," Olaf said. "Sorry." He turned to go, and then lingered, as if unsure of what was expected of him in this situation. He looked around the room. "Pretty quiet down here," he said, and he started chewing his lower lip, which for some reason softened Maya's ire. Olaf was much taller than he'd been last summer, and Maya had to crane her neck to look up at him.

"Yes," Maya said. She heard the librarian snoring around the corner. "Just how I like it."

"Me too," Olaf said. "Sometimes I can't stand being upstairs. All the noise in the cafeteria makes my head want to explode." He looked around again, and his gaze stopped at the chair next to Maya's. "Is it okay if I sit there?" he said, gesturing to the chair. "The light, you know, it's . . . it's better here. For reading."

Maya shrugged. "Why not?" Surely the day couldn't get any worse than it already had. Olaf nodded his thanks and sat down beside her. He was the kind of person who spent so much time and energy trying to be liked by everyone that no one liked him at all. Now, alone with him in the library, it occurred to Maya for the first time that Olaf was a person and not just an irritation.

She opened her book again—better to look like she was doing something instead of just staring—and watched him for a minute.

Olaf reached down into his bag and pulled out a magazine, and Maya noticed how long and slender his fingers were, the tiny black hairs dotting his wrist. "He would almost be charming," she thought, "if he wasn't always trying so hard."

Maya didn't want to seem too interested in what he was doing, so she turned her eyes back to her book, but they fell back on that same line—"With Natasha?"—and she snapped the book shut again.

"No good?" Olaf said. "You know, that's bad news for me—I haven't even started it yet."

He was trying to be friendly, and this was so strange to Maya—that he would choose today of all days to be chummy—that she couldn't keep quiet. "Why did you do it?" It was not a promising beginning—she wanted to project wrathfulness and strength of character, but her voice was already wavering.

Olaf looked confused. "Why did I do what?"

"Why did you have to go and tell everybody about what Alexei told us? It's already humiliating enough—I don't need everybody's pity to make it worse." The tears she'd been holding back all day were threatening to fall at last.

"I didn't," Olaf stammered. "I didn't tell anyone."

Maya glared at him. "All right, all right," he said, hands up. "I told Karinska, but I didn't tell any of the other students, I swear." He seemed sincere, and this calmed her.

"You didn't come down here to try to get more sorry details out of me?"

"Not at all," Olaf said. "I came down here because I saw you rush off and I thought you might want some company." For once, he spoke truthfully. He'd admired Maya ever since he arrived at the Vaganova, and even thought she was prettier than her sister, though he didn't have the courage to tell her this. His posture softened. "I know how it feels, you know—to be alone." He stared at his shoes, and Maya, knowing how little he was liked, changed the subject.

"What are you reading?" she said.

Olaf looked up guiltily, and she thought she'd caught him reading one of those black market, flesh-stuffed magazines that sometimes blew down the sidewalk like vulgar tumbleweeds. Without her wanting to, Maya's eyes darted over its pages and saw nothing but text and, in one corner, a photo of a balding man in profile, gazing haughtily toward her.

Olaf looked over one shoulder and then the other. "Promise you won't tell anybody?"

Maya nodded. A boy was about to confide in her. This day was so full of new things that it was making her dizzy.

Olaf shifted toward her. His shoulder grazed hers. "It's from Paris," Olaf whispered. "My uncle brought it back for me. It's about dancers in America."

"Oh," Maya said, deflated. The magazine was about ballet, and as such it couldn't have been more off-putting to her if it had been made of toenails. She didn't want any more reminders of her failures today. She opened her book to page one and started reading in earnest.

Olaf, thanks to that sharpened intuition that often gifts itself to the lonely, understood Maya's embarrassment. He closed the magazine. "Listen," he said. "I'm going to tell you something."

Maya put down her book. She steeled herself for another lecture, one thing she couldn't take any more of today. She turned to tell him as much, but his eyes were so unexpectedly kind that she kept quiet.

"I think the company is making a mistake."

Maya squinted. "What?"

"By not taking the two of you."

It was too much, him saying this out loud. He'd confirmed her worst fear: that everyone assumed Maya would be the odd one out. She turned away. "Natasha's just better," she said softly, hoping he would contradict her. "I can't compete with her."

"You can't, or you won't?"

Maya looked back at Olaf, who spoke like he'd been thinking about this for some time. "Natasha's the flashier dancer, sure," he said, holding out a palm as if weighing her in it, "but you've got talent too. I've seen it. When you did that pas de deux with Sophrony last spring, I couldn't stop watching you. You've got some kind of fire in you—a quiet fire, like a coal that burns slowly, you know? To me, that's a stronger sort of fire than a flash. That kind of fire can last through anything."

Maya was stunned. All her life, she'd been compared with her sister, but never in a way that favored her instead.

Olaf tapped his finger on his chin, as if puzzling through something. "You know," he said, "I bet all you'd need to best her would be a little extra training. You know, to boost your confidence. Karinska's going to pair all of us up in a couple weeks—maybe your partner could train extra with you."

"Maybe," Maya said. Perhaps if she was paired with Pyotr, he'd have no choice but to fall in love with her. Perhaps then everyone would see how remarkable she really was. Perhaps she'd even realize this for herself.

Olaf, judging by Maya's rapt face that her attention had wandered elsewhere, settled back into his chair and opened the magazine again. "Besides," he said, "everybody knows that you'd never defect. If I was in charge, I'd be worried about Natasha going to the West. People like that are too talented for their own good, you know? It makes them do reckless things. Like Balanchine."

"Who?" Maya felt stung a little at this high praise of her sister.

"Balanchine." Olaf looked over his shoulder again and then leaned in close, pointing to the man in profile in the magazine. "He was a Soviet like us, this genius choreographer. Really, really good. And what did he do with all that talent? He left, and now he's giving it all to the Americans. Those lucky bastards."

Maya looked at the picture again. Balanchine. She rolled the syllables around in her mouth—*Bal-an-chine.* The name sounded like an incantation.

The grandfather clock behind them struck eight. "Christ, really?" Olaf looked at the clock. "We'd better go. Want to walk together?" He stood and extended a hand to Maya to help her up.

"Sure." Maya caught his hand and, distracted by this experience—the sensation of a boy's warm fingers on hers—let her bag slip toward the floor.

Olaf caught it. "Let me," he said, and he looped Maya's bag over his shoulder and started for the door, looking very pleased with himself.

When a boy carried a girl's practice bag at the Vaganova, it had certain implications. Maybe Olaf was aware of this. Maybe not—after all, he hadn't been here very long. Maya considered chasing after him and insisting on carrying it herself. She didn't want to give him the wrong impression—or, worse, give other people the wrong impression about her.

But it was late, and she was tired and felt a little more hopeful than she had when she'd descended the creaky basement stairs, and so, under the grandfather clock's watchful eye, Maya decided two things: she would stay at the Vaganova, and she would let Olaf carry her bag, if only for tonight.

CHAPTER THREE

Being seventeen is an exercise in cruelty. Those unfortunate enough to be so know a little of the world, a little less of love, and less still of themselves, but not enough of any of these to avoid heartache.

The senior dancers at the Vaganova found themselves in an unusually privileged, if also confining, situation. Though their parents, at seventeen, had fought in the war (or scavenged to avoid starvation), and their grandparents, at seventeen, helped stage a revolution (or fled from it), these eleven dancers had no responsibilities beyond the Vaganova's yellow walls, and because of this, those walls contained the whole world. As the school year crept along, and the first hints of frost curled around the windows, everything within the dancers' little world loomed large. Slights became insults; hurts became blood feuds; trifling disagreements that would have been laughed about the year before became life-altering fissures.

But the senior dancers busied themselves the same as always: they went to class; they leapt and spun and were commended; they stumbled and were scolded; they sat in history class and pinched their legs to try to stay awake; they stole naps in the library between classes; they snuck away to the storage closets and made love to each other, or pressed an ear to the door and listened to lovemaking and wished they were the ones inside; they ate too much; they ate too little; they sewed ribbons onto new pairs of pointe shoes and seared the ends with matches; they lifted rusty dumbbells in the gymnasium; they fell into bed and slept so hard it made them, somehow, more tired.

For Natasha, a little light had gone out of everything. Ever since the disaster at the teahouse, Maya had avoided her—as much as was possible, given that they shared a room. She never spoke to Natasha except in monosyllabic answers to questions, sat at the opposite end of the cafeteria table, and stayed out of their room until the last possible second every night. Ivan was happy to distract Natasha from this unpleasantness, whisking her away to walks by the river and the dark corners of the school's attic, which were more exposed than the storage closets but also much more comfortable. "There is more dignity," Ivan said, leading her by the hand up the stairs, "in making love on the Nutcracker's throne than against a tangle of dirty mops."

"More dust, too," Natasha said, waving away cobwebs. The throne in question, though gilded and grand, had sat undusted since being stowed away. But Ivan pulled out a handkerchief and made a big show of wiping the throne down for her, and he sat on the throne and pulled her to his knee, and she let him, more pleased by being wanted than pleasure itself.

She was proud that she had lost her virginity and Maya had not. There had never been any real romantic competition between the sisters—Ivan told Natasha over and over that she, being blue-eyed, was his type—but still, he chose Natasha, and this was an honor, and pride helped Natasha push away her gnawing fear of pregnancy every time they crept up to the attic. He always assured her they were taking the proper precautions; he'd make jokes about Rubber Product Number 2, pull the thick, uncomfortable condom out of his pocket with a flourish, and say, "Proof of my love."

Once, last summer, she'd been late. Though this was common enough among dancers—many of them were so thin that they didn't menstruate at all—Natasha barely slept for days, agonizing over what to do. Here she was, facing the same terror her mother had faced: Who would she be if she couldn't dance anymore?

Unlike Elizaveta, Natasha could walk into any number of state clinics and be freed from her predicament—yet she was still frightened. On the third day, when she woke up to a crimson stain on her sheets, she felt such a relief that she began to wonder if all the pleasure was worth the perpetual terror. But she was young, and prone to forgetfulness, and the next time Ivan sat on the Nutcracker's dusty throne and pulled her to his knee, she forgot that she'd ever asked herself such questions.

Still, Natasha was not used to spending all her free time in the company of a man. Ivan was gentle, but he was also demanding. "I need you," he'd say, in an imploring tone, but this did nothing to endear him to Natasha. She didn't want to be needed—by him, by Maya, or by anyone at all. Natasha's idea of a good life was having the freedom to do whatever she wanted, unencumbered by anyone else's needs.

After a few weeks, Natasha began to get tired of the stuffy attic and even their time outside it. Ivan was no conversationalist—sometimes, it didn't seem like he listened to Natasha at all. Once, while Ivan skipped rocks in the river, Natasha tested whether he was paying attention, spoke of purple elephants she'd seen dancing in the sky. Ivan didn't even notice. He only said, "Mm-hmm," and sent another rock skipping out over the black surface of the water, and Natasha wished she was on that rock, hurtling away from him.

Maya had never ignored her like this. When Maya listened to you, she embraced the task with her whole being; she looked you squarely in the face and attended to your words as if you were the only person on earth. Natasha missed her sister's companionship, the feeling they often had of being one person, united against the school, the strangers around them on the street, the world itself. She never felt such unity with Ivan, and after a few weeks of their solitude, she began to feel like an accessory to him.

It was around this time that their literature instructor, who knew he was far from everyone's favorite teacher and hoped, against his better judgment, to raise his students' opinion of him, took his class on a field trip to see the American film *War and Peace*.

What a mercy that we can't read one another's minds. If the instructor, who believed that literature was essential to his students' lives and that they would be grateful for this chance for cultural enrichment, had seen his students' thoughts when he announced this field trip, he would have given up teaching altogether. Olaf thought of the taste of the sunflower seeds they served in the movie theater and wondered if Maya liked them; Anya wondered if she could somehow smuggle a bottle into the showing; Ivan thought only of the erotic potential of sitting beside Natasha in the dark. Natasha, who did not see Ivan's gaze flicker over her breasts in lustful anticipation, resolved to use this outing as an opportunity to sit beside her sister, if only for an afternoon.

This proved more difficult than Natasha had expected. At their literature instructor's request, they all walked as a group to the House of Cinema, a grand movie theater that had been renovated over the summer. As they walked, Natasha waited until Ivan turned to Sophrony—the two were debating the attractiveness of Audrey Hepburn, with Sophrony firmly anchored in the anti-eyebrow camp—and slipped forward to search for her sister, but Ivan caught her hand as she stepped away and held her back.

They turned the corner and the stately theater came into view. Green columns lined the facade, and a pair of gold lions—which were, for some reason, winged—guarded the roof. As they came closer to the theater, Natasha stood on her tiptoes and saw her sister walking near the teacher, wearing a knitted cap. Natasha had never seen this particular hat before, and she felt sad that they were growing so far apart that Maya now owned accessories she didn't even recognize.

Natasha tried to catch her sister's eye as they walked under the watchful roof lions. Maya was in front of the group, looking around for somebody—maybe for her, Natasha thought. She shouted Maya's name. Maya looked over her shoulder and then turned, holding her sister's gaze. The two of them stood there, six feet apart, the crowd of students and moviegoers parting and shifting around them. Natasha waited for her sister to smile or for the right words, words that would heal whatever rift was growing between them, to pop into her head. But neither of them said anything, and Maya turned around and disappeared into the darkness of the theater.

Maya didn't want to be with her. Natasha hadn't been rejected by much of anything or anyone in her entire life. The experience was new to her, and she didn't know what to do with it. Her body, equally perplexed by this new emotion, experienced rejection as akin to cold, and she shivered.

Ivan, who'd just finished defending Audrey Hepburn's loveliness—a pair of beautiful eyes overcame all flaws, he said, even enormous eyebrows—put an arm around her. "Come on, solnyshko," he said, and he walked her into the theater. He once told her—with typical teenage-boy earnestness that sometimes embarrassed Natasha—that he called her that, his little sun, because she warmed his heart. Natasha appreciated the kindness of his gesture, and his arm around her should have warmed her, but she felt like he was taking heat from her body.

The theater was crowded. The students, in their little factions, scattered themselves throughout the remaining empty seats. Vasili and Vasilia sat in the very back of the theater, hoping to do who-knows-what out of sight of their teacher. Sophrony settled into a seat behind Anya and Kira and Olga, planning to flick peanuts at them when no one was looking. Maya had her heart set on sitting next to Pyotr (this was the reason, she told herself, that she snubbed her sister, though she knew this was not true). Next week, Karinska would announce the pairings for partnering class, and Maya thought building a friendship with Pyotr would increase their chances of being partnered. She settled in an empty row in hopes that he would come find her, sitting up as straight as she could in an attempt to make herself more visible. But Pyotr sat in the front row all by himself, and Olaf came and sat beside Maya instead. Olaf pulled a large bag of sunflower seeds from his pocket and offered them to Maya, who took a modest handful and then realized with disgust that she was going to be sitting next to someone spitting shells onto the theater floor for the next three hours. Life had never seemed so long.

Ivan ushered Natasha into a row in the middle of everything. "Right in the action," he said. He raised the armrest between them, and Natasha resigned herself to her fate and nestled in beside him. After all, there are worse things than sitting in the dark with an attractive boy who loves you. The lights went out, and Natasha breathed in the familiar mothballish scent of Ivan's sweater and thought, at least for a moment, that she was lucky.

The movie was terrible. The Americans, in their eagerness to produce something for the uncultured masses, flattened all the life out of Tolstoy, resulting in a swoony caricature as dull as it was long. Within minutes, the literature instructor regretted this excursion, and after half an hour, a third of the audience had fallen asleep.

Natasha was not one of these: she was too irritated to be drowsy. Her first hope for the afternoon foiled—she stared at the back of her sister's head and wondered how in the world Maya ended up next to Olaf—she fixed her attention on the film, hoping she'd feel a kinship to this character who shared her name.

But the literary Natasha annoyed her; she laughed too much and made terrible decisions. And it was absurd, the idea that this Natasha would fall in love with Pierre. The actor who played him must have been fifty years old, with worn lines around his mouth and beady little eyes behind glasses, and he delivered his lines with a stodgy attempt at youthfulness that made her cringe. Audrey Hepburn was almost too beautiful to be real. Who could believe that she would marry him?

Yes, she is beautiful, Natasha thought, as Hepburn's two-story smile lit up the screen. There was something about the slant of the actress's eyes that reminded Natasha of herself, though even she wasn't vain enough to dwell on this too long.

Natasha found a brief respite from her boredom when the false-Natasha danced a waltz at her very first ball. While Maya, three rows ahead, memorized the patterns of dancers on the screen—the space between them, the shapes they made—Natasha basked in the scene's sensuous beauty: the cascade of jewels in the actress's tiara, the diaphanous swirl of her gown. Audrey Hepburn was graceful—it was no wonder that anyone would fall in love with *her*—and Natasha turned around and watched all of the people watching her, the delight on their faces. How glorious it would be, Natasha thought, to have a life like Audrey Hepburn's, whose job was to be beautiful for the benefit of everyone else, to be admired all over the world.

There was more to it, of course, than being beautiful—Audrey Hepburn was a storyteller, an enchantress. She bewitched the audience into believing she was a young girl in nineteenth-century Russia and not a twenty-seven-year-old in Hollywood. She told a story with her eyes, with her body, with her whole self, just like Natasha had learned to do in pantomime class. "Perhaps," Natasha thought, "she and I are not so different."

Natasha turned back around in her seat, and her admiration simmered into something closer to envy. Surely Audrey Hepburn was rich—being rich was all Americans cared about. Surely Audrey Hepburn lived in a palace like a tsarina, with fluffy little dogs and a cook and a closet the size of a trolleybus. Natasha could never have a life like that, simply because of where she'd been born. Everyone had everything in the West. Not for the first time, Natasha longed to see it for herself.

After this, the film lapsed back into dullness. Natasha had no interest in smoke-filled battles on bright green hills, and she fell asleep at several intervals—much to the delight of Ivan, who felt strong and capable each time Natasha's head lolled onto his shoulder. It had been a long week, and Natasha, as she was at the end of every week of dancing, was very tired. But halfway through the movie, a series of laughs and snorts woke her. She thought, rather groggily, it was very strange that such a serious film would have snorting in it—maybe the French had stumbled into a field of pigs—and then she saw a couple figures in the side rows to their right, hunched over in laughter. Irritated, Natasha leaned over and tried to see who was being annoying. Perhaps Ivan could give them a good talking-to—he was very good at being the arbiter of peace. But it was too dark to make anything out. Then a bright scene of sleds driving through the snow threw brilliant light on the laughers.

It was the stilyagi, the same gang of them that Natasha had seen strutting down the street weeks before. She recognized their leader—the boy with yellow hair. He, along with a boy from their crew and a girl she didn't recognize, was laughing at something.

Ivan, who was caught up in the glories of the Napoleonic War and relished seeing such a thing with his girlfriend asleep on his arm, felt

Natasha move and wished that she could have slept just a little longer, so she wouldn't know he'd been crying. (Ivan cried often, but only when nobody could see him.) When he saw what she was looking at, the muscles in the back of his neck tensed involuntarily. "Assholes," he whispered, hoping Natasha would hear him. He hadn't liked it when they'd stolen her attention at the teahouse, and he didn't like it now.

Natasha shushed him. "They're just young," she whispered, though she wasn't any older. The boy with yellow hair must have heard them—he turned around and winked.

"Definitely assholes," Ivan said. Natasha didn't respond, and she didn't turn her gaze away from the boy with yellow hair, even when he returned to watching the movie.

"What is it with you and that guy?" Ivan said.

Natasha turned to him slowly, too slowly to seem innocent. "What do you mean?" She knew exactly what he meant, and in her mind, she dared him to say it out loud.

Ivan was irritated, but he didn't want to make a scene in the theater. "Never mind," he said, and he pulled Natasha a little closer.

An interminable amount of time later—maybe hours, maybe years—Moscow had burned, Napoleon had been vanquished, Pierre and Natasha had been reunited at long last, and it was time for everyone to go home. The literature instructor, irate at seeing his favorite novel bastardized by Hollywood, cracked his knuckles and started mentally composing a letter of complaint to the Minister of Culture, demanding *War and Peace* have its own Russian adaptation. Olaf, honored that Maya had sat beside him for the entire film, offered her the rest of the sunflower seeds—an act of great magnanimity, because they were his favorite and he purchased them only on rare occasions—but she declined. Anya and Olga and Kira wiped their eyes and made for the exits; thanks to Sophrony's terrible aim, they had noticed none of the peanuts chucked at their heads, much to his chagrin. And Vasili and Vasilia, buttoned up again after some sort of misunderstanding, rose with burning cheeks and filed separately out of the theater.

Natasha stayed seated, under the pretense of fidgeting with her scarf but really to see the stilyagi, and the boy with yellow hair in particular. There was something about the stilyagi that fascinated her. They seemed so open with one another, so free. They seemed to operate under no one's expectations but their own, living however they wanted. The girl stilyaga laughed in the way a girl can only laugh if she knows that she's the prettiest of all her companions. Natasha hated her.

Finally, Ivan nudged her and they rose to leave. The boy with yellow hair still sat in his row with his friends, throwing a peanut in the air and trying to catch it in his mouth. He didn't even look at Natasha as she walked by. An icy lump of disappointment rolled into Natasha's stomach.

It was not a far walk from the House of Cinema to the school, and for this, everyone was grateful—the last warmth of summer had given way to unrelenting cold. Natasha took Ivan's arm and shivered. It was all the same to her, being cold, being unhappy. Why not feel the same way inside and out?

Ivan reached over and rubbed Natasha's shoulders. "You poor thing," he said. "Are you freezing? Did that movie freeze my solnyshko?"

"I hated it," Natasha said. "The only part I liked at all was when that beautiful girl was dancing. You know, the movie Natasha. I wish I looked like her."

Someone spoke up behind them. "You do look like her," he said.

Natasha turned. It was the boy with yellow hair, walking just behind them, alone. Natasha swallowed. Ivan's grip tightened on her arm—out of fear rather than protectiveness, for Ivan was terrified of losing Natasha, though he did not yet know or acknowledge this himself. “Like who?” Natasha said, feigning ignorance in hopes of being told by this presumptuous stranger just how beautiful she was.

“Audrey Hepburn,” the boy said. “That’s the name of the actress. You look just like her.”

Natasha’s cheeks burned. “Thank you,” she said. She thought so herself, but it was more pleasing to have somebody else say it.

“Except you are prettier,” the stilyaga said, strolling up beside them. The stilyaga, who was at the age when the world extends only to the tip of one’s nose, had two great loves in life: picking needless fights and flattering the vanity of simple women. Sensing he was about to succeed at both, he winked at the girl in the shabby blue coat. “You have those sparkling blue eyes.”

Ivan stopped walking. “Fuck off,” he said, and his grip on Natasha’s arm tightened hard enough that she winced. The boy with yellow hair suddenly seemed a foot shorter, and Ivan a foot taller.

The stilyaga, who, in addition to being pompous and vain, was a shrewd judge of character, saw Ivan’s clenched hand and Natasha’s wince and immediately saw an opportunity to drive a wedge between them simply for the fun of it. “You don’t own her,” he said, taking the tack of the noble and enlightened gentleman, though really, he couldn’t care less. “She’s her own person.”

“I know that,” Ivan said, sounding angrier, but his grip on Natasha’s arm loosened. Despite appearances, he was gentle at heart, and he respected Natasha deeply, though he resented being reminded of this by a person who was flirting with her.

“Stop it,” Natasha said. She tugged at his arm. “He’s not bothering anybody. Why do you always have to make a big deal out of nothing?”

Ivan stared at her for a moment, incredulous that she’d scolded him in front of a stranger. We all have our shameful secrets, things we work our whole lives to conceal; Ivan’s was that, though he looked like a man, he had the woundable heart of a child, and Natasha had scolded him as if she knew this, as if she thought he was only a little boy, and now the stilyaga knew this too. Embarrassed, he glanced at the stilyaga, whose smirk only wounded him further. "My mistake," Ivan said. "I thought that he was bothering you. But I see I was wrong." He shrugged off her arm.

"Ivan, don't—"

He ignored her. He hurried up the empty street alone, and soon his tears returned, and an old woman watched from her window and pitied him.

Natasha stood for a long time and watched him go, much like she'd watched the stilyaga on that first evening she'd seen him. The stilyaga, his heart still racing from the confrontation, stayed beside her and, when Ivan disappeared around a corner, introduced himself. "I'm Ilya," he'd said. Taking her silence for encouragement (he was a vain and foolish person, used to swift and easy successes with girls), he tried to slip an arm around her shoulders. A trolleybus rolled by just then and blared its horn at a cat trying to creep across the street, startling Ilya. As he flinched, he grazed Natasha's right breast by mistake.

Natasha, whose eyes had filled with tears when Ivan left, whirled around and slapped him. "Asshole!" she said, and when he cowered and covered his face it frightened her—she had never hit anyone before, let alone a strange boy, let alone on a public sidewalk—and this fear made her even angrier, and she slapped him again. "May a dick grow on your forehead!" Then she, too, hurried alone down the sidewalk in tears. The old woman who'd watched Ivan weep from her window saw Natasha too and felt sudden gratitude for being very old, safe once and for all from the heartaches of the young and foolish.

CHAPTER FOUR

To be a dancer is to live in paradoxes. A dancer has to build her muscles in order to appear weightless. She must conform to her craft, but respect the uniqueness of her body. Yet every dancer, no matter how short, how tall, how quick, how spry, has to learn how to be a partner, and at the Vaganova, they learned this from Madame Karinska.

You couldn't just pair any two dancers together. A girl with muscly legs, a jumper, couldn't get partnered with a quick and weedy boy—it would look like a weasel lifting a kangaroo. And the boy has to be taller than the girl, always, even when she's on her toes. But beyond the physical, there are less tangible qualities to be considered, and detecting these qualities was the skill upon which Madame Karinska particularly prided herself.

Karinska, who had taught at the school for thirty-seven years, had recently begun to slow a little. The skin on the undersides of her arms, which she'd worked so hard to keep slim and strong, now sagged; she could not hop from thought to thought as quickly as she once had, and sometimes, while she walked down the hallways, her breath seemed a step or two behind her, and her knees seized up, and she had to stop and sit at one of the many green upholstered benches that lined the hallways until both breath and knees caught up with her. This embarrassed her very much—that she, once known for her quickness, for having abundant energy that never ran out, had become an old woman trapped on a bench. So she did what she always did: she tried to make it appear that she'd chosen this bench on purpose, that she was lying in wait for someone.

Like a spider crouched in its web, Karinska watched the students and teachers walking up and down the halls, and when the eyes of the folk-dance teacher wandered over to her little green toadstool, she pounced, waved him over and invited him to sit, and the teacher obliged. Everyone knew about Karinska's maladies, and her pride; they loved her, so they played along. These interactions always went the same way: before the victim's rear end reached the seat, Karinska would launch into a long-winded analysis of one of her teaching philosophies. Of these, the art of choosing partners was her favorite—and particularly on her mind this afternoon, with the senior students waiting to be paired.

"It's much more than the height," she said, leaning in toward her victim, who was engaged in the art of feigning interest while clandestinely checking his watch. "It's much more than the appearance at all. It's like matching up the grain of wood in the pieces of a table. You can't just tell the grain by what it looks like. You have to use your hands, and your soul. You have to know how it *feels*."

Like every part of the dance, there was a universal method to how partners were to reach for each other—an offer and acceptance, a giving and receiving—that was as formal as it appeared natural. All dancers are taught this as children: when first reaching for each other, the partners' hands must be firm, but not stiff; welcoming, but not languid; offered, but not forced. Karinska claimed she could see past these required formalities into the physical realities of the dancers' bodies—the way, known to the dancers or not, that their bodies were perceiving each other, accepting or rejecting the overture. This perception appeared independently of the dancers' actual feelings for each other, which was one reason that the dancers feared Karinska's pronouncements. Sometimes when two real-life lovers touched, Karinska declared there was no actual fire between them, only flatness and indifference. And sometimes, when two enemies clasped hands, Karinska saw a spark fly, and this spark would bind them, and they would go on dancing forever, to the Kirov and beyond, even if they went on hating each other offstage.

"And the spark," Karinska said, leaning much too close to the folk-dance teacher, "is what makes a good match." The folk-dance teacher, despite growing late for class, found himself drawn in by the twinkle in Karinska's eye—it was the same twinkle, after all, that had gained her a hundred conquests in her younger years—and as he listened, part of him forgot that she was forty years older and fell a little bit in love with her, though he wouldn't ever admit this to anyone.

The spark could not be taught, Karinska said. It could not be corrected. Nor was there room for middle ground: a boy and girl either liked each other from the start or they didn't. Once this mystery had been uncovered—as it could only be uncovered, by Karinska herself—there was no changing or disputing it.

As Karinska cast her spell on the folk-dance teacher, the senior students waited in the school's largest studio, the yellow-walled Petipa Room, named for the venerable nineteenth-century choreographer who'd fathered so many dances for the Kirov and the ballet world at large: *The Nutcracker*, *Don Quixote*, *The Sleeping Beauty*. This bright, two-storied room, with its sloped floor modeled after the Kirov's, was the nursery of Petipa's genius. School patrons sometimes sat in the second-floor balcony behind a calligraphic wrought iron banister and watched for future stars of ballet, as they had since Petipa's time. Here, where Aurora first woke from her sleep and the

Sugarplum Fairy first waved her wand, the senior students would take their final partners.

Out of necessity, every boy had danced with every girl for years. It was good for each of them to learn the subtle differences of other bodies. You never knew the obstacles you'd face in professional life: the foreign guest dancer with peculiar habits, the understudy swapped in just before the curtain rose. But on this afternoon, each dancer would be matched with their best partner, with whom they would dance every day for the entire year—and possibly, if they were exceptional together, at the senior gala in the spring.

There was no use selecting the matches before the senior year; even at seventeen, the dancers were still young, susceptible to the sudden and irrevocable whims of puberty and genes. Anya and Olga and Kira weren't the only ones who came back to the school in different shape than they'd left it; everyone's bodies had been changing over the summer, and as they warmed up for class, the dancers sized up one another.

Some of them had simply grown more like themselves. Sophrony and Ivan, whose families lived near each other in Leningrad, spent the summer lifting weights and running along the Neva at dawn and became even more muscular—but not so much that it spoiled the slim lines of their figures. Vasili and Vasilia, as skeletal as ever, looked like lovers wasting away for each other. They were the kinds of dancers that made mothers shake their heads when they passed them in the street and hope to heaven that none of their children would take to ballet. "Skin and bones, like they're on a hunger strike," the mothers would say to one another. "It isn't good for a body to be like that." Olaf had spent the summer trying to bulk up like Ivan and Sophrony, and as he ran up and down the stairs in his grandmother's apartment building, carrying sacks of flour on his shoulders, he'd imagined he was really training with them—but all he had to show for his effort was little lumps of bicep, visible only to him, and only when he flexed so hard that his jaw hurt from clenching.

Some of the dancers, as happened every year, had returned looking like entirely different people. Though Anya and Olga had barely gained a couple pounds between them, imperceptible to the average person, these few pounds made them look much more like ordinary people than ballerinas. Because of this, they (and Kira, with her newly ample bosom) were the most nervous people in the room—except for Maya.

Studying herself in the mirror, Maya had trouble discerning any differences in her own body. She looked over at Natasha for reference. For weeks, she'd done her best to speak to Natasha as little as possible: she could not be both competitor and confidante to her sister at once, and a separation was necessary, even if it was only temporary. Natasha was apparently happy to oblige this; she now spent every waking moment she could with Ivan. Maya could not remember a time when she'd felt this different from her sister.

But in the nakedness of the mirror, wearing only their leotards, Maya and Natasha looked exactly the same—the same narrow hips, the same little breast buds, the same spindly limbs. As she watched her sister warming up at the barre, Maya noticed that Natasha even had that same extra little bit of reach in her port de bras for which Maya had been proud. Maya sighed. Nothing was truly her own—not even her body.

When Pyotr entered the room, Maya immediately looked down and tried to busy herself with straightening her shoe ribbons. Pyotr walked over to the boys' side of the barre, slow as ever, and started to stretch on the floor, doubling his body over itself. Like the others, he'd changed over the summer. His arms had certainly thickened. Surely Maya would have remembered the ropiness of his calves, the broad swoop of his shoulders, if they'd looked like that last spring.

Maya looked around the room. There were only so many possibilities for her partner, and the height problem made things worse. Maya was far too tall to be paired with Sophrony. Vasili wouldn't be bad—but then she would live under the heat of Vasilia's ire for an entire year, and with everyone already pitying her as it was, she didn't want any more trouble. Then there was the distressing problem of there being too many girls—one too many. Someone would have to share a partner, a humiliation Maya hoped she would be spared.

Olaf waved at her from across the room, and she returned his wave without enthusiasm.

Pyotr, doing great lunges across the floor, came across Maya's line of sight and either winked at her or happened to wince while turned in her direction. Before Maya had time to decide which, Karinska walked to the center of the room and clapped her hands, and the accompanist launched into something brisk of Bizet's, their signal to begin work at the barre.

Maya followed the exercises with precision, but her mind wandered—and, when she was able, her eyes wandered, too, over to Pyotr. Maybe if she danced with him, she could become great. Maybe he would know how to take her adagio and turn it into something that even the Kirov could not resist. Being very young, and in the throes of infatuation, Maya began to think the sorts of sentimental thoughts that would make her groan when she remembered them later—that if Pyotr would have her, she could blossom under the shelter of his love, and other bits of flowery nonsense.

After they finished at the barre, Karinska paced the room with the slow but deliberate air of a panther stalking its prey. She'd pondered every match for months—had thought of boys taking girls' hands while she slept, while she washed her hair, while she clipped her formidable toenails—and now her moment had arrived. It was the highlight of her year: later that evening, she would uncork a bottle of sherry she'd saved for the occasion and drink the whole thing in celebration.

The boys lined up on one side of the room and the girls on the other, and as Karinska continued to pace, the dancers scoped out their prospective partners. Vasili and Vasilia smiled twisted little smiles as if they shared some amusing secret. Ivan looked over at Natasha, who stared at the ceiling to avoid his glance. And Maya, whose limbs were beginning to radiate with nervous energy, as though whatever Karinska said would cause her to involuntarily leap into the air, looked straight ahead into the mirror and tried to remember to exhale.

Everyone knew what was about to happen: knowledge of the tradition had been handed down from student to student over the years, shared in dormitory hallways and while brushing teeth and while ice-skating out on the Neva, the younger students paying the same deference to the elder ones as they had when the elders explained some particular theory of drinking or the art of reproduction. This was how it would go: Karinska would call the pairs out one by one, would invite them to reach for each other. This was the first test. The second was a very brief pas de deux that the couple would perform while everyone else watched. This was when Karinska, who honed her matches like a mathematician develops a formula, tested her proofs.

Karinska stepped forward with the conviction of someone about to perform a rite both secret and sacred. She gave them twelve counts of steps: a supported arabesque and turn, several lifted pas de chat—"I want to see you boys *returning* the girls gently to the floor," Karinska said, "I don't want to hear a single footfall"—and finally, a two-handed lift in which the boy raised the girl to sit on his shoulder. At the announcement of this lift, the boys glanced at one another anxiously, knowing their strength was about to be tested, which was exactly the point.

Karinska nodded to the pianist in the corner, who played twelve counts of Glinka so the dancers could mark their steps. Then she raised her hand as if to conduct an orchestra. "Vasili," she said, letting her hand fall again, "and Vasilia."

Karinska was a romantic—you don't have a hundred lovers without believing in love—and for this reason, Vasili and Vasilia were particular favorites. She knew before anyone else when they were on the outs and when they'd reconciled; she'd explained once to Olaf that when they quarreled, Vasilia's dancing became so taut that it was brittle, as if she were steeling herself against her coming rejection, and when they made up, Vasili's leaps reached heights that they never did otherwise.

Vasili and Vasilia, looking as cool and proud as white marble, met in the center of the room. Vasili offered his hand, and she took it, and they swept through the steps with such ease that Maya wondered if they'd somehow learned the choreography ahead of time and practiced it on their own. Karinska nodded in a way that implied she'd expected nothing less. "Excellent," she said, satisfied, and she directed them to wait by the piano in the corner.

Karinska worked her way through the ranks: Sophrony was paired first with Kira and then with Anya, who, hungover again, was breathless by the end of the choreography and nearly stumbled as Sophrony readied her for the lift. "Heavens," Karinska said, eyebrows arched. "What if he dropped you? Your spine could snap." She shook her head. "Wait there for a minute, Anya, while I watch Natasha and Ivan."

Maya glanced at her sister. Natasha wore the same blank mask she always did before performing, but Ivan looked nervous, and perhaps this was why he tried to take Natasha's hand before he'd offered his own.

"Stop!" Karinska said. "Good Lord, Ivan, have I taught you nothing in all these years? *Offer* your hand. Be a gentleman."

Ivan, appearing chastened, nodded to Karinska and tried again. Natasha took his hand, and they began. Ivan was timid and stiff, but it was Natasha who looked the most out of place in the pair. She missed Ivan's hand during the turn and was half a beat ahead of him during the pas de chat. They danced like violins playing in two different keys, and their asynchrony set everyone on edge.

Karinska sighed. "Ah, well," she said. "I think we can get more out of you, but time will tell. Ivan, you will practice with Natasha and Anya both. We'll see how it turns out by the end of the year."

Ivan's face burned red, and no one thought it was because of exertion. Natasha turned to the barre to stretch before Maya could read her face.

Maya swallowed. With Vasili and Ivan paired, the only boy left who could be tall enough for her was Pyotr, unless—

Karinska eyed the remainders. "Pyotr—"

Maya's stomach fell.

"—and Olga."

Maya didn't even watch them dancing. She tied and untied her shoe ribbons, pretending to struggle with the knot so no one could see there were tears in her eyes—not even Natasha, who she felt looking over at her. Maya knew she had exactly twelve counts to pull herself together.

The pianist finished, and Karinska, humming some unknown tune to herself, waved Olga and Pyotr off to the corner with a smile.

"And last, of course," Karinska said, "Maya and Olaf."

Olaf, who had been standing in the back of the room, panicking that he wasn't going to be chosen at all, that everyone else would be matched up and he would be left all alone, or kicked out of the class, thought at first that he'd misheard, and Karinska had to repeat herself. Pyotr snickered. Maya, whose pride was now beyond humiliation, resolved to prove herself worthy to Pyotr, to show him what he was missing, and she strode out to the middle of the floor as if it were the Kirov stage itself and not a practice room.

Olaf, noticing this change in her deportment, her haughty eyes and lifted chin, thought they signaled her pride at having been chosen as his partner, and his own pride rose to the occasion, and his shoulder blades followed: the hunch that had bent him since he set foot in the school disappeared, and he looked several inches taller and a good deal more handsome. He and Maya matched perfectly, like two larks or a pair of gloves. The rest of the class stood suspended between confusion and disbelief. Was this really Olaf, the same Olaf who was nobody's favorite and the butt of everyone's jokes? No one could believe his confidence, the look of solemnity on his face, the particular triumph and ease with which he lifted Maya at the end. For once, he danced like someone who knew his own worth. (Ivan leaned over to Pyotr and whispered something profane about being mistaken about Olaf's preferred gender of partner. "Better for him," Pyotr whispered back, scratching his elegant nose. Olaf reminded him of a cousin who'd once ended up in prison thanks to his paramours. "Keeps him out of trouble.")

Later, when Maya remembered this moment—when she tried, in vain, to sleep that night, or while she waited for a train at age twenty-two, or many years later, when she was an old woman telling stories in an empty café—she would not remember a single thing about the choreography, or the way she felt when Olaf spun her through the turn, or his hands on her hips as he lifted her overhead—so effortlessly, Karinska would say later, when she related this story in the teachers' lounge, as though Maya was made of air.

When Maya was older, and she longed to return to a time when the world was simpler, when her life had not felt fractured, she would remember that when Olaf extended his hand to her, he looked at her as if she were the woman he'd waited to dance with for his entire life. Was it possible that she was someone worth waiting for?

Like any Russian, Maya believed in fate. Fate was an unseen hand weaving the tapestry of her life, and she was powerless to control it. Fate had decided her lot was to live and dance within her sister's shadow. But on that sunny afternoon in the Petipa Room, when Olaf finished the lift and lowered her gently to the ground, Maya saw Karinska's painted lips hung open, saw all her classmates staring at them—at her—and even Pyotr caught in wonder, and it occurred to her that Fate may have been wrong.

It was true that stage presence could not be learned, as Alexei had once declared; you either had the power to seduce an audience or you didn't. But seduction is indelibly linked to desire, and Maya had never had anyone she wanted to seduce—until now. When she and Olaf danced, no one—not Sophrony, not Pyotr, not Ivan, not even Karinska—could look away. Only Natasha knew the reason for her sister's transformation: Maya wanted Pyotr's love. For some reason, it made Natasha envious.

Karinska was too stunned to wave Olaf and Maya into the corner and turned to Natasha instead. "My dear," she said, "you have a lot to learn from your sister!"

Without answering, Natasha sat on the floor and started untying her ribbons. "Who cares," she grumbled, under her breath but loud enough that Maya could hear her. "They won't take both of us."

CHAPTER FIVE

There is a particular gloom that takes hold of human hearts around the middle of November—especially in a place like Leningrad, where by winter the days grow short and dark, and the sun is down by the time children finish school. Leningrad was famous for its White Nights, summer days that began at three in the morning and stretched on for what felt like forever, days that were celebrated with carnivals and festivals and ample good cheer. But the other time of year, when the pattern reversed, had no name and no festivals to lighten its burden. The students of the Vaganova dined by the light of harsh electric chandeliers that hung low in the dining hall and cast ominous shadows over everyone's expressions. Dark days, for thinking dark thoughts.

This was part, though not all, of the reason that Natasha and Ivan began bickering. The loss of daylight ended their walks on the Neva (Ivan said being out at night made him nervous) and flooded the once-quiet taverns with people (Ivan said he couldn't hear himself think in such places) and left them with only the attic. Even that had tarnished; now they went up there mostly to argue, Ivan sitting solo on the throne in his rolled-up trousers in the manner of an off-duty monarch.

These arguments, like all arguments between couples, hovered around the same two or three subjects—proxy wars for what neither of them wanted to confront, which was what awaited them after graduation. They squabbled over whose fault it had been that partnering had gone poorly. The arrangement with Anya meant Ivan and Natasha had less time than usual to dance as partners, which made them stiff and brittle when they were paired in class. They also argued over whether or not Natasha should return to Komsomol meetings, which she had recently stopped attending. Often, both of these subjects devolved into spats over who'd started the argument in the first place.

Finally, on a dreary, joyless afternoon, the true conflict made its presence known. Ivan and Natasha sat in the attic in their usual corners; he on his dusty throne, she at an old dressing table with a cracked mirror. Earlier that afternoon, the senior class had visited the Kirov to watch a rehearsal, Alexei's remedy for the usual dip in morale that cropped up this time of year. He'd hoped that seeing professional dancers would remind the students that all of their efforts and injuries could amount to something someday. For most of the students, this attempt at lifting spirits had been successful: all through dinner, the Kirov, and the glories that inevitably awaited each of them, was the sole subject of conversation. Even Ivan momentarily lifted his head from his gloom. But when Natasha watched the dancers of the Kirov rehearse the same steps over and over and over, she saw only drudgery. An old back injury had been bothering her more than usual, and as she sat in the darkened theater, enduring yet another muscle spasm, she noticed that nearly every dancer had a bandage somewhere on their body.

Injury was part of every dancer's story: everyone had some sort of minor or major catastrophe that split time into a "before" and "after"—a slip on the stage, a trip on the stairs, a botched lift, a careless landing. Tendons could tear; muscles could sprain; bones could snap. Every dancer knew this. It was the price you paid for being glorious, and every Vaganova dancer had paid their due. Maya was prone to bursitis in her pinkie toes. Olaf once injured his shoulder trying to lift Olga (an incident that did nothing for Olga's self-esteem). Anya, when she was very young, tore a ligament in her knee and missed half a school year. If you were lucky, injuries taught you to be careful, to avoid improper form, to build yourself back up again from nothing if necessary. But everyone heard stories of students and even adult dancers who had once walked into a studio or onto a stage and were carried off on a stretcher, never to return.

For some reason, Natasha had hoped that when they were all older, and more experienced, and more skilled, dancing would be easier on their bodies. This was foolish: even the teachers at the Vaganova wore battle scars. All of them either walked duckfooted or had bad backs or spent their summer vacations at hot springs, searching for cures. No, to be a dancer was to live forever in some sort of pain, and Natasha, watching the Kirov dancers with their bandaged legs and feet and shoulders, wondered for the first time in her life if anything could be worth that cost. Now tucked away in the attic, she made the mistake of admitting this to Ivan.

At least, this was what she'd wanted to express. What she actually said to him was, "I wish that I could run away."

This was the worst possible thing one could say to a young man whose mother had abandoned him. But Ivan, momentarily cheered by the visit to the Kirov and the buoyant spirit of the dinner table, was in a decent mood, and he was used to Natasha's exaggerations, so he treated her wish like a game and asked her where she wanted to go.

This question made Natasha pause. She hadn't meant what she said—not literally—but now that she'd been questioned about her destination, she realized that she not only had a genuine desire to run away, but knew where to run to: a place that came to her at once, without her searching for it, borne of foreign movies and, above all, her desire for beautiful things. "To America," she said.

Ivan, who had been looking at the ceiling, dangling a leg over the arm of his throne, sat up. "What, you're serious?"

Natasha turned to him. "Can't you picture it?" she said, her eyes wide. "Can't you see me dancing in New York?" Surely, in America, dancers were not forced to dance when they should be resting and were thus injured less often. Surely, in America, you had everything you needed and were always warm and safe. Surely everyone lived and looked like Audrey Hepburn.

The West Natasha imagined was not the real West—Indianapolis and Cincinnati can't live up to the romance of their names—but the Imaginary West, which existed only in the imaginations of young Soviets. When she thought of the West, Natasha thought of stacks of bangle bracelets and exotic varieties of perfume and sunny afternoons spent drinking Coca-Cola on boulevards. Nobody caught colds in the Imaginary West; nobody toiled away at dimly lit desks or had to do their own laundry. To live in the West was to be happy forever, and all Natasha had ever wanted was to be happy.

"Of course I can't picture it!" Ivan snapped. "Don't you know what happens to your family when you defect?" Ivan himself knew all too well. After Ivan's mother disappeared, his father was interrogated over and over again, always in the middle of the night, always returning a little more diminished. Ivan's father limped home on those nights, crossed the threshold without a word, and winced as he unlaced his shoes. He was demoted at work, lost half his friends—who judiciously crossed the street so as not to share a sidewalk with him—and never slept soundly again, and for years afterward Ivan lay awake deep into the night, listening for a knock at the door. "What you're asking me to do is dangerous and selfish," Ivan continued, swallowing a lump in his throat and trying not to think about his father's feet. "It's a betrayal of everyone we know."

Natasha, irritated to see her castle in the air torn down so soon, bristled at his words. "I haven't asked you to do anything. I haven't said anything about you at all."

And this was when Ivan began to realize that he could lose Natasha—might be losing her already, just as he'd lost his mother. "It's him, isn't it?" he said. "That boy from the movie theater—"

"What are you talking about?"

"He must be the one putting these ideas into your head. You've been sneaking off with him, haven't you?"

"I've never even seen him again!" This was true, though Natasha had often thought of Ilya and the others. They possessed so much of what she wanted: beautiful clothes, a carefree life, the ability to do and say and wear whatever you pleased.

But Ivan did not believe her: he couldn't accept that Natasha would want to leave her home, her family, or him without someone else poisoning her mind, and that someone had to be the stilyaga. As he continued to interrogate her, Natasha turned away from him and looked out into the darkness of Leningrad and wished she could fly away into it.

Two floors down, Maya blessed the winter darkness. The longer nights meant more time to practice, more time to edge closer to the Kirov.

At Karinska's encouragement, Maya and Olaf had started training together every night in a classroom Karinska herself had arranged for. "Give that sister of yours a run for her money," she'd said.

They practiced in one of the smaller classrooms, and every time Olaf snapped on the lights, Maya's heart lifted, no matter how tired she was. She replayed Karinska's words in her memory over and over: *You have a lot to learn from your sister.* For the first time, Maya felt it was possible that she could outperform Natasha, and she returned to the classroom with Olaf night after night, even though each day left her wrung out and exhausted and her toes often bled. She was ready to do anything to make it to the Kirov.

Every night, Olaf set a portable record player on a chair (yet another gift from his uncle, who was making quite a reputation for himself as a genteel smuggler of imported goods) and wordlessly, to canned waltzes and mazurkas of the Leningrad Symphony, they guided themselves through a brief barre—Maya followed Olaf from behind—and practiced dancing together.

Olaf was a confident partner, gentle but firm. Maya never wondered if he'd waver when he caught her, or if his hand would be there waiting when she came out of a turn. Her favorite of all were the guided pirouettes. Maya had never felt as free as she did on those long winter nights, with Olaf's hands on her hips. He never tried to stop her from attempting an extra turn, and his strong hands supported her instead of holding her rigid, as other partners had done.

Olaf had been waiting his whole life for someone like Maya, someone who would treat him like an equal, like a friend. As far back as his memories went, he'd always been two steps behind everyone, late to the joke. He hadn't taken comfort in the company of other outcasts; the people who interested him the most were the people who liked him the least, even as they made fun of him or ignored him altogether. For many years, he had, on some level, accepted this as a sort of curse. He imagined himself as the tragic hero in a folktale, one who'd been turned into a wolf or a bear and had to convince somebody that he was really a man. Only the love of another would reveal his true form, and this was why he danced with such confidence when he was with Maya. She was the first girl who seemed to enjoy his company rather than just tolerate it. He fell a little more in love with her every time they danced.

At first, they danced excerpts of pas de deux from memory, steps that had been ingrained in their bodies and minds from a lifetime's worth of classes and performances. They'd memorized snatches of classic ballets like American teenagers devoured the words of Elvis. Every girl wanted to grow up to dance as Kitri from *Don Quixote*, and every boy the titular lead, and sometimes, those long moonless evenings Olaf and Maya spent together felt like play. It was as if they'd become children together.

After a few weeks of this, however, these familiar steps began to feel stale. Maya's limbs ached for something new, and when Olaf suggested she dance Kitri for the third evening in a row, Maya shook her head. "Let's do something else," she said.

"Like what?"

Maya shrugged. "Put some music on and I'll think of something."

Olaf thumbed through the worn records of his gifted collection and pulled out Tchaikovsky's Serenade for Strings. He held it up for Maya's approval. "Like this?"

"Anything," Maya said. As Olaf pulled the record from its paper sleeve, Maya turned from him and started wandering toward the mirror. It had been less than a month since Karinska's pronouncement, but she already felt transformed. She did an arabesque en pointe and was astonished, once again, by how much longer her extension looked than it had a few weeks ago. It was as if she'd taken a deep breath and, instead of filling her lungs, the air lingered in her limbs. Perhaps she could learn how to float if she just inhaled deeply enough.

She looked like someone who could be loved—someone, perhaps, that Pyotr could love. Pyotr still hadn't noticed her; in her naivete, Maya had hoped that as she became a more beautiful dancer, the scales would fall from Pyotr's eyes and he'd see her at last. That it hadn't happened yet was just proof that true love took time.

The record crackled and spun to life and then sputtered. "Sorry," Olaf said. "It must be scratched." He futzed and fussed with the record until he found a place that wouldn't skip, which happened to be Maya's favorite movement of Serenade—the waltz. Olaf turned and caught Maya studying her arabesque. "Look at you!" he said, with his hands on his hips, and he smiled with such a warmth that Maya, with the egocentricity of love, let herself imagine what it would be like if Pyotr smiled at her that way. If that smile had a sound, it would be tender and pure, like these strings reverberating through the practice room.

Someday, Pyotr would be hers, and this hope poured out of Maya and into movement. Instead of walking back to Olaf, she danced to him, in a grand series of piqué turns that sent her flying across the floor. She didn't think about keeping her arms rounded as she opened and closed them or about pulling her foot into the high place her teachers always nagged about, though she executed each turn perfectly. She just saw someone she wanted to be near and danced to him, as a child takes his first steps toward some object of affection, and when she came close to Olaf, she reached for him—the waltz had cast a spell—and guided his hands to her hips. "Follow me," she said, and she danced, and he did.

She'd never done this before—had never combined her own steps to music, but her limbs moved as if somebody else was moving them, as if they'd always waited for this chance to show her what they could do. For once in her life, she was not thinking, and with the split second of deliberation gone, her dancing became more musical than it ever had. She knew this piece of music so well—it was a favorite both of the Vaganova's teachers and accompanists—and she began to feel like the notes themselves tumbled out of her, that her limbs made the music. She was not just dancing, she was making a dance, and she was too caught up in a fantasy to realize it.

The record skipped again, and the spell was broken. Olaf left her arms and rushed to the phonograph. The moment had passed, and Maya hadn't even recognized the significance of it.

Olaf pulled the needle from the record. "That was wonderful," he said over his shoulder. "What was it from?"

"What was what from?" Maya said, panting, hands on her head. She never got truly tired until she stopped moving.

"What we just danced."

Maya sat hard on the floor and started untying her ribbons. "I don't know," she said. "I guess I made it up."

"Well!" Olaf said. He folded his arms and smiled. "She dances and makes dances! It's as if you're a long-lost daughter of Balanchine. Ah! That reminds me, I wanted to show you something." Olaf walked over to his bag and pulled out a magazine. "My uncle went abroad again," he said, "and he brought me back this. You remember Balanchine, don't you? You know, that choreographer I told you about back in the library?"

"Of course," Maya said, though she didn't. She lay on the floor and tried not to think about how early she had to get up tomorrow.

Olaf sat beside her and put the magazine in her hands. "Well, here he is again," he said. He pointed to an image of two dancers in practice clothes. "Look what his dancers are up to this time. Something called *Agon*."

Maya studied the photograph. The dancers' bodies were pivoted against each other in contortions that Maya had never seen. There was something off-kilter about it, as if the ground had shifted beneath the dancers' feet just as they entered their pose. "I don't know if I like it," she said. She handed the magazine back to Olaf.

"I don't know either," he said, "but it's causing quite a stir in the West." He laughed. "What if Balanchine really was your father? It'd explain your giftedness."

He was teasing her. Maya laughed too, because she was fond of Olaf and she was grateful to him for the long hours they'd worked together. But she did not think his joke was very funny. "So what if he was?" she said. "A lot of good it's doing me now."

"Of course, he isn't," Olaf said. "He's much too old." He held the magazine up next to Maya and compared it with her face. "You don't look a thing like him, except maybe your nose."

This comparison did nothing to improve Maya's mood: the man in the magazine had a horrifically large and beaky nose. "Thanks a lot," she said, and she took the magazine from Olaf and smacked him with it.

Natasha lay awake in bed. Maya was out late again, as had become her habit. These sudden absences seemed strange to Natasha. Her sister had never been a night owl, nor prone to excesses of any kind. She didn't have any friends, let alone boyfriends. And she certainly wasn't spending time with Pyotr—Ivan had recently revealed that Pyotr wanted someone else, though he wouldn't tell her who. Natasha burrowed into her blankets and wondered if Maya stayed out late just to avoid her.

She couldn't blame her if she had. She knew that if Maya were in her shoes, and if she were the one getting left behind, she would despise her sister too. It wasn't fair, the way they'd been put into this situation. They were all being pitted against one another, turned into animals—a crowd of starving circus bears, charging after a single bowl of food. And now, with Ivan turning against her, Natasha had nobody at all. The only person who had said a kind word to her in the last few weeks was Ilya, when he'd said she looked like Audrey Hepburn.

The door creaked open. Natasha knew that creak well: she'd always tried to push past it quickly so it wouldn't wake Maya. Now she was the one in bed, pretending to be asleep.

Even buried in blankets, Natasha heard her sister sigh. She peeked out from under the covers and saw Maya silhouetted in the dark, gathering things for the shower.

"You're out late," Natasha said, with the voice of an irritated mother.

Maya jumped. "God," she said, "what are you doing, creeping in the dark? I thought I was about to get molested."

"What do you mean, what am I doing? It's the middle of the night! I'm in bed!" Natasha sat up and folded her pillow in her arms.

Maya sat on her bed and pulled off her tights. "It's not the middle of the night," she said. "It isn't even ten o'clock yet."

"Even so," Natasha said. "Where have you been?"

"Practicing," said Maya. She laid her tights on the radiator in the same careful way she had as a little girl.

"Practicing—alone?" There was no hidden meaning behind the question—this was the most they'd spoken in weeks, and Natasha wanted to see if they were still capable of sustaining a conversation.

"Yes," Maya said. Her head was turned away, and Natasha could not see her smile, but she heard it in Maya's voice. She'd always been a terrible liar.

"Good for you," Natasha said. "You know, maybe someday you could try teaching dance instead of performing—if that was something you wanted. You've always been good at explaining steps to people."

"Thanks for your permission," Maya said dryly. "I'll keep that in mind."

"You're welcome," Natasha said, too dozy to be bothered by sarcasm.

Maya wriggled out of her leotard, wrapped herself in a towel from the hook on the back of the door, and slid her feet into a pair of worn slippers. She put her hand on the doorknob.

"Maya?" Natasha crawled to the edge of the bed. "Listen, do you think we could meet at the teahouse tomorrow, like we used to? I need to get away from Ivan for an afternoon. And"—Natasha swallowed—"I miss you."

Maya didn't respond. She stood there in her towel for so long that Natasha wondered if she'd heard her. The evening stillness, which a moment ago had seemed comfortable and familiar to Natasha, evidence of the hundred students sleeping down the hall, now felt oppressive, and Natasha's own breathing obnoxiously loud.

"Please?" Natasha said. "After Karinska's class?"

"Yes," Maya said quietly. "I think we could do that."

"Good." Natasha was so relieved that she decided to stay awake until Maya returned from the shower so they could keep talking, even though she was exhausted. She lay there, nearly exhilarated by this new possibility, and tried to come up with a suitable subject of conversation—anything to keep this rift from widening. Maybe if Natasha thought of the right thing to say tonight, some thread that both of them could cling to, a visit to the teahouse would weave them back together again.

But when Maya came back a few minutes later and got into bed, she introduced a subject of her own. "Does it ever bother you," Maya said, "that we don't know who our father was?"

Many students at the Vaganova didn't have fathers, or any parents at all. The war took someone from everyone, and there was a long tradition of ballet students and dancers being illegitimate heirs of some dignitary or other, so Maya and Natasha didn't feel out of place for being fatherless. Katusha claimed she didn't know who their father was—though she said he'd asked Elizaveta to get rid of them, which certainly didn't endear him to the girls.

If Natasha had been more awake, the suddenness of Maya's question would have startled her, would have alerted her to the fact that Maya was in a peculiar frame of mind. But she was very tired. "I don't know," Natasha said, rubbing her eyes. "Not really."

Neither of them said anything for a minute. "Why?" Natasha asked.

Maya stretched out her weary limbs. "Sometimes I wonder if things would have been better for us if we did."

"Better how? We still would've come to the Vaganova, wouldn't we? I don't see how it would have been any different."

"So if we could find out who our father is—you wouldn't want to know?"

Natasha yawned. "He didn't want us to exist. Why would I want to meet someone who wished I didn't exist?"

"I don't know," Maya said. "Maybe he's changed his mind."

"I think if he'd changed his mind he would've shown up by now."

"You're probably right," Maya said, and Natasha, considering the matter settled, succumbed to sleep at last.

But Maya lay awake, staring at the ceiling. How little the human heart can know itself. Maya thought she wanted a father, and she constructed her thoughts along these lines—*if I had a father, if I knew who my father was*—but Maya, having no experience with fathers, could not imagine one with accuracy. What she really wanted, though she could not have articulated this herself, was a lineage, a history, something that would stretch back in time and fill the past with meaning and project hope into the future. Something that would anchor her in destiny. She was young and frightened, and she wanted something to hold on to, and for this reason she fell asleep full of questions about Balanchine and his kingdom of American ballet.

CHAPTER SIX

Days that turn out to be earth-shattering rarely announce themselves as such in the morning. This particular day, which was to rattle every relationship in Maya and Natasha's little circle, appeared unremarkable in its early hours, though it brought a swift change in weather. This day dawned bright and clear and cold—the sun shone, the air was sharp, and when Yeltsin, the skinny old errand boy, dragged the previous day's trash out into the alleyway, the hairs inside his nostrils turned to tiny icicles. Soon, the daily snows would descend; soon, the river would be frozen over, and skaters all over the city would rejoice. Children would toboggan on old pewter trays; snowshoes would be tied onto feet of all sizes and tromped all over the city, leaving wide, checkered tracks in their wake.

Inside the school, nothing much changed when it was winter. The students wore the same gray uniforms in the studio all year round, whatever the weather, though when it got cold, they took greater care to warm up their muscles before class, and they wrapped themselves in cardigans and covered their arms and legs with warmers that their mothers had knitted. (Natasha was particularly proud of her maroon cabled leg warmers, which Katusha had given her on one of their rare visits home. Knitting the cables had given Katusha a great deal of trouble—more than once, she stayed up all night unraveling mistakes and muttering obscenities—but she loved her goddaughters, and she especially loved the look of delight on Natasha's face when she gave her presents, that face that looked so much like her mother's.) It was cold, but a far cry from the old days, when the classrooms were so poorly heated that the students could see their breath at the barre.

Winter was a stressful time at the school—everyone had been dancing for months and was getting very tired, and the arrival of frost also meant the arrival of the inevitable colds and flus and various other ailments that would make their rounds in the dormitories and grind the Vaganova's weary students (and teachers) even further into the ground.

If a student was going to drop out during the school year—and every year, at every level, at least one student did—it was going to be now. Winter break was only weeks away. Some poor souls, with weary spirits and gnarled feet, would lug their belongings over the school's threshold around New Year's and resolve never to cross it again. Alexei, the school director, walking his morning commute, shivered and wondered who it would be this year, who he wouldn't have to bother casting in the coming spring gala.

But despite this, despite the cold and everything it heralded, something sparked in nearly every senior student's heart when they woke up that morning and saw the first snowflakes begin to fall. After all, it hadn't been very long since they'd been children themselves. The snow felt like a promise to them, the arrival of some great and long-expected magic, a magic that promised something different for everyone. Vasili and Vasilia thought of the long, cold nights when they'd sneak past the dorm mothers and fathers and into each other's beds for warmth. Kira and Olga thought of the smartness of their new wool coats, discreetly smuggled from Paris and trimmed with fox fur. Olaf, having awoken too soon from a pleasant dream, imagined hurtling snowballs at Sophrony and Ivan and astounding them with his powerful throw, maybe even bruising Ivan's arm. Natasha, waking alone, thought of Maya's promise to meet her at the teahouse that afternoon, and this gave her the strength to brave the cold bedroom floor.

Not everyone welcomed the arrival of cold and snow. Anya, waking up with her usual headache, peeked under her bed: her bottle of vodka was empty. She cursed it and kicked it and then cursed her own stupidity because it felt like she'd broken a toe. Sophrony watched the snow fall and thought of his grandfather, who had died last December during a blizzard, and left the window with tears in his eyes. Ivan, too, left his window in sadness—snow meant the school year was nearly half over, and what would be waiting for him and Natasha when it was gone?

Maya didn't watch the snow at the window. She headed off to breakfast early in hopes of catching Pyotr alone. Weary of waiting, she'd decided she needed to take matters into her own hands. It was time to be overtly flirtatious, and to this end, she put on her favorite sweater—blue, the wraparound kind that tied at the waist and accentuated what little breasts she had. Her book bag bounced against her hip as she hurried down the hall, and she imagined what it would be like for Pyotr to carry her bag, as Olaf once had.

The hallway was lined with framed lists of the names of every dancer who had ever graduated from the school. There were also pictures of notable alumni, students who had returned and become teachers, both loved and despised, and many, many stars from the Kirov. The photographs were arranged alphabetically by name, and sometimes Maya stood in front of the spot where her mother's photograph would have been, if she'd lived long enough to be famous. Maya had decided this was her duty: to live the life Elizaveta would've had if her daughters had never been born. Elizaveta's ghost whispered this to her in her sleep, ran a cool hand down Maya's neck in empty hallways, demanded it. Maya had to earn her own place on this wall. It was the debt she owed.

The aroma of porridge floated down the hall. Maya followed it into the cafeteria and then she wished she hadn't—there, sitting at their usual table, sat Olaf, alone. She thought about turning around and waiting for Pyotr in the hallway, but she stood there too long deliberating, and Olaf saw her and waved her over. As much as Maya disliked small talk, she disliked disappointing people even more, let alone someone who'd been as kind to her as Olaf. She gathered her breakfast and joined Olaf at the table.

Olaf, who'd slept well and dreamed even better—ah, the humiliation of waking in a room full of others after dreaming of Maya in the way that he had—was so happy to see her that he was nearly exultant. Though he knew better, he let himself pretend she'd come here just to be with him. "Good morning," he said in a deep morning voice, trying on this new role as a person whose company was sought after.

"Morning," Maya said. Her stomach turned a little at the way Olaf was smiling at her—crookedly, like somebody had been startled while drawing a mouth on a scarecrow. He had nice eyes, she thought—he could find a girl if he just relaxed a little. She made herself swallow some tea for the sake of having something to do. "You haven't seen Pyotr this morning, have you?"

Olaf shook his head. "He's probably off with Anya. He went to see her as soon as he woke up."

"Why?"

Olaf shrugged. "I don't know. He said she needed something from him." He looked up from his breakfast and winked at Maya in a most dreadful way. "Everybody's got to keep warm somehow, huh?" This innuendo was as loathsome to her as if he'd farted into her porridge.

Maya became very, very still, still enough that Olaf thought that his wink had made her feel amorous. "Is he in love with her?" she said.

Olaf, who was thrilled to be asked any question by anybody—particularly someone as pretty as Maya, whose face he'd taken to thinking of as he was falling asleep, which explained his dream—launched into one of his overly confident explanations. "In love with her! She's all he talks about. You know, I'm tired of the whole subject, honestly. All he does is moon around and mope about it. She doesn't want anything to do with him. And you know, all the better for him, I say. She won't be around much longer anyway."

Maya knew better than to indulge Olaf's penchant for gossip. But it was as if she'd picked off part of a scab and couldn't leave the rest untouched. "Why do you say that?"

"Don't you know?" Olaf said, even though he knew that she didn't—no one knew, except him and Karinska, who'd sworn him to secrecy knowing full well that Olaf couldn't keep a secret if he tried. "She's a drunk. Apparently, her mother is sick or something, and she's taking it hard, so she drinks. Alexei's furious at her—he said that if she sticks another toe out of line, he'll kick her out."

This news should have produced pity in Maya. It should have made her concerned for her classmate, whom she'd known since they were both nine years old and hadn't even gotten their first pair of pointe shoes yet. And as late as three months ago, she would have felt sorry for Anya. But the idea that Pyotr was in love with her, and the memories of Anya's petty cruelties, took all the energy Maya would have put into feeling sorry and crystallized it into something hard and sharp and hateful.

"I hope she does get kicked out," Maya said. "There's no excuse for such behavior."

Olaf, who looked a little startled, found himself in the surprising position of defending Anya. "Her mother is sick," he repeated. "She's taking it hard."

"So what?" Maya said. "My mother is dead. You don't see me fucking around."

Olaf put down his spoon. "What?" Maya had a reputation in the school for being a soft, unobtrusive sort of person. It wasn't that Olaf had never heard her say something like that—it was that *no one* had, because she'd never said such a thing in her life. If there had been other people sitting at the table, they would have put down their spoons and stared at her too.

"She's going to make us all look bad," Maya stammered. Even she was surprised by her words. "If she's going to make a fool of herself, she might as well get it over with."

Olaf swirled his spoon in his porridge and pondered this. "I hadn't thought of it that way," he said. Thus explained, Maya's spitefulness endeared her to him. She seemed to be confiding in him, or at least colluding with him. He wished he had a way to cheer her up, to make her see him as more than just a partner. He wanted to be someone she could rely on.

The silence—which was tainted with a sense of anticipation, whose nature Maya vaguely understood but did not want to acknowledge—was making Maya's skin crawl. She wolfed down the rest of her porridge and excused herself, leaving Olaf to finish his breakfast alone.

Maya didn't look at anyone as she hurried back toward her room. She tried—and failed—to ignore Olaf's report. Perhaps Pyotr's affections were directed elsewhere—it would explain all her fruitless months of waiting—but Maya didn't want to believe it. "Olaf makes things up all the time," Maya thought as she neared the door to the dormitories. Only yesterday, he'd told her that Vasilia was pregnant. Everyone knew she was too skinny to have periods.

Just as Maya reached out to open the door, it burst open and Anya tumbled through, knocking Maya to the ground. Anya tripped over her and fell, scattering a handful of something in the process.

"Lord, woman, watch where you're going!" Anya said, getting to her feet. "Or are you as blind as you are ugly?" She reached down to pick up the things she'd dropped—little yellow pills.

Pyotr ran up to the door. "There you are, you naughty girl!" he said to Anya, out of breath but looking amused. "Give those back! You don't need that many." He held out his palm.

"Naughty girls don't do as they're told," Anya said, and she dashed down the hallway and Pyotr took off after her, both laughing, both as interested in the chase itself as its end.

Maya, still on the floor, sat up and rubbed her throbbing knee. So, Olaf was right. Of course. Wasn't this the way her life had always gone? There would always be someone prettier, more talented, more deserving of love. If the choice was between her and someone else, Maya would always be the one left behind.

Maya got to her feet and felt something crunch under her shoe. There, surrounding her foot, were three of Anya's pills. Maya picked them up and rolled them around in her palm. Lucky for Anya that she'd found them and not one of the dorm mothers—with Anya on such thin ice, as Olaf had said, who knew how she'd be punished.

Anya and Pyotr's laughs echoed down the hall. This was when Maya began to understand that she was capable of doing terrible things.

While Maya hurried to her room, Ivan stood outside the hallway that connected the boys' and girls' dormitories, bereft of hope. He and Natasha had been fighting for weeks, and every day he woke up believing a little less in the fantasy he'd concocted for the two of them, that they'd go on loving each other for the rest of their lives.

On this particular morning, he woke up with the kind of idea that men of all ages encounter but only adolescents (or those who never mature past adolescence) entertain: he would test her.

He leaned against the wall with his jacket over his shoulder like the leading men he'd seen in American films. Elsewhere in the world, the people who passed by would have thought that he looked like James Dean. But this was Leningrad, not Los Angeles, and everyone who hurried past him thought only that he looked sad.

Girls of all ages streamed in spurts through the doorway like blood from a wound. The littlest ones, eight- and nine-year-olds, who were somehow always running late, rushed through clutching bags half their size. Eleven-year-olds, only recently put in toe shoes, hobbled down the hall, wondering how long it would be until their beleaguered toenails would fall off. The fifteen- and sixteen-year-olds, much more like women than girls, tossed bashful glances up to Ivan, who had for several years enjoyed a prominent position as one of the most attractive boys at the school. One of these older girls, a little black-haired thing whose tiny waist made her head look enormous, smiled at him and, turning to her companion, said suggestively that she couldn't wait 'til she was a little bit older. Ivan's chest rose a little higher after that.

As the stream of students trickled away, Ivan became so anxious that his skin on his arms prickled. He took a deep breath and began reviewing his plan in an attempt to calm himself. Any minute, Natasha would come through the door. Late, as always. She would be in a hurry, which would either be an aid to Ivan's test or suspend it altogether.

He would catch her by surprise. He would tell her—truthfully—that their constant bickering was driving him crazy and—less truthfully—that he'd found a cure, and he would produce from his pocket a little pewter ring he'd once taken from his mother's bureau. He would propose marriage as a solution to their problem.

They couldn't get married right away. They would have to wait until they graduated. But when Ivan proposed this to Natasha, he would be able to see, once and for all, if she really loved him.

Ivan took the ring out and slipped it onto his pinky. His mother had been tall and big-boned, like him, and he wondered if the ring might be too big for Natasha. But the ring itself wasn't the point, he reminded himself. The point would be how she reacted.

The hallway was deserted now. Ivan could hear the thrum of students in the cafeteria, though it was down a flight of stairs. He glanced at the clock and saw with alarm that it was much later than he realized; if Natasha didn't turn up soon, he would miss breakfast. He considered the feasibility of doing an entire morning's worth of classes on an empty stomach. Maybe, if he ran back to his room, he could grab a few cookies from the box Sophrony always kept stashed under his bed and still dash back in time to see her. Ivan began putting on his jacket in preparation.

Natasha came through the door, looking haggard. She'd slept terribly—her old back injury had somehow worsened in her sleep, and she walked slowly, tenderly, hoping not to aggravate it further. All she wanted was to drink some tea and dance the whole day and forget herself for a little while. This is why, when she saw Ivan, she frowned. She was not in the mood for a confrontation.

Ivan swallowed. "Good morning," he said, trying to smile.

"I'm late," Natasha said, still walking, "and I'm hungry."

Ivan was very hungry too, and this was not an encouraging beginning, but something in her loveliness—something he himself could not articulate or understand—pushed him toward his foolish test. "Natasha," he said, and the tenderness in his voice made Natasha stop walking.

She sighed. "What is it?" she asked, still facing away from him.

"Will you turn around?"

She did, and she saw Ivan standing there, holding out a little pewter ring, and she thought that her day could not possibly get any worse. She had a headache, a back injury, an empty stomach, and now this—a boyfriend playacting as a grown-up. When Natasha had woken up that morning, she'd thought to herself that it might be time to let Ivan go. This confirmed it. She knew he didn't really want to get married. She knew he was proposing as some sort of puerile test of her affections.

And yet, and yet. He was looking at her with such hope that she couldn't make the words come out of her mouth.

Ivan had planned a whole speech for her—a sincere one, full of all the things he liked most about her, that he wanted her to be the mother of his children, things he'd always imagined saying to her when the moment was right. This, he realized as he stood there waiting for her answer, was not the right moment.

"Well?" Ivan knew what Natasha was going to say before she said it. He wanted to keep his dignity. He wanted to get it over with.

Natasha lowered her eyes. "I'm sorry," she said. She wanted to run away, to go anywhere, but her feet refused to move.

"For what?" Ivan said, and his voice cracked. He was still stretching the ring out toward her. He wanted to fling it to the floor, but his body, like Natasha's, was rebelling against him—perhaps, after countless hours spent in closeness, their bodies were eager to avoid a separation—and his thumb and forefinger would not release.

The hallway traffic started picking up again. Everyone was running to class or back to their bedrooms to pick up their bags. Breakfast was over, and this realization, along with the sudden presence of witnesses, enabled Ivan and Natasha to master themselves and snap out of their frozenness. Ivan stuffed the ring back into his pocket, and Natasha turned to go. "It's him, isn't it?" Ivan said. "You're leaving me for him." Ivan referred to Ilya, and he did so not in search of answers—a part of him believed she'd never seen Ilya again—but in a panicked attempt to grasp at the familiar, at what had once joined them together. Even their old fights would be better than being alone. But his fear contorted his face, and the bigheaded girl who'd admired Ivan before glanced discreetly at the warring couple and sided with Natasha.

Natasha spun on her heel and faced him. She'd never seen Ilya again, not once, and she knew that Ivan knew this, and this made her angrier than anything. "No," she said. "I'm leaving you to be with anyone else." And she left him alone in the hallway.

Karinska could not understand what had come over her students. Natasha's ankles shook so badly during relevés that Karinska made her sit out the rest of the class, and when she swapped Anya in to dance with Ivan, the two of them didn't do any better. Even Maya and Olaf stumbled once or twice. It was as if the snow had scrambled everyone's brains. Vasili and Vasilia were, for reasons unknown, absent.

After twenty minutes of this, Karinska threw up her hands. "I give up," she said. "You're all a mess today. If I push you, you will hurt yourselves, and I'll be blamed for it, and I'll be damned if I let a bunch of snotty-nosed brats push me out in my prime!" Olga and Sophrony both chuckled at this—it was very unusual for a teacher at the Vaganova to use such language—which made Karinska so angry that a vein bulged on her forehead.

Karinska came out from her usual perch by the piano and stood in the center of the room, swiveling her head around like an owl. "Do any of you understand what's actually at stake here?" she cried. "Do you? You live here where it is safe, where there's always enough to eat, nobody to worry or antagonize you. If you are hurt, someone comes to care for you. If you are sick, someone makes you well. Do you think this is how it will go for the rest of your lives if you are lazy? Do you understand what it's like out there"—she shook her enormous fist in the direction of the great half-dome window—"for everyone else out in the world?"

This was a rhetorical question—they all knew about the outside world, they all had cousins and siblings who had less food and far more troubles—but Karinska could tell from the faces of everyone in the room that her intended point had not registered, so she continued. "If you do not press yourselves, if you do not work as hard as you can, if you do not rise to the top as the very best artists that this country has to offer—artists that our country can be proud of, can parade around the world—then you are nothing. No, you are worse than nothing, because you were given everything and you will have squandered it. If you leave this school and make fools of yourselves, there will be nobody to help you. You will work in crowded offices where nobody cares about your once-promising childhood. You will have nothing, you will have worked for nothing, and it will be nobody's fault but your own."

This was a longer speech than Karinska had given in a long time, and her lungs and knees both complained. Not wanting the students to see her weakness, she headed for the door. "If any of you ever come to my classroom with this attitude again," she said, breathlessly, over her shoulder, "I will see to it personally that each of you is expelled." She slammed the door, and the worried accompanist hurried after her.

Nobody dared move after this exhibition. They had been yelled at before—each of them had been scolded, insulted, and most had even been slapped, but nothing like this. Everyone stood stock still, afraid that Karinska would rush back in with Alexei at her side and all their lives would be over.

And then Olga sneezed, and everybody turned to her, alarmed—as if they were only safe inside the classroom because they'd been quiet—and this communal motion made them realize they were probably being silly, and the room came back to life again with stretching and cooling down and shucking hot shoes from feet.

Natasha turned to ask Maya if they could still meet at the teahouse—now she needed it more than ever—but Maya was already gone.

Alexei hung up the phone and sat alone in his chilly office. The moment he'd walked in the door the Minister of Culture had called and given him yet another earful about the duties of his role, the importance of his work, what would be lost if he failed (the reputation of Russia as a world ballet power, the respect of his colleagues, his very reputation, etc., etc.). Nikolai, always insistent and often shrill, was even more insistent and shriller than usual. "You must take your work seriously," he said, though Alexei was the most serious ballet master in the country and both of them knew it. "They're asking me if the Kirov is ready to go abroad. They won't need many students for their corps, as you know, but they have to be the best. You have to tell me, Alexei—I have to know, and it is your duty to tell me—if yours will be good enough. In the spring, I will sit in the box at the student gala myself, and I will tell you that my standards are going to be very high." Nikolai spoke as if some great weight was lying on his shoulders and he was desperate to pass it off to someone else.

Alexei sat at his desk and rubbed his forehead. He had seen his father crushed under the weight of bureaucracy, and his father's father; he'd lost many uncles and the fathers of friends to the Year of '37, their wives and children carted off to hard labor and orphanages. Thankfully, he thought, things were different now, and the only thing he was in danger of losing was his job. Alexei did not listen to the small part of himself that warned things could be otherwise.

Alexei rose from his desk and walked to the little samovar he kept on a side table. Though it had been nearly an hour, he still hadn't warmed up from his walk to the school. The back of his throat felt raw and scraped, and he'd sneezed every six or seven minutes since he'd arrived—twice, during Nikolai's call, he'd hidden his nose in his sleeve. He hoped—hoped to the god who did not exist—that he wasn't getting a cold. His wife had called before Nikolai and informed him that he'd better be home for dinner, even though he always came home for dinner, because this was her way of saying that she'd gotten the children out of the house and they'd have it all to themselves, and she had certain expectations. She was always convincing herself Alexei was having little love affairs with students, though he'd been faithful to her for many years, and these evenings were a sort of test for him. Alexei felt as if everything he loved was brittle, including himself, and it would all fall apart if he didn't hold it together. He threw back his head and sneezed so hard that one of his eardrums started ringing—a mighty sneeze, an unmistakable first-real-sneeze-of-a-cold kind of sneeze. "Oh, God," Alexei cried, and it sounded like a plea. Being a man, he was a big baby about colds.

Karinska poked her head in the door, wearing enormous sapphire earrings and looking very much like an aged bird of paradise. She'd sat in her office and had a cup of tea before coming to see him, and her anger had simmered down into annoyance. "Alexei, dear," she said. "The seniors were a mess today, just unspeakably bad, and I sent them all to their rooms for an hour of rest. Don't worry—of course, I gave them all a good talking-to. And you know, maybe you need some rest yourself, my dear, or some hot soup. You look near death. Goodbye!" And then, before Alexei had the chance to let a single sound escape from his scraped throat in reply, she was gone.

Alexei groaned and put his head in his hands. His sinuses began to throb. Under no circumstances was it appropriate for a teacher to simply cancel class, especially not without his permission. What a mess this year had handed him. The history teacher had told him he'd heard students fighting in the attic, which was worse than the usual lovemaking in the closet. Vasilia had gotten pregnant and had been whisked off by her mother that morning to get an abortion at one of the women's clinics. And Anya—wretched Anya—had gotten drunk so many times that he worried she'd ruin the spring gala. If these sorts of things kept up, he would be out on his rear end by the start of summer.

The wind picked up, and a draft billowed through the window and set the office curtains to dancing. Alexei stood, intending to draw the curtains closed. He looked out the window and saw the long ancient edifice of the academy, the same pale yellow it had been for nearly two centuries, the same view that had been seen by Petipa and every ballet master since.

Alexei straightened his shoulders. He was not a pawn in anyone's game. He was the ballet master of the Vaganova Ballet Academy, a strong and capable man. He had been chosen for this job over many others, and he had kept it for many years despite the difficulties, and he would continue to keep it. Yes—he would lay down the law if necessary.

Someone knocked. He crossed the room and opened his office door and there was Maya, trembling, holding something in a closed fist that she held out in front of her body as if she were afraid it would set her on fire. "I have something to show you," she said, and she uncurled her fist and revealed a bunch of sticky yellow pills.

Alexei stood there, still holding the door, and waited for Maya to say something else, and when she didn't, Alexei realized this was going to be one of those conversations when he had to draw everything out of the student. He sighed and cleared his scraped throat and asked her to come in.

While Maya took a shaky seat across from the ballet master, Natasha passed beneath the window of Alexei's office on her hurried walk to the teahouse. The snow had fallen swift and thick since morning, and Natasha, bundled in her faded blue coat that she despised, found no satisfaction in the squeaking sensation her footfalls produced on the now-invisible sidewalk.

There is a particular kind of loneliness that comes from being alone in a room or for an afternoon. There is a sharper, deeper kind that comes from feeling lonely in the presence of another person, a loneliness made thicker and more frightening (but all the more common) if the person is someone to whom we are very close. But the worst loneliness of all was the one that Natasha was now experiencing: to be alone and lonely in a great mass of people enjoying themselves.

Everyone in Leningrad seemed to be outside, as if Karinska's pronouncement of an hour off had been for the entire city and not just the dancers. Groups of children pulled toboggans, heading for the snow-covered steps at the amphitheater on the outskirts of the city. Gangs of leggy boys and pairs of lovers tossed snowballs at one another and worked up a good sweat despite the cold. And families formed dark little bundled lines, holding hands to keep the littlest ones from getting lost in the fray. Everyone here had somebody. Everyone but her.

Natasha's toes ached from the cold. She trudged on through the snow, relieved by the thought that in just a few minutes she would find Maya at the teahouse, and then everything would be better. She felt gratitude and relief for having been born with a twin, a person who could always be hers to rely on. Natasha needed her sister more than ever.

But Maya was not at the teahouse. Natasha sat and she waited, and she drank an entire pot of black tea and she waited, and she went and used the bathroom and she waited, and Maya did not arrive.

Natasha sat with her head in her hands, her nerves fizzing from all the tea, and wondered when it was exactly that she'd become so lonely. She had nobody now, no friends, no Ivan, not even a sister who cared. Nobody loved her or noticed her or understood.

It was at this moment that Ilya walked into the teahouse.

Who we become in this life depends on much more than our desires. Others begin telling us who we are the moment we're born and then go right on telling us until we die. Natasha, for months, through subtle hints and not-so-subtle accusations, had been told by Ivan that she was in love with Ilya, that she was obsessed with him, that she cared about nothing but being with him. When Ilya walked into the teahouse and found Natasha, abandoned and alone, she invited him to her table, not because she loved him but because she had been told so many times she was his lover, and that was who she became.

CHAPTER SEVEN

That year, when spring came to Leningrad, it came suddenly. One day everyone was bundled against the cold and the wind; the next, the ice on the Neva cracked and people unwound the thick scarves from their throats and musicians came and played on the streets and robins competed with their songs. A week later, the ice on the Neva, the same ice on which people had walked and skated for months without even thinking about what a marvel that was, splintered into little icebergs, and people came and watched the icebergs sail off into the Gulf of Finland. The great thaw had begun.

For Alexei, this was the busiest time of year. The senior gala was in just a few months, and the Kirov auditions, which he personally oversaw, were only days away. Both required long nights and weekends, and his wife packed him little dinners in wicker baskets with pickles and buckwheat salad and potato and scallion pirozhki. For the rest of his life, even when he was a very old man who remembered little of what he'd done or who he'd been, the taste of scallions made Alexei feel tired and a little despairing, like there would never be enough time in the day to do what needed to be done.

And there was much to be done. Students had to be coached in their roles for the gala, teachers had to be placated and encouraged, sets and costume designs for the gala had to be approved, along with a host of other things that Alexei remembered and then forgot again on a daily basis.

Despite all this, Alexei felt unusually calm. His life was not at all as irritating to him as it had been last autumn, when everything seemed on the verge of falling apart (including himself). He went through his daily affairs with unusual serenity. He thought he was simply maturing into a more gracious man, surer of himself and better respected within his community. That the irritating phone calls from the Minister of Culture had suddenly stopped coming certainly helped. But that wasn't the real reason either.

The real reason for Alexei's calm was simple: the senior class had settled down. No longer did Alexei have to deal with Vasili and Vasilia's crises or reports of Anya's drunken escapades. The storage closets were left alone. No one was shouting in the attics. Even Olaf, often appearing in the guise of greeting Alexei's assistant Nonna but really on the hunt for gossip, had ceased to haunt the hallway. For once, Alexei's entire job was just doing his job, and he was very good at it.

It had helped that Maya found Anya's drugs. Alexei had wanted to throw Anya out for months, but he needed a good reason, and Maya delivered it by hand. The timing was ideal—it was almost as if Maya had known this and waited to come into his office until just the right moment. If any of the other students did such a thing, Alexei would have questioned their motives, would have wondered if they were acting out of competitiveness or jealousy—but Maya was above reproach. Everyone who knew her understood her to be a sweet and simple person, one who could not be deceitful if she tried. So when Maya said she'd seen Anya taking the drugs, Alexei took Maya at her word and sent Anya packing that evening. That night, Alexei came home and made love to his wife—even she was surprised by his sudden energy—and slept better than he'd slept in a year, and he continued sleeping well even into the spring.

Alexei would have tossed and turned on this April evening if he'd known that Natasha was, as he dreamed away, sneaking out into the night alone.

A small group of younger girls who, out of boredom or admiration, had taken an interest in Natasha's nocturnal wanderings crowded around a dorm window and watched her slip out the door.

"There she goes," whispered a second-year. "Third time this week!"

"How does she get past the night watchman?" asked a first-year with a furrowed brow. She was at the age when the world was full of frightening things and grown-ups still inspired awe, and she didn't understand how anyone could be as fearless as Natasha.

"Easy," said a third-year, whose knowledge of the things of the world never ceased to amaze her younger neighbors. "She waits until he takes a leak and then she goes."

"How does she know when he's going to take a leak?"

"He's an old man. He's always about to take a leak."

This produced a series of indecent titters, and the young girls, who, unlike Natasha, slept in a large room under the watchful eye of a night matron, were shushed and told to go to sleep, and Natasha stole down the sidewalk without further observation. Each girl, as she settled down into her bed, imagined Natasha striding down the dark sidewalk alone and tried to picture her destination. Maybe Natasha had taken up with the People's Patrol Brigade and prowled the city, seeking out ne'er-do-wells with a club in hand. Or Natasha was having a love affair with a high-ranking Party official who could only meet after his wife had gone to bed. One girl convinced herself Natasha had gotten a job as a bartender and was saving up money for something outlandish and wonderful.

Though this last rumor, like the others, had no evidence to confirm it, it provided a possible explanation for another mysterious circumstance in Natasha's life. Since the winter, Natasha's wardrobe had stealthily improved, with no obvious cause. She was subtle about it: a pair of suede gloves here, a new pair of leg warmers there—but Maya noticed these things, because she was as accustomed to her sister's uninspired clothing as her own, and Natasha's new possessions were nicer than anything they'd ever been able to afford or even glimpsed in shop windows.

Once, when Natasha arrived at history class wearing a beautiful white mohair sweater, the kind of thing that nobody had ever even seen except on movie stars, Maya snuck over and asked her where it had come from. Natasha looked at her like she was crazy and then glanced around at everyone and said, a little too loudly, "What are you talking about? Katusha gave me this sweater for my birthday. You remember." But Maya didn't remember, because it wasn't true.

Maya felt further away from her sister than ever. After she'd accidentally stood her up at the teahouse, Natasha hadn't repeated the invitation, and now they spoke even less than before. When they went home over winter break, Natasha stayed out all day and only came home when everyone else was in bed. Katusha, who was hurt by Natasha's absence but didn't show it—the flighty girl, with her strong resemblance to her mother, had always been her favorite—advised Maya to be patient. "Natasha's just parted ways with her first love," she explained. "That makes everyone a little crazy. Let her go off on her own for a while—she'll come back to you."

It was easy advice to accept: now that they were back at school, with graduation just around the corner, Maya had enough things to worry about, and she resolved to stay out of her sister's affairs. Because Natasha always waited until her sister had drifted off to sneak out, and she always returned before the morning, Maya didn't know about her wanderings. The little girls who watched Natasha, proud of having a secret all their own, kept their knowledge to themselves, and the night watchman had a terribly enlarged prostate, and Maya was a very heavy sleeper, and because of all this, Natasha's nocturnal adventures remained undiscovered.

In the daytime, everything carried on at the Vaganova with remarkable smoothness. Anya's disappearance, the cause of which was universally understood and surprised no one, had an immediate rearranging effect on the social structure of the senior class. Now lacking Anya as the prospective third partner, Natasha and Ivan resigned themselves to being partners only onstage and, as a result, their dancing rebounded. They knew each other's bodies better than anyone else in the class—even Vasili and Vasilia, whose chemistry had fizzled somewhat after Vasilia's mysterious disappearance some months back. Pyotr had, as was fitting for a boy of his melancholic disposition and artistic temperament, mourned the loss of Anya for months on end. His dancing took on a note of the tragic hero, jilted in love and slower than ever, and his soulful partnering impressed even the Kirov impresario who had stuck his head in the door to see how Alexei's young saplings were coming along.

Maya had grown stronger and quicker and more commanding in her presence on and off the stage floor. Everyone noticed it—sometimes, during class, the adagio teacher's eyes wandered over toward her legs and lingered there a little too long. Maya carried her head higher now, didn't cower when called upon, didn't immediately turn when someone spoke her name. Something new was in her, and everyone could see it.

Everyone, that is, but Pyotr. Maya stood by patiently while he mourned the loss of his first love, accepting that Anya would always hold some place in the shrine of his heart, a candle burning in front of a tarnished old icon. She even admired him for the depth of his mourning and melancholy, wondering expectantly what the light of this great passion would stir up when it shone on her instead. But when the days of mourning turned into weeks, and weeks into months, Maya began to find it difficult not to slip into despair herself.

Every now and again, Maya wondered if Pyotr's lack of interest in her was her punishment for what she'd done to Anya. Maya tried to convince herself that she hadn't acted out of vindictiveness but out of concern for a friend. It was for her own good, Maya always told herself as she began to fall asleep. "If she'd kept dancing and drinking, she would've hurt herself. Luckily, I swooped in and saved her." Her heart thus hardened against guilt, Maya entered a much more dangerous phase of transgression. She began congratulating herself for acting righteously.

But she still wished Pyotr loved her. Sometimes she stayed alone in the classroom after her practice sessions with Olaf and stared at herself in the mirrors, searching for some flaw Pyotr must have found in her. Was she not lovely? Was she not worthy? Had she not improved herself in every possible way, paying more careful attention to her hair and dress, gleaning methods of flirtatiousness from observing Kira and Olga and Vasilia?

Maya had lost the myth of her life. Distant from her sister, and loverless, she decided to invent a new fate for herself. She would tour the world with the Kirov. She would meet Balanchine in America, who'd recognize her for who she truly was—if nothing else, someone like him, someone capable of greatness. She would remind him of his duty to his mother country—a country that had raised him and given him his craft, just as it had for her—and he'd be so chastened that he would repent of his apostasy and return with her to Russia and make her his great pupil out of gratitude. Maya borrowed Olaf's magazine with Balanchine on the cover and kept it in her dresser drawer, and at the end of every day, when she came back to her room to change for dinner, she took it out and greeted her idol. "Don't worry," she said, tracing his profile with her fingers. "I'm coming to you soon."

Audition day arrived. Thanks to the long-standing relationship between the two institutions, the audition took place in a Vaganova classroom instead of at the Kirov. The senior students did not speak to one another as they lined up in the hallway. The boys and girls would audition separately, with one group sequestered in the hallway while the other faced its trial. The girls stood in a silent cluster and watched the boys file into the classroom as if heading off to war. The boys gave one another glances that seemed to say both "Best of luck to you" and "Goodbye." Younger students, on their way to class, nodded respectfully to the seniors as they walked by and felt fortunate to have a few more years before facing this calamity.

Only two Vaganova staff were allowed inside the audition room: Alexei, who'd been coaching the seniors himself, and Tatiana, a new teacher who had only begun with them that spring but whose fifteen years at the Kirov gave her a sharp eye for women's dancing, and for what the Kirov wanted.

From Alexei's point of view, the conditions could not have been better. The boys had plenty of time to warm up at the barre. No one was sick, which was a rarity at these events—the year previous, the entire class had come down with croup, and two poor boys, aching with fever, slipped in puddles of their own sweat and sprained their ankles. The Kirov ballet master and his staff were kind and encouraging, which buoyed the boys' spirits, and afterward, when they'd done a barre and exhibited their technical proficiency and performed the assigned choreography with abandon, each boy filed away a secret hope of having his name on the list that would be posted on the community bulletin board later that week.

It was rare for a student not to perform well at these auditions, but Alexei felt relief when it was over. He gave each boy a stern nod as they left the room in exaltation. Now that the calamity had passed, the boys walked with exaggerated swagger; they wanted to give the impression that they had never been anxious at all—not about this or about anything else in their lives. The soldiers had gone to battle and didn't see what all the fuss was about.

Olaf winked at Maya as he walked past her. "Not so bad," he said. "Just like everyday class."

This pronouncement encouraged all of the girls, but they discovered it wasn't quite true. No one class determined the course of your future. No class was attended by the ballet master of the greatest company in the world. No class had the capacity to take your nerves and shred them within seconds.

The audition covered every element of dancing they knew—every leap, every turn, every placement of hands and feet and head. At first, the students performed in groups of five or six. Alexei watched and, though he tried not to, made private predictions of how far his students would go. This was an annual pastime of his, and his intuitions were usually right. He made his predictions not from the appearance of the students' bodies, but from their shadows. The students' expressions were distractions—a mediocre student could thwart Alexei's intuition with her prettiness—but the shadow could not lie. When Alexei saw his students' shadows, he knew whether or not they would be worthy of a spotlight.

The girls' shadows were, for the most part, easy to read. Kira was sweet and eager to please; Vasilia was icy, but strong; either could be chosen for the corps. Olga, who had desperately tried to lose fifteen pounds over New Year's by running up and down the stairs ten times every morning but hadn't succeeded, wobbled through her pirouettes; Alexei imagined her teaching a little crew of fur-clad Siberians to plié. But when he watched Maya and Natasha's shadows, Alexei came up empty; his imagination laid out no future for them, grand or mundane. For once, he couldn't make a prediction at all.

The auditions would end with fouettés, great whirling turns in which a dancer, standing en pointe, extends her right leg and snaps it around, creating a torque unmatched by anything else in ballet. It was among a ballerina's greatest challenges, and some dancers became world-famous for doing fifty at a time. Somehow—whether by coincidence or at Alexei's suggestion, who'd warned the Kirov officials that the girls were sisters—when it came time for fouettés, Olga, Kira, and Vasilia were put together, and Maya and Natasha were paired for last.

Olga, Kira, and Vasilia did their best, which was just well enough, Alexei supposed, to meet school standards, and he was right; the officials looked pleased. Alexei relaxed when the three girls passed through their last turns. But when Maya and Natasha stepped up, everyone seemed to hold their breath at once.

Six months ago, it wouldn't have even been a question. Maya would have squeaked by with a bit of luck, and Natasha would have been the star, and the decision would have been easy. But now, as the girls began their turns, the change that had snuck up over the winter became obvious. Maya had not only caught up with her sister but threatened to overtake her: as Natasha finished up her thirtieth fouetté (which was all that was required), Maya finished her thirty-first. Even the Kirov officials seemed impressed.

Tatiana leaned over to Alexei, who was standing by the piano and absently beating out rhythms with the palm of his hand. "How is that going to turn out?" she whispered. "They can't both get in."

Alexei shook his head. "I'm more worried about what will happen to the one who's left behind."

The audition now over, the girls were beside themselves with relief, and they left the classroom just as transformed as the boys. Olga and Kira started crying and held each other. Vasilia ran over to Vasili and leapt into his arms. Maya and Natasha caught each other's eyes for a moment—just a moment—and Natasha furrowed her brow and was about to say something, but Alexei and Tatiana came over and shook hands with them all, and when the handshakes were over, Natasha had gone.

Maya sat heavily on a padded bench in the hallway. Sweat had glued her shoe ribbons in place, and she peeled them off her legs like strips of skin after a sunburn. Six months ago, she would have been ecstatic to best her sister at fouettés, but all she felt now was emptiness. She pried her damp shoes from her feet. Her toes ached. She wanted to disappear into a steaming bathtub somewhere without having to speak to anyone ever again. She rubbed her left pinky toe, whose nail was in deep danger of falling off, and imagined herself in a bathhouse someplace, wrapped in a fluffy white towel, dozing away while someone massaged her shoulders and someone else brought her hot tea with lemon on a gleaming silver tray.

"Dreaming?" someone said, startling her. "Sorry," Olaf said, looking bemused. "You seemed so happy."

Maya pulled rough cotton socks over her tender feet and winced. "I'll be happy when I can run away and join the circus."

Olaf laughed and crouched down low beside her. "Your talents would be underappreciated there," he said. "I'll bet you were wonderful today." He offered her a hand up. "Shall we celebrate?"

"Of course," she said, and then she worried that the "of course" sounded like arrogance—*of course I was wonderful*—and not an acceptance of his invitation. "Of course we can celebrate," she stammered as they stood.

"Excellent," Olaf said. "Pyotr was just telling me about someplace—where has he gotten to? Pyotr!"

Olaf waved Pyotr over, and the closer Pyotr got to them, the more Maya's spirits rose. Whether the invitation was a coincidence or a selfless gesture of friendship on Olaf's part, Maya didn't know—but either way, she was grateful Pyotr was coming with them.

Soon the three of them left the school, headed to some mysterious and original place Pyotr claimed to have discovered. "Be excited," he said. "My brother said this place is really good."

Olaf rubbed his hands together. "The best blintzes, you said?" His actual level of excitement was indistinguishable from his desire to make a good impression on them both.

"The absolute best," Pyotr said. "So good they'll make you want to blow your brains out."

Maya shivered, even though it was a warm day and she was wearing her practice sweater. Jokes about suicide nauseated her, made her wonder things about her mother that she wished she wouldn't—Katusha had never told them how her mother had ended her life—but for now putting up with Pyotr's coarseness was the price of time with him.

The sun was out, and everyone's spirits seemed lifted. On their way to the very best blintzes, which were farther from the school than Maya usually wandered, they passed pairs of old women in kerchiefs, housewives with baskets over their arms, and a group of children playing some sort of elaborate game involving marbles and coins. Later, when Maya had grown up, she'd remember that afternoon had been so lovely—the gift of strolling down the sidewalk in the sun, flanked on either side by a handsome boy—that she'd felt like a character in a comedy film. Any second now somebody would say something that would make them all laugh—and maybe, if Pyotr was laughing, he would look down at Maya and see, at last, how lovely she was, and she would look back and pin all of her happiness on this one moment.

But that moment never came. Instead, a young man with red hair exited an alleyway far down the road from them. He stood out like a firefly: his hair was slicked up and over his forehead in a ridiculous wave, which, owing to the scarcity of hairspray, he'd glued in place with sugar syrup, and his yellow suit was as bright as his hair. He turned from the alleyway and started walking in their direction, head held high.

Everyone else on the sidewalk avoided looking one another in the eye: living when and where they did required an aptitude for staying out of trouble, which meant minding your business at all costs. But the boy with red hair met the gaze of every person he passed. He greeted everyone who passed him with a jut of his prominent chin.

"That dick," Pyotr mumbled under his breath. He shoved his fists deep into his pockets. "Thinks his clothes make him somebody important."

"He probably is somebody important," Olaf said. "You know, Karinska told me most of these smart-dressing kids are the sons of bigwig Party members. That's how they get away with it—nobody wants to cross their fathers."

"I can't believe he's just walking out in the open like this," Pyotr said, with an edge to his voice that made Maya look up in surprise. "Haven't you seen all of the posters? You'd think he'd know better. People who act like that should be arrested. It's unpatriotic."

Maya had seen the posters. Though nearly every block and alley in the city was wallpapered with messages urging viewers toward some virtue (usually involving hard work, sacrifice, and scythes) or away from some vice (drinking, gambling, loose women), the anti-stilyagi posters were impossible to miss because they were the most colorful. One poster depicted a stilyaga as nothing but an empty hanger of flamboyant clothes—clothes just like those on the boy walking toward them. *A sold soul,* the poster had said. Another decried the stilyagi for their bourgeois tastes in music, tastes that could only indicate something sinister. *Today he dances to jazz*, it said. *Tomorrow he will sell his homeland!*

The boy was now close enough that in a minute, they would be the targets of his chin-juts. Maya felt Pyotr tense up beside her as the boy got closer, and she worried that some sort of confrontation would break out when he reached them.

A group of tall, burly young men passed them on the sidewalk and stopped in front of the stilyaga. They were all dressed in the same gray uniforms Maya and the others wore to Komsomol every week.

One of the men stepped out from the group. "Tell me, friend," he said, "would you care to have a discussion?" The man's voice was a rich bass; if he'd been born sixty years before, he would have been recruited as a chanter in a church, where his voice would have warned parishioners to turn from their sins and avoid perdition. But, most of the churches long shuttered, the man's intimidating voice had been conscripted to serve in another capacity. "My friends and I would like to ask you about your aesthetic tastes."

The boy with red hair, who, as Olaf had predicted, was the child of a Party member who'd encountered few difficulties in his life, had just joined the stilyagi a week before: in fact, he was wearing his new suit of clothes for the first time, and in his naivete, he was flattered that they'd gotten him attention so quickly. "Of course," he said. He smiled with the usual cockiness and obliviousness of rich young men and pulled open his lapels, revealing the green checked lining of his jacket. This was a touch he'd asked the black-market tailor for himself, and he was particularly proud of it. "As you can see," he said with the same smile, doing a little spin on his heel, "my aesthetic tastes are impeccable."

The bass-voiced man looked over his shoulder and nodded at his friends, one of whom pulled something silver and gleaming from his pocket—the largest pair of scissors that Maya and Pyotr and Olaf had ever seen.

The boy's cries were heartrending. He screamed as if the men were cutting the flesh from his bones, which at first was what Maya thought was happening. And then it was over as soon as it had begun, and the scissors were returned to their pocket, and the group of men dropped the boy from their grasp and left him on the sidewalk, sniveling, his hair cut short with tall tufts poking out on all sides, his wide-legged pants in shreds. His jacket, which they'd torn off his body, had been sheared into ribbons and tossed a yard away.

Maya and Pyotr and Olaf had not moved an inch while it was happening. Like everyone who walked by, heads down, they knew better than to get involved. But Olaf also knew how it felt to be miserable, and he was the first to move. He bent down to pick up the boy's jacket. "Here," Olaf said, and he offered him a hand. The boy, who could not have been any older than them but now, with snot trailing over his lip, looked considerably younger, wiped his nose on his sleeve and stood with Olaf's help.

"Rocky!" Someone called out to the boy from across the street. "Rocky!" It was another stilyaga, a boy dressed as flamboyantly as the redheaded one. He was flanked on either side by two heavily made-up girls, one in bright red, one in blue. The redheaded boy took his jacket from Olaf and mumbled his thanks and trudged across the street to join them.

"What, there's more of them?" Pyotr said. "Disgusting. This place is infested." He glanced down the street as if to summon back the Komsomol men.

"Maya," Olaf said, quietly. He pointed across the street. "Isn't that—"

The stilyagi girls fussed over Rocky, smoothing his hair, lamenting his shredded jacket. One of them, the one in the bright blue dress, with huge hoop earrings and brick-red lipstick and her hair piled high on her head, was Natasha.

Natasha looked up just then, as if she felt Maya's gaze. When she noticed her sister and classmates staring at her from across the street, her coquettish smile disappeared. She folded her arms over her chest as if trying to hide her bright colors.

"Natasha!" Maya called, not knowing what else to say or do. Surely there was some explanation for the way her sister was dressed. Surely she wouldn't be so foolish as to associate with such people—people who, as Rocky proved, put themselves in danger. Surely Natasha would come across the street and explain it all in a way that'd put Maya at ease.

Natasha stood there, arms still folded. She returned Maya's stare, but not her greeting. The other stilyaga, who was Ilya, approached Natasha and put his arm around her. He followed Natasha's gaze and saw Maya and the others across the street. He pointed toward them and asked Natasha some question Maya couldn't hear. Natasha shook her head, and the four of them turned down a side street and began to walk away.

Maya shouted her sister's name again, cupping her hands around her mouth. Ilya looked back at her, but Natasha did not. A truck rumbled down the street between them, and when it passed, the stilyagi were gone.

"My God," Pyotr said, "what the hell was your sister doing, dressed like that?" His slender nostrils, which Maya had often admired, flared in disgust.

"She must not know what she's doing," Maya said. "She must be confused—"

"How can you defend her?" Pyotr said. "She's dressing like an American whore!"

"Pyotr!" Olaf said. "You can't talk about her like that."

"She's my sister," Maya said. "I know her. She'd never do something dangerous on purpose." She started to cry. Ten minutes ago, she never would've imagined she'd be defending the person she loved most from the person she wanted to love her.

"Sister or not," Pyotr said, "you saw what happens to people who act like that. They get what they deserve. Ungrateful bitch—I should call our Komsomol officer right now."

"Don't, Pyotr. It's none of your business," Olaf said. "Calm down—they're just clothes."

"What, you want to be one of them too?" Pyotr said. "I should have known—I always thought you'd be the type to dream of pretty things. Both of you are idiots."

A lesser man would have punched Pyotr in the face. But Olaf, more concerned with Maya's tears than proving his manhood, set his jaw and muttered, "Asshole." He put his arm around Maya and started to walk her home.

When they got to the school, Maya brushed off Olaf's attempts at consolation. She needed to be alone. She needed to wait for Natasha. She went to her room and lay on her bed so long that it grew dark, even though the spring sun never set until very late in the evening.

The quiet was welcome. Maya had so much to think about that she could have lain there for a week. Her admiration for Pyotr, which she'd nursed for two years, had completely dissolved. He'd never once encouraged her. He rarely smiled or said pleasant things to anyone. But Maya, like many women before and after her, had understood his moodiness as evidence of a sensitive and artistic temperament, one that would soften into something brilliant if nurtured by love. Now she saw him for what he really was: a self-absorbed idealogue, one who didn't speak because others weren't worth speaking to. Perhaps he was right—perhaps it was dangerous to dress the way Natasha had. Perhaps it was an affront to their country's values. But Maya could never love someone who'd spoken about her sister that way.

Natasha snuck in just after midnight, opening the door slowly so the hinge wouldn't squeak. Maya sat up and snapped on the light.

"I'm not staying," Natasha said, as if Maya had asked if she was, as if it were an ordinary day and nothing strange had happened between them at all. She pulled off her shoes. "I've just got to change. We're going dancing." She turned around for Maya to unzip her dress, which Maya rose and did out of sheer habit. Natasha stepped out of her dress and reached under the bed and pulled out a yellow dress so bright that it hurt Maya's eyes. She'd never seen Natasha wear a color so vibrant, even on the stage.

"What do you think you're doing, wearing these clothes, hanging out with these people?" Maya said. "What are you trying to prove?"

"I'm not trying to prove anything," Natasha said. "We're just having fun."

"Fun?" Maya remembered the redheaded boy thrown to the sidewalk, his clothes cut to ribbons. She remembered the boy's cries, the hatred on Pyotr's face. "You saw what happened to that boy today—going out like that is dangerous. If you go out dressed like that, I won't sleep for a second until you get home."

"What are you, my mother?" Natasha said, stepping back into her shoes. "Oh, wait—she's dead."

Neither of them had ever spoken about their mother like this before. Elizaveta's death was a shadow that lurked in the center of their lives—never to be acknowledged, never ventured into—and now Natasha was dancing out into the middle of it, laughing as she went. Maya didn't know who this new woman was, flaunting the law, speaking as if she had no heart at all. The stilyagi had eaten her alive.

"Somebody has to be your mother," Maya said. "You're acting like a little child."

Natasha, apparently undeterred, continued with her preparations, which were identical to the way she'd get ready before a show—smoothing her hair, touching up her lipstick. She was wearing as much makeup as she would have under stage lights. "Don't worry," she said. "In a couple months, after I get into the Kirov and leave this awful country, you won't have to worry about me anymore. I'll be able to wear whatever I want, and I won't get into any trouble."

"What is that supposed to mean?"

"Use your imagination," Natasha said. "You've always been good at pretending." She stood, staring at Maya with a proud defiance that felt familiar, like posters praising steel manufacturers or Soviet workers' resolve, or maybe advertising American movies. Yes, that was it—Natasha was playing a part, like a girl on James Dean's arm. She was dressing, speaking, and acting like a teenager in New York.

America. She was going to defect to America.

"You can't leave," Maya said, grabbing the corner of the dresser to steady herself. "You can't run away."

"Why not? I've got nothing keeping me here."

Nothing. It was so much worse than saying "no one." Maya wasn't even a person in her eyes. Not even a thing to be considered.

Natasha pulled a hideous pink purse out from under her bed and tossed her lipstick in it. She had been leading Maya around all their lives—pulling her while Maya clung to her, like that day long ago when they'd learned to waltz. But soon she'd be leaving, and she could not take Maya with her. It was time to cut her loose. "I'm tired," she said. "Tired of all this. Tired of looking after you. Tired of having to take care of you, protect your feelings. Elizaveta thought it was better to die than to spend her whole life taking care of us, and I'm beginning to understand it—so I'm just going to tell you the truth."

She snapped the purse shut and stood eye to eye with her sister but looked at her forehead. She knew she could only break free if she was cruel, but she couldn't look her sister in the eye while she did it. "I'm better than you, Maya. I'm always going to be better than you. Everyone knows it and nobody wants to tell you. Even Olaf knows it, but he's keeping his mouth shut because he wants to fuck you."

"That's not true," Maya said.

"Be grateful," Natasha said. "Somebody wants you at last." She turned and walked out the door. Maya stood in disbelief for a moment and then hurried after her, but it was too late—Natasha was already in the courtyard, where Ilya was waiting, and the couple slipped into the dark.

CHAPTER EIGHT

No season in a young person's life is quite so perilous as the departure from school. It's less like leaving a nest and more like exiting a womb.

The Kirov auditions over and done with, everyone's attention turned to the coming gala in June. Alexei, who'd avoided assigning gala roles until after the auditions, now doled them out like balloons at a parade. The ballet in question, *Stone Flower*, was expected to be a citywide sensation: its premiere run at the Bolshoi sold out for weeks on end, and the students' rendition was going to be the first in Leningrad.

Ivan and Natasha were cast, predictably, as Danila and Katerina, lovers whose pas de deux ended with a challenging one-handed lift; Maya as the jealous Queen of the Copper Mountain; and everyone else as villagers and woodspeople and fantastic creatures with varying degrees of solos. Olaf received his assignment as the lecherous Severyan and was astonished at his good fortune, having never had such a prominent role in his life.

Olaf was not the only one who was astonished that day. Alexei, having announced the roles and retreated quickly to his office in hopes of not being petitioned for changes, had an unexpected visitor. His assistant, Nonna, poked her head through the door. "The Minister of Culture wants to talk to you," she said.

Alexei sighed and picked up the phone, bracing for another blistering conversation with Nikolai that would waste both time and energy.

"No, no," Nonna said, her voice suddenly dropped to a whisper. "She's here."

"She?" Alexei said.

Before Nonna could answer, the door was pushed open and a short, squat, and overall formidable-looking woman entered the room, casting a cool glance at Nonna as she walked by. "Foolish woman," she muttered, looking askance at Nonna's imported shoes.

The woman, whose name was Furtseva, had no time for foolishness. She walked with brisk, solid steps to Alexei, shook his hand so hard he winced, and introduced herself, sitting behind his desk without it being offered. "Sit, sit," she said, offering Alexei the chair opposite the desk—the one students usually sat in when they came to be reprimanded.

Alexei was dizzy, but he did as he was told. So, there was a new Minister of Culture. This news was either good or dreadful, and it could not be anything in between. Sometimes, when new ministers came to power, the arts enjoyed a temporary increase in funding and prestige: if something new and momentous was going to happen, it would be after such a shift. But other times, the new ministers came in with ideas of their own, and in these cases, they often cleaned house. Alexei realized that his day could contain far worse disasters than caterwauling students.

Yekaterina Furtseva was fifty years old with graying hair piled discreetly on her head. She'd once been the most powerful woman in Moscow, a member of the Politburo, and had since fallen from grace for reasons that were never revealed, a fall that grieved her so much that she'd attempted suicide. She resented her new position, and she especially resented all the people now under her charge. She'd come of age at a time when production and practicality were the nation's highest virtues; she had little respect for artists. Soon, she would learn that, though she would never regain her former power, she could wield considerable clout through the arts; they, too, could become political weapons, and she would become their greatest ally.

But all of this was unknown to Alexei, who sat opposite her and waited for her to say something that would indicate his fate. Furtseva said nothing. Instead, she put her feet on the desk and crossed them at the ankles—heavy ankles, Alexei noticed, the kind that would have her cut from an audition line in seconds—and lit a cigarette. She stared at him, furrowing her brow as if trying to suss out his level of cowardice, and Alexei worried he would come up wanting.

Furtseva took a drag off her cigarette, looked around for an ashtray and, not finding one, tapped her ashes to the floor. Alexei tried hard not to think about the rug beneath his desk, the one he'd inherited from Petipa's grandson, grayed with ash.

At last, she spoke. "I want to come to this gala of yours," she said. "They tell me it's a very big occasion."

"Yes, of course," Alexei said. "We would be honored to have you." Nikolai had always come to the graduation gala, along with half of Leningrad: anyone who cared anything about dance would be there.

Furtseva narrowed her eyes again, and Alexei had the impression that everything he'd done and said so far had been deemed merely foolish. "I understand there's been some trouble with the students lately."

"Nothing out of the ordinary," Alexei said, though he knew she was talking about Anya, whose swift exit he'd hoped to keep as quiet as possible. "They are teenagers, after all—"

"Drugs," Furtseva interjected. "Illicit affairs. Abortions. I was a teenager once, and I assure you that when my peers and I were their age, we engaged only in the fortification of our country. Such behavior is unacceptable. These students should know by now that as artists, they are ambassadors for our country, for our very way of life."

"Of course." Alexei said these words, but he did not hear them; he was getting so nervous that if she'd asked him for his firstborn, he probably would've said "of course" to that too.

Furtseva prepared to tap her ashes again, and Alexei darted to his cupboard and found a teacup to spare his rug from the ashes, bringing it to her just in time. He expected her to say thank you, but she only stared. Alexei sat down again and wondered if she was about to fire him. He dug a handkerchief from his pocket and mopped the back of his neck, a gesture that pleased Furtseva. She enjoyed making people sweat.

She cocked her head and smiled at him. "There is no need to be anxious, comrade," she said to him, putting out her cigarette and leaning over the table. "Despite all these foibles, I have heard very good things about this school, and that is why I am here. As you know, the Kirov is soon being sent abroad. Everyone is expecting you to have excellent newcomers to contribute. There's no need to get all pale like that, comrade. Not too many newcomers. Just a few. I've been told male dancers are a particular concern. Consider this your factory inspection. Are they ready?"

Alexei thought of Ivan and Sophrony, of Maya and Natasha. Even Olaf had surprised them lately. "I think they had many good options to choose from," he said. "We have an especially talented class this year."

Furtseva snorted. "I will be the judge of that," she said. She took her feet down from the desk. "Reserve a box for me at the gala. If everything goes well, then you will have nothing to worry about." She rose and left the room without saying goodbye.

Alexei didn't want to know what would happen if everything didn't go well.

Later that week, when Maya woke up early one morning, Natasha was already gone. Maya had become accustomed to waking up alone. Her sister was now more of an absence than a presence in her life. The only evidence that Natasha still lived in this room at all was the perpetual shifting of her belongings—Maya would wake up and Natasha's bedclothes would be rumpled, and a pair of pointe shoes would be drying on the radiator, or a leotard would be draped over the desk chair, still ripe with sweat.

Maya hadn't slept well since the night Natasha threatened to defect. Even now, even after the terrible things Natasha had said to her, she couldn't imagine a life without her sister in it—let alone the danger that might await her and Katusha if Natasha made good on her threat.

Olaf, noticing the bags under Maya's eyes (as he noticed everything about her), had tried to tell her not to worry. "Just because she's threatening to be foolish doesn't mean she'll actually do it," he said. "The best thing you can do to protect her is practice." He'd squeezed her hand and given her a look that was familiar to her, a look she now realized expressed a little more than kindness. Natasha had been right, at least partially. Olaf was doing all this because he wanted to be with her. Maya filed this realization away to deal with later, the way one notices a leaky faucet and admits that, eventually, they'll have to call a plumber.

Jumbled voices and footfalls floated by Maya's door, her usual cue to get up, but she ignored them. She was weary, and she was not ready for classes and rehearsals and who knows what else. The Kirov casting list was going to be posted any day now, and she was terrified to see the results. She knew she'd studied and trained to her very limit. She did not know if it would be enough—enough to save her future and enough to save her sister from herself. Olaf meant well, but he was wrong. Practicing didn't matter now. It was too late—either she'd gotten in or she hadn't.

If there was any fairness in this world, she had. Hadn't she spent night after night sweating through rehearsals while Natasha gallivanted about with Ivan or her strange new love? Hadn't she done thirty-one fouettés to Natasha's thirty? The Kirov directors would have to be idiots not to appreciate that. Surely they'd understood that Maya was devoted to her craft, while Natasha only exploited it. Surely they'd sensed Maya's loyalty to her country, the gratitude she felt for this place that had raised her, and would reward her for it.

Yes, it would be Maya's name on that list, and not her sister's, and this victory would be all the sweeter after the cruel things Natasha had said to her. She, and not Natasha, would be the one going abroad, sending money home to provide for the rejected sister. Maya resolved not to gloat when Natasha got the bad news, but inwardly, she was already rejoicing. She would be the one to take up their mother's fate and live it out as it should have been lived.

Maya opened her eyes and saw the sun coming in strong through the window—not the dim yellow glow of the long winter but a brightness, one that looked like it could warm her if she let it. Perhaps she would look back and regret that she'd wasted so much time worrying. Maya took a deep breath and let herself imagine that this was the moment before everything in her life set itself right at last.

Someone knocked heavily, startling Maya. Olga's voice came through the door—the Kirov list had been posted. "We're all going to look at it together," Olga yelled. "Hurry up!"

It had been posted early that morning. Alexei, who was used to the emotional fallout that always accompanied such news, had locked himself in his office afterward, sipping vodka and waiting for the usual spate of tearful students.

There was reason to be tearful. Furtseva had not exaggerated: the Kirov only needed a few students, and no more. Vasili and Vasilia looked at each other, shrugged, and mumbled something about preferring Moscow anyway. Olga and Kira, who didn't have the patience to wait for Maya, cried a little, and Kira put her arms around her and said, "Now we can rest, my friend, and you can eat as much as you want," which sent Olga weeping down the hall. Kira ran crying after her.

Olaf appeared in their wake, and once he'd read the list, the blood drained from his face—because there, in plain black letters, was his name. Just his, and Ivan's, and Natasha's.

Sophrony and Ivan, who arrived next, looked at the news and then at each other. They stood there for a moment, scratching their heads and stretching, unsure of how to react to this news in each other's presence. "Want to go to the gym?" Ivan said. Sophrony nodded and they trudged off together, convinced that only lifting weights could express the depth of feeling each of them carried without offending the other.

Natasha, who had eaten a hasty breakfast alone, found only Olaf standing at the board, and when she read the letter, she grew even paler than he was. Pyotr, arriving just after her, looked at the list, scratched his nose, and muttered congratulations before heading off again. Natasha didn't say anything at all, didn't even nod. Olaf thought she was going to faint and, anticipating an occasion for gallantry, offered to get her some water. "No, thank you," she said, and she offered no congratulations, deeply disappointing Olaf, who for the first time in his life had done better than his peers and, having lived most of his eighteen years without any real companions, was beginning to think that success was the loneliest experience of all. Hanging his head, he left for the cafeteria in hopes of finding Maya there, or Karinska, or anyone who would be excited for him.

Maya arrived last, though she'd dressed as quickly as she could—her hair hung loose around her shoulders—and found Natasha staring at the bulletin board. Maya read the list and took a long step back, then another, as if something was reaching out from the board's surface, trying to hurt her. She turned to Natasha, expecting some sort of consolation, some words of comfort or even a pitying look, but Natasha didn't say anything, didn't even look at her. Natasha turned and walked away, and Maya knew, from her sister's silence, from the way she carried herself, from the determined pull of her shoulder blades, that Natasha would do what she'd said. She would run away to America. She would abandon Maya, just as their mother had done.

For as long as she could remember, Maya had feared that something terrible would descend upon her world and ruin her family. When she was a child, she feared the same things that all children fear: that a mysterious disease would drain the life from Katusha, that a trolleybus would swing loose from its cable and crush Natasha as she crossed the street. But since that New Year's Eve when she'd learned the truth about her mother, Maya's fear had become much more concrete. From then on, she understood that the something terrible would not descend upon them from above, but would gnaw them from the inside out. Maya's great fear became that her sister, her beautiful sister, who'd inherited much of what had made her mother magnificent, had also inherited her darkness. Darkness had clouded her mother's mind and made her choose death over life; darkness, too, warped her sister's understanding. It was the only explanation for why Natasha would flee the country—an act of treason so unforgivable it could be punished with a lifetime in prison, or even death—and leave her family to face the consequences. Maya did not know exactly what happened to you when someone in your family defected, as Ivan's mother had—it was the sort of thing you didn't ask about, as if asking itself was dangerous—but she'd heard you could be interrogated, even arrested. If Natasha was willing to risk that, she could not be trusted with herself.

It is uncertain if Maya would have seen her situation in this light if she, too, had been accepted to the Kirov; if the news of her sister's success hadn't come on the heels of her own failure, perhaps she would have arrived at a different conclusion. As it was, all of Maya's thoughts and fears and consciousness concentrated themselves into a razor point; she felt that she could rip open the very fabric of existence if she pressed hard enough. She turned this razor point toward her sister, and all at once, she understood what she had to do.

There was no use confronting Natasha. She was past reason. She'd made her choice, and no one—not Maya, not Katusha, not even Alexei himself—could dissuade her from it. If Maya did nothing, if Natasha went off with the Kirov and toured the world, she would never come back again, and their family would be ruined. Neither of them would be in the Kirov, taking up their mother's unlived life, and Elizaveta's ghost would haunt her forever. Later, Maya would tell herself she had no choice, but in truth, she'd faced her own decision: to destroy her sister or let herself be destroyed. A year ago, she never would have even entertained such a choice. She would have accepted that Natasha was better, would always be better, and moved on. But things had changed. She had worked too hard, she had waited too long, she had wanted too much to be left behind again.

Maya once more understood, as she had before betraying Anya, that she was capable of doing terrible things. She told herself that virtue was the result of circumstance as much as choice. Anyone, given the opportunity, given the justification and the need, could do something terrible. This gave Maya hope, because she couldn't save

Natasha alone, and she went off in search of the only person who would understand.

Ivan was alone in the cold and damp gymnasium. He and Sophrony had sat there in stony silence with dumbbells at their feet, feigning interest in lifting them, but a few minutes of this awkwardness was all that Sophrony could stand. He muttered his excuses and left for his room, where he would look at dirty pictures until the day's classes began. You had to take comfort where you could get it.

Ivan sat on a padded bench and squeezed his fingers with his right hand. Fate had smiled on him, but he did not feel happy. The Kirov wanted him, but Natasha didn't. He wondered if he could make her fall in love with him again. Maybe she'd feel differently about him in Venice, or London, or someplace suitably romantic. Surely it was possible, though he couldn't picture it. The rest of his life stretched out in front of him like a sea—not of infinite possibility, but infinite emptiness, and he started to cry.

This was the state in which Maya found him a few moments later, the dumbbells still lying unused at his feet. His tears surprised and embarrassed Maya so much that she almost gave up on her mission before she'd begun. But then he looked up and saw her, and it was too late to turn back.

She sat beside him on the bench and picked at her cuticles. She had never been this close to Ivan outside of the classroom, and now, sitting alone with him, so near that his arm would brush hers if he sat up straight, she could not think of how to begin.

Ivan, whose entire idea of himself was built on being dependable, pounced on the silence as a chance to regain his composure. He brushed his eyes as if they'd been stung by sand and not tears. "So," he said, "you saw the list?"

"Yes," Maya said. She stopped picking at her cuticles and laid her hands in her lap like an obedient schoolgirl. "Congratulations."

"Thanks. And I'm sorry," Ivan said, grateful at the chance to console someone else instead of broiling in his own confusion. "I wish they were taking more of us."

"Me too," Maya said. She looked at the clock above the door: she only had a few minutes to say what she needed to say to Ivan, but saying it out loud felt impossible.

Ivan sighed. "I guess there's always the Bolshoi. Don't you think you could be happy there?"

Maya didn't answer. She turned to Ivan so their knees were nearly touching. "I'm worried about Natasha," she said, biting her lip, hoping that the mention of her sister's name would not upset him.

Ivan looked away. "Why?" he said. "She's a big girl. She can take care of herself. She's made this abundantly clear to all of us."

The truth burned in Maya's throat; keeping silent had become painful. She looked at the open doorway, which was empty. No voices echoed down the hall.

Maya bent her body close to Ivan's and put her hand close to his ear like a little child. "She's going to defect," she whispered. She felt instant relief at sharing this dark secret with another. The problem wasn't just hers anymore.

"What?" Ivan shouted, pulling away from her. Maya shushed him, and he came close again. "How do you know?" he whispered, facing her. Anyone who walked by at that moment and glanced in the room would have thought that they were lovers.

"She told me herself. She told me that if she got into the Kirov, she would run away to America."

"She wouldn't do that," Ivan said. "She wouldn't leave all of us behind—she wouldn't leave you, surely—" In his mind's eye appeared memories he'd worked so hard to push away: his father limping home, his wince, the knocking in the middle of the night.

"She would," Maya said. She swallowed hard—what she had to say next was the most difficult part. "She's in love with a stilyaga. They're going to run away together during the tour."

Maya knew that this would be painful for Ivan. She did not know, of course, that this was the very thing that Ivan had feared for months. He was too shocked to speak. It was like losing his mother all over again: it was worse than that, because somebody was choosing another over him, somebody was volunteering for exile, maybe arrest and imprisonment, even death, over being with him. Natasha's decision was not as simple as this—like all of her decisions, she had made it thinking only of herself, not Ivan or Maya—but Ivan, blinded by love and self-pity, could not imagine the depths of her selfishness. He thought that her decision was solely a reflection of him, and his unworthiness, and his failure to rescue her from her own foolishness. He hid his face in his hands, which were bright pink, and wept like a small boy.

Maya didn't know what to do. She knew that Ivan had cared for her sister, but she never expected him to react like this. It was as if she'd unplugged some sort of cosmic drain and he was slipping down it. She felt so miserable watching his great, muscly shoulders shake with sobs. To put an end to it, she said, "We have to stop her. I know that you understand the danger she's putting herself in—"

Ivan hiccupped and wiped his eyes with his enormous red thumbs. "I do," he said hoarsely. "And it's not just her. My father—they ruined him, Maya. They could ruin us too." Maya reached into her bag and handed him a clean handkerchief, which he accepted gratefully. "But what can we do? I can't talk to her," he said. "She won't listen to me."

"She won't listen to me either," Maya said. "If we try talking to her, she'll just deny it. She's not thinking straight."

Sophrony appeared in the door. His dirty pictures had had the desired effect of cheering him up, and he wanted to pass them on to Ivan in a gesture of goodwill. But seeing his friend's eyes were red, and Maya beside him, he lost his mettle. "Class starts in a few minutes," he mumbled, hiding the contraband behind his back. "You'd better hurry." And then, not waiting for an answer, he scampered down the hall, his own tears rising at the sight of his friend's.

Seeing Sophrony undid all of Ivan's efforts at dignity, and he wiped his eyes with his thumbs again. "We have to do something," he said. "If she goes on that tour, she's going to put all of us in danger. I wish you had gotten into the Kirov instead of her." Ivan groaned and covered his face with the handkerchief. "How am I supposed to dance with her now?" he said. "It was hard enough before. Now we have to do this gala as if nothing had happened at all."

Maya, who'd turned to the door when Sophrony stopped by, turned back to the wall. She clenched and unclenched her jaw a number of times. "Yes," she said, in a calm voice much deeper than her own. "And it's a very difficult dance. You have to lift her so many times, even with just one hand."

Ivan looked at her, his brow furrowed. He'd never heard her speak in this strange voice, and he did not understand why she sounded serene all of a sudden. He'd always thought of Maya as a mouse—little and sweet, frightened at the first sign of danger. He wondered if she was commenting on his strength. "I can lift her just fine," he said, offended.

"Of course you can," Maya said, her face expressionless. "You have trained very hard. Everyone would expect her to be safe in your strong hands."

He stared at her as if he were watching something far off without being sure of what it was. "Yes," he said, more to encourage her to go on than to affirm anything.

"And everyone knows that you are very careful, no matter who you're partnering."

Maya still faced the wall, and she looked at him out of the corners of her eyes without turning her head. "You would never let anything bad happen to her. You would never want her to get hurt."

Ivan, who had started winding the handkerchief around his wrist like a bandage, became very still. His hands froze midair as if already burdened by Natasha's weight. He squinted and then slowly turned to Maya to confirm what he already knew: she was waiting for an answer.

The graduation gala was held on a warm evening in June at the Kirov Theatre. The grand box, draped with turquoise satin curtains and topped with golden cherubs, had sheltered generations of tsars and tsarinas and was now reserved for government dignitaries. Alexei gave the ushers strict instructions to save it for Yekaterina Furtseva, who'd called again this week to remind him that she would attend. He kept anxiously sticking his head out the side curtain to see if she'd arrived, but at quarter to seven, the box was still empty.

The audience, which packed the opulent theater to its aisles, was made up of equal parts eager parents and siblings and aunts and uncles and grandparents, curious balletomanes who liked to pick out rising dancers as their favorites before anyone else knew about them, and Leningrad dignitaries, Party officials, minor celebrities, and any member of the local elite who felt it was their privilege or their duty to attend. Also in attendance were the Kirov ballet master and his wife, who were seated beside old friends of theirs from their university days, the filmmaker Sergei Bondarchuk and his wife Irina, who were visiting from Moscow. The ballet master leaned over to Sergei conspiratorially. "Wait 'til you see this little girl we just hired," he said. "She's a minx."

The little girl was, at this particular moment, backstage in a brightly lit dressing room, emptying the contents of her stomach into a plastic wastebasket. No matter how excited or calm she felt, Natasha got sick just before performances, always had, and the normality of this occurrence comforted her. She wiped her mouth, swished and then spat a cup of water to wash the burn of acid from her throat, and sat on the floor to catch her breath. The green satin ribbon tied around her hair had slipped onto her forehead, and she reached up to straighten it. The site of her old back injury, just along her spine, twinged in protest, and she stretched her arms overhead to quiet it.

Natasha breathed deeply and leaned her head against the wall, resting her hands in her lap. "Everything," she thought, "will be perfect." She'd passed her examinations. She'd made it into the Kirov. The boy who loved her was going to run away with her to Europe, and then to America, where they would live forever. Ilya planned to open a bar someplace, "introduce them to real good vodka," as he put it. Natasha would get hired by an American company, maybe in New York—Ilya had assured her that New York was full of dancers—and dance as much (or as little) as she wanted. More and more, she found herself curious about life outside of dance. What was it like, she wondered, to deliver mail, or teach children, or even act in films, like Audrey Hepburn? In America, she could try to be anyone she wanted. She could save her body before it was broken beyond repair.

Natasha did not exactly know what would happen to Maya and Katusha when she defected. She knew, from the way that Ivan refused to talk about it, that something awful had happened to his father, but that was a long time ago. "Things are different now," Natasha thought. "It's nothing like it was in the old days." Besides, Maya was capable, and she was a good dancer. She'd be able to take care of herself, and of Katusha. And maybe, someday, when Natasha was very rich and very famous, when she'd become the second Audrey Hepburn, she would be able to pull some strings and bring them over to America, too, and wouldn't they be thankful to her then?

Kira and Olga walked by with their arms around each other's waists, a sisterly sort of gesture that made Natasha's chest constrict. "She'll understand," Natasha said to herself, running a flat hand over her scalp. "She'll understand." And to prove this to herself, Natasha rose, reapplied her stage lipstick in the dressing room's blinding lights, and went in search of her sister.

Ever since their earliest performances, when they played mice in *The Nutcracker* or sea urchins in *Little Humpbacked Horse*, Maya and Natasha had done the same little preshow ritual to calm themselves. It was partly a limerick, partly a secret handshake, and partly a pantomime that, because they'd invented it when they were six, involved imitating birds in a manner so bizarre it was best not done in front of others. They always snuck off to a deserted corner backstage to do it.

The orchestra was warming up—all of the students, for the rest of their days, long after they'd stopped dancing, would feel a pang of anxiety and excitement whenever they went to the ballet or the opera or the symphony and heard that joyous cacophony, because it meant something wonderful was about to happen. Alexei stuck his head through the curtain again and saw that the imperial box was still empty, and a wave of relief rippled through him. Maybe Furtseva wasn't coming after all. Maybe she'd decided to leave him alone. Feeling ten years younger, he headed for his seat in the audience.

Backstage was crowded with dancers in various stages of preparation—dipping their pointe shoes in rosin, swinging their legs this way and that, doubling over in deep, contorted stretches. A crowd of little children dressed as gypsies hurried by and pinned Natasha to the wall. Natasha peered over the sea of tightly wound coifs in search of her sister—always recognizable from behind by two little curls at the nape of her neck that sprung out no matter how much Maya tried to mat them down—but she didn't see her.

Natasha pushed up her hair ribbon, which had slipped again, and stuck her head through the stage door, peering down the hallway. There, near the dressing rooms, was Maya, talking for some reason to Ivan. Dressed in folk costumes with heads bent close, they looked like a peasant couple exchanging secrets. Natasha hurried toward them.

"Come on!" she said, tugging at Maya's arm. "We've only got a second to do it!"

"Do what?" Maya said, frowning and pulling back her arm. Her heavy kokoshnik headdress, intended to make her seem queenly, rocked on her head, and she put a hand up to steady it.

Natasha frowned too and cocked her head, hoping to appear bird-like, and when that failed, flapped her arms a little. "You know," she said. "Before the show."

Maya turned to Ivan, who was leaning in a doorway with arms folded. Both of them looked at each other solemnly for a moment, and then Ivan turned and walked away.

Natasha shook her head after he'd gone. "That silly boy," she said. "He's never gotten over me."

"Don't be pigheaded," Maya said, unusually sharp. "He's got his own problems to worry about."

Natasha, not wanting to waste time on her ex-boyfriend, grabbed her sister's arm again. "Let's go," she said, and Maya did not resist her.

They snuck behind the stage, hidden by four layers of backdrops, and began their ritual. Natasha recited one half of the limerick, and Maya the other—some nonsense about leaping like frogs and chasing hedgehogs, words they'd repeated so many times over so many years that they didn't hold any of their original meaning anymore. They slapped each other's hands six times, grabbed each other's elbows twice, and tapped each other on the nose. Natasha's ribbon fell into her eyes, and when she pushed it up again Maya was crying.

"I'm sorry," Maya said, her mouth contorted. "I'm sorry."

"For what?" Natasha said. She wondered if Maya and Ivan had become lovers. Of course her sister would feel sheepish about that. But later, in the days and weeks and years to come, when Natasha's life had fallen to pieces and she found herself flailing, trying to understand what had happened to her, she remembered her sister's apology, and she understood how her life had come to be the mess that it was. That her sister could have done this, this old and sacred ritual of theirs, knowing what was going to happen to her afterward, was unforgivable.

But here, crouched backstage at the Kirov Theatre, these thoughts did not occur to Natasha yet; she was young and whole, with a promising future. Maya's apology confused her, but the orchestra came into tune with itself—every dancer knew that single strong A was the signal to get ready to go onstage—and Maya ran off.

Back in the auditorium, the sounds of the orchestra coming together hushed the audience into watchful expectation. As the orchestra launched into the lively *Stone Flower* overture, everyone settled into their seats and, with their bodies relaxed, their minds took the opportunity to roam free before the performance began. Ivan's father glanced anxiously at his watch and hoped that the performance would not go too late—being out after dark made him nervous. Katusha wrapped her coat around herself and shivered, even though the auditorium was warm—perhaps Elizaveta's ghost was here tonight. Olaf's grandmother glanced proudly through the program, though it was too dark to see even for young eyes, and breathed a sigh of satisfaction when she found her grandson's picture in the dim light. "Such a good boy," she thought to herself, stroking the photograph with her finger. "He's turned out so well after all."

Despite not wanting to, Alexei turned around to look at the imperial box, and just as he did, an usher helped a squat and formidable-looking lady into it. Regretting that he'd looked, Alexei turned around in his seat and looped his arm around his wife and whispered something naughty in her ear to try to calm himself. She smiled and swatted him with her program, and thus satisfied that everything would be all right, Alexei's shoulders relaxed for the first time that day.

Yekaterina Furtseva waved away the usher's offer of an ashtray. "I can damn well smoke without one," she said, in an attempt at a whisper that was loud enough for heads to turn. She lit her cigarette and leaned back in her chair, resting her enormous feet on the same gilded guardrail where tsarinas' gloved hands once lay.

She flipped through the program without really looking at it and sighed, hoping that the overture would be brief. "Damned waste," she muttered to herself. "Once I was running the entire country, and now I'm stuck chasing tutus." She closed the program and tossed it onto the chair beside her. She fidgeted with her sleeves, pushing up one cuff and then the other, and took a long drag off her cigarette. "No matter," she thought. "Just wait until they see what I can do. I will bring them films, concerts, dances like they've never seen before. Every damn man and woman in this country will know my name."

Yekaterina Furtseva leaned back in her chair and watched the curtain go up.

PART II

CHAPTER NINE

NEW YORK CITY, AUGUST 1962

George Balanchine sat in the first-class cabin of the last Pan Am flight out of Newark, twiddling his thumbs. The plane, which had taxied for twenty minutes, was getting warm, and his damp palms stuck to the blue vinyl armrests. He'd only been away from his apartment for an hour, and he already wanted to go home. Some people thought this plane was taking him home, but he knew better. That Russia didn't exist anymore.

It wasn't the idea of flying that made him sweat. It was the significance of this flight in particular, a flight that would take him and his entire company, the New York City Ballet, to Europe, where they would spend five weeks touring the great capitals—Hamburg and Paris and Rome—and then, in October, Moscow and Leningrad.

The last time he was in Russia, his name was Georgi Balanchivadze, and he was twenty years old, all skin and bones and ambition, with a head of floppy dark hair that conquered hearts. The last time he'd been in Europe, a mere six years ago, Tanny had still been able to walk, and to dance, and to love him.

Those six years had aged him twenty. The wrinkles in his large, round forehead, long abandoned by the floppy hair, had deepened, his hair receded to wisps. His slightly beaky nose was larger. But George dressed the same way he had for decades, in a sharp suit with a string bolo tie, just like the cowboys in the Western movies he'd admired as a young man. He costumed himself as an American, for that, more than anything, was who he wanted to be.

Though he was now fifty-eight, George moved with the grace and confidence of a much younger man, and none of the other first-class passengers eyeing him over their newspapers had successfully guessed his age, though several recognized him from his pictures in the press. But if George didn't look his age, he felt it, especially when he was trying to remember things. It was as if his mind had grown old and forgotten to tell his body. Twenty-one years later, after Balanchine had died, a pathologist would examine a slice of his brain and discover evidence of Creutzfeldt-Jakob disease, a degenerative neurological disease resulting in muscular difficulties, dementia, and death. But on this day in 1962, as Balanchine's plane continued taxiing up and down the sizzling tarmac, that particular pathologist was only ten years old, and Balanchine's brain was still inside his skull, and he was still healthy, if fifty-eight, and he had no idea what would kill him.

The plane lurched forward in a promising fashion and then stopped altogether. Balanchine stopped twiddling his thumbs and looked toward the back of the plane, where the rest of the entourage—the dancers, a doctor, the costume ladies, several chaperones, and a dance critic from the *New York Times*—was tucked away in coach. He didn't like being so far from them.

"Stop fussing," Lincoln Kirstein said, returning from the bathroom. Lincoln was cofounder of City Ballet, and putting everyone else in coach had been his idea. He climbed over Balanchine and folded himself into the seat beside him, trying to tuck his enormous legs under the next row. "You're the most valuable thing on this damn plane, and their leader besides, and it's good for them to remember that every once in a while." Lincoln had been born wealthy, and he was the kind of person who, while claiming to be an egalitarian, enjoyed subtle reminders that class distinctions still existed in the twentieth century.

Balanchine, who had been born in a modest home, become poor after the Revolution, and survived his boyhood by subsisting on the rats and cats and dogs of Petrograd—the last of these, an ancient beagle with mournful eyes, gave him nightmares for a decade afterward—thought that this remark of Lincoln's was foolish, but he didn't reply. This was the oldest habit of their thirty-year relationship and one of its foundations: Kirstein would say something, and Balanchine would ignore it. Balanchine respected Lincoln very much, and for the rest of his life, he would be deeply grateful to him for bringing him to America, for making him an American, for helping him found his company after decades of stops and starts. But Lincoln said too many things and shared too many opinions for Balanchine to take them all into account. To be friends with Lincoln, filtered ears were necessary.

Lincoln had not, for instance, approved of his marriage to Tanny. "For fuck's sake, George," he'd said, with a studied coarseness that made Balanchine cringe (Lincoln was as self-conscious of his silver spoon as he was proud, and he tried to cloak his pedigree with profanity.) "She's a baby. And your student. Why do you have to marry her? Can't she just be your little something on the side? Aren't you tired of getting married?"

This was a reasonable question. Tanny was Balanchine's fourth wife—fifth, if you counted Alexandra Danilova, whom he'd common-law married in his twenties. His list of wives read like a playbill—every one of them dancers, every one of them astonishingly beautiful. Tamara Geva, when he was seventeen; Vera Zorina, when he was thirty-four; Maria Tallchief, when he was forty-two. Balanchine grew older, but, in the way of successful men, his wives stayed young. He'd noticed Tanny while she was still a student. Even then, a light shone from her. At this age, the best dancers in the class still behaved like little girls, screwing up their faces when the teacher corrected them, scratching themselves between pliés. But Tanny stood still and calm, a model of serenity, looking much more like a woman than a child.

They'd married when she was twenty-three. When she was twenty-seven, she flew with him to Copenhagen, where she performed with the rest of the company. And then, polio. And then, paralysis. And then she hadn't loved him anymore.

This was how George told himself the story—but, as humans are wont to do, he told it in a way that took all blame from his shoulders and cast it off on others. The truth was that Tanny had grown weary of him long before the European tour—or, rather, they'd grown weary of each other and his eye wandered, as was his habit. And George Balanchine was nothing if not a man of habits. His life was a series of traditions conducted as steadily and seriously as a liturgy: post-performance blintzes and caviar at the Russian Tea Room with his friends, preparing an annual Easter feast for this same entourage, purchasing perfume for his company favorites so he could smell them coming down the hall—and, above all, molding mere women into dancers and then falling in love with them, over and over again. Perhaps it's more precise to say that he needed to mold them in order to love them; women were his clay, fresh and malleable, and when Tanny's legs went dead, his love went brittle also.

The plane still taxied, making long, slow loops around the tarmac, like the tourist trams at Hollywood studios where Balanchine first worked in America—and then, again, it stopped. Everyone groaned. Late-August sun streamed through shoebox-size windows, which refracted and focused the light onto everyone's faces. They were ants under a magnifying glass, unable to crawl away. Some of the passengers discreetly removed exterior articles of clothing and draped them over the backs of their seats, which did nothing to improve the stale air. An elderly lady across the aisle produced a large Spanish-looking fan from her bag and created a sizable windstorm with it, lifting the hairs Balanchine had combed over his pate with such care and exposing his creeping baldness.

Balanchine turned, very slowly, to the woman and reached out his hand. "Perhaps, madam," he said, not without courtesy, "I may fan you?"

The woman, unsure of whether to be offended or flattered by this request from the handsome gentleman of unknowable age, began to protest, but a tall young man came tromping up the aisle and interrupted. It was Jacques D'Amboise, City Ballet's strapping young star. He looked like the kind of man who would be as at home lifting barbells in a leopard skin as he would be in an opera box.

"Say, Mr. B," said Jacques, leaning over the back of Balanchine's seat with a Cheshire-cat grin, "don't you think you can get us up in the sky any faster?"

Balanchine pointed to his shoulder. "Look," he said, twisting around. "Do you see wings on my back?"

Jacques, who was bored and tired of being cooped up, stood there and chatted a moment until an anxious stewardess in a pillbox hat emerged from the front of the plane and asked Jacques to return to his seat, which gave Lincoln an undeserved sense of satisfaction. "Beat it," Lincoln said, and Jacques did.

Balanchine turned and watched him galumph back down the aisle. He liked Jacques. He was as talented as he was kind, a rarity in the dance world, and he possessed a warmth that drew everyone to him, including children. Someday, with the right kind of coaching, he could become a very great teacher.

"You know," he said, turning to Lincoln, "that's the sort of man I could see running things after I'm gone." He'd entertained many such thoughts of late—the anticipation of this trip had exacerbated his tendency toward the morbid. He'd wondered if the Russians had invited him to their theaters just to cut him down.

"For Chrissake," Lincoln said. He had put on his sunglasses and did not take them off again when he spoke. "You're not even sixty. I'm not convinced you'll ever die. Make it through this tour first, and then we can talk succession."

"All right," Balanchine said. He sighed. "I still don't even know why I'm going."

The sunglasses came off. "For Chrissake," Lincoln repeated. He got very irritable when he traveled, or drank too much, or ate too much, or was tired. He was irritable most of the time. "We've been over this a hundred times. The government begged you to go."

This was not an exaggeration. Two state department officials, in navy blue suits with little presidential seals on their lapels, had come to Balanchine's apartment for coffee. Tanny wanted them to stay for dinner, but he'd refused, uneasy with the idea of any official sitting at his table. "Mr. Balanchine," they'd said, stumbling over the name like they weren't sure how many syllables were supposed to be in it, "the Russians have us in a bind." It pleased him, how they'd phrased it—"The Russians"—as if they were something other, as if he weren't one of them.

Still, he hadn't wanted to go. He didn't want to leave Tanny, even though she'd insisted she'd be fine—in fact, she'd made it very clear that she wanted him gone. Beginning a journey was not as sweet when the homecoming threatened to be painful. And when he'd left

Russia, all those decades ago, he'd sworn to himself that he would never return.

At first, even the officials in their imposing suits had not succeeded in convincing him otherwise. "Mr. Balanchine, we're in dire straits," they'd said. "The Kirov were a smash when they went to Europe. Everybody's crazy for Russians, for ballet. We've got to get over there and beat them at their own game. And nobody can show them better than you."

He was not immune to flattery. After that, he'd agreed to let the company go—why not show the Soviets the fruits of his labors, how he'd taken the beauty of his heritage and brought it to the world—but he still refused to go along himself. He could not bring himself to return to the place where he'd become a dancer and a man and then nearly starved. He'd already witnessed his hometown overrun by Bolsheviks, its beauty marred by Soviet grime and the blood of thousands. The Russia he had known and loved was dead, and the Soviets had killed it, and he would not be paraded around by its murderers.

Lincoln spent long hours in Balanchine's office, trying to convince him. "Listen," he said, "what harm does it do if you go? It's not like you'll never come back. They can't keep you."

This was what really worried Balanchine, so much so that when he finally acquiesced and agreed to go, he requested a Marine guard to accompany him abroad (which he was refused). He was afraid that the Russians would capture him somehow, would force him to work for them—the godless, sneering lot of them. That his orphaned company would fall apart without his care. That everything he'd built and everything he loved would be lost. Though he'd defected decades ago, every now and again he woke up with a gasp, his striped pajamas soaked through with sweat, having dreamed that a KGB agent had crept around a corner in Manhattan and paralyzed him with a poison pellet discreetly injected from the tip of an umbrella.

If he'd been faced with such a fear when he was young, he would have believed that God would protect him from danger. He'd been haunted by God since his childhood, when he'd attended his uncle's ordination and witnessed the grandeur of the transformation from man to bishop, had sensed the majesty of God in gilt icons and swirls of incense. During the years of famine, he'd felt like the prophet Elijah, saved from starvation by miracles—if not morsels dropped by birds, like the holy man, then crumbs of bread stolen wherever he could find them. And hadn't God conducted his safe passage out of Russia, and eventually to New York, and given him all his heart's desires?

All his heart's desires but one. When Tanny got sick, Balanchine quickly conjured up the faith of his boyhood. He stockpiled icons and blessed oils and relics, covered his living room with holy goods until it looked like a tiny cathedral. He prayed and prayed, both to Christ and to his Mother, but nothing happened, and now he didn't feel he could ask for anything anymore. Not even to visit his home. Leaving home the way he had meant setting it on fire.

"Hey," Lincoln said, tapping Balanchine's arm. "Are you all right?"

George's hands ached. He looked down at them and, seeing his knuckles were white, realized he was gripping the armrests. "Yes, yes," he said, relaxing.

"You're going to behave yourself, aren't you?"

Balanchine turned to his friend. The sunlight glinted off Lincoln's severe sunglasses and made him squint. "What do you mean?"

"I mean—" Lincoln appeared to search for words that would both be respectful and convey the importance of his message. "You'll be nice to them. Your countrymen."

Balanchine bristled. "They aren't my countrymen," he said, with such vehemence he nearly choked on the *C*.

"Right," Lincoln said. "Sorry. But you know what I mean, don't you? You'll comply with them, a little? You'll answer their questions—"

"—I will answer no questions—"

"—about your techniques—"

"—they don't deserve them—"

"—and you'll be gracious to them—"

Balanchine huffed. "—the pigs—"

"—and you'll represent our country well."

The plane had started up again. "I will serve my country," Balanchine said, raising his voice over the roar of the plane as it picked up speed. "I will do it for America."

Lincoln reached over and, in an uncharacteristic show of gratitude, patted his friend on the wrist. "Attaboy," he said, and the plane rose at last and shot off over the Atlantic.

As one plane bore America's best dancers over the sea, another sat on the tarmac at Sheremetyevo International Airport in Moscow, where a host of technicians and kerchiefed cleaning ladies readied it for its most auspicious journey to date. For this was the plane that would soon carry the Kirov to America.

It was an exchange, one that had been planned by both countries in a display of goodwill, a show of generosity that would, in the not-so-distant future, appear unbelievable. Behind closed doors, the Soviet and American governments had decided to send their prized dancers abroad simultaneously, both to avoid competing with each other for prestige and patrons and to give reporters on both sides the chance to judge who was superior. Neither side expected their dancers to come up wanting.

This was not a new phenomenon: for nearly two decades, America and Russia had sent their artists to war. The United States had once shuttled Louis Armstrong and Dave Brubeck through the Soviet Union's neighboring states to demonstrate their cultural superiority, and Khrushchev responded in kind, sending singers and folk-dance groups all over America.

No, what was unusual about this cooperation was not its existence, but how incomprehensible it would come to be just two months later, when the two nations would stare each other down in a face-off that nearly ended the world.

But it was August, and no one in Washington knew what Khrushchev was planning in Cuba, and Balanchine did not know that in a few weeks, his dancers would be in grave danger, and nobody in the Kirov worried that they were about to leave their country and never return.

Several young Kirov dancers gathered at a party in a crowded Moscow apartment—a private apartment, the communal ones being out of fashion here in the capital—where their old school friends toasted to their coming adventure. Pyotr and his wife Elena, both corps members at the Bolshoi, scurried in and out of their kitchen, loading their tiny dining room table with bowls of piroshki and cabbage salad. Ivan and Sophrony, who hadn't seen each other since graduation, sat on the sofa, swapping tales of life in their respective companies—Sophrony also in the Bolshoi, and Ivan in the Kirov. The further this group of dancers drifted from the Vaganova, the more their shared past drew them together. Even Maya, who once couldn't imagine sharing a meal with Pyotr again, was happy to see these familiar faces after another wearying day of rehearsals.

Ivan loved talking about the first leg of the Kirov's ambitious tour of Europe, which was both grueling and remarkably well received. He was telling Sophrony how many curtain calls they got at the Paris Opera. "So many that I thought we'd never leave the stage," he said. He turned to Maya, who was sitting alone in the corner. "I forget—was it twelve or thirteen?"

"Thirteen," Maya said. "They gave us thirteen curtain calls."

Not everyone from the Vaganova class of 1959 had been so fortunate. Kira and Olga, who had auditioned for four or five regional companies and not been accepted by any, had been assigned as teachers at a dance school in Siberia, where they married exiled jazz musicians. Vasili and Vasilia joined the Perm Ballet and, according to letters received by Pyotr, split up shortly after arriving. No one knew what had happened to Anya.

But Olaf had the most surprising fate of all. He had quickly proven himself a strong and capable dancer; even while he was in the corps, Leningrad critics noticed and praised him for his fiery spirit. Within weeks, he was getting solos. Eight months after being hired, Olaf was promoted to soloist and, along with Maya and Ivan, was chosen to take part in the Kirov's tour to Western Europe.

Three weeks later, after being feted by the French and deposited once again at Le Bourget, Olaf went straight to a French policeman sitting at the airport bar and asked for asylum.

It took Olaf six steps to walk from his party to the policeman. He counted them as he walked, six steps that he knew would cut him off from everyone he'd loved forever. The consequences back home were swift and severe, particularly at the Vaganova. Karinska was fired—her sudden departure was euphemistically referred to as a "retirement," which, considering her age, wasn't much of a stretch, but Karinska shook when she walked the streets. She closed herself off from the world, rarely receiving visitors and refusing to speak of former students when she did, as if the very walls had ears. Olaf's grandmother was questioned and forced to write Olaf long letters reprimanding him for his betrayal. Alexei was taken in for interrogation over and over again, always at night, and forced to appear in Moscow to publicly denounce his former student. By some miracle, he managed to hold on to his job, but the interrogations took their toll. He returned to the Vaganova that fall looking thin and weary, and he never had quite the same spark again.

Olaf's flight was the chief subject of conversation at the dinner party Elena and Pyotr hosted for their old friends that evening.

Pyotr had, for some reason, taken the defection as a personal affront. "I never thought he'd betray us in this way," he said, setting down a bowl of peanuts with such force that a few of them escaped onto the table.

"Why?" Ivan said, scooping one of his enormous hands into the peanuts. "He's always been weaselly. He cared more about getting ahead than anything." He looked to Sophrony for confirmation, who nodded and stuffed his own mouth full of peanuts as if to prevent himself from having to say anything about it.

Elena, who always moved like she'd just walked off the set of *Les Sylphides*, appeared from the kitchen and swept the spilled peanuts into her dainty palm. "He sounded like a nice boy to me," she said, perhaps in hopes of provoking her husband's ire.

Pyotr glared at his wife, who glared back and then retreated into the kitchen. They had the kind of relationship in which spitefulness is mistaken for passion. "You don't know anything about him," he said, and then, as if a sudden thought had occurred to him, he turned to Maya, who'd been sitting by herself in a corner all evening. "You, though," he said, gesturing to Maya with his elegant nose, "you two were always running around together. Did you suspect anything? How long had he been planning it?"

Maya's attention had wandered as soon as Olaf entered the conversation. She felt envious of Olaf, roaming free—and then felt foolish for feeling envious. After all, hadn't she gotten what she wanted? Wasn't she dancing in the Kirov, fulfilling the future her mother should have had? Wasn't she about to see America and half the world?

And yet, this was not the life she'd wanted. Maya had only been dancing in the corps for a short while, but she'd already gotten tired of it—the bit parts, the monotonous drudgery of rehearsals, the endless repetitions of *Swan Lake*. She was weary of the stilted, formal choreography, of the predictable plots and set pieces—how was it that every classic ballet required tutued virgins to dance chastely in the moonlight?

Nor had her career proven the quick ascent she'd hoped for. Nearly two years, and she'd yet to be given a single solo. She'd gotten so despairing that, a couple months ago, she'd gone to see Alexei at the Vaganova and asked if she should quit. Once, she'd thought her mother's ghost compelled her toward the Kirov, no matter the cost. Now Maya understood the truth—she hadn't obeyed Elizaveta, but her own ego, and she wasn't the only one who'd suffered for it.

Alexei, to his credit, encouraged Maya to stay put but keep her eyes open. "Maybe you could think about choreography," he said. "Olaf once told me you were gifted in that way."

She did think about choreography—all the time. She couldn't watch anyone dancing without rearranging the steps in her head, like Olaf had joked late one night in the Vaganova classroom—*it's as if you were a daughter of Balanchine*. What a pity that Balanchine would be in Russia while she was in America. If she and Olaf had known this, rehearsing all those years ago, they would have laughed at the irony. But remembering Olaf was painful now, and Maya's pain ended her reverie. "Did someone ask me a question?"

"Did you know he was going to leave?" Pyotr said.

"No," Maya said, which was true, but not entirely so. The night before they'd flown from Paris, Olaf came to visit her in her hotel room, and he said the thing she'd known he wanted to say but always hoped he wouldn't. She knew he was going to say it the moment he came into the room—that familiar look that was a little more than kindness. "I love you," he'd said. "I've loved you for a long time." Actually, he'd said he "gloved her," having downed seven shots of vodka to bolster his courage. He said this to her standing at the foot of her bed, swaying unsteadily.

Maya was flattered—she knew many girls in the company would be overjoyed to find themselves in her position. But she refused him. "You don't want to be with me," she said. Olaf was very dear to her, and she knew she could love him if she let herself—but that was something she could not risk. How could she, who had betrayed the person she loved most, be trusted to care for anyone, especially anyone as kind and good as Olaf? "You deserve someone better."

Olaf sat heavily at the foot of the bed. Maya felt sorry for him. She knew so well what it was to be rejected—how strange to be on the other side of things. She put her hand on his shoulder, but he pulled away. "I can't be near you and not love you," he said. "It's unbearable." He told her that he had to go away, and at the time Maya thought he meant away from her, to sleep alone. But the next morning, at Le Bourget, when Olaf turned to her and waved sadly before he walked up to the policeman, Maya understood what he'd meant.

"Remember how much he loved Karinska?" Sophrony said.

"I think you mean, remember how much Karinska loved *him*," Ivan said, with lewd implications, and everyone groaned. "All right, all right. What was that piece of music Karinska loved so much? The one she used in every class?"

"It was Bizet," Maya said. "Bizet's Symphony in C." She hummed a few bars. Such an energetic opening, perhaps designed to startle you—Karinska had known it was the perfect thing for rousing sleepy teenagers.

"I remember the way Karinska led us through port de bras," Pyotr said. "She told us to move our hands as if we'd dipped them into water."

"I remember that too," Sophrony said. "Remember how deep her voice got when she got angry? *'If you don't work hard, you will be worse than nothing!'*"

"Remember how well Vasili and Vasilia always partnered after they got back together?" Ivan said. "You could always tell when they'd started fucking again."

Everyone laughed but Maya. Part of her longed for those days—the simplicity of all of them, lined up at the barre, convinced that every step they took was moving them closer to some glorious future. Everything was simpler then: everyone was young, and pure, and whole, and no one's hopes had been shattered.

And Natasha had no reason to hate her.

CHAPTER TEN

The human body is remarkably resilient. Bones heal; muscles reknit themselves; cells regenerate as we sleep. Under the right circumstances, a hand can even regrow a lost fingertip. But when Ivan dropped Natasha at the graduation gala, she broke much more than a bone.

She was blinded twice, first by stage lights and then by agony, by a pressure right where her rib cage met her spine that was so forceful and deep she thought she'd fallen through the stage and suffocated under its weight. She heard someone screaming far away and did not realize it was herself. Everyone who heard that scream—the thousand people in the audience, the dancers in the wings, the stagehands, the costume mistresses, the little boy selling peanuts in the lobby—hoped they would someday forget it, but none would. Especially not Maya and Ivan. It wasn't the sound of the scream that was most horrifying—it was its duration. No one understood how a single pair of lungs could hold out for so long.

He had dropped her in the middle of a one-handed lift, dropped her from the highest reach of his extension, and she landed right on her tailbone, her spine absorbing the full force of the impact. It was as if he'd waited until the worst possible moment and then let go. Later, when Natasha lay in the hospital for ten weeks and thinking was her only occupation, when the pain gave way to an all-encompassing numbness that swallowed up both body and brain, she realized that was exactly what had happened.

For years, she had dedicated herself to the sculpting and strengthening of her body, to acquiring extraordinary flexibility and range of motion. Even outside the classroom, while attempting the simplest task—reaching across the table for the salt, walking down the sidewalk, washing her hair—her body spoke ballet, her limbs reached out, out, *out*. Then she was encased in a full-body cast, both legs bound and sealed off in an attempt to coax her shattered vertebra—*burst* was what the doctors pronounced, crushed in all directions—back into itself. Her beautiful, promising, enviable life shrank to the size of a hospital bed.

At first, there was no end to the visitors and well-wishers bearing bouquets and meals and cards and notes and favors—like Alexei's arranging for Natasha to be treated at a private hospital exclusively for Party members and their families, where she had a room of her own instead of a bed in an open ward. For the first couple weeks, Alexei came to visit her every day on his way home from work, always referring to her as "our girl."

"And how is our girl feeling today?" he'd ask, with a kinder, gentler voice than he'd ever used at school. "How is our girl getting along?"

At first, the visitors and well-wishers brought in only encouragement and good cheer along with their note cards and roses. Olga and Kira visited her twice a week, bringing chocolates and magazines with pictures of handsome film actors. "You must try to enjoy your recovery," Olga told her. Katusha brought Natasha cheerful striped leg warmers and currant tea from home.

Vasili and Vasilia, though somber, brought her books of poetry. "Poetry is like rest for the soul," Vasili said, prompting an admiring look from Vasilia.

All of the students who had seen Natasha's fall were badly shaken by it; they needed her to get better as proof that there would be hope for them if they were injured someday. So at first, recovery wasn't something Natasha experienced alone: she was part of a great wave of hopefulness, crashing toward the shore. She was a heroine.

But as the days turned to weeks, and the weeks turned to months, and it began to become clear to everyone that Natasha's abilities might never return, the voices around Natasha's hospital bed became hushed. The doctors and nurses hurried; they did only what they had to do, said only what needed to be said, using phrases like "long-term" and "compensation." The visitors came for rushed and apologetic visits, not wanting to linger in the sadness of Natasha's fate. Alexei, who always grew busiest at the end of the year, only came to visit once or twice a week. The students who visited didn't speak to Natasha like she was one of them anymore. Vasili and Vasilia, immersed in their own dramatics, stopped coming altogether. Kira and Olga told her about everything she missed at the Vaganova, the graduation ceremonies and the ball afterward and their plans for their future—a future in which, as was becoming clear, Natasha would have no part. Even Katusha looked anxious every time she came in, as if afraid Natasha would ask her a question she did not want to answer. Natasha waited for some sort of pronouncement to be made about her future. Some part of her knew, deep in her bones, that to dance again was impossible. But waiting for the news was even worse. She didn't know how she'd react to it, whenever it came. She was afraid she wouldn't be strong enough to face the truth. Her mother, after all, had chosen death over not dancing.

There were three people whose absences from Natasha's bedside were the most noticeable. Ivan's was easily explained: he was an ex-lover even before the accident, and his carelessness—that was what everyone called it, "carelessness"—had crushed her. Ilya also never turned up at the hospital, nor any of the other stilyagi. Violent incidents, like Rocky's humiliation by the People's Patrol Brigade, were becoming more common. Perhaps Ilya and his crew were afraid of appearing in public. Or perhaps he'd realized what Natasha had: they hadn't loved each other so much as the idea of an escape.

But the most conspicuous absence was Maya's. Katusha made excuses, said Maya was so busy, that the Kirov's rehearsal schedule was grueling—but Natasha knew the true reason her sister was absent, and it was the same as Ivan's. The two of them did this to her. When, on the night of the gala, Natasha saw Maya and Ivan whispering backstage, she'd thought they might be lovers. Uncomfortable as this was, it was nothing compared with the truth. Natasha eventually realized Maya had apologized to her for causing the accident before it had even happened. "I'm sorry," she'd cried, her kokoshnik wobbling on her head. "I'm sorry." Now, her body and her future crushed beyond repair, Natasha understood.

Lying in the hospital bed night after night, Natasha flipped through her memories like unwelcome picture albums, trying to understand what she'd done to deserve this. It was impossible that Ivan and Maya were seeking revenge—revenge for what? She had never wronged them. Her love affair with Ivan had come to a natural and inevitable end; teenagers had been pairing and parting for as long as there had been teenagers. The only conclusion Natasha could come up with was that both of them were jealous of her, and that Maya envied her acceptance by the Kirov—envied it enough that she'd destroy Natasha just to take it. Settling on this cause brought Natasha no comfort, and it was just as well that Maya never came to visit her. Natasha was not sure she could ever see her sister again without doing something terrible.

After eight weeks, the cast came off, and the brief joy and terror Natasha felt at seeing her legs—her own familiar goose-pimpled skin, though now pale and gray—dissipated when she understood how weak she was. She had to learn to walk again, first between raised bars at the physical therapy clinic, then with a walker, then, for a few weeks, with a cane, which made her walk with a swoop, as if she might break into a waltz at any moment, which only added to her humiliation.

She had been told she needed, for the rest of her life, to be careful. She had been told that she was lucky—if she had been dropped from a slightly different angle, or landed in a different position, she might have been paralyzed. But Natasha had lost too much to feel grateful. The core strength she'd spent a lifetime building was gone, likely never to return. Her remarkable flexibility, which had been the envy of every girl at the Vaganova, and even some of the teachers, had vanished. Her vertebra had healed, but the injury left a permanent stiffness in her back, along with a shooting pain that in the years to come would become as familiar to her as the shape of her fingertips.

One morning, in an examination room that she knew all too well, Natasha's favorite doctor delivered the worst of the news—news she had been anticipating for weeks and praying would not come. "Your nerves will take years to heal," he said. "Some may never heal at all. In the meantime, you must be extremely cautious. You must promise me you will not try to dance again."

The doctor who said this to Natasha was young and had always spoken kindly to her. She even thought him, with his green eyes and long and slender face, a little bit handsome. As her visitors had dwindled, Natasha looked forward to the afternoons when he visited her on his rounds. He'd often brought her cartoons that he'd clipped from the newspaper and sat on her bed and read them aloud to her as if she were a child.

For months, Natasha had waited for him, or anyone, to tell her the truth. The issue of her dancing had been skirted over and over again. When she'd asked about it, the doctors and nurses said something like, "Don't worry yourself over that just yet. First you must get well." But, as time went by, and the looks on their faces changed from kindness to pity, Natasha braced herself for some sort of final declaration every time one of them entered the room.

And now, here it was: her future, or the lack of it, staring at her in the form of a young doctor with a wrinkle between his eyebrows, who looked a little too sure of himself to be of any comfort to her.

The doctor had been very nervous to share this news with Natasha. Part of the reason the chief surgeon at the hospital had given him this task was that he was still very young and green, and he needed to practice the art of ending people's hopes. "Don't be subtle about it," the chief surgeon had said. "Don't take your time getting there. Prick it like a balloon, and let all the air out at once. Above all, don't act like you pity them. The weak hate to be pitied. They'll thank you for it." This had struck the young doctor as rather cruel, but he trusted the chief surgeon and wanted to impress him, so he followed his advice.

Dancers' careers are very short. Natasha had always known this. The lucky ones last until they're forty; most last much less. Natasha had heard plenty of stories from her teachers, many of whom walked with hobbles or limps from their career-ending injuries or, at the very least, with feet splayed out like penguins. She'd known from a young age that, if she was fortunate, she would have a brief and brilliant career, one that either ebbed away or ended in some sort of catastrophe—like her mother's.

A little part of her, too surprising and shameful for even her to acknowledge except when falling asleep, felt immediate relief that her dancing days were over. She'd known she didn't want to dance forever, even if she could, and now nobody would judge her for wanting something else.

But it wasn't supposed to have happened this way. She wanted to leave because she'd chosen it, and now the choice had been ripped away from her, and far too soon, by people who had claimed to love her. Ivan betrayed her. Maya stole her life.

The doctor, who had many more visits to make and needed to relieve himself, decided he had waited long enough for some sort of response and took Natasha's silence as a sign of acceptance. "Very good," he said, reaching over and patting her hand. "I knew you would be a good girl about it." He winked at her and got up and left the room, shivering as he stepped into the hallway because he'd noticed a chill had taken up permanent residence in Natasha's room—a chill that was not an indication of temperature, but of hopelessness.

A few weeks later—nearly three months to the day after the accident—Natasha went home to live with Katusha in their communal apartment, not unlike the one in which she had been born and in which her mother had died. That it was the same place where she had spent so many summers with her sister only made things more painful. In the hospital, a place where neither she nor Maya had ever set foot, it was easier for Natasha to pretend Maya didn't exist. But every corner of Katusha's apartment reminded Natasha of her splintered sisterhood. There was the tiny bedroom where they'd slept on twin beds—why did they have to be called twin beds?—and whispered confidences about the boys they loved, all their Ivans and Pyotrs and Pinkys. There was the kitchen table where they'd sat and sewn their pointe shoe ribbons before the first day of school—Maya always with her tiny, perfect stitches. Even the ancient sofa, which looked like it belonged in a museum of early Soviet history instead of a home, made Natasha think of Maya: the girls hadn't ever sat there without one of them playing their old game, trying to pin each other's toes to the ground. Everywhere Natasha looked was proof that someone had once loved her, and then decided that love was worth nothing.

Oh, the paradox of love: Natasha loathed the thought of her sister, but her body craved Maya's nearness like a phantom limb. Her hands missed the slope of Maya's scalp as she helped her pin her hair. Her feet missed the familiar press of her sister's toes. Natasha lay awake at night and listened for Maya's breathing in the dark, though she knew she wouldn't hear it. She was a body, halved. No, more than halved—her sister had taken her dancing body, leaving behind only what could shit and eat and sleep.

When Katusha went to work, Natasha sat in the corner of the sofa and stayed there until she came home again. No one came to see her. She did not go to visit anyone. She was, for the first time in her life, completely and utterly alone. Katusha did her best to keep her company, as she had for Maya when Natasha fell for Ivan, but she was unequipped to provide any sort of solution to Natasha's problem, which was who, exactly, she was supposed to be, now that she had lost everything.

Seeing Natasha so listless frightened Katusha. Sometimes, she liked to pretend that the girls were hers as well as Elizaveta's. If some miracle of science had mixed their genes, it would have produced children like this: Maya, dark-eyed and pensive like Katusha, and Natasha, blue-eyed and bright like Elizaveta. Now, Natasha's expression looked too much like her mother's in her last few days at the Kirov. It was the look of someone who wanted to give up.

But Katusha would not give up, even if Natasha did. She had been too late to save Elizaveta, but she could save her daughter. In the first weeks of Natasha's return, Katusha plied Natasha with distractions. In her mind, all that was needed was some meaningful task—a hobby to pull Natasha's mind from numbness. She brought Natasha needlework and knitting supplies, oil paints and brushes, a portable loom. She even scrimped and saved and bought her a guitar. Nothing captured Natasha's attention—which, after a while, exasperated Katusha. "Why can't you just choose something?" she said, after the guitar and all her other failures had gathered dust in the corner.

A month after she'd come home, at the urging of both Katusha and her doctors, Natasha began to take walks. She hated these at first—she'd never been one for wandering out alone, and the surrounding neighborhood was as soaked with memories as Katusha's apartment. Her sister's ghost was everywhere: in the shop where Katusha sent them to buy kasha and grains, in the dingy little shoe store where they'd had their street shoes resoled, on the sidewalk itself. Until last summer, they'd gone to all of these places together. Now Maya was off discovering a new world and had left Natasha back in the old one to rot. Though she didn't know it, Natasha spent her days thinking the same thing as Maya: this was not the life she'd wanted.

Natasha's misery during her walks was physical as well as spiritual; the days were short and the air was cold, and it hurt to bend down and tie her shoelaces. She shrank back from other people in the street, afraid that they'd bump into her and shatter her spine all over again. She tensed her back muscles as they passed, trying to protect it, which only worsened her shooting pains.

Gradually, these feelings passed. Natasha learned to relax her muscles when people passed her in the street, to breathe through pain until it subsided, and she started taking new routes to avoid old haunts. She came to love these strolls, the peaceful hum that came over her body as her limbs warmed and remembered what it was to be useful. And in this way, walking through snow and through rain, through light and through dark, Natasha survived the first year.

Like a cat sunning itself near its favorite window, her mind basked in the pleasure of coming to know the intimacies of a small corner of the world—the particular dip of the sidewalk as she turned off Katusha's street, the daily habits of the squirrels who busied themselves outside the window, the comings and goings of the barber next door, and the concentration of the fishmonger two blocks down, who always stood working near the window, decapitating carp.

One afternoon, Natasha had menstrual cramps—a monthly occurrence now that her body had the necessary fat to regulate itself—and did not go on her walk as usual. The next day, when the irritation had passed, she headed out into the warm spring morning, relieved to resume her routine. As she passed the fishmonger, she was astonished to see him look up and wave. "Wondered where you were yesterday!" he shouted through the window. And in this way, Natasha made a surprising discovery: she was not invisible. She was still a part of the world around her, despite her perceived lack of usefulness to it. And this discovery made Natasha suddenly ravenous to be back in the world again.

How, she did not know. She could have found some sort of work. But despite everything she had gone through, everything she had lost, some indivisible element of Natasha remained steadfast at her core, and this part of her refused to work in a dark office, hunched over a typewriter, or to be tucked away in Katusha's basement costume shop. She wanted to be around lots and lots of people.

A connection to the world proving elusive, Natasha decided to bring the world home to her. She began reading the newspaper every day. Back at school, she'd sometimes passed the teachers' lounge and seen the grown-ups leaning over tables full of newspapers, arguing over who knows what. She'd shuddered then—there was nothing beautiful or even interesting in those papers. Adulthood seemed so dull. But now Natasha read *Pravda* like it was an oracle, every day seeking some sort of revelation from its pages. She knew she was foolish for doing so. She was behaving like some poor, maligned character in a fairy tale, looking for her fortune.

Natasha's ache to dance had receded into numbness. Two years had passed since her injury, and you can only sustain an ache for so long. But when Katusha came home with the news that Maya was leaving for the Kirov's American tour—"Directly from Moscow," Katusha said, disappointed, "with no time to come home"—she felt tempted to lapse into her old sadness again. She, who belonged to no one. She turned to *Pravda* with more than a little sorrow that day, thumbing through articles about Khrushchev and the price of grain with no interest at all. She noticed, for the first time, how dusty the paper felt, the whiff of chemicals that came up every time she turned the page. She turned the page again, to try to replicate that experience, and saw a photograph of a dancer. Something about an American company coming to visit. Natasha's insides went rigid. It was the first time she'd seen a picture of a dancer since her accident: everyone had thought it best to keep her safe from such things—which, judging by the nausea Natasha now felt, had been a prudent decision. She folded the paper into quarters, ink staining her fingertips, and tossed the paper into the wastebasket. Not even her walk gave her its usual pleasure that day. When she got home, she retreated to her habitual corner of the couch and munched an apple, envying its rosy perfection.

Katusha came home not long after, smiling cautiously and crouching over her goddaughter as she always did. She tucked a stray hair behind Natasha's ear. "Feeling poorly today?"

Natasha shrugged. "Every day is the same," she said, though lately this had not been true, and Katusha knew it—knew that, before the news of Maya's tour, Natasha's days had been getting better and better.

"There, there," Katusha said, and she kissed Natasha on the head. "Let's clean up, shall we?" she said, pointing to the apple core, which Natasha had left on the arm of the couch. Natasha sighed and heaved herself off the couch, snatching up the apple core as she went. She opened the wastebasket and froze. There, on the back of the newspaper she'd thrown away an hour before, was an advertisement that asked, in big black letters, *Are You Natasha?*

It was a casting call for a film. The director's impassioned plea was printed beneath a photograph of himself—and not a flattering one either, Natasha thought, shuddering at his beetly eyes. *Help us capture Tolstoy's genius and the spirit of Russia on film*, he said. *Come be my Natasha*. The smaller print beneath gave the details: young women ages 18–25 were invited to send their photograph to Mosfilm to be considered for the role of Natasha Rostova in Sergei Bondarchuk's *War and Peace.*

"What is it?" Katusha said, alarmed. "Did you hurt yourself?"

"No," Natasha said. She looked up with a gleam in her eye that Katusha had not seen in two years and asked to have her picture taken.

CHAPTER ELEVEN

Yekaterina Furtseva sat at her desk in her apartment deep within the Kremlin walls, framed on one side by a portrait of Lenin and, on the other, by a square of unfaded wallpaper where Stalin's portrait had once hung. She wore an emerald dressing gown dotted with nut-brown cigarette burns. The desk, which faced the door, was buried in old letters and newspapers and invoices from the hundreds of projects she'd been asked to oversee. Though it was barely past dinner—she hadn't eaten yet—the sun was already setting.

Yekaterina Furtseva had a headache, and it was all on account of the animals—endless animals, hundreds of them, obscure ones, and she had to acquire them all by September. To start, there were the horses—fifteen hundred of them, all battle ready, capable of being saddled and harnessed and ridden by actor-soldiers and sent out onto the mock battlefield. Furtseva, despite all her wheeling and dealing and occasional threats, had come up short by six hundred. Not all of the farmers and breeders were willing to comply when they learned that the horses might not be returned—the cost of playing at war.

Then there were the hunting dogs. Beagles were easy enough to come by. Though just after the war, it would have been near impossible to find any edible animal, the last decade of peace and (relative) prosperity had returned pets to the Russians. Furtseva secured the promise of five dozen beagles with very little trouble.

It was the borzois that were giving her a headache. Until Sergei Bondarchuk, she had never even heard of a borzoi, and after he described them to her, she still couldn't understand the fuss he was making about them. "They're sleek and slender," he'd said. "Real hunting dogs."

Furtseva, being a practical woman and mindful of the million rubles she had already distributed for this project, suggested they use greyhounds instead. But no—Bondarchuk insisted on borzois because *Tolstoy* wrote of borzois. This was why she was sitting at her desk without dinner, waiting for another obscure breeder way out in Tashkent to return her call.

He was an obstinate man, Bondarchuk. He'd been chosen to direct this film in part because of this obstinacy. After the Americans released their version of the film—soporific, Furtseva had thought, so ridiculous that Audrey Hepburn would have married someone as ancient as Henry Fonda—Bondarchuk had been one of the many Soviet artists who'd raised their voices in protest. He'd written to Furtseva about it. "Why is it that this novel, the pride of Russian national character, was adapted in America and released in their cinema halls?" he'd written in a sloping, angry-looking hand. "Are we ourselves not able to adapt it? It's a disgrace to the whole world!"

When Furtseva shared this letter with the Politburo, it—along with a growing consensus among artists and novelists and filmmakers that the Americans' overture must be answered—led to a decision: *War and Peace* needed to become a Russian film. And it needed to be unfathomably grand.

Furtseva hadn't minded this. Indeed, such a project, on such a scale as was being discussed, would greatly raise her profile. An epic film, seen by millions around the country—and the world—would draw far more attention to her efforts than the piddly ballets and dramas she'd been tasked with for the last three years.

But she'd bristled when Bondarchuk was suggested as a director. For one thing, he was a newcomer: he'd been an actor—and a mediocre one at that, Furtseva thought—before he'd turned to directing, and he'd only directed a single film. For another—well, she just didn't like him. He was the sort of man who made her despise men—cocksure and arrogant, belligerent if provoked. She'd held out for weeks in hopes that someone else would arise. But then he won the Lenin Prize for his piddly little film, and then a whole host of cinematographers started a letter-writing campaign to secure Bondarchuk the job and—well, time and energy were finite, so Furtseva gave up and gave in.

She had been instructed to spare no expense—never, in Russia's history, had the government lavished so much on a single film—and she'd given Bondarchuk a generous stipend so he could write the script. Even she had been impressed with the result. Bondarchuk was a smitten Tolstoyan at heart, and the script he produced bore the marks of his love: every detail had been researched, every voice-over and line of dialogue matched up to Tolstoy's text. The script's most noticeable attribute was that it was long—far too long for a single film, and after approving the script, Furtseva made the decision that it would be released in four parts. Bondarchuk immediately requested her help with preproduction—and more money—and hence, the phone calls in search of horses and beagles and borzoi, along with inquiries to museums and armories and purveyors of antique costumes and china.

This project was not Furtseva's sole obligation. There were so many other things to do. The American ballet tour alone could have kept her working all hours, and it often did. The Americans stunned her with their fussy requests—why on earth did every dancer need such large portions of meat with their dinners, and rooms with a private bath? She hoped fervently that the Kirov dancers heading abroad wouldn't make such a terrible impression. Russian dancers were made of sturdier stock—well, with the exception of that troublesome Kirov soloist, whose defection raised such a stink for Furtseva that she'd considered retiring young.

The phone on Furtseva's desk rang, its shrillness muffled by the old issue of *Pravda* that had fallen over it. It was the farmer from Tashkent, answering her inquiry about borzoi. "I haven't even heard of them," he said. "Are you sure you're spelling it right? Are you sure you don't mean *beagle*?"

Furtseva set her jaw. She was always getting questions like this—the kinds of questions people would never dare ask her if she were a man. The subtext, too often, was menstrual in nature: *Are you sure it isn't just your uterus clouding your thoughts?* She spat back a harsh reply and hung up the phone, crossing out the farmer's name on her list in thick black pen and making a mental note to raise a motion to stop all agricultural aid to Tashkent at the next Politburo meeting.

Her stomach grumbled. "Hush," she said, as if it were something outside of her, like a dog, and she dialed Bondarchuk's number.

"Yes," he said, in an urgent sort of whisper.

Furtseva rolled her eyes—Bondarchuk didn't seem capable of speaking in a normal voice. "I'm calling to inquire about the casting," she said. "How is it going?"

"Terribly," he said, which was nearly true. Sergei Bondarchuk was the kind of man who ate when he was stressed, and right now he was very stressed. At his doctor's admonishment, he'd given up chocolate and cookies and all other sweets two weeks ago and had been left with fresh fruit as his only indulgence. Half an hour before Furtseva called, he'd consumed an enormous quantity of cherries (they reminded him of his childhood, when he'd wandered around orchards and imagined he was Chekhov looking for inspiration) and iced milk and now deeply regretted both.

Furtseva shook her head. "You always exaggerate," she said. "Who are you still missing?"

"Andrei," Bondarchuk said. "The last actor I cast flaked out again. We're going to have to do auditions for Natasha without him. Not that the search for her is going any better," he said. He tried—and failed—to cloak a burp in his sleeve. "That godforsaken newspaper advertisement didn't do a damn thing—except bury me in photographs of very young girls."

Furtseva's gaze fell to the old copy of *Pravda* lying on the desk, which featured Bondarchuk's advertisement for his future Natasha. Though he had sat for a special portrait in a brand-new suit and tie, Furtseva knew there wasn't a camera in the world that would have prevented him from looking like a mole. Bondarchuk glanced off to the side in a dreamlike pose as if he were still an actor and not the director of the most expensive film in the world.

"What's wrong with very young girls?" she asked.

"Everything," Bondarchuk said. "They all look brainless. My Natasha has to be innocent, but she also needs to think thoughts. And don't forget how much she'll need to grow in the picture! She'll have to be thirteen and seventeen and nineteen and bereft."

"And graceful," Furtseva said. She lifted up the newspaper and found an agenda from the Kirov's tour. "Have you thought about a dancer? We have plenty of those around, and it would be convenient—aren't there a couple scenes where Natasha has to dance anyway?"

"I would never cast a dancer," Bondarchuk said. It might have been Furtseva's imagination, but she felt like she could hear him scowling over the phone. "I need an actor, not a ballerina. And begging your pardon, Furtseva, if you'll excuse me, I have to keep combing through these pictures. Goodnight." And he hung up without waiting for permission.

Yekaterina Furtseva drummed her hands in the lap of her burnt dressing gown and sighed, staring down the list of animals she had yet to obtain. "This man is going to be the death of me," she said, and she rested her weary head on her desk.

Yekaterina Furtseva was not the only woman looking at Bondarchuk's portrait that night. Nearly five hundred miles away, in Leningrad, Natasha laid her head on Katusha's tiny dining room table—in the same manner as Furtseva—where the weeks-old issue of *Pravda* sat wrinkled before her too. On the day she'd sent in her picture for the auditions, she leaned the paper against the salt and pepper on the table and left it as a sort of shrine. She believed this film would be her chance to have the life she'd wanted, a life like Audrey Hepburn's. She believed that she, too, could bewitch the world into loving her. But she'd been waiting for a reply for two weeks, and with every day that passed, this dream became a little harder to hope for.

Katusha had been accommodating enough in getting Natasha's picture taken (despite the check Maya sent them every month, things were always stretched thin, as they were for everyone in those days), but she was wary of Natasha's hopes. "You've got your whole life ahead of you," she said while darning a sock. "Why pin all your hopes on this one thing?"

Natasha bristled. Ever since the accident, people had been saying this sort of thing to her: *You're still so young, you've got so much life ahead of you*. What none of them understood was that time could be a burden as well as a gift, and she had too much of it on her hands. The future weighed her down and left her listless. "My whole life," Natasha said, idly picking up a fork and letting it drop to the table with a clang, "is worth nothing if there's nothing in it." An idea struck her and she dropped the fork again, this time by accident. "What if I just went to Moscow?"

"To do what?" Katusha's needle had come unthreaded and she was straining to see its eye.

"To audition," Natasha said.

Katusha put down the needle. "Didn't the advertisement say they'd contact you if you were invited?"

It had said that, and it did still, sitting on their table. The fine black print was so sure of itself—it seemed to mock her now. "Yes," Natasha said, barely audible. "But I could go just to see."

"We don't have the money for a train ticket," Katusha said, her voice sharper than before. "You know that." She was weary of Natasha's malaise. It made sense that nature provided children with two parents—if one of you lost patience, the other could step in. Maybe Elizaveta would have been better at handling her spirited daughter. If Elizaveta were sitting with them, what would she say?

Katusha glanced at the empty chair beside her and her eyes welled up. Even now, thinking of Elizaveta, imagining the life they could have lived together, made her ache. She craved a moment to sit alone with her grief. "Why don't you go check the mail? Maybe it came late today."

Natasha rose without replying and bounded down the stairs—or came as close as she could to bounding these days. She still walked with a tiny lilt, imperceptible to strangers on the street but recognizable to anyone who had known her before, and every now and then a terrible pain still radiated from the center of her spine. Her back twinged a bit as she reached the bottom of the stairs, where the mailboxes were, and she resolved to walk back up more carefully. Though it had been two years, she was still frightened of injuring herself again.

Natasha stood in front of the mailboxes for a minute, readying herself. A nervous energy rose in her throat. She hoped there wouldn't be a letter from Maya, describing the wonders of America. No, this was it now, she could feel it. Something big was coming. And of course it was, because she was Natasha, after all, the one everyone had had such hopes for.

Thus prepared for a miracle, she inserted the key into the mailbox and opened it.

There was nothing inside.

The nervous energy that had risen in Natasha's throat sank back down again, turning cold as it went. She couldn't face Katusha with this news—inevitably, Katusha would have some sort of pat wisdom to share that would only make her feel worse. Natasha dropped the key into her pocket and skulked outside.

Though it was a hot, clear evening, the rot of late summer was already in the air, warning everyone that soon the leaves would fall and unrelenting cold would return. Natasha dreaded the thought of another winter spent gathering dust in Katusha's apartment. She wished she could get away, and the wish was so fervent and strong that it was almost a prayer. She wished so hard that she stopped paying attention to what was around her and bumped into a man in a gray wool suit coming around the corner.

The man swore—Natasha had scuffed his shoes, which he'd taken great care to polish before heading out for the evening—and then stepped back, astonished. "Natasha?"

It took Natasha a moment to match the familiar voice with the serious-looking fellow before her. The last time she'd seen him, he'd worn a yellow suit so vibrant it nearly glowed in the dark. But now Ilya didn't look like himself at all. His hair was cut short, and he wore the plain gray uniform of a Komsomol officer. Still, she was so happy to see him—to see anyone from her old life—that she embraced him without thinking about it. Ilya accepted this embrace, but rather stiffly, and when Natasha pulled back, he looked relieved.

"My God, Ilya," Natasha said, "what happened to you?"

Ilya laughed—not the ready, boyish laugh of before, but the way a man laughs at a joke told by a child. "I decided it was time to grow up," he said. This was almost true. After Ilya's father got word of Rocky's public denouncement, he'd beaten Ilya until his face was a meaty pulp. (Natasha, if she had known this, would have realized Ilya's nose was newly crooked.) "No son of mine will bring our country shame," he'd said, and he swore to keep Ilya under lock and key. Ilya, whether out of sincerity or simply having no choice, repented for his lack of patriotism, cut his hair, and became an officer at the Komsomol. The group of stilyagi, like so many of their counterparts around the country, disbanded, resigning themselves to dull clothes and ordinary adulthoods. Ilya told Natasha a shortened and somewhat sanitized version of this tale that made him out to be something of a patriotic hero. A hero who was, as it turned out, engaged—to the daughter of a high-ranking Party official.

"Congratulations," Natasha said, trying to appear like this news didn't sting. So even Ilya got a happy ending. "I hope you get everything you wanted."

Ilya noticed the shift in Natasha's voice and, revisiting a guilt he'd carried for two years, apologized for never coming to see her. "When my father found out what had happened, he told me I could never see the old gang again," he said, lowering his voice. "You understand."

"Of course," Natasha said, although she didn't. Not for the first time, she felt lucky that she didn't have a father.

"But I can't say goodbye without hearing about you," Ilya said, hoping Natasha would remember him as a kind old friend rather than someone who'd abandoned her. "What are you doing these days? I'm so happy to see you're walking again."

Natasha, attempting the self-preservation and self-aggrandizement necessary to speak to a former lover, told him all about Bondarchuk and *War and Peace*. "I'm certain they're going to call me in for an audition any day."

"Ah, yes, I've heard of that film," Ilya said. "They've got very high hopes for it in Moscow." He chuckled. "So, you've decided to shill for the motherland too, eh?"

"What do you mean?"

"The state's pouring a lot of money into this film. They want to show up the Americans—they're even using real soldiers for the battle scenes. I guess you'd be a sort of soldier too—but you already were at the Vaganova, weren't you? Ballerinas are our best diplomats."

"I don't know," Natasha said. "I don't care about any of that. I just want to be an artist. This might be the only chance I have left."

Ilya looked wistful. "I understand," he said, quietly. "You said you've got an audition?"

"No," Natasha said. "I'm waiting to hear back from them."

Ilya, hands in his pockets, leaned back on his heels, considering something. "You know, Natasha," he said, "life in our country isn't all that bad. There are so many things we don't have to worry about. We're a nation that believes in taking care of our people. But sometimes you need to take care of yourself, too."

"What do you mean?"

Ilya looked over his shoulder. "I mean," he said, his voice dropped low, "that our motherland is very good at watching out for us. But even the most excellent mothers can get frazzled and overlook us now and again, yes? No mother wants her child to go hungry. So sometimes, if you notice she leaves a cupboard open, you have to help yourself."

He stepped closer. "I still want the same things you want," he whispered. "I never stopped wanting them. But I gave up on trying to get away, because I realized you can never really leave the place that made you. You'll carry it wherever you go. But you can still live the life you wanted, even here. You just have to build it for yourself. You have to play the game. Don't wait for anyone to come along and take care of you, Natasha. If you see something you want, reach out and take it."

Katusha knew better than to say anything when her goddaughter came back up the stairs empty-handed. She knew Natasha preferred to be alone in these moments of disappointment. Without a word, she made Natasha a cup of currant tea, kissed her on the top of the head, and went into her tiny bedroom to put herself to bed.

Natasha didn't even notice the tea. She considered the possibility that this was how it was going to be for the rest of her life—waiting around for a miracle that would never happen. She didn't want an ordinary life like Katusha's. She wanted the life she'd been fated for from the beginning—to be rich, to be famous, to be adored by thousands of people. That was her destiny. She'd earned it, and it had been stolen from her. So now she must steal it back. Wasn't this exactly what Maya had done? She wondered if her sister had felt justified, even righteous—was it really stealing when the thing had been yours in the first place?

Natasha crept to the back of the kitchen and lifted an old cracked jug from the shelf, the one that Katusha kept all of her money in. She rifled through the worn bills. There were only twenty kopecks in the jug. How much was train fare to Moscow? Ten kopecks? Doubting her ability to make such a judgment, Natasha took all but three rubles, put them in her pocket, and left for the next train to Moscow.

CHAPTER TWELVE

New York City smelled terrible. Maya wondered why on earth nobody had warned them about this. It smelled like someone had taken all the world's rotting fish and garbage and then baked it and spread it over the late-summer sidewalks. It was September, but the air was hot and dry, and the stench cut into Maya's nostrils the moment she got off the plane. Some of the other dancers gagged. Even a few of their handlers held handkerchiefs over their noses.

Despite the stench, six weeks into the US tour, it was the presence of the handlers that most irritated all the dancers. Everyone knew they were KGB agents, but they'd been instructed to refer to them as "chaperones," as if this tour was just a gathering of hormonal pubescents and not an act of cultural warfare.

Before the tour, the entire traveling company had been lectured on the importance of what they were about to do. The logistics alone were enough to intimidate even the more seasoned dancers: a three-month tour, visiting nine cities, with six performances a week. But there was more being risked than exhaustion. Yekaterina Furtseva climbed on top of a chair in Sheremetyevo International Airport and reminded them all that dancing on this tour was an act of patriotism, a solemn duty. "The whole world will be watching you," she said.

It was never stated explicitly why the handlers were there—most of the meeting had been spent exhorting them to spread the Soviet gospel, to insert their country's accomplishments and innovations into conversations with foreigners at every opportunity—but everyone knew they were there to keep the dancers out of trouble, to ensure they behaved in a manner befitting their duty, and, above all, to keep anyone from defecting. Olaf's flight had reflected very badly on the Soviet state, and he was not the only one to flee; how good could this country be, the foreign papers reasoned, if people were so eager to leave it?

In any case, Furtseva reminded them that they were forbidden from having any contact with Olaf, or any of the Russians who'd defected—warning that the "corrupt American government" would attempt to "ensnare them" through such means. Hearing this, Maya shivered and hoped that the letter she had recently sent Olaf—to the last address he'd left her in Paris—had never reached him. It was not that she'd said anything she regretted—not anything the government would object to, anyway. She'd said only that she missed him, as she missed everyone from those days at school, the simplicity of those years, and that she had a lot of regrets. By this she meant what she and Ivan had done to Natasha, but Olaf did not know that, and later, Maya wondered why she'd written to him at all.

Ever since the party at Pyotr's, Maya had been thinking constantly about their days at the Vaganova—their simple gray uniforms, the time at the barre, the particular litany of exercises. As a professional dancer, Maya took company classes and rehearsed every day, even on tour, but it felt different than her student days. When professional dancers did their daily barre, it was part of their job. At the Vaganova, the barre felt more like a religion, and their teachers were their priests, promising that if they were good now, heaven waited for them down the road. Karinska in particular had excelled at uncovering the spiritual in the physical. "You are not just exercising your muscles," she'd say as they struggled through a grueling set of repetitions, often to her favorite Bizet. "You are exercising your will. You are strengthening your soul. You are not just reflecting beauty—you're becoming beauty itself." From the looks on everyone's faces, even the sweatiest and most disillusioned among them—Anya, Kira, even Natasha herself—had felt some sort of kinship with what Karinska was saying. All of them were here because they believed they were part of something good. Maya missed that certainty of purpose. Perhaps she'd been a pawn in a grand scheme of propaganda at the Vaganova too, but she hadn't quite realized it then. Or, perhaps, she'd believed much more in the goodness of their cause—and in her own goodness.

Karinska's favorite Bizet had played in Maya's head all over America. She thought of it as she brushed her teeth in Kansas City, warmed up in Detroit, rode the bumpy train to Philadelphia. Though she was in a new city nearly every week, each new place just made her think of Leningrad, of that low yellow building on the narrow street, the only place she had ever felt at home.

Here she was, on tour with the best ballet company in the world, performing all over the country that had been the bedrock of her sister's dreams—but every curtain call only highlighted her emptiness. She didn't belong here. She was never meant to be a star—just her sister's understudy. If she hadn't been so afraid of being left behind, if she'd been able to face the truth of her life, Natasha would be the one bowing on these grand stages instead of her. The Americans' applause didn't bring her any joy. It just reminded her of how she'd ruined Natasha.

In every city they visited, Maya sat up late at night on crusty hotel beds sewing ribbons on her pointe shoes. Once, she'd felt pride in her tiny, perfect stitches, their evenness and grace. Now this, too, just made her think of Natasha. They'd sat up like this so many nights in their cozy little room at the Vaganova. Every dancer had a slightly different method for sewing ribbons, and Maya and Natasha's further proved their oppositeness. Maya carefully slipped the needle between the layers of satin and canvas so as to hide her stitches. Natasha, who was perennially impatient and easily bored, preferred to stab through all the shoe's layers at once, which was both uglier and much more difficult, but she claimed it went by faster. Natasha was like this about everything—always willing time to hurry, wanting to stuff as much into a day as she could. Maybe that's why she'd longed for America. She hadn't wanted a new destination so much as the feeling of being in motion. But now Maya was the one in America, and Natasha would never sew ribbons on her pointe shoes again.

Maya had never meant to end Natasha's career. She'd thought she would be injured just badly enough to be kicked off the tour, to be kept safely at home. But there was only so much you could control in this life, and Maya realized this too late.

Maya thought of Natasha everywhere they went—what would Natasha say about the Great Lakes, Monet's haystacks in Chicago, Atlanta's stifling heat? Would Natasha have overslept in all these hotel rooms, as she had back home, needing Maya to pull her out of bed by her ankles? Once, on a crowded bus, someone stepped on Maya's foot, and for a second, she thought it was Natasha, playing their old game.

During the first part of the tour, there had always been another rehearsal or mandatory cultural experience to distract Maya from these memories. But in New York, her sister was unavoidable. Every woman on the streets was like Natasha's ghost—that is, the ghost of Natasha the stilyaga. Women in New York wore bright pastel pillboxes and smart tapered skirts, outfits coordinated right down to the buttons. One afternoon, the eager American attachés took the female dancers to Bergdorf's, hoping to dazzle them with capitalism's excesses. While the other dancers oohed and aahed and rushed around like little girls, filling their arms with stockings and shoes (the handlers, clustered in a corner, looked on in disgust), Maya stood in front of a display of gloves, her eyes welling up. Two dozen pairs, in every imaginable shade, were laid out in a rainbow, mulberry and lemon yellow and sage and turquoise and deep amethyst. It would have made Natasha so happy to learn that gloves came in so many colors.

Still, walking the dirty streets with a scarf wrapped around her nose, Maya did not understand why anyone would want to leave Russia, especially to come here. All of the streets were gray and angular, and there were—with one exception, as far as she could see, that long strip of trees in the center of the city—no parks. Where were people expected to live?

A week later, her impression of the West had only worsened. The way people talked about it back home, Maya had half expected the West to feel like a fairy kingdom, where everyone was always happy and the streets were paved with gold. But the West was, it turned out, an ordinary place, a place where cats napped in alleyways and people hung their laundry out their windows and tossed trash into the streets. Even though it was September, it was strangely warm, and her morning walk from her hotel to the Metropolitan Opera for rehearsals left her dripping in sweat. As she walked into the opera house, she wondered why on earth her sister had ever wanted to leave everyone and everything she loved for this.

She wondered, too, why she had thought it would be worth it to swap her sister's happiness for all this drudgery. She had thought being a dancer would be glamorous. Back home, people fantasized about what it would be like to tour in America—to be pampered like queens, with fur coats and limousine rides, to parade around parties, to have your face grace the covers of fashion magazines.

Maybe this was what it was like for the star dancers—the ones for whom handsome men waited backstage, bearing armfuls of roses. But Maya was a lowly corps member, and it was looking like she might stay one forever. Last week, another dancer from the corps had been promoted to soloist. Yet again, someone had been chosen over her. She'd been working like a dog since she was a child, and all she had to show for it was injuries and disappointments. Her bursitis flared, disappeared, then reappeared again, and her left pinky toenail was going to fall off again any day now. These days she did a good deal of thinking about her feet (and how much they hurt), about her fouettés (and how her extension wasn't as long as it should be), and about Ivan—far more than she would have liked, and far more than she understood.

It had started that night at the dinner party, before they'd left for the tour. Elena had seated Maya and Ivan across from each other, and for the rest of the evening, whenever she had the temerity to look up at him, Maya found Ivan looking back at her too. It was probably just the alcohol—there was, as was often the case, far too much of it flowing that night, and the next day they'd all had headaches. But then Ivan sat next to her on the plane, and he often sat beside her when the company gathered for meals in the opera houses' basement cafeterias. One afternoon in Washington, DC, three weeks into the tour, the entire company was shuffled through the echoing hallways of the National Gallery of Art. Maya lingered in the back of the group, not because a painting had caught her eye—the endless rooms full of pompous portraits bored her—but because she was tired. Tour life was grueling: their per diems were abysmally small, even by Soviet standards, and though Maya had followed the advice of veteran dancers and stuffed her suitcase with canned peas and hard cheeses, she always seemed to be hungry. On this particular day, the corns on her left foot had become so painful that she limped, and when the tour group disappeared into yet another gallery, she deposited herself on a hard wooden bench and waited for them to come out. She knew she'd have to rejoin the tour by its end to participate in the inevitable photo op, when everyone was expected to appear grateful and content in front of the American cameras.

Maya resented all the posturing. She'd wanted to be a dancer, not a diplomat. And if the Soviet state was as generous toward its citizens as it pretended to be, both Maya and Natasha could have joined the Kirov, and it never would have occurred to Maya to betray her sister.

The ball of Maya's foot ached and throbbed. Maya made sure she was alone and then took off her shoe and examined her foot, looking for some offending rock or splinter, but as usual, the only thing causing her body pain was itself. She wished she could skip the photo op and sneak back to the hotel—wasn't touring hard enough on its own?

"Need a rub?" Ivan, who had a gift for sneaking up on people, was leaning over her with his hands in his pockets. Maya looked up so suddenly that her head collided with his chin. Both recoiled and rubbed their injuries. "No," Maya said. "But now I need an aspirin."

Ivan, who was as amused as he was embarrassed, offered his arm in penance, and he helped Maya limp into the gallery, where they melted into the crowd unnoticed.

They were often thrown together like this. After all, Maya later told herself, while she and Ivan and the rest of the company walked through the great hall of the United Nations—yet another instance of forced sightseeing they were made to do on this tour—they'd known each other since childhood. Memory was a shared language. Once, when the rehearsal accompanist happened to play Karinska's favorite Bizet during company class, Ivan looked over at Maya and smiled, and both knew what the other was remembering—that sunlit classroom in the Vaganova, yellow with half-dome windows,

Karinska's bracelets jangling in allegro vivo. They had grown up together: it was natural that they would seek out each other's company.

Still, she felt a twinge of unease every time Ivan came near her. It was impossible to be close without thinking about what she'd asked him to do in the gymnasium, without thinking about her sister falling from his arms, without imagining Natasha imprisoned in a hospital bed. When she and Ivan shared a meal or stood next to each other in company class, she did everything she could to make it clear she wasn't flirting with him. She never touched him unless they were partnered—which was rare—and she tried to avoid being alone with him if they were drinking. She even flirted with a couple other male dancers in his company to make her disinterest as clear as possible.

Despite all this, Maya allowed herself to watch Ivan while he was performing, and she stood in the wings to see him as often as she could. Watching him was a bright spot in an otherwise dreary couple months. She disliked all the parts she'd been given to dance on tour—you could only dance in the corps for *Giselle* or *Swan Lake* so many times before you grew weary of dramatic gestures and long white tutus. There was something artificial and posturing about the Kirov's dances: one night in New York, they'd been taken to see Alvin Ailey's dance company, and Maya envied their exuberance and freedom of expression, the near-nakedness of their bodies. She wondered, as she watched them, if she could capture that feeling in a dance of her own. She wanted to make a ballet, and she wanted it to feel like life at the Vaganova—a ballet that felt like it was building something that mattered. All she needed was the right idea, and the right opportunity to present it to the Kirov, and then the myth of her life would be complete.

With this aim only dimly in mind, Maya wandered down to a practice room early one morning, a Bizet record under her arm. She'd woken up with an idea: What if there were a ballet whose story was not a prince seeking an enchanted lover, or an army waging a fierce battle, but the making of a dancer? There was a certain beauty to the synchronous movements of dancers at the barre.

Maya put Bizet on the record player and tried to channel her childhood. Every plié she did on the stage was the product of thousands she'd done in the Petipa Room, and all the teachers who had corrected her, poking at the inside of her foot, nudging open her turnout—every day, for years and years and years. Surely all of this hadn't been in vain. Maya felt as if every step they'd performed had a life and a value all its own—as Karinska said, they strove not to imitate beauty, but to become it.

That morning, as Maya began the alchemy of spinning music into movement, she strove to become something new: a choreographer.

CHAPTER THIRTEEN

Sergei Bondarchuk cut himself shaving and cursed. His hands shook, and he hated himself for it. Why fear a confrontation with two hundred little girls? He had seen two hundred the day before, and the day before that, and none of them had been frightening. If anything, all of them had been frightened of him. Yet Sergei Bondarchuk found himself, while shaving in his fashionable Moscow apartment, afraid. If Bondarchuk had been in a more contemplative mood—and not groggy from a sleepless night thanks to the overindulgence in cherries and milk—he may have stumbled across the realization that he was afraid of women, that he'd always been afraid of women, had always been afraid that they would laugh at him.

Somehow, three years ago, he'd overcome this dread of the female long enough to court and woo a beautiful woman named Irina, which was a mystery to everyone who witnessed it (Bondarchuk included). She had enormous blue eyes and Norse goddess hair and she could have married any man she wanted—but she had chosen Bondarchuk, fat and oafish and clumsy as he was, and this gave him faith in life's goodness, or at least Irina's.

But Sergei Bondarchuk was not waxing philosophical that morning. He was tired, and his neck hurt from tossing back and forth all night, and when Irina asked him if he wanted coffee with his breakfast, he snapped at her. "Of course I want coffee with my breakfast," he said. "Do you, too, doubt the remnants of my faculties?"

There was no reason for him to say this to her; she'd said nothing about his intelligence. He referred to the immense pressure that had settled on him since he'd been chosen to direct *War and Peace*: all day, and sometimes at night, there were phone calls from the Kremlin, reminding him of what was at stake—not that he ever forgot it. The apparatchiks all expected this film to astound the world, and Sergei did too, though for different reasons. Tolstoy was his god, and *War and Peace* his holy scripture. He'd spent years adapting the 1,440-page novel into a script, then approving plans for ball gowns, sabers, and chandeliers, bending over his work like a monk illuminating a manuscript, attempting faithfulness—which, incidentally, required large quantities of money, which is why the apparatchiks were necessary. That they considered his great opus a piece of propaganda only compounded his distress. He thought of himself, first and foremost, as a lover of art.

Ordinarily, he was very gentle with Irina—Irina, whose figure, now enveloped in a flattering pink bathrobe, made Bondarchuk the envy of men, a fact of which she was well aware. But she was also aware of the great troubles that come with being an artistic genius, which, in her mind, her husband unquestionably was, and this helped her be patient. They'd been very happily married from the start; each of them was grateful for the other.

"Poor dear," she sighed, scratching her husband's back. She opened the tin of coffee. "You know, my love," she said, scooping the aromatic grounds into the pot, "I thought that I might be able to help you. As an actress myself—"

"And a fine one at that," Sergei said, admiring his wife's well-developed figure from behind. He realized that he had been grumpy, and he was eager to make up.

Irina turned around and smiled a knowing smile. She understood his compliment was really an apology; she was always so ready to understand him. "As an actress," she continued, "and as a woman, I think I have a good sense for talent when I see it."

"And?" Sergei said. He bit into his toast.

"And," Irina said, pulling something from her pocket, "I see it in her." She put a photograph next to Sergei's plate. The photograph was of the very Natasha who, at that moment, was sitting yawning at a coffeehouse in the middle of the city, having just arrived in Moscow.

It was not as flattering of a photograph as it could have been; if it had been taken two years earlier, before the accident, it would have given Bondarchuk a much better idea of Natasha's loveliness, and perhaps then he would have taken it more seriously. But as it was, Natasha had tried to compensate for her weariness with energy, which resulted in her smiling much too big and opening her eyes much too wide. "*Her?*" Sergei said, with more than a little disdain. "She looks crazy! Are you trying to get me killed?"

"Of course not," Irina said. "But look at her, Sergei. There's just something to her that isn't in the other girls. She reminds me of someone. I can't put my finger on whom." She tapped the photo with her index finger.

"You can't put your finger on her," Sergei said, picking up his wife's hand and kissing her finger, "because she isn't worthy of being touched by such a finger." And he kissed his wife on the neck, and she laughed, and the coffee began to boil and overflow without either of them noticing.

Six hours later, the memory of this happiness long faded, Sergei

Bondarchuk was sitting in a stuffy office at Mosfilm, succumbing to despair. Every single girl who crossed his path was wrong. They were too short, too tall, too fat, too long-necked, too peevish, too bold, too everything. What he wouldn't give for a girl who had all the necessary qualities in just the right amount.

The woman standing in front of him was redheaded, and much too old for the part, and he was tired of listening to her. Her voice droned on and on without moving him at all. But he had promised Furtseva he would let every girl who showed up have a chance—his assistant had at least gone to the trouble of screening them and making sure everyone who showed up had been invited.

When the auditions began, the line outside of Mosfilm snaked down the street. Who wouldn't want to play Natasha? She was like the Juliet of Moscow, and this film was a chance to be beloved by the entire country, maybe the whole world. But in Sergei's eyes, not a single girl's efforts matched her desires, and by the late afternoon, the line dwindled down to nothing without any hope of his finding his Natasha. The redheaded girl was the last one of the day, and he was grateful for it, because his feet ached and he was tired of everything on earth. His assistant had a dentist appointment to go to, and she was going to be late, and she kept pointing at her watch to remind him.

As the girl was finishing her lines, Irina popped in the door behind her, and she snuck around the back of the room to sit at the long table with Sergei, squeezing in between a handful of listless producers and Furtseva, who was eating an orange and pretending that she wasn't paying attention. "How's it going?" Irina whispered, but Sergei waved her off.

"Thank you, thank you," Sergei said, interrupting the redhead with another wave. "Thank you for coming in. Begone with you. Goodbye." The girl blushed to her hairline and bent down to get her bag and nearly ran out of the room.

"Sergei!" Irina scolded. Furtseva snorted. She got a kick out of seeing men like Sergei scolded by their wives. It was cathartic for her.

Bondarchuk raised his hands. "What? I wasn't doing her any favors by letting her go on and on. Was I, Furtseva? Even you have to admit she was terrible."

Furtseva leaned back in her chair and looked up at the ceiling. "Dreadful," she said, and she nodded to the handful of producers, who rose from their seats. "I'll admit to you, Sergei, that this worries me. You're already running behind schedule. With a project this big, it's not a very good sign." Having finished her orange, which had been a gift from a Cuban envoy and only the second orange she'd ever eaten in her life—such luxuries were rare, even for her—she swept the accumulated peel into her hand and deposited it in the trash. She stood and started to walk toward the door, motioning the producers to follow her. She turned around and raised an eyebrow at Sergei. "This problem has to be fixed."

Sergei, who had risen too, nodded. "I understand," he said, color blooming in his face. "But you can't ask me to make compromises. It's too important of a part to—"

Furtseva, who wanted to go outside and smoke and was not interested in becoming embroiled in another argument with Bondarchuk, walked out without acknowledging him. Irina stood up and rushed after her. "Let me handle this," she said to her husband, because she and Furtseva were old friends, but mostly because Irina, beloved by all men, was overconfident in her ability to handle other women.

Just moments after Irina walked out the door, a slender, dark-haired girl with bags under her eyes rushed in. "Excuse me," she said, "I'm Natasha."

Sergei had bent over and rested his forehead in his hands and he did not look up to see who was speaking to him. "No, you're not," he said. He had been hungry for an hour, and the exotic smell of Furtseva's orange lingered in the air and worsened his hunger, and this made his voice more gravelly than usual. "I've seen two hundred girls today and none of them are Natasha, and neither are you. Go away."

"But that's my name," Natasha said. Having spent the morning wandering all over Moscow, looking for the studio, Natasha was so tired that she wanted to weep, and she couldn't stand the thought of leaving now, the shame of having stolen Katusha's money for nothing. "My name is Natasha."

"Oh," Sergei said. He looked up at her, and he immediately thought that she looked familiar, though he could not remember why. "Did she tell you to go in?"

He meant his assistant, who by this time was already in the waiting room at the dentist and was dreading the thought of having her teeth drilled. But Natasha thought he meant Irina, whom she had passed in the hallway and who had been the one to direct her to the stuffy office, which now smelled both of oranges and stale sweat. From this day on, whenever Natasha encountered the strange smell of oranges she would feel a sense of dread. "She told me to come here," she said.

Sergei sighed. "All right then," he said, and he motioned her over and handed her a thin script. "I've been doing lines with the actors myself," he said. "It gives me a good sense of how the scene would actually be. Would you prefer to sit or stand?"

Natasha, who had never auditioned for any sort of acting role before, desperately wished she knew the right answer to this question. Sensing none, she didn't respond, and Sergei got impatient. "Sit!" he barked, and she obeyed him like a spaniel.

The scene they were to read from was late in the film, after Natasha had already fallen and lost the love of Prince Andrei, and Pierre delivers this news. But Sergei, being tired and irritable, did not explain any of this to Natasha, so she filled in the missing details of the story with the details of her life. When Sergei asked her if she had been in love with "that vile man," Natasha thought not of Tolstoy's Anatole, but of Ivan—Ivan in the dusty attic, pulling her to his knee; Ivan, standing in the hallway holding out a pewter ring; Ivan, hunched over backstage at the gala, whispering something to her sister, about to ruin her life. Bondarchuk repeated his line—"Were you in love with that vile man?"—and when Natasha replied, "I don't know, I don't know," she answered truthfully, and when the script instructed her to cry at this moment, she had no trouble summoning tears. Her back was stiff and sore from the train ride. She was certain that she'd already muffed the audition somehow and that her chances at the part were over. Her life was fading into gray again.

She jumped when Sergei continued with the scene and said, with a tenderness that startled her, "We won't speak of it again, my dear, and I beg of you—think of me as your friend." He said these words so sincerely and convincingly that Natasha forgot she was supposed to be acting and gazed up at him in gratitude. She looked lovelier than she ever had in her life, and Bondarchuk saw it, felt ashamed of himself for how long he let his eyes linger on this young girl who had, only a moment before, been nothing but a roadblock between him and his dinner.

He cleared his throat and continued on. "I'll tell him everything, and I beg you," he said, looking at the script—though he had the lines memorized, he wanted to remind himself what he was doing, why they were there—"consider me your friend. If you want help or advice," he said, stepping toward her, "if you simply want to open your heart to someone—not now," he said, watching her wipe her eyes, "but when your mind is clearer—think of me," and he reached down and kissed her hand. This gesture was not called for in the script, but he knew instinctively it was the right thing to do, and he made a mental note to add it to the script as soon as he was able. "I should be happy if it is in my power—"

Natasha, who had seen Irina and Furtseva come back through the door behind Bondarchuk, turned back to the script in alarm, worrying they would misunderstand his gesture. "Don't speak to me like that," she said, her alarm inserting itself into her voice. "I'm not worth it!" Even if Sergei was pretending, she couldn't think of the last time someone had spoken to her with such tenderness. She stood and tried to walk away from him. Sergei did not let go of her hand.

"Stop it," Sergei said. His hand felt so steady and strong wrapped around her small one. "You have your whole life ahead of you." He wished that he could remember why she looked familiar.

You have your whole life ahead of you. The dreaded words that Katusha, the doctors, everyone had been saying to her. Words that said nothing except, *Your misery is making me uncomfortable—would you direct it someplace else?* She turned to Bondarchuk, paler now. "Ahead of me?" she said. Ahead of her was only misery and darkness. "No. For me everything is finished."

Sergei remembered then how he knew Natasha. Not the picture Irina had pulled from her pocket—though soon, he'd remember that too. She had been the dancer, the sweet and cocky little dancer, whose horrible accident he'd seen at the Kirov years ago. He'd been struck by her the second she took the stage—so young, yet she knew how to keep a crowd's attention. Even her catastrophe had been graceful: she'd fallen from her partner's hand like a pebble into clear waters. He was so moved by Natasha's sincerity and loveliness that he wanted very badly to launch into his character's next speech—if he were free, if he were the handsomest, cleverest man in the world—but this was the end of the scene, and Natasha, not knowing what else to do, sat down abruptly.

Bondarchuk shook his head and tossed his script onto the table, astonished that his search had ended at last. "You were right," he said, incredulous. "You are Natasha."

Irina walked up to her husband and kissed him on the cheek, both in congratulations and out of a desire to mark her territory, because the girl was very pretty. "Well done, my dear," she said. "You found her." Startled, Sergei bristled at the kiss, and then, worrying his wife would misunderstand—he'd reacted like a man caught in impure thoughts—he smiled at Irina and kissed her hand too. "*We* found her," he said, remembering that his wife had presented him with this very woman's photograph that morning.

"Not so fast," Furtseva said. She pulled out a cigar as if preparing for a celebration, but did not light it. "Has she acted before, Sergei?" The girl's beauty boded well both at home and abroad—but something about her unsettled Furtseva, though she didn't know why.

"I don't think she has," he said, looking to Natasha for confirmation, who shook her head. "But she's performed, she studied at the Vaganova—that's practically acting experience, isn't it?"

"The Vaganova?" Furtseva said, squinting. "My God, you're that poor creature who fell at the Kirov, aren't you?" She put the cigar back in her pocket. "What are you thinking, Sergei? This woman can't dance. I'm amazed she can even walk."

"Well, if she can't dance," Irina said, sounding oddly cheerful, "that'll never do."

"Stay out of it," Sergei snapped, giving his wife a very particular sort of marital glare. "You saw how many people we looked at, Furtseva—we're not going to find anybody better."

"I *can* dance," Natasha said, in a voice that made the others turn to her and even surprised herself with its authority.

Furtseva raised an eyebrow. "I was told you had permanent injuries."

"Physical therapy," Natasha said. "Years and years. The doctors were just as surprised as you are—but I worked very hard and I'm much better now."

This news produced a different reaction from each of the others. Irina seemed disappointed; Sergei, immensely relieved; and Furtseva, eager to consider the matter solved and get on with her afternoon, pulled the cigar back out from her pocket and lit it. She shook Natasha's hand. "Well, then," Furtseva said, "I suppose all that's left to do is to welcome you to Mosfilm. Do you live here?"

Natasha shook her head. "Leningrad," she said.

"Of course," Furtseva said. "Well, don't worry, we'll help you get settled. Come to the Kremlin this afternoon—my assistants will find you an apartment. And we'll discuss the details of your salary." She shook Natasha's hand again and turned to go, nodding approvingly at Sergei.

Every nerve in Natasha's thin body came alive at once, and her hands started trembling—which, thankfully, Sergei and Irina, who had turned around and begun discussing some private matter, did not see. Her body understood what had happened before her mind—or her mind, perhaps, aware that she had a meeting at the Kremlin to endure, kept reality at bay until she was safe to think again. Later that day, Natasha sat through a meeting in a warm, dark, womb-like office. She spoke only when she was spoken to, which made a very good impression on Furtseva's underling, who was so impressed with the sad-looking little woman in his lonely office that he decided to forgo the usual feigned bureaucratic delay and find her an apartment that afternoon.

It was only when she was in that apartment an hour later, finally alone, that Natasha let herself acknowledge what she now faced. The apartment was the cleanest and most comfortable place Natasha had ever lived in her life. If she had been more conscious of her surroundings, she would have rejoiced in them, would have been thrilled with the private bathroom, the prim little bed, and the gleaming white tile in the tiny kitchen—would have realized that, like Ilya said, there was abundance in store for those bold enough to help themselves. Overcome with joy, she would have run from one corner of the apartment to the other, would have taken off her shoes and slid around on the parquet floor in her stockings, if she hadn't just found out that it might not be hers at all. Instead, she sank to the floor as soon as the door was closed behind her and wept.

Here she was, resurrected. Here she was, for once the recipient of good fortune, having laid claim to the life of comfort and praise that had always been her due. She had played the game, and she was already at risk of losing everything again. All because of her sister. Without even reaching out her hands, Maya had blotted out this new future too.

At the thought of Maya, Natasha sat straight up and wiped her eyes with the back of her hand.

"No," she said, out loud, to the empty apartment. "This will be mine. No matter what I have to be, no matter what I have to do, this will be mine."

With this decided, she finally began to take in her surroundings, this lovely little apartment that was only hers, and she decided that nobody would take it from her.

CHAPTER FOURTEEN

Moscow felt like another planet. Natasha's first impression of the capital was grim: everywhere she went, she compared it with Leningrad, but Moscow boasted no candy-colored buildings, no streetlamp-lined boulevards along the river. Leningrad was something to be proud of—an ancient, imperial city; Moscow was industrial and tired.

In the week before production began, Natasha had time on her hands, and she wandered the streets of Moscow for hours, stopping only when her back ached. Most of the buildings she passed looked identical—concrete, compact, and squat. Every now and again she'd pass a building in one of the old styles, with gilt ornamentation on the windows and doors, and these, in their likeness to Leningrad, felt like friends to Natasha. All of the trees looked young and startled, like they'd just been plucked from a forest and were surprised to find themselves on a boulevard. The streets were wide and crowded. Natasha explored until she got hungry or thirsty, when she'd find a pierogi cart or a kvass vendor and a park bench and would rest there, watching the people hurrying around her.

Muscovites dressed in everything from headscarves and dumpy house dresses to short skirts, trench coats, boots up to their knees—

modish looks that had not yet reached Leningrad. "I'll bet Maya knew about miniskirts months ago," Natasha thought. She wondered what sorts of fashions her sister was seeing on the streets of American cities: Was everyone dolled up like stilyagi? Did they wear fedoras and broad-shouldered suits, like in American movies? Moscow, for all its grandeur, was no New York. What a waste that Maya was the one to see America.

Natasha had written to Katusha and asked for her forgiveness for taking the money, and the response was surprisingly curt. "The next time you need something," Katusha wrote, "ask one of the friends whose company you now prize so highly." Katusha had been patient and long-suffering for so long, sacrificing herself for the well-being of these girls who, after all, were not really hers, and Natasha's faithlessness had wounded her deeply. She was almost as hurt that Natasha had left without saying goodbye as she was that she'd taken her money. That the girl looked so much like her mother only worsened the blow, as if Elizaveta had abandoned her twice.

But Natasha did not stop to consider her godmother's feelings, and she did not write back—she was too caught up in her new life to think about anything but herself. There was her new apartment, for one, provided by the state, clean and compact with brand-new appliances, an unheard-of luxury. Natasha spent some of her afternoons—and more than a little of the stipend Furtseva had given her—roaming the cavernous GUM department store, looking for things to make her apartment feel more like her own. She was not a judicious shopper. One afternoon, she went out in search of dishes and came home with two teacups and a proud little china cat, which she put on the kitchen counter. "I can always just eat out of the teacups," she told herself, and she did.

It was fortunate that Natasha had settled in someplace so comfortable, because she was going to be there for a very long time.

Furtseva had told her that filming would take at least three years, maybe four—most of which she would spend here in Moscow, with the occasional trip elsewhere to shoot on location.

Furtseva had brimmed with advice when Natasha came to meet her at the Kremlin. "Do your best to get along with everyone," Furtseva said, smoking her ever-present cigarette, "and never forget the importance of what you are doing. This character is a national hero. Portray her well, and you will always be remembered."

This promise of glory thrilled Natasha—and helped suppress the nausea that arose when Furtseva described what she was about to do as an act of patriotism. Natasha wasn't a patriot any more than Ilya had joined Komsomol because he wanted to extol the virtues of the Soviet Man. Sitting in Furtseva's office, with Lenin's portrait staring at her suspiciously, Natasha made the same decision that Russian artists, athletes, scientists, and intellectuals had made before her, and would continue to make for generations to come: she would feign loyalty because she thought it was the only choice she had, the only way to live where she'd been born and still reach for what she wanted. She would play the game, like Ilya had told her to do, and in exchange the state would make her glorious.

"Shirk this duty," Furtseva continued, "and, well, no sense in discussing that possibility, eh, since Bondarchuk will squeeze the best out of you!"

Natasha was a little afraid of Sergei Bondarchuk. Bondarchuk was like the sea—serene one moment and turbulent the next. She was most afraid of him when he became quiet and gentle, because it was in these moods that he was eerily attentive toward her, like he had been during her audition.

She'd been surprised to learn that he hadn't just read with her during her audition because he was the only person in the room. He'd actually cast himself as Pierre, and Irina was to play his on-screen wife,

Hélène. Furtseva had all but rolled her eyes when she told Natasha this. "It was an unbreakable condition of his," she'd explained. "Let's hope it doesn't ruin the movie."

Natasha had not told Furtseva that she couldn't dance. She hadn't told anyone. She hadn't even really admitted to herself that it was impossible, because a small part of her still believed—still needed to believe—that she could dance again, if only in this film. Despite what the doctors had said, despite the stiffness of her spine and the dreadful insistence of her own intuition, Natasha could not imagine a life in which she was forever afraid of her body. Still, she was relieved when Furtseva told her that the ball scene, including her character's famous waltz, would not be filmed for some time. "First we'll get all those behemoth battle scenes out of the way," Furtseva had said.

By the time Natasha joined the cast, preproduction for the film had already been going on for a year. Russia's historical vaults—its armories and personal collections and museums—had emptied themselves out for Furtseva's patriotic cause, and the vast warehouses at Mosfilm filled up with dresses and jewelry and epaulets and sabers and every sort of imaginable nineteenth-century furnishing. Before filming could begin, Bondarchuk called the entire cast to assemble at Mosfilm to read the script aloud.

On the morning of the reading, Natasha woke up feeling anxious. She hadn't worked a day in two years, and she'd never worked as an actress—despite what Bondarchuk had said, she didn't feel like all her years of pantomime classes and performing as a dancer were quite the same—and she worried she wouldn't know what to do. She brushed her teeth and petted the china cat and told herself that she had no reason to be frightened. Bondarchuk, who had called her himself to prepare her, had said so on the phone. "Very little to do," he said. "We'll read through the script, but not all of it. You'll have your measurements taken. We might do a screen test or two to get the lighting right. You should be home in time for dinner."

For this first day on set, she'd given herself a present: a wool skirt suit in harvest gold. She'd stood uneasily in the dressing room at GUM, but the eager saleswoman insisted this was what people were wearing now. "You're young," she'd said. "If ever there was a time for miniskirts, it's now." But the matching tights the saleswoman had talked her into buying were not warm, and Natasha shivered as she walked to the studio, though it was only September.

The Moscow streets were bustling. Everyone looked like they knew exactly who they were and where they were going, and the squat and joyless buildings put Natasha on edge. So different than Leningrad, she thought, and there came that old pang again, the thoughts of home. But then she turned the corner and saw Mosfilm, a grand white marble building set back from the street like a palace, and she thought of all the hundreds of people waiting inside, waiting for her: scriptwriters, storyboard artists, production designers, costume mistresses, Bondarchuk himself. The curtain was rising on her life at last, and her courage rose with it. Finally, she'd have the fate she'd longed for. The fate she deserved.

An aide was waiting for her at the door. That aide took her to another aide, who'd been assigned as Natasha's assistant and who marched her straight to makeup in case press photos would be taken. A man with hair so black it was blue tweezed between her eyebrows and shook his head at the leg hair poking through Natasha's tights. "I thought you were a dancer," he said, wagging his finger. "You should know better." He turned to Natasha's assistant. "Wax it later," he said, and the aide wrote this down like it was not an untoward request, and Natasha crossed her legs and decided she had no idea what it meant to be an actress.

The aide-turned-assistant didn't leave Natasha's side for the rest of the day. Her name was Olenka, and she moved through all the meetings and check-ins and protocols like she'd been born knowing them. She whispered everyone's names to Natasha as they walked by. "That's Bolkonsky, a propman—if you ever lose so much as a handkerchief it might be the last thing you ever do. Nektarios is the master electrician. He's the one we all need most when things break down, so be sure to bribe him now and again as you can. Do you have any cash? Never mind, I do. Let's give him something now."

Olenka's confidence put Natasha at ease. Everyone in the hallways either liked Olenka or was afraid of her, and both responses served her well. They all smiled with deference at Natasha, which delighted her so much that she forgot to be nervous about the table reading, and by the time Olenka pushed her through the door of a conference room Natasha momentarily forgot who she was and what she was doing, and everybody stared.

Fifteen people, who were gathered around the kind of oblong table used for councils of war, looked up at her with solemn expressions. Everyone seemed much older than her. Natasha's confidence threatened to flag.

Bondarchuk rose from the far end of the table and greeted her politely. "Good morning, Natasha. We've all just now gotten ready. Come, sit here." He gestured toward an empty seat on his right, next to a man Natasha had never seen before, and introduced her to him. "This is Lev, our Andrei," he said.

Olenka handed her a copy of the script, thick as a phone book. As Natasha sat down, she became acutely aware of the physical presence of the man sitting beside her, whose name she had already forgotten. A small part of her noticed that Bondarchuk was addressing everyone in a rousing and boisterous tone—the kind of voice you'd use before sending your troops into battle—but she didn't hear a single word he said, because most of her being was absorbing the experience of sitting beside this man. She didn't dare look at him—it was important, she knew, that she at least appear to be listening to Bondarchuk—but her body did the looking. Her right arm told her that his left arm was near. Her right leg told her that if she crossed her legs and draped them ever so slightly to the side, her foot might dangle toward his.

Bondarchuk became more and more animated as he continued his speech, and to Natasha's delight, he began pacing up and down the length of the room, giving Natasha an excuse to glance over at her seatmate again and again. The man was broad shouldered, straight-backed—sitting up tall like he was already pretending to be a soldier. She wished she could see his face. If only she'd been more attentive when they were introduced. What she wanted to know, more than anything, was the color of Lev's eyes.

Yes, Lev—that was his name, she remembered now, that was what Bondarchuk had called him. Bondarchuk was speaking to him now, and everyone in the room looked at Lev, and she felt no shame in joining them.

"I must tell you all that I did not intend to cast someone from the country in so distinguished a role. But the alternative—the alternative was not a pleasing one, and so I have the honor of introducing Lev to you all. I hope his large farmer's hands will not prove so huge an obstacle when they are on the cinema screen . . ."

Bondarchuk was not pleased by the necessity of casting Lev—he had had another, more established actor in mind, who had slighted him at the last possible second, and Furtseva, wanting to ensure her masterpiece would not fall apart just as it was being assembled, ordered Bondarchuk to hire Lev as a substitute. Lev and Bondarchuk had attended film school together; Lev, with his quiet dignity, had a way of attracting people wherever he went, and the unpopular Bondarchuk hated him for it. Even now, every time Bondarchuk saw Lev, he also saw his younger self, lonely and unliked, sitting by himself in the school cafeteria while Lev held court at a crowded table, so he put Lev down every chance he got.

Lev was a slender, stern-looking man, with close-cropped brown hair and a long, narrow nose. He pursed his lips when Bondarchuk spoke of him. When Bondarchuk began pacing again and moved to some other subject, Natasha saw Lev draw his hands under the table and crack his knuckles rapidly, those knuckles with tiny brown hairs on them.

"I do not need to tell you all that the stakes are very high for this film. We are adapting a beloved treasure of Russian literature, one of the great artworks of our species, and this work will require us to have oneness of mind. As Gogol once said, 'Nothing astonishes one more than a perfectly coordinated agreement between all the parts . . .'"

Bondarchuk continued his eloquent speech from his chair, and Natasha could not help herself: she stared openly at Lev, at the side of his head, his hair cut so short it looked velvety. He shifted in his seat and leaned toward her a little, oblivious to her closeness, and she realized with joy that she could smell his cologne, or his hair pomade, or whatever product it was that men use to make themselves irresistible. For as long as she lived, she would remember that scent, woody and fresh, and it would make her think of how it felt to fall in love.

He turned and looked at her—green eyes! He had green eyes! Natasha thought she would collapse from happiness, and she was already imagining what she would tell them at the hospital when her poor heart gave out and they had to call an ambulance. "His eyes were green! I had to know!" That was what she would say.

He smiled at her, and if this smile happened to be the last thing she ever saw, if she had died then basking in the radiance of that smile, she would have died very happily. But Natasha did not die, and she began to realize that he smiled at her as if she were doing something very funny, and she could not understand what that thing was. Was there some jam from breakfast smeared on her face? Had she buttoned her suit jacket the wrong way? Her delight curdled into horror, and blood pooled hot in her palms.

"Natasha?" he was saying—ah, it was the first time she'd heard his voice, and he was saying her name! He was asking her a question. What was it?

She realized then that the whole room was staring at her. Bondarchuk had his hand stretched toward her in some grand gesture, the kind one uses when showing off a prized possession, but he looked baffled. He had just introduced Natasha and expected her to stand and offer some sort of remark, which she did not do. He gave her a look that said, *What is wrong with you?*—the calm sea was clouding over—and then he regained possession of himself and continued.

"As I was saying," he said, looking at Natasha over his glasses, "we are very fortunate to have Natasha playing our beloved heroine. As you all know, I searched high and low for the perfect candidate. I searched so long I began to despair of ever finding someone who had the grace and depth to play Natasha Rostova. But find her we did!"

Everyone applauded, and Natasha basked in the sound. Lev leaned over to her, and she breathed in the woody freshness again. "I am very glad to be working with you," he whispered. "I hear you are an accomplished dancer."

She started to correct him—she *had* been a dancer—and then didn't, only nodded and smiled. She would act next to this man on a stretcher if she had to.

Bondarchuk continued. "As part of the historical and textual accuracy of this film, it is crucial that the dancing be convincing, and Natasha's dancing in particular, since that is what first inspires Prince

Andrei's affection. We are very fortunate, then, to have hired a dancer as our heroine, and I've just received word this morning that because of location availability, the grand ball scene in Petersburg will be one of the first sequences we film. In November, we will head to Leningrad to film at the Hermitage."

Lev had always loved Leningrad, and turned to Natasha to say so, and when he saw how pale she was his eyes widened in alarm. "Are you all right?" he whispered, bending close to duck out from Bondarchuk's gaze.

Natasha swallowed. "Yes, of course," she whispered. "It's just very cold in here." She'd started shivering again.

Lev glanced at the thin tights covering her legs and shook his head. "And no wonder," he said, and he took off his coat and discreetly tucked it around her knees, and Natasha forgot all about her troubles.

Lev smiled at her. "Better?" he whispered.

"Much better," Natasha said, and she felt so happy that when the script reading began, she missed all of her cues and Bondarchuk had to wave his hands at her every time she had a line.

In an instant, Natasha's life became a flurry of wardrobe fittings, film tests, and makeup trials. She was tweezed and powdered and prodded into dresses. She was commanded to sit, to stand, to walk, and to speak. She was filmed and interviewed and photographed. She began to feel like some royal person's pampered and beloved exotic animal—an ostrich, perhaps, belonging to Marie Antoinette. Some of it was uncomfortably familiar—stage makeup's powdery smell, the heat of dressing room lights, and the general atmosphere of preparation made her think of student performances at the Vaganova. Once, when a novice hairdresser accidentally seared a ringlet off an extra's wig, the ensuing burnt aroma reminded Natasha of a time backstage at their first spring gala, when Kira sat too close to the mirror's naked lightbulbs and her wig caught fire. Kira, who was not known for keeping a cool head in the best of circumstances, ran around the dressing room for a full minute before a costume mistress threw a blanket over her head and smothered the flame. Maya and Natasha had laughed so hard that they nearly missed their cue.

But the overall experience was nothing like ballet, which was both a blessing—remembering the Vaganova was painful—and a disappointment. Without the stage, there was no moment of release, no applause, no post-performance letdown—just endless preparations, like a car whose engine turns over and over but won't start. Natasha tried to remind herself that all this was not the real performance. It wasn't even the rehearsal. "All this is just a prelude to making movies," Olenka told her. "A temporary phase."

What made it all bearable was the ever-constant presence of Lev. Often, he was sitting in the makeup chair beside her, or trying on a thousand different shoes while she was being fitted for wigs. Bondarchuk spent every day, and every waking hour, investigating every possible option for every aesthetic decision. There were rumors that this fastidiousness was putting the production behind schedule, and the Party ministers, including Furtseva, were getting irritated, but nothing changed. Bondarchuk had an eye for detail, and he was determined to get every detail of this production exactly right.

That was the word he used—*right*—and it didn't quite mean "correct" or "historically accurate." "Right" was an amorphous quality. An object was "right" when it matched the object in his mind. A person was "right" when they agreed with him. Very, very little was right on the first try, and Natasha and Lev tried shoe after wig after jacket, and a whole host of helpers buzzed around them like bees trying to please their queen.

They made a game out of it, Natasha and Lev. Every time Bondarchuk would fuss over something for an hour, or a day, or a week, and would finally declare it "right," Natasha and Lev would immediately look over at each other behind Bondarchuk's back and nod very slightly to each other, hands pressed together at the fingertips, replicating the gesture Bondarchuk made when he was, at long last, pleased.

It was a tiny game, and the days were long, so they repeated their ritual often, much like Maya and Natasha had pounced on each other's toes during dull bus rides and literature classes—though Natasha was much too wrapped up in Lev to notice this similarity. To Natasha, Lev's little bow seemed to say, *Look how well we get along. It's as if we've always known each other.* When she bowed her head to him, she felt like she was begging: *Love me, love me, love me.*

She did not understand what had made her fall for him so suddenly. It wasn't as though she had never been in the company of attractive men. Though boys had been in short supply at the school (and the ones who were there were shy and inward looking, or bombastic and stupid like Ivan, or not interested in girls at all), men always hung around the dressing rooms at performances, loitered outside of stage doors, crowded all the venues—some handsome, some not. At twenty, Natasha was the precise age to appeal most to men in all stages of life: very young men, who saw her as a peer; older men, who saw her as a little sparrow to take under their wings; and middle-aged men, who saw her as a worthy conquest to shore up their eroding confidence. All of them had fawned over Natasha when she was a teenager, too, and had followed her with hungry gazes wherever she walked. But with all of this attention, Natasha had never felt seen. She knew she was not a person in their eyes. She was a reflection, a symbol of whatever it was that they loved or hated most in themselves. She was the answer to whatever questions haunted each of them.

And perhaps this was why Lev felt so different to her. When he smiled and he bowed at her, when he made conversation from the other makeup chair, he didn't act like he wanted anything from her. He didn't seem to be concerned with himself at all. He gave every person who came across his path the same sort of intense attention, whether they were an accomplished actor or an electrician. His gaze was so focused that sometimes Natasha had to look away, but even then she still rejoiced, like someone who blesses the warmth of the sun even as it burns their skin.

Natasha wasn't his only admirer. Everybody, from Olenka to the costumers to the electricians to the cleaning ladies, loved Lev. When he made a joke, everyone laughed. When he spoke, everyone listened attentively. When he made a request, or asked for a favor, assistants tripped over one another to come to his aid. Many men, given these opportunities, become monstrous. But Lev treated everyone well and never took advantage of his status.

At first, Natasha wondered if this was just how it was to be an actor, particularly a good-looking one, but the costumers and the assistants and the cleaning ladies were not as attentive to the actor who played Anatole, who was taller and better built than Lev. No, there was something special about Lev that drew others in and made everyone love him.

Natasha knew she should have been shy about it, should have concealed from him and from everyone else how much she loved him, and at first she tried. But this only lasted a few weeks, because everyone noticed anyway.

Olenka was the first one to say something. Lev had just followed Bondarchuk out of the dressing room—they were all rehearsing monologues with him, one at a time—and as soon as he was out of earshot, Olenka crept over with her clipboard and a steaming cup of tea and patted Natasha on the head. "Got it bad, haven't you?" she said, and Natasha blushed and didn't reply, which was all the answer Olenka needed.

"You're not the first one," she said, nodding sagely. "All the girls fall in love with Lev, and some of the boys too. If I were a man, I wouldn't love him any less." She laughed at her unfunny joke and handed Natasha her tea. Natasha, jealous of all these invisible people, did not respond, and Olenka filled the silence as she usually did. "He seems to have taken a special shine to you, though," she said.

"Really?" Natasha coughed and nearly choked on her tea, but she didn't quite believe Olenka—much as she wanted to. Wasn't coddling one's starlet part of an assistant's job?

"Really," Olenka said, not quite paying attention as she flipped through the schedule on her clipboard. "I've never seen him laugh as much as he does when he's with you. And this is our third film together. Don't you dare say a word of it to Bondarchuk."

"Why?"

Lev came back into the dressing room, followed by Bondarchuk. Both were flushed, though the entire building was kept very cold. "You'll have to keep working at it, that's all," Bondarchuk said. Lev nodded and sat in his chair beside Natasha, who was feeling a little bold thanks to Olenka's revelation and—when Bondarchuk turned his attention to a clipboard—patted his knee in solidarity.

Antonina, head costume mistress, a pear-shaped woman with a pillowy froth of gray hair, came in. She wore the costume woman's uniform of a white jacket and kerchief, and she had a diaphanous gray-blue dress draped over her shoulder. "Here we are," Antonina said. "Natasha's dress for the ball."

Bondarchuk ran the hem of the skirt between his fingers. "It's decent," he said. "But I think it might be too transparent for her. Can you replace it by Tuesday?"

Natasha started, and her teacup shifted in her lap and nearly tipped over. "Tuesday? But I thought we're not filming that scene for—"

"Just for a fitting," Bondarchuk said, without looking at Natasha. He was still inspecting the dress. For some reason, he sniffed it. "And maybe some blocking. It's a complicated scene, you know, and one of the most important."

Antonina and Bondarchuk fussed over the dress for a few minutes. Antonina draped it over Natasha, and then held it up high so Bondarchuk could better see the folds. Though she was still in the room, Natasha hardly noticed. The dress looked like a ghost to her now, something that would haunt her and steal all of her happiness.

Now Lev, who had evidently noticed her distress, leaned over to Natasha and patted her on the knee. He raised an eyebrow as if to ask what was the matter, and when she waved him off, he tilted his head toward her and gave her such a pitying look that it made her melt into her chair a little. She would stay sad for the rest of her life if only he would stay there leaning toward her, looking at her pityingly like that.

Lev gestured with his head toward Bondarchuk just enough that it would be noticed only by the two of them. Then he leaned over closer and whispered in Natasha's ear. "Watch," he said.

She watched. Bondarchuk strode around the dress with one hand behind his back and one hand over his mouth, like someone in a comic play. His finger tapped rhythmically on his lips, as was his habit. He looked displeased, as was also his habit. "It's not . . . quite . . ."

Lev looked over at Natasha mischievously, winked, and then turned to Bondarchuk and said, "Right?"

"Yes, yes, exactly," Bondarchuk said, still not looking away from the dress. "Not quite right."

He was delightfully predictable, Bondarchuk. It was as if they knew what he would do before he himself knew. The comfort of this knowledge, and sharing it with Lev, gave Natasha such a feeling of at-homeness—a feeling she hadn't known for so long—that she lost sight of herself for a moment, lost self-consciousness altogether, and when Lev winked at her again, she laughed. And when she laughed, her teacup slid farther and farther down her lap, unnoticed, and when it finally fell off, Lev reached and caught it, and the tea splashed all over him, and Lev started laughing too. His eyes crinkled when he laughed, and his forehead creased, and Natasha realized for the first time just how old he was and loved him for that too. He was seasoned and dependable, her Lev. As their laughter settled down, she allowed herself to look at him with a little more than kindness in her eyes.

"What?" Bondarchuk said. He was not looking at the dress anymore, and neither was Antonina. He stared at the two of them. The lights from the makeup mirror reflected off his glasses and they couldn't see his eyes at all. He looked like a blind and weathered mole, squinting into the sunlight. "What is it?"

"Nothing," Lev said, dabbing at his dampened shirt, "just a little accident." He held up the emptied teacup as if in explanation.

This episode, small and unremarkable to any passersby, had an immediate and lasting effect on everyone in the room. Antonina looked like she had just witnessed something she'd long feared. Lev, ever implacable, puffed his chest out a little more than usual, perhaps in Bondarchuk's direction. Bondarchuk furrowed his eyebrows so deeply they nearly met in the middle. Natasha looked at Lev's hand, warm and heavy, which had come to rest on her knee.

Bondarchuk followed Natasha's gaze and saw the hand, which, as if come to life, sprang away to join its mate on Lev's teacup. "Forgive us for laughing," Lev said. "We have this game, Natasha and I—"

"I do not want to hear about Natasha and you, and the games that you play, or anything at all from you," Bondarchuk said. Bondarchuk had hoped that now that he was a famous film director, one of the most powerful men in Mosfilm, he'd overcome the social challenges of his school days, would gain the respect of his peers—but he was wrong. Lev was still everyone's favorite, even his protégé's, and Bondarchuk felt once more like that lonely boy in the school cafeteria—though now with a grown man's rage. "All I want to hear from you from now until the camera is first pointed at your fat farmer's face is your lines, rehearsed every day until you sing them in your sleep every night and your wife whips you with a pillow to get you to stop."

His wife? Natasha looked at Olenka for confirmation, who nodded in a sad and apologetic sort of way. His wife? No one had ever said he had a wife.

Lev stood. "I beg your pardon," he said, in a brittle voice Natasha did not recognize. "I did not mean to offend." He handed the teacup to Natasha, nodded to them all, and left the room.

CHAPTER FIFTEEN

Leonid Yakobson, choreographer of *Spartacus*, peeked out from behind the curtain at the Metropolitan Opera and rubbed his palms in anticipation. Patrons stuffed the opulent theater, to Yakobson's great relief—he'd engineered *Spartacus* and all its spectacle with American audiences in mind. Everyone knew that Westerners loved gladiators and sandals and swords—why not a ballet with all three? Yakobson had all but guaranteed it would be a success, and he'd cast his son in the lead role. Time to prove to the Americans that they could outperform them in everything, even wearing gladiator skirts.

Maya, whose dancing slave-girl character didn't go on until the third act, stood in her usual spot in the wings and watched crew members roll a gilded chariot toward the stage. The orchestra filled the great hall with a brassy overture. A chorus of male dancers, bound at the hands and chained to the chariot, warmed their legs with anxious tendus and hops. Ivan was at the end of the line, and he grinned at Maya as he walked toward the stage. Maya wanted to wish him luck, but the curtain went up and the great chariot was wheeled away, slave dancers in tow.

Maya ran her fingers over the black curtain beside her and prepared herself for the pleasure of watching the dancers—Ivan most of all. She liked watching from the wings, observing the patterns of dancers forming and dissolving. She'd slip into a reverie, imagining how she would rearrange the formations and movements if the dance were in her hands. More and more, this was what she dreamed of when she watched ballets—not dancing, but directing the dancers.

Maya's eyes wandered back to Ivan again. She'd always thought he was good-looking, and he was especially good-looking leaping in front of thousands of Americans, taut skin gleaming under the stage lights. (All of the men had oiled their chests before going onstage.) Maya absentmindedly ran her fingertips over the edge of the black curtain and let herself admire him.

She didn't get to daydream for long. A rumbling sound broke out from the audience, loud and deep and so unexpected that it took Maya a moment to recognize it. The audience, dressed in spangled evening dresses and crisp black ties, was booing.

Maya's heart dropped and she looked at Ivan, who danced as if oblivious. The booing grew louder and louder, but not a single dancer onstage betrayed any knowledge of this. "Maybe they can't hear them over the orchestra," Maya thought, but when she saw Ivan's mouth twist in an awkward way, she knew he had.

After the performance, a heavy atmosphere loomed backstage. The dancers had struggled on despite the booing and finished the ballet as if nothing had happened—but as soon as the curtain went down, disappointment clouded everyone's faces. Some dancers glanced anxiously at the handlers, worried that some sort of retribution was at hand, but none came. After all, it wasn't the dancers' fault. They'd danced well, had done so with patriotism and love. The audience was just engaged in a patriotic act of their own.

The United States and Russia, which had not been on friendly terms since the end of the war, were quickly stumbling toward a more serious escalation. After Kennedy tried and failed to quash Castro's revolution at the Bay of Pigs, Soviet leadership had grown anxious over Kennedy's ambition, and the day before *Spartacus*'s ill-fated performance, the Soviets warned the Americans in no uncertain terms that any further aggression on Cuban soil would have swift and severe retribution. Any possibility of friendship between the nations was beginning to feel like a fantasy, and the audience's severe reception of *Spartacus* reflected the death of that dream. The Cold War was threatening to turn hot.

When the curtain fell on the first act, Maya's first instinct was to rush to Ivan and embrace him, to try and offer whatever comfort she could. But she worried what she would do if she let herself touch him. She hid herself in her dressing room until she was called to the stage, and when she danced, she did so distractedly—like she'd stepped into someone else's body. As soon as the ballet was over, she hurried back to her dressing room, hoping to avoid Ivan if she could.

She shared the room with three other dancers, who always waited 'til the last minute to change out of their costumes (there were often admirers to be flirted with in the corridors). If she hurried, she could have some time to herself before they arrived. She opened the door, freed her feet from her pointe shoes, and lay down on the red carpet, exhausted. After a few deep breaths, she sat at the vanity and took a cotton pad from her makeup bag, soaked it in baby oil, and patted at the foundation melting in orange streaks down her neck.

Someone ran past the dressing room, squealing, which reminded her that she didn't have long to be alone. Maya hastily removed her eye makeup, and when she had finished, she noticed a bouquet on the white countertop—a bouquet of roses in an unnatural shade of salmon pink, so bright they seemed to glow. A tiny envelope was tucked among the blooms.

Maya stood fast, which made her dizzy, and she had to clutch the edge of the countertop to keep from toppling over. They couldn't be from Ivan—he wouldn't have had that sort of money, and it wasn't his kind of gesture besides—but this unlikely hope still made her tear eagerly into the little yellow envelope.

The note was short, and it was written by hand—probably by the florist, Maya thought—on a tiny note card with a cluster of pink roses printed on one side. "I miss you too," it said. "Will you come join me where we can be free? All my love, Olaf."

Maya's heart, which had already been beating fast, tripled its speed. It was one thing to get an unwanted love note. But Maya was also abroad, in an enemy country, in a time of cold war, when she had been explicitly warned against speaking to people like Olaf. And now, she held incriminating evidence against herself in her hands.

Someone knocked. Maya jumped and stuffed the note into the bodice of her leotard, where it stuck to her damp skin. "Come in," she said. She hoped it was just one of her roommates, waltzing in with some new paramour.

It was Ivan. She could tell before he even opened the door—could feel him there without even seeing him. This alarmed her, and when he came into the dressing room she put on her bathrobe. Though a thousand people had just seen her in a leotard, she didn't want Ivan to see her bare legs.

Ivan had changed into street clothes, and though he was no less handsome for it, he looked weary. "Can I sit down?" he asked, gesturing toward the extra chair in the corner.

"Of course," Maya said. She wrapped her bathrobe around herself a little more snugly, and sat in front of her dressing table. Ivan limped over and sat down.

"Oh, no!" Maya said. "What happened?"

"Oh, it's just this tendon that keeps acting up," Ivan said, reaching down and rubbing his calf. "I think it would get better if I could just rest it for a while, but there hasn't been time for much rest lately."

"Maybe you should ask to get taken out of tomorrow's performance," Maya said. "You don't want it to get worse."

"Do you think they would let me sit out? I don't want to get yelled at."

Maya shrugged. "It's worth asking Yakobson."

"Maybe." Ivan exhaled heavily and leaned his head against the wall. "This is nothing like I thought it would be."

"The inside of a girl's dressing room?"

"The tour," he said, without smiling. "Is this what you thought it was going to be like?"

Maya reflected on the past six weeks—the train rides, the meager food, the thin envelope of cash in her suitcase. Her eyes went involuntarily to Olaf's roses on the counter. "No."

"You're lucky," he said. "You at least have something of your own that you're working on. How's that ballet of yours coming along?" Ivan had caught Maya one night in yet another practice room, setting steps to Bizet, and she'd confessed her hope of becoming a choreographer.

"I think it's almost ready," Maya said.

Ivan smiled. "I'll bet you're lying," he said. "I'll bet it's done and perfect and you're just too scared to do anything with it."

"You're right, you're right." Just that morning, as she'd worked on it in her hotel room, the last piece had clicked into place. "It's done, and now I'm terrified."

"You're the one who needs to talk to Yakobson! You should ask him if they'll use it in the program."

Maya shook her head. "Why would he want a dance from me? I'm just some girl from the corps. And anyway, it's too contemporary and not grand enough for Kirov tastes. Everyone will just be in practice clothes." She described what she'd figured out that morning: after the barre, it would end with several acrobatic solos she'd devised over the course of the tour. "It'll be like the graduation exercises at the Vaganova."

"God, those graduation exercises." Ivan closed his eyes and rolled the back of his head on the wall. Maya noticed for the first time that little wrinkles had cropped up on his forehead. "Sometimes, I think about all of us at school—and I wish I could go back in time and warn us off."

"What would you say?" Maya worried he was about to say something about Natasha.

Ivan smiled to himself, his eyes still closed. "I would tell us all to become mechanics." He started chuckling under his breath, and Maya leaned over and smacked his arm.

"You don't mean that," she said. "You wouldn't last one day as a mechanic."

Ivan opened one eye. "I think I'm insulted," he said. "Should I be?"

Maya thought for a moment. What would Natasha have said in a time like this? No matter how disheartened or frightened Maya was about the future, Natasha had always known what to say. Maybe that was what Ivan wanted from her—someone to act like her sister. "All I'm saying is—nobody should take stock of their vocation on a night like this. You can't judge your life by its worst days."

Ivan shrugged. "Why not? That seems like the best way to judge your life to me. And I have a lot of regrets." He sat up and looked over at Maya. His gaze lingered on her long, bare calf, which was sticking out from underneath her bathrobe.

Maya tucked her offending leg behind its twin. She knew what he was saying—of course she did, because his regrets were her regrets too. Perhaps he, like her, still saw Natasha falling when he closed his eyes. He probably wished that Natasha was sitting with him in this stale dressing room instead of her.

They were skirting something dangerous, and Maya knew it. But when Ivan drew his chair close to hers and kissed her, she decided not to feel guilty. It was just a kiss—they didn't have to love each other to enjoy each other. Ivan reached out and pulled her onto his lap, and Olaf's note crinkled in her leotard.

Ivan pulled back. "What was that?" he said, laughing. "Hiding chocolate on your person like Olga?" Their Vaganova classmate had been notorious for sneaking contraband of all kinds into the school—chocolates, little bottles of vodka, cigarettes—stuffed into her bosom.

Maya's face, still caked with sweat, grew warmer. Nobody could know what Olaf had asked—not even Ivan. "No, no," she said, trying to laugh, too, to seem at ease, "just a good luck charm," and she pulled the crumpled note from her leotard and threw it in the trash.

They drew close again. Both of Maya's roommates burst into the room, still wearing scanty slave-girl costumes, tuxedoed strangers on their arms. "Well," one of the dancers said, putting her hands on her tiny hips, "it's about time you two got together!"

"Really, Ivan," said the other, raking her fingers through her companion's hair, "I'm surprised you're in the mood after how terrible tonight was."

Ivan lifted Maya from his lap and stood, frowning. He was, after all these years, still a bashful sort of person; he had hoped for this moment with Maya for a long time, and he was angry that it had been spoiled. He didn't respond to the girls and their teasing. "I'll see you later," he said to Maya, and he left to go find Yakobson.

The ballet master was, at that moment, in an office down the hall, getting an earful from Yekaterina Furtseva, who'd telephoned from the Kremlin and instructed him to pull *Spartacus* from the company's repertoire. News of the booing had reached Moscow. "It's shameful," she said. "You can't possibly perform this for the Americans again. Tomorrow's your last night in New York, so you've got one last chance to impress them. Don't you dare bring out the feathers and tutus for this one, Yakobson. The American audiences are expecting something new, something modern like their Balanchine." Furtseva dreaded the thought that Balanchine, the prodigal, parading his avant-garde dances on Russian stages, could look fresher than the Kirov itself. "If you fail, I'll have you on the next plane back to Moscow." Furtseva had reason to be anxious: relations with America were deteriorating, and this cultural tour was more important than ever—though even Furtseva did not yet know how important. Yakobson insisted he couldn't possibly pull this off in one day, that they didn't have anything contemporary prepared, but Furtseva hung up before he could finish his sentence.

Ivan, who'd heard the end of the conversation, knocked on Yakobson's open door. He grinned. "So you need something contemporary, eh?"

The other dancers were skeptical when the choreographer told them the news at the next morning's rehearsal. A mere member of the corps de ballet, directing them for a performance that very evening? It was unheard of. But Maya instructed them with such gentle confidence (a confidence she did not feel, being thrust into her dream much sooner than she'd expected) that they soon felt at ease. As she guided them through a barre, she thought of that night with Olaf in the practice room—Tchaikovsky's Serenade and the movement that had poured out of her. She was not instructing the dancers to take on characters, or to perform roles, but to be fully themselves—to fully inhabit their bodies and display the skills they had sacrificed everything to acquire.

Maya's ballet opened the Kirov's performance that evening. It was unlike anything the company had ever done. There were no sets, no backdrops, no eerie blue lights signaling the presence of the supernatural: just dancers—with Maya among them—performing their barres to Bizet in simple practice tights and leotards. Yakobson walked in between the barres, correcting here, directing there, just as any teacher would during a class.

The audience, most of whom had never set foot in a ballet classroom, watched this unfold with great interest. It was like seeing the underside of an opulent tapestry or putting an X-ray to a painting: even the building blocks of this art form were beautiful. Later, the barres were taken offstage, and when the Kirov's soloists began the series of acrobatic spins and leaps Maya had designed for them, some in the audience gasped. Stripped of the trappings of theater, tutus and tiaras cast aside, the dancers' bravura shone strong. It was, as it turned out, more impressive to watch a dancer pull off forty fouettés as a mere woman rather than as a princess. The audience—at least, judging by the level of their applause—felt being a mere woman was impressive enough.

The next morning, when Yakobson handed her a newspaper review that declared her work "Balanchine-esque," Maya knew she'd found her destiny at last.

CHAPTER SIXTEEN

After several more weeks of fittings, screen tests, line readings, and rehearsals, Bondarchuk at last gave the announcement everyone had anticipated for so long: they'd begin filming tomorrow. Cast and crew alike received this news with joy. That evening, Oleg, a young actor who played one of the Rostovs, called Natasha with an invitation. "We're all gathering at my house for drinks tonight," he said. Natasha tried to turn him down, but her fictional brother insisted. "You've got to come! It won't be a real cast party without our Natasha."

Our Natasha. Living alone in Moscow, Natasha didn't feel like she belonged to anyone anymore, and Oleg's kindness drew her in. As she changed into her most festive dress—a green striped one she'd purchased shortly after arriving in Moscow—she tried to ignore the only reason she'd agreed to come, which she'd resisted asking Oleg on the phone: Would Lev be there too? She'd barely seen Lev since the day she found out he was married. Whether this was by accident or by Bondarchuk's design, Natasha wasn't sure. Natasha couldn't decide if being away from him made her feel better or worse.

She was relieved when she stepped into Oleg's shabby apartment and saw that none of the older cast members were there—only people who played young Rostovs and Cossacks and Katharina, the solemn young woman who played Prince Andrei's sister.

The young Rostovs and Cossacks were deeply immersed in a drinking game loosely involving chess (but mostly involving vodka) and they invited Natasha to join them, but she was already exhausted from the long week she'd had and declined, heading toward the kitchen where she spotted Katharina sitting alone.

But as Natasha entered the kitchen, she realized Katharina was not alone. Lev sat on the other side of the table. When he looked up at her and smiled, half of Natasha wanted to run to him and the other half wanted to dart toward the door. She didn't take the chair Katharina offered her and stood uncertainly by the table.

Raucous whoops and hollers erupted from the other room. "I swear," Katharina said, shaking her head, "those boys are going to break a glass and cut themselves." She got up and went into the living room to investigate, shouting as she went.

Lev lit a cigarette. "You look a little down," he said. "What's bothering you?"

"Nothing," Natasha said. She didn't know where to look—at the table, at the ceiling. Anywhere but directly at him. Finally, her gaze rested on his shoulder. "I guess I'm just nervous about filming—and the waltz scene too. I've never done this before. I don't know how I should prepare."

"I do," said Lev, barely audible above the whoops and reprimands coming from the living room. He stood and stamped out his cigarette.

"You do?"

Lev nodded. "You should come with me." He offered his arm, and Natasha took it, and they left the kitchen and walked through the living room, which was full of such chaos—Oleg juggling glasses and Katharina scolding him and the other boys watching the both of them and laughing so hard they fell onto the floor, spilling their drinks as they went, which made Katharina scold them more and the boys laugh even harder—that no one saw them leave the apartment.

The night was quiet and cold. Natasha shivered, and Lev noticed and clucked his tongue. "You have a knack for never dressing for the weather!" He handed her his heavy tweed jacket and then put two fingers in his mouth and whistled so loudly that Natasha jumped. A taxi rolled up immediately.

"Where to?" the driver said.

"To the Metropol Hotel," said Lev.

The Metropol was the largest and grandest hotel in Moscow, with a storied history to match. The Bolsheviks and White Army used it as a battleground; Lenin's government conscripted it to serve as a dreary bureaucratic hall; later, when Muscovite officials began to realize the usefulness of having an impressive place to host foreign dignitaries, it was made glorious again and opened to the public once more.

With a steady arm, Lev led Natasha into a restaurant the size of a ballroom where thousands of love affairs had begun and hundreds of lives, whether at the hands of the KGB or the vagaries of war, had ended. The ceiling was a patchwork of stained glass in golds and ochres and reds. An orchestra played on a raised platform on one side of the room. Everyone was dressed elegantly, and the sweet tang of alcohol and imported perfume clouded the air. It was the kind of place that she and Maya had dreamed of visiting when they were younger—this was what they'd hoped adulthood would be like. Natasha felt like she'd stepped into an Audrey Hepburn movie.

She turned to Lev in alarm. "I'm not done up enough for this! You should have let me go home and change!"

Lev smiled and surveyed the room. "You're right," he said. "Do you want to go home?"

Natasha took in all the elegance—ladies with furs and silver-rimmed plates and the orchestra's starched collars—and she shook her head. She smiled. "No."

A solemn waiter with a long upper lip seated them in a gray velvet banquette. Lev ordered champagne, and when the waiter brought the bottle, Lev insisted on pouring it himself. Natasha, sitting in a beautiful restaurant, with a handsome man pouring her champagne, realized that she'd somehow obtained the kind of life she'd always wanted—for tonight, at least.

Lev slid her glass toward her. "What are you thinking about?" His knee touched hers under the table.

"Nothing," she said, moving her knee away and remembering why she hadn't wanted to be around him in the first place. Why was she always wanting things she couldn't have—to dance, to leave Russia, to be with a man who belonged to someone else? Natasha began to wonder why Lev had brought her here. Some part of her conscience warned her to be careful.

But if Natasha had ever excelled at anything, it was ignoring her conscience. The champagne made her giddy, and soon, she was telling him about her whole life, how she'd never known her mother, how she'd wanted to see the world after leaving the Vaganova.

And she told him about the accident. It was a story she'd recited many times over the last couple years—everyone wanted to hear the sorrowful tale of the fallen dancer—and she usually described it in clinical terms, the full-body cast, the exercises. She never talked about how she'd felt in those days, only what she did. But to Lev, she admitted everything, including that she'd contemplated suicide. "I never thought I was going to be able to walk again, let alone dance. I lost everything. And if Bondarchuk finds out, I might lose this, too."

Lev nodded. He had a way of making her feel like he was listening, even if he didn't say much in return. It was something in his posture—he leaned far back in his chair, his head tilted toward her—and his gaze, which never left her, even when a waiter dropped a glass and the orchestra conductor sneezed mid-concerto. She had never seen someone so good at paying attention, not since—well, not since Maya. If Natasha didn't discard every thought of Maya as soon as it entered her mind, she would have noticed this about Lev the moment they met. Now, a little drunk, she saw it clearly.

Loosened by the champagne, Natasha stared at Lev and remembered the first time they'd met, how badly she'd wanted to know the color of his eyes. It was delicious, getting to look into them as much as she wanted.

Lev poured her another glass, which she drank more quickly than was wise, wanting to silence the part of her that told her to be careful, to remember that this man could not be hers. "And the worst thing about it," she said, swirling the last golden drop in her glass, "was why it happened."

Lev leaned forward. "Why did it happen?"

"On purpose," she said. "My sister and my ex-boyfriend planned it. They were jealous of me."

Lev squinted, as if he didn't quite believe her. "How could anyone do a thing like that to a person like you?"

Natasha didn't know what to say. How could she tell him about their mother and her desperation, which had entered Maya and Natasha's blood before their birth and turned into ambition? How could she tell him about Maya's surprising ascent, her thirty-first fouetté that made no difference at all? How could she tell him what it was like to be doubled, to grow up with the other half of yourself an arm's length away, to know with certainty that you will never be understood or seen or loved like you are by this person, and then to have that person betray you? Even sober, it would have felt like too much to explain. Drunk, it was impossible, and Natasha merely shrugged. "I got in her way."

Lev shook his head and lit a cigarette. "Why women do these sorts of things to each other, I'll never know. I've never understood your sex."

"You must not, since your wife's home alone and you're out here with me." Natasha meant this playfully, but Lev's mouth hardened.

"She's not alone," he said.

"Oh, no?"

"No," he said, putting the cigarette, unsmoked, in an ashtray. "She has a lover. And she's leaving me."

Natasha—who was by this time unquestionably drunk, and in love, and even sober was prone to overreactions—started, because this revelation meant so many things to her all at once. She knocked over her glass, which was conveniently empty and toppled onto its side without even dampening the tablecloth. "How could someone—how could they do this to a person like that—to you?"

She was too drunk to make sense, but Lev picked up on her meaning. His gaze wandered over toward the orchestra, which had started playing again, and the couples gathering to dance. "She had her reasons."

Natasha, again not knowing what to say, watched the dancers too. Most of them were fat Party members and their wives, and few of them were graceful: one woman stumbled on her partner's wayward feet, uttering curses, and two men stepped on the hems of dresses. But Natasha would have given anything to dance again, even if she looked ridiculous. None of these people, many decades older than her, knew what she would have given to be one of them.

You have your whole life ahead of you. "And what good," she wondered to herself, with the sudden gloominess of wine, "is such a life?"

She felt Lev staring at her and turned to him, blushing. "What?"

He looked at her as if he knew something about her that no one else did—something she herself didn't even know. "I have something to tell you," he said, extinguishing his cigarette in the ashtray. He leaned so close to her that their noses were inches apart—perhaps he was a little drunk too. "I don't think you should let those doctors dictate the rest of your life."

Natasha, finally noticing her toppled glass, righted it and ran a finger around its rim, only half listening. She couldn't bear being so close to him. "What do you mean?"

"I mean," he said, pushing back the glass, "that I think you should try to dance." He stood and held out his arm to her and gestured toward the dance floor. "Shall we?"

Natasha's back tensed as if in protest. "I can't."

"How do you know? Have you tried?"

"No," Natasha said. "But they told me that if I tried, I could damage things permanently."

"Well," said Lev, leaning in and offering his arm, "we'll be very careful."

It might have been the kindness of his gesture, or the recklessness of it, or the champagne that was leaving her dizzy—who can say for sure? Whatever it was, whatever it is that makes us try things that are dangerous and frightening but could be very, very good, Natasha stood, and she accepted his arm, and she followed him out to the dance floor.

It was a slow song, and the number of couples had thinned, which helped put Natasha more at ease. "Less risk of being bumped," she thought, and she put one hand in Lev's hand and the other on his shoulder. Anyone could see that she was nervous. Bondarchuk, if he had been present, would have clapped his hands and eagerly called for a camera, noticing the similarity between Natasha's grand waltz in Tolstoy's novel and this one, in the real world, with the real Natasha about to dance.

If Bondarchuk had been there, he also would have noticed the way that Natasha looked at Lev, and this would have made him call off the cameras in disgust. But Bondarchuk was not there, and Natasha had not danced yet, not even swayed. She was afraid to take a step. She looked up at Lev uncertainly.

"Come on," Lev whispered. "If you stumble, I'll catch you."

The song ended, and a new one began—a waltz, a coincidence that would have sent Bondarchuk and maybe even Tolstoy himself into ecstasies—and Lev took a step back, gently pulling Natasha to follow him. How strange it was to be led. Dissolving yourself into one-two-three, one-two-three required a certain abandon. You couldn't learn to float if you worried your partner would spin you into the wall. No wonder Maya had clung to her when they'd learned to waltz all those years ago. To be led required total trust.

The tread of Natasha's shoe caught on the parquet—it was winter in Moscow, and despite Natasha's vanity (after all, she'd been raised in the snow) she was wearing winter boots. She breathed in sharply, and her back muscles braced against the pain she knew would come.

But none came. Lev's arms kept her steady, and they began to move together, and this was how Natasha, after years of being told otherwise, realized that she might dance again after all.

CHAPTER SEVENTEEN

OCTOBER 22, 1962

Maya sat on the floor of her room at the Fairmont Hotel in San Francisco, watching the president's speech. John Kennedy looked tired, and he did not sound particularly confident that the naval blockade he'd sent to Cuba would amount to anything good.

Maya's English, though improving, was not perfect. She couldn't make out every word he said, but this made the intelligible words that drifted through all the more startling—words like *destruction, threats, nuclear war*.

And, of course, *the Russians*.

There had been rumors—in the papers, from the bellhops, on the streets—that some kind of conflict was coming. The Kirov's performances at the War Memorial Opera House, a grand, columned old hall that made Maya ache for Leningrad, were poorly attended. A wave of tension descended every time the curtain rose; it was not clear what attending a performance of the Russian ballet meant in such times, and between dances, the members of the audience stole glances at one another as if to ask, "Why are *you* here?" Everyone—dancers, audience, ticket takers—was suspect, and as a result, the company's reception was chilly. That night, after the performance, a heaviness hung over the dressing room, and that heaviness followed Maya home and sucked up all the space in her lonely hotel room.

Before the Kirov had left for the tour, Furtseva told them they were envoys of everything Russians held dear. Maya had felt a little bit of pride at this. But here, sitting on the dingy floor of her hotel, realizing missiles from the motherland could strike at any moment, Maya recognized what she really was to the state that claimed to mother its own: expendable.

This was when Maya missed her sister most. Natasha had always known how to comfort her when she was frightened, to make jokes about the sounds Maya made when she snored, to tease her about her first love—whose name Maya still couldn't remember. Natasha, even now, would insist it was Pinky. "I'm absolutely certain of it," she'd say. "You used to practice writing out your married names: 'Mr. and Mrs. Pinky.'"

But Natasha wasn't here, and there was no one to tell Maya that everything would be all right. The young president finished his speech, and the local news commentators dissected it with the grim enthusiasm of vultures who must peck apart a friend to survive. The rapidity of their speech hurt Maya's head, which was already on the verge of throbbing—a thunderstorm rumbled low over the bay—and she turned off the television and sat back against the bed.

He'd said big cities would be targeted. San Francisco was big, Maya thought. She wondered if everyone back home was safe. Had Alexei gathered all the younger Vaganova students that morning and broken the news in an assembly? Were Kira and Olga watching their jazz-musician husbands play in a Siberian nightclub, totally oblivious? Were Pyotr and Elena bickering over whether or not to build a bomb shelter? Soviet newspapers were loath to admit calamity, even in the direst circumstances, and Katusha and Natasha might not even know what was going on. How would anyone find out if something terrible happened to her? Would Natasha even care? Other than Ivan, nobody from the Vaganova days even talked to her anymore—nobody except Olaf, and even him she'd pushed away.

Maya fingered the slippery coverlet on the bed and wondered how she would be remembered if her own country's weapons reduced her to ash. Her choreographic dream was only a fledgling. Just yesterday, somebody had produced a newspaper column that had singled her out: "Such effortless taste hasn't graced the stage since the days of Anna Pavlova." That was her: a choreographer with taste.

But taste was not itself an accomplishment; nobody would remember you for your taste. And this hour, spent alone in a hotel room in America—her roommates had gone out in search of some pre-apocalyptic bacchanalia—could be her last. Maya turned off the television and crawled into bed. Time went by; it melted and flowed around her without any indication of its passing. She did not know how long she lay there alone.

Somebody knocked on the door—softly, as if they weren't sure they wanted to be heard. Maya, who was both lonely and uncertain if she could tolerate company at this moment, was grateful for the knock's humility—surely nobody dangerous would knock like that—and went quickly to the door and there was Ivan, holding a bottle of wine.

He did not say hello. "I thought," he said, looking for some reason at her left ear, "that you might like some company."

"I would," Maya said, and saying this made her realize it was true. She stepped back and let Ivan in, wishing she'd smoothed the rumpled bedclothes. Ivan took off his shoes and sat cross-legged on the bed. Maya got plastic cups from the bathroom, Ivan opened the bottle of red wine, and they drank in silence until the bottle was nearly empty. It was quiet, though the hotel was in the middle of the city: it felt like the whole world was holding its breath, waiting for some news.

Heat prickled on the back of Maya's neck. The room felt stuffy after all the wine. Gathering all of her courage—she never liked being the one to speak first in a conversation, let alone with a man, let alone a man whose attractiveness couldn't be ignored—she asked Ivan if he was scared.

He shrugged. "Doesn't matter if I'm scared or not," he said. "It still might happen."

Maya understood and even admired this. "No sense in getting riled up," she said. "It might all come to nothing."

"It might all come to nothing," he repeated, whether to affirm her words or examine them, Maya did not know. He shook his head. "We're too young for all this," he said. "I know it's very selfish to think of ourselves at a time like this, but we're all much too young."

"Yes," Maya said, grateful that someone else was also thinking in this way. There was nothing selfish about wanting a long life. "There's much more that I wanted to do."

Ivan turned to her. "Me too," he said. "What else did you want to do?" And then, as if answering the question himself, he slid his hand across the bedspread and touched her thigh.

How quickly the rest of it happened was a great surprise to Maya, and something she would marvel at for years afterward—how everything in your life can change in the span of time it takes to wash your hair. They jumped into the act as if they'd been practicing for it all their lives, as if it were something they'd been discussing and preparing for since the Vaganova. Maya was not a virgin—a shy soloist had taken care of that her first year at the Kirov—but she was not particularly experienced, either, and she was astounded by her own boldness. They went about it with an urgency, like they were afraid they would be interrupted, like if they stopped or slowed they would realize what they were doing and their courage would falter. Maya thought that no matter what happened, everything would be all right, even if sirens began to wail as they rocked, even if the walls around them began to melt, even if it was the end of the world.

But it was not the end of the world—not yet. They finished, and sirens did not wail, and the room did not burst into radioactive flames. They finished, and they had not been transfigured; they were still just two dancers, stuck in a foreign country, trapped in the middle of a war. Before Ivan pulled out, he looked at Maya and appeared startled, as if he'd expected to see someone else's face. Maya was only a stand-in, just as this coupling was an imagined happy ending to their shared mistake. They both knew the truth: they didn't love or even want each other. They were just two people who had ruined someone's life and were trying to make something good from it. Even naked and alone, half a world away from home, both of them still felt Natasha haunting them, still heard her scream from the stage floor.

There was no need to say anything. Ivan took a shower, and then he put his clothes on as quickly as he'd taken them off, and he left Maya alone in the little hotel room, just as he'd found her.

As Maya drifted off to sleep, as unaware of the revolution within her as Washington was of the nuclear submarines drifting toward Cuba, Sergei Bondarchuk sped through a busy street in Moscow, bracing himself for another day of filming. The previous day had been a disaster. Lev, who had taken to wearing gloves to make his "farmer's hands" seem smaller, had muffed his lines in twenty-two takes—why, Sergei wondered, was it so difficult for him to get people to do anything he wanted?—and then threatened to quit the production altogether, though a producer had convinced him to stay. Sergei was tired and anxious; his whole being felt disordered. The only thing that could fix it was hurrying home at the end of the day and eating an enormous bowl of cherries.

This cheered him—the thought of the sweet cherries, a luxury straight from the country, which Irina kept stocked in the freezer just for him, and the thought of his sweet wife, with her welcoming shapeliness, handing him the bowl—but as he turned the corner, he saw the American embassy, and a large, angry-looking crowd seething outside it.

Bondarchuk was a man of the world. He possessed a shortwave radio, which he kept in the bathroom; sometimes he listened to the BBC as he shaved. His English was poor, but he was better at listening than speaking, and he'd caught a little of Kennedy's speech that morning. The issue of *Pravda* that had arrived on his doorstep had been ominous: "The Ruling Circles of the USA Are Playing with Fire."

As a man of the world, but also as a veteran of the last war, Bondarchuk knew better than to go borrowing trouble when he had enough of his own. He sped past the embassy so quickly that he nearly clipped a tall young man stepping off the sidewalk.

The tall young man was Jacques D'Amboise of the New York City Ballet, who, after having been hit by a streetcar in Hamburg that broke five of his ribs, was still very jumpy around foreign vehicles. He shook his fist at the back of Bondarchuk's car, swearing. "Mother Mary," he shouted, and people stopped to stare at the angry American, and Jacques hung his head. If his very Catholic mother had heard him take the Holy Virgin's name like that, she would have disowned him on the spot.

Nora Kaye, a wiry City Ballet prima, took him gingerly by the arm. "You okay?" she asked, with the air of someone inquiring after a child who'd fallen off a bicycle. When Jacques nodded, she tugged at his sleeve. "Come on," she said, dragging him toward the embassy. "I want to see what this ruckus is all about."

They did not get the chance to find out. As they skirted the edge of the crowd, a man in a black knitted cap, who recognized Nora from the newspapers, strode up to her and extinguished his cigarette on her arm, looked her in the eyes for one terrifying moment—green eyes, she would tell people later, green and bright as artificial grass—and then ran away before Jacques could throw a punch. Nora cried out and Jacques, who was fond of Nora and very protective of all the female dancers, started to dash after him, but Nora pulled at his sleeve again and they hurried off to rehearsal.

The whole story was later relayed in great detail to Balanchine, who already knew what the dancers did not: the United States and Russia were locked in a nuclear standoff, and the whole world was watching. Even Balanchine did not know that the next morning, as the United States began its naval blockade in Cuba, seventy-two American B-52 bombers would be perpetually in the air, ready to unleash a nuclear arsenal on Russian targets at a word. But he knew that his dancers were in danger, and that night, he and Lincoln Kirstein and Betty Cage, the company's general manager, wore out the already-threadbare carpet in his suite at the Hotel Ukraina. Nearly all night long, they paced and plotted, keeping vigil much as Khrushchev and his men had the evening before—catching snatches of sleep in their clothes on the couches and making escape plans in between. A handful of options were proposed, dissected, and discarded, including chartering a plane, in hopes they could escape before a missile struck.

"The embassy would tell us first, don't you think?" Betty asked Kirstein, her generous mouth drooping, and Kirstein only shrugged.

They could keep their tour bus on call and sneak the company into the embassy. And what if all was lost, and war was declared too quickly for them to do anything about it? Nobody liked discussing this potentiality, but Betty managed to find a sliver of hope in it.

"Isn't the Kirov in the US right now?" she said. "Maybe they'd let us go if they came home—you know, swap our guys for theirs."

Balanchine sat wearily on the edge of a burgundy damask sofa that looked as tired and haggard as he did. Even before all this, the tour had been eating him alive. All the people on these Soviet sidewalks looked like automatons to him, mechanical and unhappy. It nauseated him to see Tolstoy and Tchaikovsky's homeland reduced to a godless wasteland, a place without color or joy. Every interview enraged him; the journalists all tried to cut him down and prove the superiority of their ideologies, but Balanchine was undeterred. A cocky young journalist made the mistake of dismissing Balanchine's choreography as "soulless," which made Balanchine want to upend the table like Christ in the temple. "You're an atheist!" he'd shouted. "What do you know about souls?" It made him sick to see shuttered churches everywhere, all those onion-domed cathedrals converted to warehouses and factories—if they still stood at all.

All this took a toll on his body. His bursitis flared up so badly that he winced every time he moved his shoulder, and he was barely able to sleep. He was counting down the days until after Leningrad—Lincoln was insisting he go home for a little while to rest. And now, on top of all this, a catastrophe was brewing, and Lincoln and Betty were looking to him for a solution. "Don't tell the dancers any more than you have to," he said, standing, an indication that their congress was over. "They have enough to worry about as it is." He patted Betty on the back. "Don't you worry, either," he said. "The government is probably planning our escape right now."

He did not mean this, and both Betty and Lincoln knew it, but it brought them comfort anyway, which was why he had said it.

In the midst of this, ordinary life continued, as it always does—particularly in Moscow, where accurate updates were hard to come by. Like the Americans, the Russians had long been warned that they lived in the crosshairs of the enemy. They hadn't constructed fallout shelters or stockpiled radiation test kits, but they—or their parents and aunts and uncles—had lived through war, and they did their best to ignore the conflict. So Natasha's world, at this time, was much quieter and calmer than her sister's, and her immediate concerns were much more pedestrian. She still hadn't told Bondarchuk she'd been ordered not to dance. The doctor's pronouncement might not be right, but it wasn't entirely wrong, either: the day after she and Lev danced at the Metropol, Natasha woke up with such a searing backache that she'd been two hours late for rehearsal. She realized she'd been foolish. No one jumped right back into dancing after a terrible injury and two years of convalescing—they never would have let anyone do such a thing at the Vaganova. Students who hurt themselves ended up in the physical therapist's office for weeks before they were allowed to set foot in the classroom. When Anya tore a ligament, she'd done nothing but rehabilitative exercises for several months. No, if Natasha was going to dance again, she was going to need help, probably professional training—but she was still too scared to ask.

When Irina called her later that week and asked her to come to their house for dinner, Natasha felt caught. She imagined that the Bondarchuks' entire house would be a lie detector: the moment she walked through their door, they would know she'd deceived them.

Bondarchuk did not want Natasha in his house. He preferred a line of separation between his home life—his wife, his secret radio, his well-worn slippers—and his work life, because this allowed him to feel like a man at home and a director at the studio. "A director is like a god," he had explained to Irina. "He is tsar and god."

Irina had smiled her sly, winsome smile and put a wooden spoon in his hand. "If you are tsar, then I am tsarina," she said. "Stir the borscht." Natasha was invited for dinner that Saturday evening—October 27, 1962.

Irina had not invited Natasha to supper out of altruism—though this was how she'd framed it to her husband. ("She's all alone, Sergei," she'd said. "We can't let her face such a terrible time by herself.") She'd noticed the way her husband sometimes looked at Natasha, the way he skillfully avoided mentioning her in conversation at home. Irina decided there was no better way to put Natasha in her place (or to soothe her own jealousy) than to give her a seat at the table: nobody could admire a little girl like Natasha when *she* was around.

A dinner party between employer and employee is always a fraught affair, and the particular circumstances of this evening gave it the potential for even greater disaster. Each of the three at the table had a secret they wanted to conceal at all costs. Sergei did not want his wife to know he found Natasha attractive; Irina did not want Sergei to know that she knew; and Natasha, who was completely unaware of the marital minefield she'd walked into, did not want either of the Bondarchuks to know that she might not be able to dance, though the eventual disclosure of this information seemed inevitable.

The house was stuffed with secrets, and the world outside was too: the nuclear submarines, with their orders to retaliate if attacked first; Kennedy, with his hopes for the elections and the survival of the world and the chance to bed Marilyn Monroe before he died, whenever that would be; Khrushchev, who did not want a war and had never meant to start one; and the U-2 pilot seeking air samples in the North Pole who had been blinded by the northern lights and was now drifting into enemy territory, hounded by Russian bombers and invisibly guarded by American planes armed with nuclear missiles.

So much that could have happened did not happen. The U-2 pilot, who had run out of fuel, glided safely back out of enemy territory and landed in the snow, where he was just as grateful to relieve himself as to be alive. Kennedy, whose advisors and chief of staff had been pushing toward aggression and war, did not let his migraine reduce him to a murderer. Khrushchev, who was known for being mercurial and had threatened to nuke the White House when he heard of the naval blockade, did not order a first strike—not yet. The whole world watched and waited.

Inside the Bondarchuks' spacious and comfortable apartment, the unhappy trio of diners also waited. The conversation was stilted, the soup grew cold, and just as soon as the rules of etiquette allowed—Bondarchuk was a stringent observer of etiquette; it was one of the requirements of tsarhood—Bondarchuk excused himself, retrieved his shortwave radio from the bathroom, and took it to the living room, leaving the two women alone.

This was a great relief for Natasha. She was much more afraid of Bondarchuk than she was of Irina, and Bondarchuk's absence also meant the end of the meaningful glances the couple had been shooting at each other all evening.

The experience had reminded her of an awkward evening at the Vaganova dinner table when she'd been trapped between Vasilia and Vasili in the middle of a fight. Nothing outrightly hostile had been said; Vasili had asked Vasilia to pass the salt, Vasilia had commented that the potatoes were salty enough and refused to hand it to him. "You should learn to enjoy what's in *front* of you," she'd said, pronouncing the words with such articulation that she sprayed Natasha's arm with little drops of spittle.

Sergei and Irina behaved in the same way: everything they said to each other seemed to mean something else. To Natasha, marriage looked like a never-ending sequence of indecipherable codes. She didn't think she would ever understand it.

So when Bondarchuk left for the living room, Natasha stood, too, intending to thank her hostess and excuse herself from the uncomfortable evening, but Irina pulled down an enormous samovar from the top of a cabinet and asked her to stay for tea.

What could she do? She didn't want to risk making Irina mad, and nobody waited at home for Natasha except her proud china cat. She sat down again and accepted.

Irina filled the kettle and started clearing away the dishes in a great hurry. Bondarchuk's radio crackled in the other room. Natasha did not understand how she fit into this domestic picture at all, and she tried to help with the dishes in an attempt to find a place in it. But Irina, ever the hostess, would not let her. "Sit, sit," she said. "You are a guest in my house." She emphasized those last two words—*my house*—with such vehemence that it was nearly a shout, and Natasha, who felt she was being punished for something without understanding what, obeyed.

"So, my dear," Irina said, in perpetual motion—washing a dish, putting leftovers into the refrigerator, wiping down the counter—"do you have a boyfriend?"

"Well—"

"Surely a pretty girl like you can't be all alone. When I was your age, I had dozens of men vying for my attention." Here, Irina stopped, and she looked over at Natasha, watching her as if it were Natasha's face and not her words that would answer her question.

Natasha didn't know what to say to this. There was no sound but the drone of Bondarchuk's radio, which became louder and louder, and at first Natasha thought Bondarchuk was turning the radio up, trying to drown them out, but soon it became clear that the sound was not just getting louder, but coming closer. Bondarchuk entered the room, carrying the radio. "They've downed a plane," he said. He suddenly looked fifteen years older; his face was white, and his arms hung limp at his sides.

Irina froze. "Who has?"

"We have," Bondarchuk said. He said it with remorse, as if he, himself, had done it.

He and Irina looked at each other without saying anything for so long that Natasha wondered if they remembered she was still with them. "Will they bomb us now?" Irina said.

"I don't know," Bondarchuk said, and he looked at his wife so sadly and so tenderly that it made Natasha blush. For a horrifying moment, Natasha thought that he, this famous and lauded director, this great bear of a man whom she feared and admired, was going to cry. He glanced quickly at Natasha, perhaps remembering her presence, then turned his back to her and left the room. "Probably," he said over his shoulder, and he waited until he was safely alone again to wipe his eyes.

Irina lowered herself heavily into her chair and then was still. The teakettle started howling, and she did not rise to tend to it.

Natasha stood, and for once she was not told to sit down again. She poured the hot water into the samovar, inhaled the tea leaves' woody fragrance, and returned to her seat. She numbered all the accoutrements of the Bondarchuks' married life: the pink tablecloth, edged with hand-crocheted lace; the crystal water glasses; the pewter vase of hothouse chrysanthemums. To her, their life seemed full and rich. She could not understand why anyone who had what they had could be unhappy.

The radio became louder—this time, Bondarchuk really was turning it up, so no one could hear him weeping—and Natasha heard the phrase "total annihilation." It was a phrase she did not think she could understand, or anyone could understand. The Bondarchuks, if worse came to worse, would be able to say that they had everything they wanted. Everything she wanted kept slipping from her fingers—or, perhaps, Maya kept pulling it away from her, bit by bit. But even bitterness seemed untenable in a time like this. Natasha wondered if Maya was safe. The world was so fragile. After everything Maya had done to get to the Kirov, she might disappear if a man in Moscow lost his temper.

What was the point, then, of keeping secrets? Natasha had nothing to lose. She leaned over to Irina and told her that she had something she needed to confess.

Irina looked alarmed when Natasha said this. Perhaps, humbled by being in the Bondarchuks' home, the girl was about to confess sins of a venial nature. But there were no such sins to confess, and when Natasha told her the truth, Irina was so relieved that she started to laugh, and Bondarchuk, thinking the stress of the moment had cracked his wife's sanity, sprang up and ran into the kitchen. Irina just kept laughing and waved him back into the living room.

"I'm sorry," Irina said, sitting back at the table and wiping her eyes, "you'll have to explain it to me again, dear. What did you say?"

All Natasha had said was that she'd lied—she couldn't dance, and she had no idea why such a simple (and embarrassing) statement would have provoked such a reaction—especially from Irina, who seemed like an implacable fortress of serenity. "I haven't danced in years," Natasha said. "The doctors told me I couldn't dance ever again." She whispered, afraid that Bondarchuk would make one of his sudden entrances again. She decided that pleading her case would be easier if she told Irina the full truth, and she told her the entire story: Maya's jealousy, Ivan's vengeance. "She took everything from me," Natasha said. "She even took my spot at the Kirov." Saying this out loud made it feel more real, which hardened Natasha's anger and fear into a firm resolution. "I never want to see her again."

"I can certainly understand that," Irina said. She sighed, calculating the headache this was going to cause for her husband. "So you can't dance in the film, I take it?"

"I don't know," Natasha said. "Maybe, if I had a little training, I might be able to."

"We'll see," Irina said. She retrieved a plate of honey cakes from the counter and set it in front of Natasha. "For now, let's just try to survive the evening."

That night, as Natasha rode home in a taxi and the Bondarchuks got ready for bed, as Khrushchev paced in his office and Kennedy watched *Roman Holiday* in the White House theater while he awaited Khrushchev's answer to his ultimatum, the world was nearly ended and then saved through a series of accidents. The captain of a Russian submarine, mistaking a low-flying American plane for an act of war, gave orders for a nuclear warhead to be launched, which would begin the end of the world. But another officer, standing on the deck of the submarine, happened to look up at the night sky one last time and, seeing the Americans' signaled apology, realized they were not under attack after all and shouted below deck to cancel the captain's order, and it is because of this man that the world still exists today. His name was Vasily Arkhipov.

Back in Moscow, Bondarchuk wasn't thinking of saving the world but of saving his opus. Irina told him Natasha's news the moment the girl was out their door, and he immediately called Furtseva. Though it was nearly midnight, he had a feeling she would still be awake, given the circumstances, and she was. Wearing the same green dressing gown as always, the one stamped with cigarette burns, Furtseva jumped when the phone rang. She thought it was the apocalypse.

But it was only Bondarchuk—which, for once, was a relief to her. She listened to his problem and shook her head at the foolishness of her job. "Everyone else is off trying to save us from the Americans, and I'm stuck here minding fannies," she muttered to herself.

"What was that?" said Bondarchuk.

"Nothing," said Furtseva, and she stamped out her cigarette in a globe-shaped ashtray. "What do you want me to do? It's too late to replace the girl."

"She's healthy and strong," Bondarchuk said. "And she was once a very good dancer. We just need someone to help her remember."

Furtseva nodded, though there was no one in the room to see it. "Leave it to me," she said, and two days later, when it was clear that the crisis had passed and that such a call would not be perceived as a breach of loyalty, she called George Balanchine.

CHAPTER EIGHTEEN

While the rest of the cast was packed off to film scenes in a remote palace, Natasha was sent to Leningrad to study with Balanchine, who had recently arrived with City Ballet.

Natasha visited her godmother when she arrived in Leningrad—Furtseva had put her up in a hotel near the Vaganova—but Katusha seemed remote. The only time Katusha became animated during Natasha's short visit was when she read Maya's latest letter aloud. "That ballet of hers has turned out to be a great success," Katusha said, her eyes lit up. "Now the Bolshoi has commissioned a dance from her too!" Maya had even included a newspaper clipping with a photograph of herself with the Kennedys, posed next to Jacqueline behind a table piled with green beans and turkey legs and potatoes. Jacqueline and Maya were the same height, both wearing stylish cocktail dresses and smiling at each other like old friends.

As is often the case with photographs, the image of Maya smiling next to Jacqueline Kennedy did not capture the actual experience of her life. Before leaving New York, one of the handlers had cornered Maya and asked her if she'd spoken to Olaf recently, which she hadn't—but the handler's tone implied he thought otherwise.

"What would you do if he sent you flowers?" the handler asked. He was a tall, gaunt man with a sandy mustache that always seemed to have crumbs in it. "Would you throw them away?"

"Of course," Maya said, remembering the note Olaf had sent her in his bouquet. Later, Maya's roommate told her she'd seen one of their handlers going through their trash. "They do it every night," she'd said. "Didn't you know?"

From then on, Maya was never really alone. If she was walking down the street, if she was touring an automobile factory in Detroit with the rest of the company, if she was scooping mashed potatoes onto her plate in yet another basement cafeteria, she felt someone's eyes on her back. She even thought they watched her while she slept; often, while lying in bed, she heard a car engine running through the open window.

Maybe it was this, maybe it was the humiliation of her evening with Ivan, but for the rest of the tour, Maya had a perpetual stomachache. Her appetite waned away, and she could barely force herself to eat enough to dance on. At the luncheon in the photograph Maya sent home, which the Kennedys hosted in an enormous house on the horn of Cape Cod, Jacqueline Kennedy chided her for how little she'd put on her plate. "Come on, then," the First Lady said, picking up the serving tongs herself and piling three more strips of beef filet on the elegant china. "American food can't be all that bad." Truth be told, Mrs. Kennedy had noticed her husband eyeing the dancers, as he was wont to do, and she wanted to fatten them up. Maya was feeling bashful, and her English was not good enough to respond anyway, so she only nodded and took her plate to the table.

Natasha would have been so much better at all this, Maya thought. She had no trouble talking to strangers. She would've said something witty and charmed Mrs. Kennedy. Perhaps if Natasha had been there, she could've ended the Cold War with cocktail chatter. Maya, picking at various unappetizing things swimming in gravy, felt like a poor understudy. She didn't belong here—in the Kirov, in the Kennedys' living room, in America itself.

Someone laughed in the back of the room, and though Maya knew who it was, and that she should ignore him, she looked over anyway and saw Ivan standing in a group of Jackie's pretty slim-suited aides, telling jokes through an interpreter. Ivan's jokes were rarely funny in their original language, and it was doubtful that they gained humor in translation, but he was handsome, and he laughed at them, so the aides laughed, too, and Maya hated all of them.

Later that afternoon, when liquor swelled conversations to uncomfortable volumes, Maya slipped out to the beach to watch the waves. After a few minutes, Ivan appeared at her side. They stood together, shoes in hand, the cool water lapping at their gnarled dancer toes.

"Listen," Ivan said. His body looked tense, as if he expected to break into a sprint at any moment. "About the other night—I don't want you to get the wrong idea."

"I didn't have any ideas," Maya said. "We're grown-ups. We both knew what we were doing." She'd seen the way he looked at her just after—startled, as though he'd been imagining someone else's face. There, too, she was a poor substitute for Natasha.

Ivan's shoulders relaxed, and Maya knew she'd said what he hoped she would say. "Now we can put everything behind us," he said, as if that was possible. He'd always been fond of Maya. Surely it wasn't easy being the lesser sister. But now, he couldn't look at her without thinking of Natasha, the feeling of her weight leaving his arms, the dull thud as she hit the stage floor. He couldn't hear her voice without remembering Natasha's screams. Bedding Maya was his attempt at an exorcism. Until the end of his days, he'd assure himself it had worked.

After that night, Ivan stopped seeking out Maya's company. He stood elsewhere during the morning barre; he didn't wink at her as he went past in the wings. Instead, he quickly took up with Nina, a black-haired soloist known for her possessiveness, and stopped greeting Maya in the hallways. Maya hadn't expected to become his lover, but she hadn't expected this either—to be treated like someone who didn't exist, to be made invisible. A few weeks later, when the company stopped in Las Vegas, Ivan and Nina shocked everyone and got married by an Elvis impersonator in a neon-lit chapel. Maya heard from others that the couple was thinking of leaving the Kirov after the tour and starting their own studio in Yekaterinburg. Maybe this, Maya thought, would be better than having to see Ivan all of the time. Maybe it would be easier to pretend he didn't exist.

Spurned by Ivan, and finding no relief in the company's stale repertoire, Maya took solace in choreographing. At least, in this, she was appreciated: the company commissioned two more works from her, and the Bolshoi commissioned one as well. On the planes and trains and taxis between cities, Maya filled little green notebooks with ideas. She thought of Balanchine, the hero of her girlhood, bent over a piano score with Stravinsky, sketching figures in a notebook just like hers.

Balanchine was famous for his plotless ballets, a concept that appealed to her. She was tired of story ballets stuffed with pantomime and exaggerated faces. Even at the Vaganova, everything they'd done had been like this. They'd shuffled from classical forms to folk-dance class to rehearsing some ballet that had been choreographed some sixty years before, back in the days of the tsars. But even those antique ballets had been groundbreaking in their day. What was the point of being a twentieth-century person if you had to dance like you'd take a horse and buggy home?

Maya wanted to do something new. After Ivan, and Pyotr, and every other man who had made her feel lesser or slighted or small, she wanted to create something that would make everyone sit up and watch. Between rehearsals and shows, between bus rides and yet another tour through yet another American wonder of commerce and industry, Maya worked late into the night in hotel rooms that smelled of cigarettes and fried foods, dreaming of something that would shake up Moscow.

On a frigid morning in Cleveland, Maya arrived early at the company's makeshift practice space, a dark classroom beneath an opera house stage, to try out some steps. The room was so cold that Maya kept on her street clothes over her practice garb. She had not eaten breakfast in hopes that this would calm the stomach pain that had become her unwelcome companion. She had no music except what was in her own head.

The song she had decided on was Maurice Ravel's "Bolero." She had heard it at a concert by the Chicago Symphony Orchestra, a forced cultural expedition that had turned out not to be a waste of time. The music's peculiar structure intrigued her—no dramatic swells or flourishes, just a slow and steady building, a pulse you felt in your bones. Though highly structured, there was a hidden wildness to it, and this is what endeared it to Maya. She, too, standing at the barre in this dark and frigid little practice room, felt wild. She decided she would pattern each section of her dance after some sort of untamed creature or element—a jungle cat, a slithering fish, the sun itself.

First would come the crab. Maya wanted to make herself hard and impenetrable. Thinking of Ravel's crisp snare drum, she raised her arms high overhead and snapped her wrists into angles, like pincers. The pulse of the music came out of the balls of her feet: she shifted her weight from one foot to the other in perpetual motion. She had visions of a woman on a red table, with men seated around it, rapt in attention. She decided she would dance it herself. The music would build and build and build, and she alone would be under the spotlight, and no one would be able to look away. No one could make her invisible.

The men seated all around the table would watch her transform herself from one creature into another—from crab into sun, from sun into fish. As the music rose, they would stir, and they would rise from their chairs and mimic her movements. Maya could see it all so clearly—now she just had to bring it out of her body and birth it into the world. Still, the ecstasy she'd felt when dancing to Serenade with Olaf was nowhere to be found. Her limbs felt filled not with air but with rage, a seething heat deep in the pit of her stomach. She had been practicing for nearly half an hour before she began to realize that the pain she felt was not just psychological, but physical—even empty, her stomach roiled, and she sank to her knees and onto the floor, too sick to move anymore.

It was in this state that the company class director found her a few minutes later. He insisted she go to the doctor immediately. "You won't do us any good all broken up," he'd said gently, and he packed her into a taxi and sent her away.

An hour later, Maya was sitting on a cold examination table in a medical office, waiting for the doctor to come in. The exam room was spartan and fluorescent-lit and a particular shade of pale green that made Maya's nausea double. She tried to distract herself by stacking and restacking the little pile of magazines the nurse had brought in. "A busy day," the nurse had said. "You might as well get comfortable," and she'd handed her the magazines, a hospital gown, and a cup to urinate in as if they were the solution to this problem.

Maya did as she was told. She filled the cup, placed it in a little metal cabinet in the wall, and put on the gown. A few minutes later, a different nurse came in, took her vital signs, listened to her description of her complaints, and then left her alone again.

She was used to wearing little, even in the presence of strangers, but the thin gown did nothing to shield her from the chilled office air, and unlike stage lights, the fluorescent panel buzzing overhead offered her no warmth. Maya shivered and pulled out a fashion magazine she'd already thumbed through and started turning the pages without really looking at it. She hated being in doctor's offices. They made her think of Natasha, stuck in a hospital bed for all those months. What a coward she'd been for never going to visit her. If Natasha hadn't already figured out what she'd done, that alone incriminated her. Perhaps Maya had caught some sort of awful disease as punishment, and now she'd serve out her own hospital sentence. Perhaps this would be her new life—shivering in a papery gown, waiting under fluorescent lights for some doctor to come in and reveal her fate.

Just when Maya thought she couldn't sit on the chilled table another minute, the doctor entered. He was neither old nor young, and he wore thick black glasses and a lime-green tie beneath his doctor's coat. "My God," Maya thought. "Even the doctors in America dress like stilyagi." She sat up straight, trying to give the impression that she was implacable.

The doctor did not say anything and began performing a hasty examination with a stern look on his face. His hands, to Maya's relief, were warm, and she even felt a little thankful for them as he palpated the lymph nodes on her neck. But he acted as if he weren't looking for answers but confirming something that he already knew, and this made her anxious.

After another minute, the doctor concluded his investigation and sat on a stool in front of her, scribbling notes onto a clipboard. His silence made Maya want to scream.

"Well, doctor?" she said. She realized that she would quickly reach the limits of her English and decided to speak in short and direct sentences. "Am I going to die?" She meant it as a joke, but her voice cracked, and the doctor looked up at her in amusement and smiled.

"Today?" he said, grinning. "No." His face grew stern again. He set the clipboard aside and folded his hands around one knee. "Listen, you're not married, are you?"

Maya's face flushed. Americans were always asking impertinent personal questions like these. Where did they get the nerve? "No," she said, and then she began to worry that the doctor was going to proposition her, and she crossed her legs and tucked the gown beneath her thighs.

The doctor shook his head. "Third one today," he said. "I swear, the world's gone to hell. Nobody's got a sense of decency anymore."

"Third one what?" This was another American trait—using fifteen words when one would do. "What is wrong with me?"

The doctor stood and folded his arms. "You've gotten yourself into trouble."

Maya's mind skipped from one horrific possibility to another like a secretary flipping through files. How could it be her fault if she was sick? Maybe she wasn't really sick—maybe she'd been poisoned. She began to wonder if this was some sort of trap, if this doctor with the ridiculous tie was really a KGB agent come to take her home. She tried to tug the hospital gown farther down her leg. "What trouble?"

The doctor, clearly exasperated at having to spell things out so clearly, shook his head. "You're pregnant," he said, miming a round belly above his own.

"No," Maya said. She hadn't recognized the word—not in English—but the gesture was unmistakable. She wrapped her arms around herself as if to keep this bad news out, as if her not believing or accepting it would make it not true. "No."

"Have you had sexual intercourse recently?"

Maya shook her head. She'd felt too sick to even think of men, let alone sleep with one, let alone get herself pregnant.

"About a month ago?"

And then, she remembered it, the red carpet of the hotel, the bottle that they'd emptied, Kennedy's face on the television. Ivan.

The doctor, seeing that Maya had understood, began giving her a host of instructions: "You're too thin. You're going to need to work on that. Make sure you get plenty of vegetables and some organ meats—liver, if you can stomach it . . ." but Maya did not hear any of them, nor did she see the prescription for vitamin pills he put in her hand, nor did she hear the door close behind him. She was so wrapped up in her thoughts that she did not know where she was until the nurse popped in and, surprised to still see her there, demanded she get changed.

Maya left the clinic in a daze. Snow fell thickly, sticking to her hair and eyelashes, but she did not notice, and she did not brush it away. Cold as it was, the world was not loud enough to compete with the roar in her head.

She was pregnant, and Ivan was the father. They had shared misery and made a child.

This was not how children were supposed to appear. It was not love that had drawn her and Ivan together on that terrifying night. It was not even lust. It was their shared fear that Natasha hated both of them. Even now, even thousands of miles away, Natasha was the great sun they orbited around, the center of their world. She, and not Maya, was meant to carry Ivan's child. She, and not Maya, was meant to be on this tour. Like a fool, Maya had fought her fate. She had taken Natasha's place and upset the natural order of things, and now the world had come undone, and now a new person would bear the brunt of it.

The snow crunched under Maya's feet, a sensation that reminded her of home, which depressed her but brought surprising clarity. She would never, ever, tell Ivan. They'd been linked in guilt once before, and it had nearly broken them. To have a child, to be forever connected through a child—that was unthinkable. No, let Ivan go to Yekaterinburg with his wife. Let him disappear.

But could she imagine having a child at all? Maya dug her hands into her pockets and shuddered. She'd forgotten to ask how far along she was and what her options were in America. She tried to picture herself with a baby, living in Katusha's abysmal apartment, or anywhere. How could she dance if she was a mother? How could she bring forth beautiful things from her body if another person depended on it to stay alive?

"After everything I've done," Maya thought, "I have turned out like my mother." Elizaveta must have asked herself all these questions so many years ago—and as the Nazis encircled the city. No wonder she'd chosen to do what she did.

Ever since she'd learned about her mother's suicide, Maya had thought there was something wanting in her, that if she'd only been prettier or quieter or pinker or rounder as an infant her mother wouldn't have chosen death. Now pregnant herself, and alone, Maya understood that Elizaveta's decision hadn't been about her at all. No child could have willed Elizaveta to live. She'd been lost long before her daughters were born.

Maya, buttoning her coat around her belly and whoever lay inside it, felt new compassion for her mother. Perhaps Elizaveta's death was less an abandonment and more an acknowledgement of insufficiency. Surely she'd known her children wouldn't be left to die, that Katusha or the man who lived down the hallway would discover them. Maybe she'd loved them the only way she could.

Uncertain of her destination, Maya wandered from the sidewalk and began to cross the street, stepping into another set of footprints to keep her ankles dry. She reached the other side and then kept following the footprints, step by step, as if someone had left these tracks here for her to follow, as if they'd lead back to her fate.

CHAPTER NINETEEN

George Balanchine sat in a mildewy hotel room in Leningrad, arguing with his wife on a transatlantic phone call that was costing him the equivalent of a tin of good caviar.

Establishing the connection took an hour, and when the call finally went through, Tanny was not happy to hear he was coming home. "Just stay there," she said. "We both know you're not lonely." She knew, as everyone did, that Balanchine was never without a muse in the company, and that the current season's muse had come with them to Leningrad.

But Balanchine was in no mood for flinging marital daggers, and he spent the entirety of the call with his hand over his eyes. He lived in a waking nightmare. His days were a monotony of irritating interviews and press appearances so contrived his skin crawled. His shoulder bursitis was now so agonizing he could barely pull on his shirts. He never felt at rest or at peace, knowing full well that everywhere he went was bugged—even now, he knew that agents listened to his phone call, which both enraged and embarrassed him—and he slept even less than he had in Moscow. Important work awaited him back home—his true home, not this false one: a palatial theater was being constructed for the company at Lincoln Center, and without him there to supervise, the orchestra pit had been built too small, and now he had to go back and correct this.

But none of this moved Tanny. She refused to let him come home, and when the connection cut off, Balanchine lay face down on the bed, still fully dressed, and turned off the lights. In his exhaustion, he did not stop to wonder what the agents who'd bugged his room thought of his pitiable situation. It's better that he didn't think about this, because the agents, who were excited to eavesdrop on a man feted for his ways with women, were laughing at him: This famous man, a Russian who called himself an American, was kept out of the house by a crippled wife? Balanchine lay on the lumpy bed and tried not to think or feel anything, and in the suite two floors above him, the agents laughed and laughed and laughed.

He slept fitfully, plagued by the unease that had begun haunting him again the moment the plane landed in Moscow. He'd held his own for the first leg of the tour, bolstered by the pride he felt in representing America. It helped that he'd never spent much time in Moscow, and he didn't have an idealized image of the city in his mind. The busyness of his schedule kept him from sinking too far into sadness.

But his defenses were no match for Leningrad. He insisted on referring to it as "Petrograd," as he had in his childhood, even when other Russians corrected him. For decades he'd thought that, by doing so, he was helping keep the city's true spirit alive. But then the train pulled into the city, the place where he'd grown up and learned to dance and married Tamara Geva as a teenager. As soon as he stepped out of the train, he knew that Petrograd was lost. Still possessing its imperial shell, it was a sadder sight than Moscow: so many edifices had been torn down or lost in the war or built over with depressing cement facades that made even the grandest halls look like decrepit bunkers. It was like seeing the decaying carcass of your mother—the familiarity only made it more horrifying.

Kazan Cathedral, now a shrine to the atheist cause, broke his heart. Zealous Bolsheviks had pried the icons from the cathedral walls—the same icons his uncle had venerated after being ordained a bishop—and replaced them with propaganda posters decrying religion's horrors: red-eyed cannibals eating Christ's corpse with jagged forks, gap-toothed grannies pulling children to church by their hair. Even places that retained a sense of themselves, like the Vaganova, which was virtually unchanged from the day he'd left it, depressed him. He'd hurried to his old school almost as soon as he'd stepped off the train, but when he arrived at that familiar yellow building with its beautiful oak door, he stopped on the doorstep. He could not go in. The past wasn't just past—it had been obliterated.

In a perverse twist, the company's reception—and his own—was far warmer here; he was feted and fawned over and celebrated even as he felt himself sinking further into despair. He met many people from his past, people he'd missed and dreamed of seeing again, but this depressed him too. His old friends lived in decrepit little apartments, even more cramped than the ghettos of New York, and his brother, whom he hadn't seen since their childhoods, was a frumpy, doddering old man. Time had even caught up with his beloved dance teachers; these heroes of his boyhood were no longer the beautiful and glorious young men and women of his memories but elderly has-beens, bent and wrinkled and worn. That he himself was also aging only compounded his horror. He had an abhorrence of age and ugliness, and in Petrograd, these things surrounded him on all sides. Even Nevsky Prospect brought him no pleasure—it made him think of living on the streets during the war, of seeing a horse collapse and then be picked clean by starving passersby.

He had wept for an hour before calling Tanny, and now, in bed in his rumpled black suit, he cried and he cried until his voice went hoarse.

He still sounded raspy the next morning, when he had to return once more to the Vaganova. This time, he would have no choice but to go in; Furtseva insisted he coach some student there. At first, he'd refused—why did Furtseva call him, of all people, for such a small task?—but a call from the American embassy persuaded him. "Please," the envoy begged. "Things are still so tenuous. Don't cause a ruckus."

No, she was not a student, he corrected himself on the walk there, his hands sheltering in his pockets from the crisp November air. She was a dancer. No, she was not a dancer, she was an actress. Balanchine approached the same oak door and paused again on the doorstep, his fists balled as if ready to defend himself from ambush. He took a deep breath and opened the door. "Whoever she is," he muttered to himself as the great oak door creaked open, "I'd better get this over with quickly."

Natasha, too, had lingered uncertainly at the great oak door, unwilling to face this place she'd known so well. She hadn't set foot in the school since the night of her accident. The only thing that gave her the strength to enter was knowing that if she didn't, she'd lose everything all over again.

Now she waited anxiously in the Petipa Room. Furtseva had made it clear that she was doing Natasha a favor by having this great choreographer come evaluate her, but his accomplishments did not interest Natasha—particularly given Maya's burgeoning success. "What's so hard about putting steps together?" she thought, observing herself in the mirror. "Anyone can do it."

No, what interested Natasha about Balanchine was that he had left Russia, as she'd once hoped to do. He'd left and made a wonderful life for himself. Ilya had told her that it wasn't possible to truly leave, that you carried your homeland with you wherever you went, that the best you could hope for was to play the game and curry favor for yourself. Natasha wondered if this was true, and she hoped that Balanchine would help her understand.

So far, Ilya's advice had served her well: she'd built a new life thanks to the government's generosity—a beautiful apartment, a promising future, a salary. Still, leaning over the barre like she had as a young girl, Natasha wondered what her life would have been if she'd left when she'd had the chance. What would it be like to be Maya in New York, posing for photographers and dining out at a hundred restaurants a year? What a waste, sending Maya to lunch with the Kennedys. She was terrible at small talk, even in Russian.

Natasha sighed and scratched at her tights. It was strange, wearing tights again, pulling on a leotard. Natasha had felt grief as she dressed that morning in her hotel, and to quiet this grief, she told herself that this might be the beginning of things, not a reminder of their end. She knew, in her bones, that she would never dance again like she had here. But she hoped to dance one last time, her elegance captured on an illuminated screen for all to see. There was something so comforting about imagining a roll of film containing images of her in motion. If Balanchine could help her, she would have permanent proof that she'd once been graceful. No matter what else happened in the world, some back storeroom would contain this proof, and perhaps that would give Natasha the strength to accept her dancing days were over—a strength Elizaveta had never found.

Natasha was grateful she'd come on a Sunday and wouldn't have to face any of her old teachers. Her sense memories were even stranger than being in the Vaganova itself. Her hand slipped over the familiar varnished barre as if they'd never been parted. Everything at the school felt the same—the shoes, the tights, the well-worn floor. The room even smelled the same to Natasha, of warm dust and rosin and sweat. She kept expecting to turn around and see Vasili and Vasilia quarreling in the corner, or Karinska whispering confidences to Olaf, or, worst of all, Maya behind her at the barre. It was like warming up in a roomful of ghosts.

She was grateful no one from the Vaganova days could see her now. In the absence of a strict regimen, and eight hours a day of dancing, she'd grown breasts. Her stomach, though far from paunchy, was much rounder than it had been when she was a student here. She hoped that Balanchine would not comment on the state of her body.

She had no idea what to expect from him. Was he going to be handsy? Dance teachers always were—you had to touch someone to efficiently tell them how to move—but some teachers' touch lingered more than others. And some great men had become great because of their cruelty and ruthlessness. Even Bondarchuk, who reminded Natasha more of a giant black bear than a man, had let his eyes rest on her breasts when she'd tried on a revealing gown. You always had to be watchful; you never knew what these sorts of men would do.

The door opened, and Natasha's spine went straight out of habit. The man who walked in looked nothing like she anticipated. He was neither tall nor handsome, but he carried himself like a prince.

He started when he saw her, taking two steps backward. Natasha blushed, thinking he must have been horrified by her body, and she wished she could shrink down into a little mouse and escape through a hole in the corner.

"Excuse me," he said, wrinkling his brow and looking intently at her, "but have we met before?" His voice was nasally, and his Russian was stilted and formal, like it was a stiff jacket he'd reluctantly put on.

"I . . . I don't think so," Natasha said. She searched her mind for any reason that she would look familiar to George Balanchine.

"You have never been to America?"

Natasha shook her head.

"Forgive me," he said, shrugging. "I must be getting old." He clapped his hands. "Well," he said, taking off his jacket and draping it delicately over a chair, "shall we get started?"

Over the next quarter of an hour, he tested each of her limbs, searching for whatever strength and flexibility she had left. It had been clear to him the moment he'd entered the room that she was never going to be a great dancer—something in her had been broken beyond repair. As soon as she moved, he spotted the stiffness in her spine. But Furtseva had said Natasha did not need to be a great dancer—she only needed to waltz. "And do a little folk dance, if that isn't too difficult for you," she'd said. It was clear from her voice that Furtseva relished delegating to him, the great prodigal, this humble duty. When Balanchine protested—surely someone else could teach this girl to folk dance—Furtseva insulted him. "Perhaps you've been so long in the West that you've forgotten your heritage," she said. Balanchine resented her insinuation. Thank God he'd soon depart this place and its graceless people.

Natasha, now unused to moving in this way, found herself sweating profusely, which was a great humiliation to her. When Balanchine asked her to do a port de bras, and she raised her arms and saw dark sweat stains covering her armpits, she flinched, and this flinching made the familiar spot in her back spasm so sharply and suddenly that she cried out.

"*That* hurt?" Balanchine said. It was not a good sign. His own muscles had tensed when Natasha cried out. As this appointment dragged on, this girl with little breasts began to remind him of some of the worst moments of his wife's recovery, when Tanny had accepted that she would not walk again, but he did not. Natasha reminded him of everything he'd tried with Tanny: every doctor, every physical therapist, every quack treatment and remedy that was brought to their door. She reminded him of calling up all his Russian friends, who filled his house with holy oils, ancient relics, and miraculous icons that exuded myrrh and smelled like his boyhood. But none of them had done any good.

He had failed Tanny, and now, alone in this room with this dancer who reminded him so much of a lost love from his boyhood, he had the feeling that he was failing all over again.

After Natasha tried a port de bras and winced a second time, Balanchine shook his head. "I'm sorry," he said. "It just can't be done. Better stick to acting, dear." He couldn't bear to see her disappointment—to witness her recognition that her dancing days were over, just as Tanny once had. He picked up his jacket, folded it over his arm, and strode out of the room before Natasha could respond. As he left the school, the heavy front door slammed behind him as if in surprise at his sudden exit. He picked up his pace until he was nearly running, and as soon as he was safe in his room, he picked up the phone, called Lincoln Kirstein, and told him to book him on the next flight home.

The second call he made was to Furtseva. "Very sorry, but she's too far gone," he said. "Why not hire a dancing double? It's what they did all the time back when I worked in Hollywood. You'd be amazed how many beautiful actresses have feet of lead."

Bondarchuk balked at this suggestion when Furtseva called him with the news. "Natasha's essence is so vibrant and pure—like a clean sheet of paper," he said. "How could we possibly find a dancer who can replicate that?"

Irina laid a hand on her husband's shoulder. "Dearest," she said, "I know just the girl."

CHAPTER TWENTY

Everyone always expects sea changes to descend gradually, as if there were encoded into the decency of the world some kind of law requiring calamities to announce themselves. This desire is not unnatural; if tidal waves followed some sort of emblem in the sky—a reverse rainbow appearing before the flood—fewer lives would be ruined and lost.

No, not an unnatural desire, but an impossible one nonetheless: it ignores the hard truth that many of the changes that happen in the world do not rain down from the sky but come from the hands of men—capricious men, self-serving men, men whose decisions sometimes depend more on the digestibility of their breakfast than on sense.

Men, for instance, like Nikita Khrushchev, who, after seeing several nipples at an exhibition of abstract art in Moscow, declared that no obscenity would be allowed in Soviet art any longer—an impulsive declaration that changed the course of Russian art for good. "What is hung here is simply un-Soviet," he said, swinging his arm toward the paintings. "It's amoral. Art should ennoble the individual and arouse him to action. And what have you set out here? Who painted this picture? I want to talk to him. What's the good of a picture like this? Wallpapering a urinal?"

"Gentlemen," he said, narrowing his eyes at the artists as he strode from the gallery, "we are declaring war on you!"

The deputy minister of culture, who had witnessed Khrushchev's ire and knew full well who would bear the brunt of it, hurried back to the office to warn Furtseva, who had been busy working on reportage of the Kirov's tour of the United States. Pictures of Maya's choreography littered her desk, and Furtseva leafed through it as Khrushchev called and hung her out to dry—and this is why, later, when she saw Maya for the first time, she intensely disliked her at once, though she never realized the correlation. Khrushchev shouted at Furtseva so loud and so long that her ear rang long after she put down the receiver.

"Of course something would happen like this," Furtseva thought. She began grinding her teeth, a habit to which she turned only when she was afraid. "And right when I'm about to make my masterpiece." She was referring to *War and Peace*, which, though behind schedule and immensely over budget, was fully underway. After the Hermitage had been deemed too plain for the set of Natasha's waltz—three decades before, the government had sold off some of the museum's most glorious paintings in a desperate grab for cash—a soundstage at Mosfilm had been outfitted as the interior of an opulent palace. Furtseva was supposed to go over and inspect it later that week.

Yekaterina Furtseva leaned over her desk, turning Khrushchev's words over and over in her mind. He'd insisted that lewdness and indecency were taking over Russian art. "I won't have it, Furtseva," he'd said. "No more sexual nonsense on any stage or screen or page or canvas in this whole fucking country. If I find so much as a single pubic hair in anything coming out of your office, I will send you someplace so miserable that you'll wish you'd never met me." She wasn't sure if he referred to an awful clerkship or something worse. She did not want to find out.

Furtseva began to rub her forehead with her palms—thanks to Khrushchev, she was very late for lunch, which had given her a headache—and her elbow slipped on a glossy publicity photograph lying on a pile on her desk. It was of Maya, dancing in her own ballet in America, her leg extended straight in the air. Maya gazed right at the camera with her signature seductiveness, the same gaze that had given her such power over Madame Karinska's classroom.

Over Furtseva, however, Maya's gaze held no such power. She had been raised long after Soviet free love was dismissed as an outmoded and even dangerous sensibility; such ideas were outlawed and then disappeared from the public mind altogether, along with the civic conveniences, such as the easy obtainment of abortion, that had made these ideas sustainable. She had little use for sexuality of any persuasion; her marriage, though politically advantageous, was loveless, and after her marital relations had produced the child she was expected to have (after all, the population must be sustained), she ceased engaging in them altogether.

Even before this, she'd never been one of those women who had an easy time obtaining lovers. In her childhood, she'd been ridiculed for her frownish mouth and thick ankles. As a young woman, she'd been ignored in favor of girls who smiled readily and had tiny, waifish waists and slim legs—legs, she thought, though she was not entirely aware of it, like Maya's. She crumpled up the picture and threw it in her wastebasket.

As Maya's desecrated image settled into its new home among cigarette butts and paper scraps, the real Maya boarded a stale-smelling bus to Mosfilm and the set of *War and Peace*, where she was expected for a costume fitting. She'd flown in from New York the night before and was jet-lagged and worn out in anticipation, knowing that, after leaving Mosfilm, she had to head to the Bolshoi for a rehearsal of her new *Bolero* ballet. Her nerves felt frayed; they hummed with a frazzled energy, and every time the bus stopped, it filled her with dread. Maya was weary, but no longer because of nausea; since she'd learned she was pregnant, her symptoms had mysteriously disappeared. Still, she was acutely aware that every time the bus stopped and then lurched forward again, it was hurtling her closer to a meeting that she'd successfully avoided for nearly three years.

And yet, she'd felt a twinge of relief when her company director pulled her aside on their last day in America and told her, with no small measure of pride, that she'd been chosen as her sister's dancing double in *War and Peace*. After all, she was still pregnant and did not know what to do about it; after all, Natasha was still her sister—to whom can we turn in moments of great indecision if not to our siblings? Of course, she wouldn't tell Natasha who the father was. She didn't need to know.

As she debated her ability to keep such a secret, Maya looked out the window and saw two little girls jumping rope with the same length of twine. One of the girls got distracted by the passing bus and tripped on the rope, and her little friend went to comfort her. Maya winced. Natasha had once been the only person in the world in whom she'd confide. Natasha had always listened to her with patience and love.

Maya was indulging in the habit of those who have not seen a relative in a long while; in the absence of contact, members of splintered families flatten their relatives into demons, whose virtues have been resented into nonexistence, or angels, whose faults do not and could never have existed. Maya's guilt edged her toward the latter.

Maya might not have been so nostalgic if she hadn't met an old friend on her connecting flight to Moscow. She'd settled into her aisle seat—all the better for trips to the bathroom, whose frequency was beginning to be comic—and then heard her seatmate exclaim her name. The woman was about her age, the hints of lines just beginning to form around her eyes and mouth. She laughed at Maya's puzzled expression. "Ah, of course you don't remember me," the woman said. "It's Anya. From the Vaganova."

Maya's body stiffened. After all, she was the one who had ratted Anya out—but, judging by Anya's enthusiasm, she'd never learned this. For the rest of their flight, Anya jumped from memories of their school days—did Maya remember the way Karinska's bracelets jangled as she led them through pliés, or the particular viscosity of the potato soup?—to gushing about her new life. After the Vaganova, her father apprenticed her to a seamstress in Sarajevo, where she'd become a costume designer. Now she was flying home to interview at the Bolshoi and the Kirov both. "Personally, I hope it's the Kirov. They might even take me along on the tour to Europe next month," she said, clapping her hands on her face. "Can you imagine? I'll tell you, getting kicked out of the Vaganova was the best thing that ever happened to me. At the time, I thought it was the end of the world, but it made me sober up. Sometimes you need a kick in the pants to find your fate."

Remembering this conversation gave Maya courage as she sped ever closer to her sister. The bus rounded a corner so sharply that Maya knocked knees with the elderly man beside her. "After all," Maya thought as the gentleman recoiled out of a sense of propriety, "she's made a good life for herself. Maybe things turned out all right in the end." A deeper, wiser part of Maya knew this was foolishness, knew there was nothing noble in ruining someone's life, but Maya ignored it. She leaned away from the window and settled more easily into her seat.

The bus pulled up to Mosfilm, the largest film studio in the country. Its grandiose campus had first been erected in the 1920s after a group of young Soviet filmmakers had returned from a trip to Hollywood with ambitions to make Moscow the film capital of the world. Its layers of white stone put Maya in mind of a giant cake, evidence that her appetite was returning.

As Maya stepped into the large, high-ceilinged lobby, swarming with people who all appeared to have some urgent business to do, she even began to wonder if she'd done her sister a favor by ending her ballet career. At best, her own career would only last a handful of years before her body started to give out, even without the pregnancy. But Mosfilm, with its air of solidity and permanence, felt like a place that could guide an artist from young adulthood to old age, a place that could sweep you up in its current and never let you go.

Perhaps, Maya thought, she had not only saved her sister from defecting but had given her the key to her happiness, just as she had for Anya. As she pushed her way through the crowded lobby, she began to imagine the luxuries that made up her sister's new life as an actress—new clothes whenever she wanted them, a palatial apartment, endless evenings in glamorous restaurants spent on gentlemen's arms—luxuries that suited Natasha's taste much better than the hardships Maya had known in life on the road. Maya had lived on canned sardines and toasted-cheese sandwiches made with hotel-room irons. She'd become accustomed to the crust of hotel sheets, the monotony and noise of a life lived in liminal spaces: airports and waiting rooms and trains. Natasha had her own apartment. Surely that was the pinnacle of happiness. Surely, Maya thought, looking around in wonder at the soundstage that had been turned into a palace, her sister lived like a queen.

But Natasha had had a miserable morning. Her eyebrows had been tweezed, her upper lip had been waxed not once but twice, after a first attempt by a stylist-in-training had proven disastrous, and her skin was red and raw thanks to an allergic reaction to expired foundation.

A little bald man with watery eyes was tending to her fingernails and pushing back her cuticles with such force that every now and again it made her yelp. A hairdresser was in the final stages of attaching a large dark wig over Natasha's hair with an untold number of bobby pins that appeared to function only if jabbed deep into Natasha's scalp. A third and final attendant was, for some reason, polishing the little white heels Natasha was supposed to wear to the ball. Natasha felt less like an actress and more like a doomed virgin being readied for sacrifice to bloodthirsty gods.

"Stop fidgeting," said the hairdresser. She'd been flown in from Paris for the express purpose of doing Natasha's hair for this scene.

"Sorry," Natasha said, but she wasn't. Today was for her. Natasha, who was prone to having unjustifiably grand thoughts on her very best days, was not deluding herself in thinking this. It was true; the entire purpose of the ballroom scene was to showcase her character attending her very first ball, experiencing life out in society for the first time, dancing her first waltz with Prince Andrei, who was supposed to fall madly in love with her on this day.

Natasha had reflected on this as she wandered through the set that morning, up the towering marble staircase with a gold scrollwork banister, through the majestic hall surrounded on all sides by mirrors, gold candle sconces, and chandeliers. Much of the finery had been constructed just for the film; Bondarchuk's office contained elaborate blueprints for fifteen different kinds of chandeliers, which had been built by hand, and an enormous army of seamstresses had worked for months to outfit the ball-goers. Everything else was borrowed; Furtseva worked her magic (dark, foreboding magic though it was) and the coffers of Russia opened themselves for this noble purpose. Fifty-eight museums, along with the jewel boxes of hundreds of ordinary citizens, had loaned their wares to the production. Once, these jewels had been precious family secrets tucked under bedsteads and sewn into coat linings by grandparents and great-grandparents during the Revolution; now they glittered on wrists and earlobes and arms for all to see—and soon, the whole world would see them, would see Russia as it once was (or, at least, as the Russians themselves imagined it).

After so many years apart from the world in her godmother's dingy apartment, after being cast from the spotlight into an interminable season of isolation and purposelessness, after the humiliation of having to learn to walk again, after losing everything, Natasha did not accept her rise to all this grandeur as an exception to the path of her life, but as her due. After all, she had been marked as someone special from her youth; the accident, though it had marred her body and broken her bones, had not robbed her of her *self,* this luminous self that all of her teachers had noticed and admired. "You are destined for great things," they'd told her. And she believed they had been right.

Outwardly, Natasha comported herself with dignity, like a regent at her coronation—as someone receiving an honor that is very great, but also inevitable. But Natasha was trembling, and not just for fear that the hairdresser would pierce her scalp with more pins. She shook with anxiety at the thought of seeing her sister again.

It was a particularly bad bit of luck for Maya that she walked in just then. Maya had been rehearsing the friendliness and ease with which she would address her sister—"Just as if nothing had happened," she had repeated to herself as she came down the hallway—and she was so caught up in her fantasy of a happy reunion that she did not notice the way her sister went pale when she entered the room, and she went ahead with her planned ease and friendliness and said, in a tone so playful it made even the shoemaker at Natasha's feet look up, "The wayward sister has returned!"

Nobody—not Natasha, the hairdresser, the manicurist, nor the shoemaker—knew how to take this, and the four of them stared at Maya for a moment as they each tried to suss out what she had meant. Did Maya mean that *she* was the wayward sister—an odd phrase, with its peculiar glaze of guilt, whose significance meant nothing to anyone but Natasha—or that Natasha was? Both meanings, as the four of them turned over the possibilities in their minds, had their own unsuitability. Maya stood there with her arms outstretched, in anticipation of what—an embrace?—even she did not know. As everyone continued staring, and Natasha did not stir from her seat, Maya's arms dropped to her sides. The shoemaker, unable to look on at the awkwardness of this scene, returned to his work with renewed vigor, attacking Natasha's spotless shoes with the same tender alacrity with which he would have cleaned the muddy boots of a child.

The hairdresser, whose name was Natalia, spoke first. "How happy you must be," she said, settling the wig into its final resting place, "to be reunited." She said this not because it appeared to be true—it certainly didn't—but because it was what ought to have happened, and everyone knew it. "I can't imagine going two weeks without seeing my sister," the hairdresser said, her speech now hampered by the presence of several pins in her mouth, which she had put there for the sole purpose of preventing herself from talking. "Yes, you must be very happy," she said, and then she stuck four more hairpins in her mouth and mumbled something unintelligible.

"Of course, we are very happy," Natasha said, with a queenly and tranquil air. She stared straight ahead at herself in the mirror. "You'll have to forgive me, Maya, but I'm under strict instructions not to turn my head until the hairdresser is finished," she said, though the hairdresser had said no such thing. Natalia, the shoemaker, and the manicurist, all understanding their roles in maintaining Natasha's regal air, finished their work and backed away from the actress, who rose, walked to her sister—who hadn't moved from the doorway—and embraced her.

It was not a long embrace. It was also not a particularly emotive one. It was just two bodies exerting pressure on each other, and it did not communicate anything to either sister except that they, despite it all, were still sisters, meeting in public after a long absence from each other's company, and as such, this was what they had to do.

They had just released each other when Antonina, the costume mistress, marched through the door, her white apron starched into stiff submission. She told Natasha, with her usual brusqueness, to take off her dress. "And that wig," she said, speaking now to Natalia, "it'll have to come off too."

Natalia threw up her hands. "I just spent half an hour pinning it on!"

Antonina shrugged. "The double's dress won't be ready 'til tomorrow, and the boss says it's more important to see how it looks on the sister, since she's the one dancing."

Whether due to the ease of the process or to Natalia's irritation—which was considerable—the wig's removal was much faster than its installation, and Antonina shooed Natasha and Maya behind the dressing curtain soon after. "I assume you don't mind changing together," Antonina said from the other side of the curtain, "your being sisters and all."

They stood facing each other, the sounds of Antonina and the hairdresser bustling around coming through the thin blue curtain. It was the first moment they were alone and, because the hairdresser had grumbled aloud all through the removal of the wig, the first moment they could really speak to each other.

Maya, whose mind was already overstimulated and fatigued from her travels, could not think of anything to say to her sister now that they were face to face. She desperately wanted to—she wanted some sort of absolution, some sort of reassurance that Natasha still loved her, and she would have said anything to this end, but she hadn't eaten in a long time and all of her thoughts crashed into each other and destroyed themselves. Natasha, who had apparently been waiting for Maya to speak as well, opened her mouth to say something, but Antonina's voice came again from the other side of the curtain and told them to hurry.

When they were little, and even not so little, Maya and Natasha had never felt any sort of shame or embarrassment about seeing each other's bodies; being dancers required it, and there's no room for bashfulness when you share a bedroom that was once a closet. But this attitude required intimacy and trust, and both of these had been broken, and too much time had passed, and both girls had become women, and they did not know each other anymore. Some sort of nonverbal understanding of this nature passed between the two of them, and they turned their backs to each other and started to undress.

Maya took off her dress with the swiftness of one who is used to quick costume changes. At the sight of her own stomach, Maya suddenly remembered she was pregnant and that being pregnant meant her stomach, which she'd spent decades honing to steely perfection, would begin to distend and swell. Was it swelling already? She put her hand to her chest and bent over in an attempt to see, which of course made her stomach stick out much more than usual.

"What are you doing?" Natasha said.

Maya spun around. Her sister was still dressed. "Nothing," Maya said.

Natasha pointed to her back, a gesture that made Maya cringe. "The zipper's stuck," she said. "Will you help?"

Maya nodded. Natasha turned around and Maya tugged at the zipper. "It really is stuck," Maya said.

"Pull harder," Natasha said. She glanced back at Maya. "They've really been fattening you up on this tour, haven't they?" she said, and Maya's whole body went cold. Her sister was inscrutable; she could have said this out of cruelty, or she could have truly seen that something was different. If Natasha could intuit such a thing, perhaps she could intuit something worse, like the identity of the child's father, but Maya pushed this thought away. She let herself believe that telling Natasha about her pregnancy could be her salvation. She could tell her, and the knowledge of this crisis could reaffirm their sisterly affection, and—

"Are you even pulling?" Natasha said. "You don't want to see Antonina mad—and I've got a lot of work to do, Maya, unlike you, I don't have all day—"

Maya tugged hard and the zipper came undone so quickly that Natasha toppled over.

"What is it?" Antonina yelled from the other side of the curtain. "You better not have torn that dress. It took my seamstresses six weeks to find that fabric."

"We're fine," Natasha said, though she wasn't sure they were. "Is it torn?" she whispered, staggering to her feet and pulling off the dress with alarm.

Both girls bent over the dress, inspecting the gauzy fabric for tears, but they didn't find any, and Natasha turned her back to Maya to give her privacy, even though they'd just seen each other naked, and held the dress out to her.

Half a dozen people were waiting for them, and Antonina's grumblings were getting louder. But Maya didn't reach for the dress. She didn't move at all. Then she said, in an even smaller whisper than Natasha's, "Does it still hurt?"

"Does what still hurt?"

"Your back."

It was the first time she'd seen Natasha's back since the accident—that back she'd known so well, the shoulder blades and constellations of tiny moles she'd memorized all those hours standing behind her at the barre. Natasha's vertebrae poked out above her slip, and Maya wondered which of them had been shattered—shattered at her own command. She wondered if she could see it if she looked closely enough. She put a hand on her sister's bare back. Ivan, perhaps, had thought he was protecting Natasha, and Maya had told herself she was too—but now, staring at Natasha's vertebrae, she knew there had been nothing noble about her own intentions. She had wanted to be Natasha, to rip Natasha's promising future from her hands and try it on for herself.

Natasha turned around and now, naked, shoeless, wigless, without the coterie of attendants who'd swarmed around her when Maya first entered the room, looked nothing like the woman who had taken Maya's breath away. Her hair was flat, her slip was stained under the armpits, and mascara flaked beneath her eyes. And now, because of her, Natasha would never stand at a barre again.

Gone was any illusion that she, by ending her sister's ballet career, had made her life better, had kept her safe. She had broken her sister, and now neither of them would ever be whole again.

"Not really," Natasha said. Her voice sounded too full, and Maya looked up and saw tears in her sister's eyes. "Not anymore." She shoved the dress into Maya's hands and went out from behind the curtain.

CHAPTER TWENTY-ONE

Rehearsing any sort of large undertaking—particularly one involving lit candles and several hundred dancing people—is a thousand times more difficult than the act itself. To fulfill its obligations to convention and cliché, the rehearsal of such an undertaking must fulfill at least two of three criteria: it must go far beyond schedule; it must prove so complicated that at least one member of the party will threaten to quit; and several people must, over the course of the rehearsal, be injured. (Fainting from exhaustion also fulfills this last requirement.) Only then can the parties involved proceed calmly to their performance, knowing that their traditional obligations of preshow disaster have been fulfilled and, having thus gotten catastrophe out of the way, the event itself will be perfect.

Fate smiled on Sergei Bondarchuk: he got all three difficulties out of the way at once. They'd allotted two hours for the extras to learn their waltz and to practice. Yuri Burmeister, the Siberian dance master who'd been brought in to teach the extras how to waltz, spent an hour and a half explaining the history of the waltz. When Bondarchuk interrupted and asked him to hurry—they only had half an hour until the crew had to go home—Yuri reacted violently, shouting that he'd never been treated like this, he'd been hired for his expertise and now was being mocked, and he would not stand for it; he would leave. In the course of delivering this tirade, Yuri flailed his arms around in protest and smacked a young extra, whose nose started bleeding and whose female companion instantly fainted at the sight of his blood.

Somehow, they salvaged the afternoon. Bondarchuk humbled himself and apologized; Yuri, chastened by the inadvertent shedding of blood, relented and ran the extras through a dance tutorial so dizzying that even the hardiest among them felt slightly nauseous, and all of the crew still made it home in time for their suppers.

Maya, who had time only to pawn an apple off an extra for her dinner, rushed to change out of her dress and into her street clothes. She was exhausted, but she still had to be at a rehearsal for *Bolero*—and, for some reason, she'd invited Natasha to come with her to the Bolshoi. Even Maya did not understand why she had done this. Perhaps she wanted Natasha to see how well she'd done with what she'd been given—that is, with what she'd taken away.

Like her sister, Maya had been cared for by the state since her childhood; it was only fitting that the Russian premiere of her work would take place here in Moscow, just down the street from the Kremlin, where the ministers of culture worked tirelessly to ensure that Soviet artists had what they needed. It wasn't like that in America: she'd been stunned to learn that there wasn't even an American state ballet company. Maya knew she was lucky. Away from the pressure and hardships of touring, she felt less resentful of her lot in life and the state's role in it. She felt a little bit like a child who'd been given a set of watercolors, eager to show her mother the beautiful picture she'd painted. Perhaps some Kremlin dignitaries would attend and marvel at what she'd created with their investment.

Natasha didn't understand why she'd agreed to come along. She pondered this decision as she and Maya walked along a busy Moscow street. For three years, she'd carefully avoided attending any ballet performances or encountering dance in any way. Watching the rehearsal this afternoon—even the amateur waltzers, with all their stiffness and clumsiness—had stung her heart. When Maya invited her, she should have said no, she should have made up an excuse—but instead, she accepted.

As they walked to the bus stop, and Maya told Natasha about life on the road—careful to share only the hardships, Natasha noticed, and none of the glories—Natasha began to realize why she'd agreed to come to this rehearsal. Maya had taken so many things from her: her career, her future—she'd even stolen her waltz with Lev. Natasha did not want Maya to think that losing dance still pained her. Instead, she smiled too wide at her sister and imagined that she was coated head to toe in some sort of enamel that no one could crack, not even Maya.

The wind was bitter, and there was not much time before the bus was due to arrive. The two girls, bundled in an array of scarves and coats and kerchiefs, hurried along so fast it was hard for them to catch their breath. Maya was in the middle of relating a long and uninteresting anecdote about a time when she and Ivan had ironed toasted-cheese sandwiches and nearly caught a bedsheet on fire. It was the kind of story that is only funny to the person who has lived it, and Maya, forgetting herself, laughed as she described the look on Ivan's face when he realized he'd seared the edges of his fingers instead of his sandwich.

Natasha stopped walking. "Please stop talking about Ivan," she said. A hairline fracture was already appearing in her implacable veneer.

Maya stopped too. "Sorry," she said, and when Natasha started her loping walk again, Maya hurried to catch her.

They passed an advertisement for the Kirov posted in a café window. Maya's name was front and center in big red letters, and beneath it, *Our new star choreographer*.

"A star!" Natasha clucked her tongue. "Aren't you lucky."

"Yes," Maya said, uneasy. "Very lucky. In some ways."

"In every way," Natasha said, much more angrily than she intended. "You've toured the world, you've met the Kennedys, you've been to all the fancy American department stores—"

"Yes, but they were overwhelming—I didn't like them—" She couldn't tell her the truth—that the stacks of sweaters, the rainbowed display of gloves, had brought her no pleasure because everything reminded her of Natasha. How could you tell someone whose life you'd stolen that you wished you could give it back?

"Stop!" Natasha said, slicing the crisp air with a fist. "Stop pretending you didn't like it. I know you, Maya. I know that everything that has happened to you is what you've always wanted."

Maya didn't know how to respond, and they reached the bus stop in silence. Then, after they had stood there for a full minute, shivering, Maya whispered, almost to herself, "Not everything."

"What do you mean?" There was something in Maya's voice that Natasha recognized—the voice a younger Maya used when she was sad or hurt and, after Natasha spent hours coaxing the truth out of her, was ready to talk. It sounded like she was on the verge of a confession.

To Natasha's surprise, she was not sure that she wanted her sister to confess. As long as the secret was unspoken between them, nothing would ever be repaired, and Natasha could continue being angry. "You don't have to talk if you don't want to," Natasha said, looking off into the distance at the coming bus so as not to appear eager. The men and women waiting on a bench for the bus stood and prepared themselves for boarding, shifting purse straps onto shoulders and boxes into arms.

Maya had been suffering inside through the entire conversation, waiting for some opportunity to unburden herself. How could she decide what to do without telling someone? And who could she tell if not her sister? "Natasha," she whispered. Her sister turned to look at her. "I'm pregnant."

The bus stopped at a traffic light, and the men and women who had stood sat back down again. An infant wailed aloud. This was not the confession Natasha wanted, and she didn't know how to respond to it, so she only said, "How far along?"

"Not long."

"Are you keeping it?" Natasha tried to hide her disappointment with questions. She did not want to give Maya the satisfaction of knowing she was hurt.

"I don't know."

They stood in silence for a minute. Their mother must have asked herself this question, once. Perhaps she'd considered visiting one of the underground clinics, the old plying the young with remedies that sometimes worked and sometimes killed. They'd never know why she'd chosen to avoid them. "You shouldn't keep it, you know. It'll ruin your figure," Natasha said, owing not to her strong feelings on the matter—she had none—but a desire to hurt her sister by any means possible. "Does the father know?"

"No," Maya said.

"Who was it? Did Pinky knock you up?" Natasha smiled a little in spite of herself, recalling their old argument about the name of Maya's first love.

"His name wasn't Pinky," Maya said, not returning Natasha's smile. "And does it matter?"

"It matters to me." Natasha did not know why she was pushing her sister to divulge this, but she kept on, though some part of her warned her not to. "It should matter to you too."

"It does matter to me."

"Well then who is it?" Natasha said. "Why wouldn't you want to tell me?"

Maya did not say anything, and in not saying anything, she said everything. The bus pulled up beside them.

The next morning, the extras and actors and crew had all been instructed to arrive early so as to make up for the fiasco of the previous day's rehearsal. Miraculously, nearly everyone obeyed, and all five hundred extras crowded the great artificial hall at nine in the morning, powdered and coiffed and bejeweled. University students, who had not lived through war, walked around with hands on their ornamental sabers, chins raised in pride. Older extras, who had lived through too much war to think weaponry a point of vanity, shook their heads, though they too felt a sort of boyhood joy in the sabers rattling at their sides. And the ladies, most of whom had never worn such fine fabrics and jewels and makeup in their lives, strolled around and noticed whether people were noticing them. It was, between the preening and the posturing, between the vanity and pride, not unlike an actual nineteenth-century ball.

So, too, was the overdue arrival of the guest of honor, who showed up twenty minutes late. Natasha, having overslept—she'd spent half the night on the phone with Lev, weeping over Maya's revelation—rushed to the makeup room, where she was placed in a chair beside her sister, who was already bewigged and in costume. Neither sister said a word to the other, which everyone around them attributed to nerves. Everybody was nervous that day. Natalia attached Natasha's wig at twice the speed she had the day before. A portly and genial makeup artist named Feodor was brought in to ready the sisters' faces for the screen and make them as alike as possible. First, he did Natasha's full face, just like the stage makeup Natasha had applied herself during her dancing years—the thick foundation, the eyebrow pencil, the black mascara stiffening every last eyelash into alertness. Feodor, bouncing around from one side of Natasha to the other, applied so much blush that Natasha thought she looked embarrassed, and then she became embarrassed, and her cheeks grew even pinker. This order of things was so familiar to Natasha—how strange to experience it with her sister sitting beside her, just as she had before every performance of their lives. Natasha wondered if Maya was thinking of the frenzied hour before their Vaganova performances, their classmates skittering all around—Anya, struggling with a false eyelash glued to her cheek, the boys trying to apply eyeliner without making themselves look clownish. The last time they'd experienced this together was the night of the gala. They'd sat beside each other, dabbing their faces with cakey foundation in the same way that they always had. Two hours later, Natasha had been pulled off the stage in a stretcher. Now here they were in Moscow, pretending none of that had ever happened.

Having finished with Natasha, Feodor moved to amend Maya's face. Their bodies were similar enough, and from a distance, their matching wigs and long, thin dresses made them look identical. If you squinted, you couldn't see the details that distinguished them from each other—Natasha's high, wide cheekbones, Maya's beaky nose. But this wasn't good enough for Bondarchuk, who wanted his stand-in to be as convincing as possible and came over to supervise her transformation himself.

"See the way that Natasha's upper lip has these two strong peaks?" Bondarchuk said, and Feodor hovered over Maya with a pink pencil, replicating her sister's mouth.

Feodor was a master of his trade, and even without Bondarchuk's interventions, he peered through his little black-rimmed glasses and saw details in Natasha's face that were so minute she'd never even noticed them herself. He plucked and thinned Maya's eyebrows to match Natasha's. He shaded the sides of her nose until its beakiness all but disappeared. Maya's cheekbones, which sat much lower than her sister's, were magically lifted under Feodor's deft brush. A pair of false eyelashes was produced to make Maya's eyes appear as large as Natasha's. The longer the two sisters sat beside each other, the more alike they became.

At long last—which was too long, considering the time crunch the production faced that day—Feodor and Bondarchuk stepped back to admire their creations, and the costume women who'd gathered to watch applauded their efforts.

"Magnificent," one woman said. "If it weren't for the eyes, you couldn't tell them apart at all."

Bondarchuk patted Feodor on the back, and he bowed like the conductor of a mighty orchestra. "You don't get to be my age in this business without learning a trick or two," he said.

Natasha felt sick. First Maya had stolen her life—now her face too? When Bondarchuk walked them down the hall and presented Maya to Lev—"Behold, your dancing partner. Maybe with a real dancer you won't trip over your own two feet"—Natasha wanted badly to correct him, to tell him that if anyone was truly Lev's partner, it was her. But she knew this would be foolish, and she knew she had a job to do, so she bit her tongue.

That day was such a massive undertaking that everyone had at least two jobs. Some of the extras picked up ladders and matches and helped the crew light the hundreds of candles that lined the walls, displayed in chandeliers, tucked into sconces, rising proudly out of massive candelabras that had once lit the rooms of Catherine the Great or stood vigil over the funerals of past dignitaries. The younger women fashioned fans from magazines and newspapers and helped cool the old, who were not used to wearing thick, heavy ball gowns and were beginning to fade from the heat of being around so many hundreds of people at once, not to mention the candles. Irina Bondarchuk, in full costume and wearing a bouffant wig better suited to Motown than to nineteenth-century Moscow (Bondarchuk, who for some reason found large hairdos arousing, had insisted on it), helped dislodge a wooden nickel a couple young boys had jammed in the kvass vending machine, much to the joy of the dozens of thirsty extras who'd lined up to wet their throats before dancing. Maya, seated in a folding chair beside her sister, kept looking anxiously over at Natasha and wondering what to say. Natasha stared straight ahead, with Lev hovering beside her. Every now and again, when Bondarchuk wasn't looking, Lev rested his hand on Natasha's shoulder.

Sergei Bondarchuk installed himself at the end of the long room and, with the help of a large white megaphone, explained to the waiting extras and actors that the day's events would follow three steps. First, they would film the grand entrance of the sovereigns. Then, they would film Natasha alone at the edge of the ball, waiting for Prince Andrei to come ask her to dance. "And last, of course," Bondarchuk said, "we must also film this great waltz between them, which is surely one of the most important waltzes in all of literature—though we do not have the means to do Tolstoy justice"—here, he glared at Lev, whose dancing yesterday had impressed nobody, and even Lev was nervous about it—"but we shall do our best."

Bondarchuk was ready. A table to his left held an array of storyboards he'd drawn up with the help of his director of photography, Anatoly Petritsky. Bondarchuk and Petritsky, who had been conscripted for the film at the last minute after the previous director of photography quit in a rage, had been preparing for this day for months. The storyboards told them everything they needed to know: the sequence of shots, the number of takes, the general flow of the scene. A squadron of gaffers had stayed up all night installing an overhead track on the set's ceiling to produce sweeping shots of the dancers from a godlike perspective.

But one thing they had not figured out was how to film in the middle of the dance floor. Bondarchuk wanted as naturalistic an approach as possible. He wanted it to feel like the camera was one of the dancers—not static, but buoyant and graceful. Petritsky went home mulling this over and arrived that morning bearing the solution, an idea of his six-year-old son: a pair of roller skates. He pulled them out of his bag and showed them to Bondarchuk. "I'll look like I'm gliding along," he said.

Bondarchuk was pleased, but he waved him off; he was only capable of thinking about one shot at a time. "First, the grand entrance," he said.

This first shot of the day was also the simplest: nobody had to be dancing, nobody had to be speaking. The only thing necessary for things to go well was for neither of the sovereigns, who, appropriately, were outfitted with even more jewels and finery than the others, to trip, which of course happened during the first take. Both sovereigns were asked to walk very quickly—they, like all weary royals, were supposed to want to get this public appearance over with as quickly as possible. The tsarina, being female, was accustomed to the cumbersomeness of constricting apparel, having run to catch buses in heels and tight skirts many times over the course of her life, and she was practiced in the art of swift but cautious elegance. The unlucky tsar, however, had had no such experience, fine Soviet menswear being identical to everyday shoes and pants, and he tripped over his wingtips and fell, and Bondarchuk slapped his forehead and muttered to Irina that today was going to be a very, very long day. Irina patted his back and slipped him a piece of sour cherry candy, which insulted him—he did not like being treated like a child—but he took it anyway and put it in his mouth and it soothed him, even though he didn't want it to.

Mercifully, the following shot, where Natasha was waiting alone as a wallflower, was much easier. It required the day's first bit of dancing, but through some ingenuity of Bondarchuk's, this appeared only in a mirror by Natasha's right shoulder, and the dancers felt much less pressure because of this, and because they felt better, they danced better, and nobody tripped or stumbled. Yes, a much easier scene.

Easier, that is, for everyone but Natasha. She had no lines in this scene; in the final film, a voice-over would reveal her thoughts, which, like most of the dialogue in the film, Bondarchuk had lifted straight from Tolstoy. But they hadn't recorded the voice-over yet, and Bondarchuk decided to have someone read the lines as they filmed so Natasha could pretend she was thinking them. And, because she was one of the only people on set who was not otherwise engaged, Bondarchuk assigned this task to Maya.

It was supposed to be a moment of great humiliation for Natasha's character. Here she was, at the first grand ball of her life, her first emergence as an adult and as a woman, and nobody noticed her. Natasha did not have to reach very far inside herself to conjure up these emotions: she was listening to her sister, who was dressed as herself and about to dance with the man she loved, read her character's thoughts—*surely they must know how much I long to dance, and how much they'll enjoy dancing with me*—while she watched a whole crowd of people doing the very thing she'd once loved and could never do again. They filmed the scene in two takes: the first was interrupted by an extra's sneeze, and the second was—in Bondarchuk's words, a word that he had not yet used to describe anything on set—perfect. "She even had tears in her eyes, without my asking her," he whispered to Petritsky. (He was wise enough to keep praise of Natasha away from his wife.) "She was perfect."

The third and final element of the scene, Natasha's waltz, was much more difficult. By this time, the room had become so hot under the scorching stage lights and the accumulated heat of hundreds of bodies that the extras' makeup started to melt off their faces, and Feodor led a little squadron of makeup artists around the crowd, wiping fallen mascara here, dabbing liquified foundation off necks and décolletage there. Between takes, an army of severe-looking women in kerchiefs and white coats descended on the set to polish new scuffs from the floor. And six times, the film stock, which was Soviet-made, shredded; it was terribly flimsy and dotted, for some reason, with mosquitoes. (Bondarchuk had fought to use American film, but the government insisted that Soviet films were made with Soviet film.) Each time it fell apart, everything—waltzers, cameramen, lighting techs, sound engineers—came to a grinding halt, and entire sequences were destroyed without warning. Years later, when Bondarchuk was very old and cinematic failures had both weakened his confidence and forced him into Party membership, he would lean over to whomever was beside him and lament the loss of these sequences, which he claimed were the best of his career.

Filming the waltz was tightly controlled chaos. Petritsky wore the roller skates as he filmed, which made his camera appear to be dancing and gliding itself. Four men pulled him around the set, swirling in and around the dancers.

Bondarchuk, who'd arrived that morning with inspiration from his wife's robust closet, added another flourish to this eccentric method. "I want the audience to feel like they are at the ball themselves," he explained to Petritsky, "with ladies' dresses brushing past them." He draped himself in an array of scarves and carried fans in both hands. As Petritsky rolled through the crowd, Bondarchuk followed, waving the fans and the fringed edges of scarves over the camera lens to give the appearance of elegant wraps and sleeves and gowns grazing the viewer. He looked like an overzealous peddler of women's frippery trying to entice an unwilling buyer.

Natasha had a tiny bit of participation in this sequence. She, to her relief, was still the one Lev was to approach when he came to ask for a dance. His approach was filmed from very far away so as to mimic her perspective: Bondarchuk smooshed the camera right up against the wall next to Natasha and had Lev walk over from the very farthest side of the room. As usual, Bondarchuk was near impossible to satisfy, and he had Lev perform this simple walk over and over again. Lev had to look at the camera in this shot, but his character was supposed to be gazing at Natasha, and Natasha felt this gaze—warm, confident, inviting—was just for her.

She was grateful to be there with him, grateful that she was still able to participate in this most important scene. Bondarchuk had decided to use Natasha for the close-up shots, so it really was her gloved hand that went up on Lev's shoulder when he asked her to dance, and Lev guided her out of the shot, and for a split second they both felt like they were back at the Metropol.

But after Lev guided Natasha off-screen, and Petritsky and his camera were hoisted onto an enormous dolly, he let go of Natasha's hand and took Maya's instead, who came rushing up from under the dolly, as she'd been instructed, and they waltzed off together to the middle of the floor, flanked on all sides by proud-looking men in epaulets and rows of women fluttering their fans like jeweled butterflies.

Bondarchuk, who was not convinced that Feodor's masterful disguise would hold up on the screen, snapped a fan or a shawl over the lens each time Maya showed her face, which Natasha noticed with great relish—it was like her sister was being censored. This helped her keep her composure as she waited for her next shot.

Weeks ago, when she'd found out Maya was going to be her dancing double—Bondarchuk, at his wife's suggestion, had announced it in front of the whole cast—Natasha had run to her dressing room and started hurtling things to the floor. Lev hurried after her, and by the time he made it to her door she'd already smashed two teacups and was about to throw a hand mirror. She wasn't crying at all. She was barely breathing—she smashed the teacups with the air of someone destroying dangerous things. Concerned crew members peered in the open door and, seeing Lev, decided to stay out of it. Actresses, they thought to themselves, shaking their heads. What a luxury to have time for hysterics.

"Stop, stop it," Lev said, catching her by the arms. "You'll hurt yourself!" He took the mirror from Natasha's hand and pulled her to the couch, sitting beside her.

"I hate her!" Natasha said, pounding her thighs with her fists so hard that later they'd pebble with bruises. "I hate her!" She slammed her heels against the couch. Her rage would split her in two if it didn't escape her body.

"Who? Who?" Lev said, trying to stop her from kicking and getting kicked himself in the process.

"My sister," Natasha said, choking on the words. "I hate my sister. I can't see her again!" Her eyes fell to the china shards littering the floor. "If I see her again, I'm going to kill her."

"Natasha," Lev said, his voice becoming stern. "Take it from someone who knows—this sort of anger won't solve anything. You hurt her, and you'll be hurting yourself—deeper and more permanently than anyone else could."

"But I can't do it," Natasha said. "I can't stand there and let her get everything I should have had instead. Not again. I have to do something, or I'm going to die." She looked up at Lev with desperation in her eyes. The strength of her anger was frightening her. "What should I do?"

Lev poured her a cup of water from the pitcher on the counter and handed it to her. "I don't like to give advice like this," he said, frowning. "But—"

"What?" Natasha held the cup of water, its coolness only highlighting how warm she was.

"It's my experience," he said, running a hand through his hair, "that people of this sort always expose themselves in some way."

"What do you mean?"

"I mean that, if you want revenge on your sister, you're not going to have to go looking for it. She'll give you the key. People who are cruel always have some sort of Achilles' heel, something that's very dear to them and vulnerable. All you have to do is find it."

Natasha drank, and the taste of water made her feel a little less like an animal. "If I could do anything, I'd just have her legs broken."

"Don't let anger make you a thug," Lev said. "If you must retaliate, do it elegantly."

"How am I supposed to do that?" Natasha said. She shuddered, thinking of her sister dancing at the grand ball instead of her.

"Just be patient," Lev said. "The solution will present itself to you."

Now, Natasha watched Lev dance with her sister. She knew that all the loving glances he gave Maya were just acting—there was an artificiality to his face that had been totally absent at the Metropol—but they still made her furious. It was bad enough that Maya had sabotaged her, but to step into the life she was meant to live? To take her place with the Kirov, to tour the cities and countries she'd longed to see, and now, to have a child with her ex-lover? It was too much to bear. Watching Maya with Lev, all of the hatred Natasha had felt for years flooded her body. She wished one of the giant chandeliers overhead would come loose and crush Maya. She wished she'd dance too close to one of the candelabras and her voluminous wig would catch fire. She wished for something to take all the suffering she'd had to endure and drop it on her sister's shoulders like an ox's yoke, heavy and inescapable.

Natasha did not hear Bondarchuk call "cut," and she did not even notice that Lev had let go of her sister and come over to her side while they filmed Maya dancing with other men. Only when Lev surreptitiously took her hand and squeezed it did Natasha come out of her daze.

Lev leaned close. "You look like a ghost," he whispered. He was so near her that she could feel heat emanating from his body. Despite her sour mood, Natasha found it exhilarating to be this close in public—and Lev's sharp white dress uniform wasn't hurting him either.

"She's poisoning my life," Natasha said, and she knew she did not have to explain who she meant. "I can't stand being around her."

"So get rid of her," said Lev, and there was such nonchalance in his voice that Natasha looked at him in surprise.

"She's pregnant," Natasha said.

"I meant send her *away*," Lev said, indicating with raised eyebrows that Natasha was monstrous for thinking he meant otherwise.

"How?"

Lev gestured to someone who had just walked up to Bondarchuk. It was Yekaterina Furtseva. Bondarchuk, who was in the middle of directing the scene, nodded curtly to Furtseva and waved her away.

"I don't understand," Natasha said.

Lev smiled a wry, cynical little smile and squeezed her hand again. "Then let me help you," he said, and he walked over and said something to Furtseva, who came over to Natasha.

Natasha swallowed. The stocky, sour-looking woman had always frightened her. She'd heard that Furtseva had been in the audience the night of her accident, and as a result she had always associated her presence with doom. In this, she was correct.

Furtseva leaned back against the wall beside Natasha and crossed one ankle over the other. "Your sister's ballet is highly anticipated here in town," she said, lighting a cigarette. "Lev tells me you've seen it?"

"Not all of it," Natasha said, not understanding the direction this conversation was taking. She wished Lev had told her more of what he was thinking before he'd gotten Furtseva to come over. Natasha worried she'd say the wrong thing and get herself in trouble.

Furtseva took a drag off her cigarette and, realizing that the appearance of cigarette smoke in the film could ruin it, hastily waved her cloud of smoke away. "Tell me what you thought of it," she said. "Lev tells me I can trust your opinion."

"I didn't see very much of it," Natasha said. She spoke truthfully: once the curtain had gone up—the first time she'd seen a curtain go up since the night of the accident—a haze had fallen over her eyes. After ten minutes, she'd taken a taxi home and called Lev.

Natasha looked over at Lev, who was standing casually behind Petritsky and Bondarchuk. Lev made an obscene gesture, the kind of gesture teenage boys make when they're feeling too young and are trying to prove their worldliness. Natasha blushed and wondered why in the world he was doing such a thing in public.

Then she remembered the night before; she'd told him Maya's ballet had been obscene, which it was—her sister was half naked, dancing seductively for a crowd of hungry men. But why did Furtseva need to know this?

"Surely you saw something," Furtseva said, narrowing her eyes at the nervous young girl. "Here is what I want to know: Is it decent? Is it something our youth can or should aspire to? We Soviets are, as you know, called to devote ourselves to purity and decency in the name of our ideals. Would your sister's ballet make our motherland proud?"

At last, Natasha understood. This was about much more than *Bolero*. Furtseva, hovering hungrily over her, needed the opportunity to prove herself, to be a righteous crusader and curry Khrushchev's favor. Like a grateful cat, Furtseva needed a mouse to pierce with her teeth and lay on her master's doorstep, an offering on the altar of her ruthless ambition. With the wrong word, Natasha could end her sister's choreographic career.

Natasha looked over at Maya, now dancing with one of the extras, and wondered how her sister had felt before deciding to destroy her. Had she questioned if she was doing the right thing? Had she become convinced of the necessity of the task, of her own self-righteousness for instigating it? Had she felt any guilt for what she was doing?

The bustle of the film set carried on around them as it had a moment before. The dancing extras tried to remember their steps without looking like they were trying to remember them. Petritsky whirled around on his roller skates, with Bondarchuk swirling scarves close behind. Propmen and costume women hurried around on the fringes, rebuckling fallen swords, wiping melted makeup from collars. Yes, everything went on as before, and Natasha didn't feel guilty at all.

She turned back to Furtseva. "The ballet was disgusting," she said. "Completely obscene. I was actually ashamed of it. That was why I left in the middle of it," she explained, astounded by her own cleverness. "It shocked and horrified me. I'm ashamed to be her sister."

Furtseva nodded slowly. This was just the sort of opportunity she'd been waiting for: a chance to show her strength, a chance to prove to Khrushchev that she was capable of punishing not only unworthy art but also the artists themselves. "Thank you," she said. "That was all I needed to know." And then she walked right to Bondarchuk's office and called the director of the Bolshoi.

A week later, Olaf trudged home from the Palais Garnier to his little apartment in the 9th Arrondissement, his hands deep in his pockets. It was a damp and cold and desolate day. Leningrad was cold, he thought, dipping his frozen nose into his turtleneck, but you could get used to it there, if you knew how to cope. Here, things alternated between loveliness and misery, often on the same day, making you crazy. A repertory director from the Royal Ballet in London had been hounding him for months, trying to get him to move to England. Olaf had been holding him off—after all, wasn't Paris the center of the world?—but now, heading home up the same sorry street, dodging the same old cracks in the sidewalk, Olaf craved an escape.

He missed Russia. He missed the ice and snow; he missed hearing his own language and not thinking twice about it; he missed waiters bringing lemon for his tea without being asked. He often lay awake at night and wondered if he'd made a mistake, especially when he received pleading letters from Karinska or his grandmother and read pain between the lines, or when someone in the audience—maybe KGB agents, maybe angry French Communists—threw glass on the stage and he nearly sliced his feet open. But as often as Olaf thought about Russia, he thought more about his other love, which was his true reason for thinking fondly of home.

He had tried to fill her place with many other women, and a handful of men, and anyone who welcomed his attention. He was like a gardener who tends a dozen little plants at once to distract himself from the one that refused to bloom. He'd tried to forget her—he'd been told by friends and lovers that he would, someday, but it hadn't happened. He'd fallen in love again once or twice, but only for a week or two. Maya, and only Maya, remained on the throne of his mind.

He had followed her ascent from afar, clipping every mention of her choreography from the foreign papers that he scouted at the newsstands. "She's becoming a woman of experience," he'd say to himself, looking over the clippings, imagining her falling for a long string of lovers—a string he hoped would make himself all the more impressive by comparison when they were finally reunited. When he found out she was in Moscow, filming with her sister, he sent her flowers again, with a plea he knew she could and would never answer: "I still love you," he said, as if the two of them had ever been lovers. He hadn't gotten a response.

Dreaming of dinner, and a cup of tea so hot it would sear his throat, Olaf threw open the door to his building and hurried up the stairs, which were lit by a single bulb dangling from the ceiling. A dark shape sat at the top of the stairs. The shape stirred, and then stood. It was a woman.

This was the sort of thing that happened often in this part of town: an unfortunate woman, past her prime, having sold herself until her looks wore away, would get desperate enough to come inside and beg. Olaf was not in a generous mood, and the woman's tangy odor—which was strong enough that it wafted all the way down the stairs—didn't help. "Excuse me," Olaf said, hurrying toward his door, but then the shape said his name, and he pressed against the stairwell and stared.

Maya almost didn't recognize Olaf herself. He was much better looking than she remembered. His arms and chest had thickened; he carried himself with more elegance and pride. His eyes, which had once verged on buggy, had sunken a little, lending him the tragic romance of a young man in a nineteenth-century woodcut. The overall effect was a pleasing one.

All day, Maya had rehearsed a speech for Olaf—it was the only thing that had kept her from falling asleep on her feet after several hours in the immigration office—but now, faced with the reality of him, his actual nearness, all of her elegant words fell out of her head, and she was left with simple ones. "I'm here," she said, forgetting to smile. "I've come to be with you."

Maya had not spent much time imagining how this meeting would actually go. Everything had happened so quickly. In the span of a single day, the Bolshoi had announced *Bolero* had been canceled and the Kirov pulled *Ballet School* from its upcoming season. When Maya called Alexei in a panic, he confirmed what she already knew: she'd been blacklisted. "I don't think your services as a choreographer will be welcome anywhere," he said. "Not even in Siberia. If making dances matters to you—well, you'll need to make arrangements."

Fearing he'd said too much—he suspected, rightly, that his phone had been bugged—Alexei hung up, and Maya understood his meaning. All these years, she'd thought she was repaying her debt to the state that had made her a dancer by dancing well enough to make her country proud, by bringing beauty to the world. Now Alexei had told her the truth: the state didn't care about what was good or beautiful or even true, and it didn't want her art as repayment. Her debt was to do as she was told, even if she was told not to dance, not to create—even, as so many thousands had been told, to die. Somehow, she'd crossed a line—weeks later, through rumors in the émigré world, she'd hear what Natasha had done—and she could not be a Russian and an artist both.

But, like her mother, Maya could not be parted from her art and still live. She had to leave the country—for her sake and for the sake of her child. Yes, her child. She would have a child. Elizaveta hadn't been able to flee, but she could; she knew, as soon as she decided to run away, that she could have a child and care for it, give it the life and love and stability she'd never had herself. But she couldn't do it alone.

Fortunately, whether by the kindness of some staffer, a desire to avoid bad press, or a simple oversight, she hadn't been fired from the Kirov, and she'd been permitted to rejoin the company on its tour.

When the company returned to Paris, she slipped from her handlers in the airport—with the aid of Anya, who'd been hired by the Kirov just in time to come along. Anya, long skilled in inappropriate manipulation of bodily functions, made herself vomit on a handler's shoe, and in the ensuing chaos Maya rushed to a policeman and asked for asylum, just as Olaf had. After a few hours in the immigration office, she was questioned and given papers and, finally, a ride to Olaf's apartment.

If Maya had imagined how this reunion would go, she would have expected much more excitement from poor Olaf, who, finding his idol in the stairway, did not know what to do with her. Unlike Maya, he had pictured this reunion over and over again, each time tracing the fantasy a little deeper into his mind until it almost became a memory: Maya would show up at his door; she would be thin and wan but as beautiful as ever; she would carry a bouquet of roses that he had sent her, carefully dried, and hand him one of the many love notes he'd written and say, "Yes." She would be so grateful to see him and would profess her love on the spot, would admit that she had been his from the beginning, since their earliest days at the Vaganova, and the two of them would make ravenous love until morning and irritate the neighbors.

Olaf's fantasy, as fantasies are wont to do, bore no resemblance to the reality before him: his idol was disheveled and dressed in frumpy clothes and had more than a little of the stench of the road on her. She looked not thin, but heavy; wan, but not as beautiful; and she seemed more desperate than grateful. But Olaf was, at heart, tender and considerate, and even if much of his affection was based on false pretenses, at least some part of it was genuine, and after recovering somewhat from the shock of seeing her, he invited Maya into his apartment.

He apologized after he turned on the lights, and he scurried from room to room attempting to tidy up, a task to which he was unaccustomed. He moved piles of shirts from one end of the sofa to the other; he stuffed a stack of magazines under the refrigerator; he did many other things with no discernible purpose, and after he had finished, the apartment looked no tidier than before, only shuffled.

He threw up his hands in surprise at this, making Maya laugh. She asked if she could make him a cup of tea.

It was a kind gesture, this reverse hospitality—Olaf should have been the one offering tea to her, and he pointed this out. But Maya already felt indebted to Olaf, and she wanted to make good on this debt before he could grow resentful of her.

Olaf showed her the teapot and the kettle. "No samovars here," he said, and he meant it as an apology, but Maya shook her head.

"We'll do fine without samovars," she said.

Olaf did not reply. He was too taken up with the strange vision of Maya in his kitchen. In the six months since he'd last seen her, the first hints of lines had appeared around Maya's eyes and mouth—lines that, though barely noticeable, were deeper than what Olaf expected to see on the face of a twenty-one-year-old. Olaf tried to conjure up some sort of physical attraction to her—the exhausted woman in front of him, not his fantasy—and found it difficult.

They stood in silence for a while as the kettle warmed. When it was ready, Maya poured water into the two cups Olaf had given her, mismatched and with puny teabags inside them, and brought them to the kitchen table. "Are you surprised to see me?"

"Not a bit," Olaf said. He crossed his legs in an effort to appear relaxed and masculine. "I always knew you'd come." This was a lie—though Olaf had stuffed his letters with confidence and bluster, with plea after plea for Maya to come away, though he'd imagined their reunions nearly nightly, no part of him had actually thought she would appear, and now that she had, he felt a little foolish.

Maya, who was too tired to notice that she was under scrutiny, cupped her hands around her mug and, when it seared her fingers, yelped in pain. Something about hearing the sound of her own voice undid her: all of the grief and fear she'd kept locked away since the plane had left Moscow came rushing at her all at once, and she started to cry.

Olaf was very kind. He knew all too well what it meant to be in exile, the pain that came from losing home forever—knew there was no real remedy or solution for this pain. Instead of shushing her, or saying something trite to ease his own discomfort, he sat there quietly beside her and, after a few moments, reached out and took her hand. Eventually, he offered her his handkerchief, which she accepted, and he appreciated then what an honor it was, that this accomplished and talented person had come to him, and he realized that he still thought she was beautiful.

PART III

CHAPTER TWENTY-TWO

MOSCOW, FEBRUARY 1969

Only three things can be depended on in this world: that hemlines will rise and fall, that regimes will come and go, and that people will never change.

This is why the Russians went on doing many of the same things under Brezhnev that they had under Khrushchev, which they'd also done under Stalin, which were the same things people everywhere have always done, no matter who exploited them: getting toothaches and falling in love, scolding their children and singing in taverns, disbelieving the news from abroad, hoarding money and wasting time, cheating their neighbors and feeding stray cats, writing terrible poetry and believing, even though they knew better, that some sort of brilliant fate awaited them.

Yekaterina Furtseva still strived for this fate, and her office window in the Kremlin stayed lit long into the bitter evenings, a beacon for the taxi drivers and policemen and stragglers roaming the city in the dark.

On this particular evening, Yekaterina Furtseva was up late because she had a problem. She sat back at her desk, smoking a cigar and watching the snow fall, and resolved not to go home until she'd found a solution.

This problem was not easily solved. She'd been sitting at her desk since dusk, puzzling over it, rolling it around in her mind like dice and examining it from every side. Her cigar, a gift from one of her superiors on the occasion of *War and Peace*'s theatrical release, smoldered between her fingers, and she stamped it out in her globe-shaped ashtray, which had once gleamed brightly on her desk—a symbol of Soviet internationalism, of bettering the world—and now sat tarnished. She cut and lit herself a second cigar. Her stomach burbled in angry protest at the injustice of once again missing dinner by several hours.

On the surface, Furtseva's problem did not look like a problem. On the surface, it looked very good, even for her professionally: after all of her travails, all the haggling over budgets and borzois and borrowed jewels, all of the sleepless nights and the hair that had fallen out and accumulated in her shower drain, *War and Peace* had triumphed, not only in Russia but also in the 117 countries where it had been screened. It had competed at Cannes, and now, in the exact sort of coup d'état that Furtseva and Bondarchuk and Mosfilm and the Kremlin itself had hoped for, the Americans had nominated it for an Academy Award.

At last, here was proof that the film—that Furtseva herself—was being taken seriously. Brezhnev called Furtseva himself when the news arrived and promised her a new summer dacha, which disappointed her—she already had a dacha that she liked very much, with rhododendrons tucked under dark green shutters, and she'd hoped, with no legitimate reason for doing so, that he'd make her a People's Artist instead. Though she was not an artist, exactly, she'd had a hand in the making of many, and she wanted to be recognized for this more than anything else. But these things would come in good time, she thought, as long as she could keep on. Some days, she wasn't sure she could.

In the meantime, there was the problem of the Academy Award. The Americans expected them to send someone to California for the ceremony. Bondarchuk was the obvious choice, but he had suffered a heart attack and was unable to travel. Lev, Furtseva thought, would also do nicely, but he was due on set in Siberia a week before the ceremony.

And there was Furtseva's problem: they had to send somebody. She'd been strictly instructed to send only one person: "Imagine the humiliation," Brezhnev had told her, "if we send half of Mosfilm and we don't win!" But who? If nobody went at all, the Americans would be insulted, and Russia would waste this hard-won opportunity to lord it over the West.

The next morning, having slept little and arrived at no conclusion, Furtseva gave up and used one of her rare calls to Brezhnev to ask his advice. He suggested something Furtseva hadn't dared to ask for on her own. "Send Natasha," he said. "It's our only option."

Furtseva rolled the remnant of last night's second cigar between her thumb and first finger. "Aren't you worried she'll be reckless?" Natasha had been kept under steady watch ever since her sister's defection—had it not been for the film's success, and Bondarchuk's interventions, she would not have been permitted to travel anywhere, even within the borders of the USSR.

"Lev will help us make sure she gets back. Besides, doesn't she have a daughter now? Motherhood makes a woman more easily persuaded." Brezhnev was fond of speaking in aphorisms.

Furtseva sat thinking for so long that Brezhnev thought the call had been disconnected, and he started muttering in complaint, which brought Furtseva back to attention. "What if her sister tries to reach her?" she asked.

"Talk to Lev," Brezhnev said. "Husbands can be very convincing." Confident that this observation settled the matter, Brezhnev hung up, and Furtseva dialed Natasha to tell her the news.

Their conversation was short—Furtseva had never been one to mince words—and after Natasha put the phone back in its receiver, she leaned against the wall and surveyed the room around her, looking for some indication that her life had just changed, but she found none. The accoutrements of parenthood were still scattered everywhere she looked: a jar of diaper pins tucked up high on a bookshelf, picture books piled on an end table, a pacifier perched on the arm of a chair. A mass of snow-white diapers—half folded, half not—lay just as they had moments ago, when Natasha had leapt up from her folding to answer the phone, to learn that she, after all this time, after everything she'd endured, was going to America.

Several years ago, this news would have flung Natasha into an urgent joy, the kind that casts all other tasks and considerations aside. She would have run right to her suitcase and started packing, even though the trip was months away. But she had become a mother and had thus learned the possible length of a day, how it could stretch out forever and ever, swallowing multitudes.

Yes, Natasha had grown up—had gotten married, had given birth to a daughter, and now every experience she had filtered through these layers. It wasn't so much like sunlight straining through a dirty windowpane as it was hot water pouring through tea leaves: her new roles had made her life richer and deeper and, above all, more complicated.

Hearing Furtseva's voice again had lifted her up out of her apartment and transported her to the overheated Mosfilm studio, air made stifling by the body heat of several hundred powdered extras, the withering glare of the studio lights, the canned orchestral music coating all conversation with a layer of noise. Furtseva's voice, though it brought her good news, news she'd awaited for years and years, also brought her back to the day when Natasha had held her sister's fate in her hands and crushed her.

But thinking about this was too much, and Natasha shook her head as if to shake these thoughts from her mind and walked to the nursery to bring herself back to the present. Elizaveta sat upright in her crib, so focused on stacking a red block on top of a blue block that she did not hear her mother come in and did not respond to her greeting. Natasha had not spent any time around babies until Elizaveta was born, and she wondered at her daughter's capacity for intense concentration. Elizaveta was only a year old, and she'd somehow learned to block out everything else around her while attempting to master a task. That the tasks were minute—the arrangement of inanimate objects, such as the blocks, and, occasionally, brief but frightening interactions with the cat—made no difference. Once, when Elizaveta had been trying to untie a knot in a loose shoelace, Natasha picked her up and set her on top of a table without breaking her daughter's concentration on the shoelace at all.

It made Natasha envious. She had not known an absorption like that since the Vaganova. Even now, for all her successes, for all the joy she'd found through acting, any time she remembered the thrill of landing a jump or pulling off a triple pirouette or an orchestra awaiting her cue, her heart smarted like a stubbed toe and she had to hobble her way back to the present, feeling bruised. Her past was dotted with land mines and barbed wire, and she had to navigate her memories carefully, the same way she now tiptoed around the scattered messes of Elizaveta's room.

Elizaveta was still transfixed by her blocks, and Natasha, jealous both of her daughter and for her daughter's attention, called her name. Her mother's name. She'd named her daughter after Elizaveta not in honor of her—though that is what she'd told everyone, even her husband—but in celebration of the fact that she'd achieved what her mother had not. She had given birth to a child and lived to care for it. Elizaveta's birth had reopened Natasha's orphan wound rather than healing it. Now that she had a child of her own—a child known and loved by two parents—Natasha better understood what she had missed, what Elizaveta's abandonment had taken from her.

The child, finally taking notice of her mother's presence, looked up at Natasha. Her little lips curled, not into a baby's brainless, toothless smile, but into a coy, close-lipped grin that said, *I know you are as happy to see me as I am to see you.* It was the sort of look Elizaveta's father had on his face all the time.

It was almost like magic, the way everything had worked out with Lev; their four years on Bondarchuk's set had been hell, but pulled them closer together. Lev stepped in after Maya's departure and then never left her side. Just before *War and Peace* was released, Lev announced that his marriage had been formally dissolved, and now he was free again. Photographs of him and Natasha holding hands at every promotional event appeared in *Soviet Screen* and all the other film magazines, and the day before the Russian premiere, he dropped on one knee and proposed. When Elizaveta was born a year later, Natasha took it as a sign that the universe was finally allotting her her due.

How quickly she'd gotten everything she'd wanted: a daughter, a handsome and dependable husband, a beautiful three-bedroom apartment in a fashionable corner of Moscow. She'd even managed to secure Katusha the apartment next door thanks to her many advantageous connections. "And why not?" she said out loud to Elizaveta, who was now in her arms, red block still in hand. After all, she'd worked hard since *War and Peace*'s release—touring the country for its promotion, lending her presence to the christening of ships and factory openings. If the Soviet state was her mother, Natasha had been a good and dutiful daughter, and now she was being rewarded in kind.

Ilya had been right: there was a good life to be had here, as long as you knew how to secure it for yourself. People suffered—that was inevitable. After Maya defected, Katusha was brought in for questioning over and over again. But fixing things was easy when you knew the right people: Natasha called Bondarchuk, who called Furtseva, who called a superior in the Kremlin and assured them of Katusha's loyalties, and the interrogations stopped. Because Natasha was famous, because, as the star of *War and Peace*, she'd served her country in a most valuable way, nothing was impossible for her. And wasn't this how it should be? Because of her—and Lev, and Bondarchuk, and everyone who'd worked so hard on this film—people all over the world were admiring Russian culture. It was an exchange of loyalties: she'd proven her patriotism through art and now, as a reward, she and her family were comfortable.

"Oof," Natasha groaned, setting her daughter on the floor. "You're getting heavy!" Elizaveta looked up with a scowl as if in reproach for this remark, then continued her careful inspection of the block.

Natasha could not believe Elizaveta was a year old already, because that meant Natasha's advent into motherhood was also a year old. She had wanted children, and she entered her new role anxious to pour into her daughter everything her own mother never had. But after the self-extinguishing exhaustion of pregnancy, followed by a year of sleepless nights and long days, she felt emptied out, unsure of who she was or what she wanted. Lev encouraged her to consider acting again, and Natasha daydreamed about this sometimes, about the glamorous life she could return to when her daughter was a little bit older and wouldn't need her quite so much. She missed the time when nobody needed her at all.

Still, she had a good life, and Natasha was grateful for it—for her husband and daughter, for her enviable apartment, but she longed to be part of the outside world, to feel free. "Maybe," she thought to herself, "this trip will make me feel like myself again." She interrupted her daughter's investigations of her block. "What do you think, Elizaveta?"

Her daughter looked up at her, a little less delighted than before—her block held some sort of crucial mystery that she was close to unraveling, and she was getting tired of these interruptions—and Natasha thought, not for the first time, that her daughter's brown eyes were just like Maya's.

Once, Natasha had sworn she would never see her sister again, but now her heart had softened. Perhaps it was becoming a mother. Perhaps it was the passage of time. Perhaps it was the guilt she felt at her own betrayal, the understanding that unthinkable circumstances lead us to do unthinkable things. Whatever it was, it depressed her to think that Elizaveta would never know the only real family Natasha had.

Elizaveta, having untangled the block's mysteries, cautiously stood and made her way to her mother. She tugged at Natasha's knee, requesting to be picked up, and her mother obliged. Natasha wished that Maya could feel the weight of her niece in her arms, but she had no idea how this could ever come about. When, at the government's insistence, Katusha had written Maya anguished letters, begging her to come home, Maya replied that she and Olaf were happily settled in London. Every now and again, thanks to sympathetic friends who smuggled letters or foreign newspaper clippings, they got glimpses of Maya and Olaf's adventurous life. The last clipping Katusha received announced that they were moving to New York, where Olaf would dance with the American Ballet Theatre.

Natasha had never been asked to write to Maya; because she'd helped get Maya blacklisted, Furtseva had vouched for her loyalty. At the time, this was a relief: What was there to say? She and Maya could never be close again, let alone live on the same continent. But after Furtseva's call, Natasha wondered if it would be possible for them to see each other again, if only one last time.

Maya descended the stairs of a Pan Am plane onto the tarmac at LaGuardia Airport in New York, shrouded in a heavy coat. The winter wind stung her face. After the mildness of London weather, which had been her companion for years, she was shocked by the bitterness of her first nor'easter. Olaf followed her out of the plane, and they hurried down the tarmac together, huddled against the cold.

If Natasha had somehow been there to witness this, she would not have recognized her sister. Maya looked nothing like the girl who'd played her dancing double and waltzed with Lev in the ballroom. Her waist was imperceptible; her eyes, which had once sparkled under the lights of every grand opera house in the Western world, had bags under them, which had appeared seven years ago and never receded.

Maya was aware of these losses, and painfully so; she'd noticed each flaw as it appeared and tallied them every day, like a debt owed. She wanted to leave her old self behind in this new life in America, so she'd camouflaged her deficiencies as best she could; she hid her thickened body under a shapeless coat, a large fur hat, and two woolen scarves; she coated her eyes in black liner and powder-blue shadow, which she knew was garish, but it gave people something to notice besides how tired she was. And to some extent, these disguises worked: the cab driver who stopped at Olaf's whistle looked at Maya through the rearview mirror and, hearing her accent, wondered who the mysterious and beautiful Russian woman was.

The lobby of their hotel was palatial, all done up in blues and golds in a way that made Maya think of Leningrad—an observation that, like all thoughts of her home, brought her pain. When Olaf gave the woman at the front desk his name, it had the usual effect, one that had become so familiar to Maya since they'd gotten married. Though Maya's defection had afforded her a brief notoriety, Olaf was the famous one—he was the one still dancing. People all over the world who knew nothing else about ballet knew his name.

Depending on one's perspective, Olaf's name was either shorthand for betrayal and cowardice or for bravery, for fearlessness in the face of oppression. Judging by the flush that crept into this woman's cheeks, she was of the latter conviction. "Welcome, sir," she said, in a voice so breathy that even Olaf was embarrassed. "We are very happy to have you and your wife with us." She bent over the reservation book and looked up again, confused. "But it says here you need two rooms?"

"Yes," Olaf said, and when he offered no explanation, the woman asked for none, handed them two keys, and spent the rest of the day wondering about the famous dancer and his mysterious wife—who, in her opinion, wore far too much eyeliner.

Maya and Olaf didn't say anything to each other in the elevator, or during the long walk down the hallway, or when they found their rooms. Maya worried Olaf would try to make some declaration before they parted ways, perhaps revisit the conversation they'd tried and failed to have over and over during the long plane ride, but he didn't—he only handed her a key and disappeared behind his door, and this relieved her. Inside her own room, Maya sat on the soft bed and felt her blood pressure lower. Being with Olaf had become so painful.

They'd moved to London three weeks after Maya's arrival, where Olaf had been hired as a principal dancer at the Royal Ballet. Maya was grateful for a change of scenery: she'd spent her time in Paris locked inside their apartment, terrified that retribution was at her door. Getting letters from Katusha, who told her Alexei had been fired from the Vaganova, did nothing to assuage Maya's nerves—or her conscience. "It's my fault," she said to Olaf, weeping. "I shouldn't have called him for advice. What if they send him to prison? And what if Katusha is in trouble too?"

Olaf, who understood (and shared) her guilt, urged her to leave these feelings behind. "We have to forget about everything back home," he said. "It's the only way we'll survive." So in London, they suffocated their homesickness and unease with the kinds of bohemian nights Soviet teenagers only dream of: dinners in crowded pubs with sticky floors, "Love Me Do" on the jukebox; parties in friends of friends' apartments, kaleidoscopic colors filtering through marijuana smoke. Maya, exhausted by her pregnancy, slept late and cooked so many foods from home that their little table buckled. They lived in a walk-up apartment that would be snug when the baby was born—they'd fashioned a makeshift nursery in the bedroom closet—but was perfect for two.

One evening, strolling home along the Thames, Olaf confessed to her that he'd always wanted a son. "I can't imagine anything more rewarding than being a father," he said. "To teach another man how to be a man. To be the strongest person in someone's life, someone you can always count on. I never had that—I loved my grandmother, and she loved me, but she was too frail to really take care of me." He told Maya that she, and the baby, made him look forward to growing old.

And then, when Maya was far along enough to be showing, the baby died. Or, to be more precise, it was discovered that the baby had died. The doctor told her it could have happened any number of weeks before. "You may have been carrying around a dead fetus for a month, as far as we know," he said. "Have you recently undergone significant stress? That's sometimes a factor." The doctor, who was no balletomane and was too busy to keep up with matters international, had not recognized his patient as the famous dancer whose photograph had been in all the papers—but seeing the anguish on Maya's face, he stopped short and cleared his throat. "But sometimes," he continued, more gently, "these things happen for no reason at all."

There was no burial—the hospital had declined to release "the remains," as they put it, in the name of sanitation. Just a procedure, and a taxi ride home, and a closetful of tiny things to pack away. Maya and Olaf were the first people in their social circle to have children, and their friends, eager to participate in a novel rite of passage, had started buying things for the baby far too early—little shirts and socks and diapers, a rubber giraffe, a tiny silver rattle shaped like an elephant. Olaf put everything in a milk crate and carried it outside while Maya waited in the living room, her eyes dry, her head heavy in her hands.

Women have been losing babies for as long as they have been carrying them. Maya knew this, and yet the experience instilled in her a horror of being pregnant. Her body had been so many things—an extension of her art, a source of pride and disappointment and pain. Now it was a place where someone had died.

Lying awake at night, Maya stared at a rabbit-shaped crack in her bedroom ceiling and thought about her sister, the person with whom she'd once shared a womb. The doctor's words haunted her. The stress of the defection might have killed her child—a stress Natasha had directly caused. Maya knew that the loss of the child wasn't her sister's intention—even Natasha wasn't that cruel. But Maya never would have gotten pregnant if Natasha hadn't spurned Ivan. And she never would have defected—another loss, the loss of home—if Natasha hadn't gotten her blacklisted.

But perhaps, Maya thought as the hours and weeks ticked by, this was the wrong way to think of things. Maya had stolen from Natasha too—a life lived for dance, an unbroken body. Maybe the defection hadn't taken her child. Maybe fate itself had, as retribution for

Maya's sins. Maybe she had ruined someone's life and another life had been taken in return.

Life is never so simple as this—our tragedies and good fortunes alike defy reason—but Maya's grief was too great to bear without some sort of explanation, so she donned blame like a heavy coat that sapped the light out of everything. She did not do the exercises that the doctors recommended for her recovery. She did not return to the raucous parties of their London life. She did not even try her hand at choreography again—after all her worry about the trouble of being both mother and artist, she was neither. She did not feel like, or resemble, herself at all.

After some time passed—enough time that this was not an insensitive request—Olaf suggested that they try again. "Maybe it would help us move on," he said, "to have a child of our own." Maya still wanted children, but the idea of conceiving again made her ill. She'd already been someone's tomb once. She didn't think she could survive a second time.

Thanks to this fear, Maya could not bear to touch or be touched by her husband, not after six months, not after a year. After two years, Olaf stopped making overtures, and they started sleeping in separate bedrooms. Maya began to suspect that Olaf discreetly took lovers from the company. He never admitted this to her, but sometimes she heard him come in late at night and she could tell—there was a certain way a man fell into a chair when he'd been satisfied.

She had no interest in confronting him about it. Their marriage, though rooted in friendship, had been created to serve a practical purpose that was no longer needed, and Maya couldn't fault him for wanting out. He still wanted to be a father. She saw the wistful way he looked at families walking past them on the sidewalk. Surely he was only hanging on because he felt sorry for her—after all, she had no money of her own, no apartment, no job. But Maya knew they couldn't go on in this stasis forever. Perhaps the most merciful thing she could do was let him go.

Maya considered this possibility for some time. The idea of being on her own again brought her more fully into the world. Cast out from her country, her occupation, her very body, she decided to refashion a new self, one who could feel fully at home in the West, and she decided to do it with clothes. She saw London women wearing miniskirts in bright shades of mango and lime, daisy-patterned shifts and paisley scarves, and she imitated them, seeking out the aids of bold makeup and loose clothing to give herself an air of sophistication. She listened to the radio and practiced her English. Having a language to speak besides her own made her feel less like an exile.

Maya's transformation took several years, and she threw herself into it, emerging from her cocoon a different woman altogether. In the early days of her defection, she rarely left the house, worried that the KGB was lying in wait for her. She didn't feel like she had lived in Paris at all—only the little prison cell of their apartment. But now, she decided to make London her own. She took long walks all over Covent Garden and marveled at its varied architecture, that a four-hundred-year-old church could be next door to a concrete parking garage. She stopped having their groceries delivered and did all the shopping herself, an experience that was at first as overwhelming as it would come to be joyful. Nothing astonished her more than the supermarket aisle with three dozen varieties of soap. She wondered why people in the West didn't look more exhausted: their lives, after all, were an unending string of choices—what to buy, what to eat, what to wear. Who to be.

She even dipped her toes back into dance again, just to see if she still felt some connection to it. She contacted a friend of Olaf's at the Royal Ballet and eventually staged *Bolero* to great success, coaching another dancer in the lead role. But even this felt stale—she wanted to make new things again, and she wondered if she was even capable of it. Everywhere she looked, she was surrounded by dead and decaying things—her aging body, her cold marriage. She wanted to start afresh, but didn't know how.

Then, in a rare fortunate twist of fate, Olaf was offered a guest artist job at the American Ballet Theatre in New York. The company's Lincoln Center home was across the way from the New York State Theater, where the New York City Ballet performed. Maya wrote to a friend in New York, asking for teaching work, and when a letter arrived two weeks later, offering her a job at Balanchine's School of American Ballet, she and Olaf agreed to move to America.

Several hours into the plane ride to New York, the stewardess dimmed the lights and most of the passengers succumbed to sleep. A hush settled over the cabin, the kind that social graces forbade one from breaking with angry or impassioned words, which meant Maya's moment had come. She turned to her husband and told him that she thought they should separate.

It wasn't a strange request, given the circumstances. They hadn't slept together in ages. One of the stewardesses even assumed they were siblings and asked if they were traveling to visit their mother. But something about saying it aloud, admitting that they didn't need to go on living together, made it feel possible that their marriage could end.

Olaf didn't say anything for a minute. He pulled a magazine out of the pocket in front of him and flipped through the pages without looking at them. "I know you think I'm unhappy," he said finally, with the air of someone who's often lain awake at night rehearsing this exact conversation. "But I'm not."

This surprised her: How could you sleep with other people and not be unhappy with a frigid wife? "But I am," she said. "We're hardly married as it is."

"I don't want to live apart," Olaf said. "I would be too lonely without you."

"You don't have to pretend for me, Olaf," she said. "I'll be able to make my own money now. You don't have to take care of me anymore. I won't be a burden to you."

Olaf slammed the magazine onto his tray table. "A burden!" The stewardess, tucking a blanket around a sleeping child two rows over, raised an eyebrow in their direction, and Olaf lowered his voice. "I can't believe you'd even say that to me."

"It doesn't matter if I say it or not. We hardly even see each other. If you wanted to be with me, you'd be home."

"I have class in the morning!" Olaf said, in an exasperated whisper. "I have rehearsals at night! You used to be a dancer. You know how this works."

You used to be a dancer. No one had ever said this to her, and it was as crushing as it was true. Maya swallowed. "No rehearsals run as late as you're out. I know you wish you could leave me and just be done with it."

"Maya." Olaf reached out and took her hand. "I haven't gone anywhere. I'm not trying to go anywhere. Why are you pushing me away?"

"You want things I can't give you," she said, pulling her hand from his. They'd heard, through a letter of Katusha's smuggled by a friend, that Natasha had a child of her own now—news that somehow made her own childlessness seem more permanent. It was yet another way Natasha had succeeded where Maya had failed.

Olaf shook his head. "I want *you*," he said. "I've always wanted you. You just decided you didn't want me."

She wanted to believe him, but she couldn't. *I know him better than he knows himself,* she thought. "If he stays with me, he'll always be unhappy."

They went on like that for the rest of the flight—Olaf making the case for staying together, Maya deflecting. They'd run out of things to say and sit in silence for a while, and then one of them would start up again, and the stewardess would walk by with folded arms and they'd fall quiet, brooding over what to say next.

By the time the plane began its descent, both of them were exhausted, and when Maya said things would be better this way, Olaf didn't fight her. "We don't have to do anything now," she said. "We'll take some time to get settled first."

Olaf stared out the window. The Manhattan skyline loomed in the distance, partly obscured by heavy gray snow clouds. Their future, a future apart, was growing nearer and nearer.

When the plane's wheels hit the runway, Maya took her husband's hand and squeezed it. "I have been very grateful to you," she said. "For everything." Olaf returned the squeeze, but said nothing.

It had all seemed simple then—but now, sitting alone in her hotel room in New York, nothing seemed simple to Maya. America was just different enough to disorient her. The city's parks were crowded with protesters, everyone's hair was long, and there was an acrid tension on the streets, which were even dirtier than Maya remembered from the Kirov tour. Nobody seemed to feel at home in this world anymore.

Maya looked out the window and watched the crowd of young people picketing in Central Park, all dressed in bright colors, the sorts of hues Natasha once risked everything to wear, and she found herself—though she knew it was impossible, that she'd burned her bridges once and for all—wishing for home.

CHAPTER TWENTY-THREE

Spring came, at last, to Moscow. For two months, Natasha attended wardrobe fittings (her figure, though still enviable, had thickened, and she needed to look her best for the ceremony), etiquette instruction (Furtseva and her crowd were very keen on what Natasha should—and, especially, should not—do and say), and English lessons (it was hoped that, if her film won an Oscar, she would astonish everybody with an acceptance speech delivered in perfect English). When the Kremlin approved her outfit for the ceremony—a long, diaphanous white dress, with the bell-shaped sleeves that were ubiquitous that season—her adventure began to feel real.

The closer Natasha got to her trip, the more anxious she became about being separated from her daughter. Since Elizaveta's birth, Natasha had never left her side for more than an hour or two: the thought of being a continent away made her throat close up. When, two days before Natasha's departure, Elizaveta contracted a runny nose—and the requisite fussiness and sleeplessness that come with infants' colds—Natasha's anxiety solidified into an urge. It was unthinkable to leave her daughter behind while she was ill, even with Katusha to care for her. That Natasha also wanted to see Maya—and introduce her to her niece—only made this urge more acute. Surely Maya wanted to meet Elizaveta too. Natasha became convinced that if she took her daughter to America, Maya would appear out of the shadows, perhaps in New York, where Furtseva, hoping for a victory at the Oscars, had scheduled a press conference the day after the ceremony.

Natasha waited until the night before her departure to tell her husband what she wanted. She knew Lev, who was also leaving the next morning to film in Siberia, would be distracted, and this was always a good time to make requests he'd otherwise decline. This was how she'd convinced him to let Katusha move next door in the sleepless days after Elizaveta was born. Lev was easiest to convince of something when his mind was elsewhere.

After the dinner dishes had been cleared and washed and Elizaveta put to bed despite her clamorous protests, Lev laid out a game of solitaire on the dining room table, as was his evening habit. Natasha watched him set up the cards and then, after he had flipped the first from its deck, she pounced. This was her moment: he would be in the middle of forming a strategy and eager to return to his game, and Natasha knew his distraction would aid her cause. She went about it casually, sat on the couch and made the pretense of flipping through a magazine. "My goodness," she said, exhaling heavily to indicate exhaustion. "I thought the baby would never go down." She glanced over her shoulder to catch her husband's response. Seeing there was none, she continued. "Poor thing—she was so fussy today. I'm worried she'll be too much for Katusha."

"Katusha's capable. She'll have no trouble taking care of the baby."

She had him now—he'd answered, but in the sort of voice that proved he was only half listening. Though her back was to him, she could hear the steady flip of his cards. "I'm not so sure," she said. She set the magazine on her lap as if struck by an idea. "You know, with her this ill, I don't think it's a good idea to be away from her. Traveling with a baby wouldn't be easy, but I could manage it if the handlers would help." (Furtseva had informed her that three or four escorts would accompany her to America. "For your protection," she'd said. "We want to keep you safe from the Americans.")

"They would never let you out of the country with the baby." And then, silence, except for the flipping of the cards.

"How do you know?"

"It's the law, isn't it? No two family members can travel at once." Each sentence was sliced in two by the flip of a card. It was a deliberate and steady rhythm, like the sound of someone sharpening a knife.

"But the baby wouldn't count, would she?"

"Of course she counts. They're worried you'll take off with her."

"What do you mean, 'they're worried'? Has someone been talking to you about this?"

The apartment suddenly felt still—too still—and Natasha realized that Lev had stopped flipping the cards, and she turned to see his hand frozen midair. For a split second, Natasha thought he'd said something he hadn't meant to, but then his hand moved again toward the deck of cards, and she decided he'd been thinking about his game.

"Furtseva visited my director while I was in his office this afternoon," Lev said. "She asked me to pass on these reminders to you."

"Well, why didn't you?"

"I just did."

Years ago, Natasha had told Lev she'd once thought about defecting, and after this he'd become jumpier around her. He sometimes clung to her hand so tightly in subway stations that she yelped—as if she were a balloon about to float away.

Natasha, seeing the tightness of her husband's mouth, felt compassion for him. It had to be hard to be on your second marriage—always on the lookout for things to go wrong again. She stood and walked over to him and embraced him from behind. "I'm not going anywhere, you know," she said, kissing his head. "I promise."

Lev looked up at her and patted her arm. "I know," he said, but he seemed relieved.

Natasha, pleased that her wifely instincts were so accurate, celebrated her victory too early. "Maybe if I told them the baby was sick, they'd let me take her. I thought about trying to see Maya—I want her to meet Elizaveta—"

Lev pulled back from Natasha's arms. "Oh, my dear," he said, sounding weary and amused at once. He tucked Natasha's hair behind her ear. "You know you can't do that."

Natasha did know this, but she didn't want to admit it, didn't want to admit that the walls around her were built higher than she'd thought. She sank into a chair. "Why not?"

"Even without the baby, the handlers would never let you within a hundred feet of Maya. It isn't safe."

"But what if I promised not to try to see Maya? I can't be away from the baby."

"Dear heart, you'll have to. There's no way they'll let you out of the country otherwise."

"But she's too little!"

"She'll have Katusha," Lev said. "She'll be fine. I promise." The phone rang and interrupted them, and Lev, after talking on their bedroom extension for half an hour, announced that his flight time had been moved up and he needed to get ready for bed. "Join me?" he said, reaching out his hand to her.

Natasha didn't move. Though none of this was Lev's fault—she knew everything he'd said was true—her helplessness needed an outlet, and it settled on him. She was too irritated to accept his overture.

Lev walked over to his wife and sat beside her. "It'll be better this way," he said. "You'll be able to enjoy America without having to worry about the baby. Natasha, please," he said, sounding unusually serious, "promise me that you won't do anything stupid."

Natasha swallowed and let her gaze fall to the floor. "I promise," she whispered.

Lev kissed her, and then he stood and offered his hand again, like a dancer beginning a pas de deux, and she took it and followed him to the bedroom.

The next morning, Natasha groggily kissed her husband goodbye before his early departure and then stumbled back into her bedroom, changing hastily. What Lev had said was true, but that didn't mean she had to accept it, and when Elizaveta's forehead felt warm, Natasha felt vindicated: no decent mother could leave a sick child behind. Surely Furtseva would understand that. Surely Lev would too—nobody could keep a promise under such circumstances. Natasha did not call Katusha and ask her to come take the baby. She shoved a few of Elizaveta's things into her overstuffed suitcase and struggled with the zipper.

It was uncharacteristic of her, to do something so flagrantly against her husband's will—they never made decisions without each other's consent, especially decisions about their daughter. But Lev was wrong, and there was no time to convince him of this, and there was no room for compromise. Natasha saw the baby's illness as an opportunity, one she knew she'd never have again, and Natasha, after all, was still herself, which was akin to being a bulldog: she wanted what she wanted, and she didn't let go until she got it—she sank her teeth into the heifer's ankles 'til it dropped.

When the doorbell rang, Natasha jumped, sure it was Lev, but it was only the Kremlin driver, come to take them to the airport. She smiled at the young man and tied on her favorite sunflower-printed headscarf, trying to appear youthful and carefree, like a girl who could be his friend, and she tucked her daughter under her arm and closed the apartment door behind her. She congratulated herself on her motherliness—unlike Elizaveta, she couldn't bear to be parted from her child.

The young driver glanced back at her as they headed down the stairs. "So we are dropping your daughter off somewhere?" he said. "I had the impression she was staying with your godmother."

"Ah, yes, that was the plan, but poor Elizaveta is a little sick today. I'm afraid she can't do without me," Natasha said. She said this with the same charming voice she used to get everything—discounted groceries, Katusha's exculpation, even Lev.

"Poor child," the driver said, not unkindly, and he helped Natasha into the waiting car. "If you'll excuse me," he said, "I just have to confirm that your flight is on time."

He headed toward a pay phone down the street, and Natasha settled into the car, feeling victorious. How pleasant it was to have people attending to your every need. She congratulated herself on attaining such a comfortable life, both for herself and for her daughter.

"You will grow up nothing like I did, my dear," she said, caressing Elizaveta's silky head. "You'll have everything, and you will be able to do anything you want, and you won't even have to break the law to do it."

Still, she kept looking over her shoulder for the entire drive, half expecting to see Lev hurrying after them instead of being on the plane to Siberia. She saw nothing of the crowded, growing city; she did not notice the traffic slowing in the streets; she did not notice towering apartment buildings that had accumulated over the last decade, as the demand for private housing had become ravenous; she did not see that the sky was overcast and gray. If she had, she would have found the gathering clouds foreboding.

Relief flooded her as they reached the airport. She'd been right: not even Furtseva would take a sick child from its mother. Natasha felt triumphant as she stepped out of the car and had no trouble looking radiant for the state publicist and photographer who awaited her outside the airport. She even cajoled Elizaveta into waving for the camera, which made everyone around them smile approvingly.

Inside, a young man in a black cap identified himself as Furtseva's assistant and escorted her into the terminal. "Your traveling companions have already boarded the plane," he explained as they walked. "To ensure your safety."

The old spot in Natasha's back tensed as if in warning, but there was no time to investigate this feeling. Thanks to the traffic, they were running late, and the assistant hurried her through the crowded terminal. When the porter at the gate asked for her ticket, Natasha swore under her breath. She hadn't flown since the baby was born, and she'd forgotten to have her ticket out and ready. She'd also forgotten to eat breakfast, and her hands shook as she handed Elizaveta to the assistant and dug around in her bag for the ticket.

Elizaveta started fussing, and Natasha shushed her as her purse fulfilled the universal obligation of purses—that is, giving up everything but the one thing required. "Shhh, shh, Liza," she said. "You're all right," and Elizaveta went quiet. Finally, Natasha found the ticket, handed it to the porter with a flourish, and turned around to take her daughter back from Furtseva's assistant, but he was gone.

Natasha dropped her bag. She looked in every direction, but she did not see the handler anywhere. She turned to the porter in a panic, but he shook his head and turned away. Then she heard Elizaveta wail, and she saw the assistant rushing toward the door, still holding her child.

"Wait!" Natasha cried, and she ran after him. Her headscarf flew off and she did not stop to retrieve it. Passersby in the terminal, waiting for flights to Leningrad and Helsinki and Tbilisi, looked up and then looked away, having learned long ago to distance themselves from any altercations. They busied themselves with their watches and their newspapers and their own children and families and turned a blind eye to the tragedy unfolding, as they'd turned a blind eye to so many tragedies before. But one woman, who had seen the black-capped young man hustle off with the baby that was clearly not his, bent down and picked up Natasha's fallen headscarf, watched Natasha run toward the door, and willed her to run faster.

Whether moved by the woman's well-wishes or her own terror, Natasha ran faster than she ever had in her life—in the middle of all this, she was astonished by her own speed—and she was only a few steps behind the assistant by the time he exited the airport. There, standing beside a waiting car, was Furtseva—and Lev.

"Madam, please do not make a scene," Furtseva said, and she gestured to Lev, who stepped forward reluctantly and took Elizaveta from the assistant's arms. "You have been given specific instructions on how to best represent our nation abroad, and we expect you to follow them. Your daughter will be well cared for while you are away."

Though she knew it was useless, Natasha turned to her husband with pleading eyes. "Lev," she said, still out of breath from the chase. "Please." She didn't even know what she was asking for—it was too late, they were trapped—but she needed him to answer. Elizaveta wailed so loud that even one of the handlers put a hand over his ear.

Lev stepped close to Natasha, and the baby calmed down a little, mucus streaming down her lip. "Oh, my love," Lev said, in a low and weary voice. He looked like he hadn't slept at all. "I tried to warn you last night." Natasha remembered the phone call the night before, the one he'd taken in the bedroom. So, they'd planned this—they'd even used her husband to coerce her. "Please, don't fight them. We'll all be safer." He kissed Natasha on the cheek, but she did not move to kiss him, and Furtseva stepped between them and ushered him and the baby into the waiting car. Natasha stood motionless as they drove away.

Furtseva's assistant put a hand on Natasha's arm. "Madam, we can't delay any longer. You'll miss your flight." Blank-faced, Natasha nodded, and she let herself be led back into the airport.

CHAPTER TWENTY-FOUR

Maya sat alone on her bed in her hotel room, watching television. Since arriving in America, she'd gotten into the habit of leaving it on all the time, both for the noise and for the education. Though her English was improving, she was eager to shed her accent, which both embarrassed her and raised the eyebrows of passersby. It was not a good time to sound like a Russian in America, and a small part of her still worried that if someone heard her accent, the KGB would home in on it like a heat-seeking missile, and she'd never be free again.

So she watched the Pink Panther scramble through his neon escapades and the Brady children chase their moplike dog, catching only about a third of the plot and a quarter of the dialogue. Most confusing of all was the lone episode she watched of *Monty Python's Flying Circus*, whose comedy did not translate well—she couldn't tell if it was satire or an ineffective educational program about trees.

That morning, she had taught her usual classes at the School of American Ballet. She'd been assigned the eight-year-olds, the youngest class at the school, which made her unhappy. It hurt her heart a bit to be around young children—her own child would've been around that age. The friend who'd assigned her this class had implied that Maya's skills were best suited for this age group, owing to her years away from dance. Maya hoped to work her way up the ranks after a while, at least to an age group that was capable of doing actual pirouettes—or getting through class without needing three bathroom breaks.

Maybe, if she was lucky, she would run into Balanchine, who sometimes came to visit the younger children's classes in search of new talent. After all these years, she had not forgotten him—a girlish part of her still dreamed that he would someday see a ballet she'd made and recognize something of himself in her, if only a shared love of making beautiful things. That same morning, a fellow teacher had told her that Balanchine was away in Mexico for reasons unknown.

Her life in America had, thus far, been uneventful. She had hardly spoken to Olaf since they'd arrived, which was something of a relief, and having spent the day with fidgety eight-year-olds, she was grateful to be having dinner alone, eating a greasy hamburger and watching some sort of award ceremony for American film. It was a beauty pageant, really, and a silly one at that—men parading in black tuxedos, women with enormous bouffants, jokes she didn't understand—but Maya enjoyed it anyway. Her back hurt from standing—it was taking her a long time to get used to being on her feet all day again—but watching the elegant ladies parade sylphlike across the screen made her feel glamorous.

The award ceremony took a turn toward the absurd. A tuxedoed orangutan scurried onstage, golden statuette in hand, and climbed into the arms of Walter Matthau, who appeared to feel very affectionate toward his companion. Maya checked the *TV Guide* to make sure she hadn't turned back to *Monty Python* by mistake. Having confirmed this was not the case, she had just gotten distracted by the *Guide*'s magically pungent perfume advertisements when someone knocked at her door.

She checked the peephole first, which made her feel like a lady detective in a film noir. She never knew who would be lurking in these hotel halls, and being alone made her jumpy.

It was Olaf. She hesitated, unsure of what to expect, or even what she wanted, and then opened the door. "Come in," she said, and Olaf stepped inside.

Maya realized she still had the *TV Guide* in her hand and for some reason hid it behind her back, which amused Olaf. "Didn't take you long to get to Times Square, I see," he said, imagining she was hiding some sort of lewd magazine.

"Oh, no, I—they have these perfume samples. The smells are printed right into the page—look!" She lifted a flap and held it to his nose.

Olaf obliged her and nodded approvingly. "Very nice," he said. "But a little sugary for you, perhaps. I've always thought of you as a musky sort of person."

She laughed, relieved they were still capable of joking around. He sat on the bed, and she joined him and wondered, for the first time, if they could be friends like they had at the Vaganova, even after everything. Maybe Olaf had accepted that it was time to move on.

Olaf reached into his jacket pocket and pulled out an envelope. "I've brought you a present," he said. "I hope that's all right."

"Of course," Maya said. She took the envelope but didn't open it. Olaf often turned to gifts when they were fighting, and she worried this was an attempt at reconciliation.

"It's tickets," he said, "to City Ballet. It's for tomorrow's show—one of Balanchine's best, they told me. *Agon*."

Maya had been trying to appear calm and detached, the way a future divorcée should be around her soon-to-be ex-husband, but this was too much. She gasped and sat on the bed and tore open the envelope even though she already knew what was inside.

"I got two tickets," Olaf said, "because—"

Maya dropped the envelope in her lap. Here it was—he was going to try to convince her to go with him, was going to make some big romantic gesture in the hope that they'd stay together.

"—because I thought you might want to take someone," he said. "You know, your friend at the school, maybe. I don't know. Whatever you want."

"Oh," Maya said. "That's very thoughtful of you. Thank you."

"Yes, well . . ." Olaf rose to his feet. "I'd better be going. I need to pack for rehearsal tonight." He grinned at the remains of Maya's burger, which was leaking grease onto the comforter. "Enjoy your dinner."

And then she was alone again, feeling oddly deflated. She glanced at the tickets in her lap. Of course, it was better that he didn't want to come along, she told herself. It would be too awkward to be together like that. Better to have a clean break. No regrets.

No regrets.

At that moment, the announcer on the television said something strange—strange not because the words he spoke were strange to her, but because they were familiar, as familiar to Maya as her own name. She looked up at the screen and there, dressed in white, with a gown as full as and hair piled as high as the others, was her sister.

In all these years, Maya had only seen pictures of her; she'd never seen *War and Peace* in theaters, not even to see herself on-screen, for fear it'd be too painful—and now, here was Natasha, climbing the stairs to the stage, accepting a golden statuette from another actress's hands. Here she was, fuller and rounder and dressed in the fashions of the day, but still herself, delivering a speech in English. "Thank you very much," she was saying to the audience. "I love you."

She was not saying this to Maya, of course. But Maya had not heard Natasha's voice in seven years, and the sound of it was unexpectedly sweet. What a relief to know that, with everything that had changed in the world, her sister's voice was still the same. Natasha bowed and left the stage, and the camera didn't follow her, and Maya wished more than anything that she could hear that voice again. That voice was the closest thing to a home that she had ever had, and Maya wanted to linger in it, if only for a minute, if only one more time.

Of course, this was impossible. Visiting Russians were kept far, far away from defectors. But after all these years, to be on the same continent again—surely Maya couldn't let the opportunity pass without even trying to see her. Couldn't they find some way to be together? Couldn't she see Natasha without putting either one of them in danger?

"Olaf would know what to do," Maya thought. He was good at solving things, good at slicing through the haze of details and seeing what needed to be done. After all, he'd managed to send her roses even when she was traveling all over the world. Maybe he'd know some way of getting in touch with Natasha, some way they could meet without being seen. Maya stood to go ask him for help and the tickets fell out of her lap, as if in response.

The glamor and luxury that flickered across Maya's television screen were just a sliver of Natasha's reality. The Oscars overwhelmed Natasha in every way a person can be overwhelmed. As an actress, she was no stranger to pomp or its pressures; thanks to all of the film premieres and press junkets, she knew well the particular exhaustion of being on display. Yet nothing could have prepared her for the sensory overload of Hollywood and its excesses. Never in her life, not in the finest shops in Moscow, not even in the costume rooms at Mosfilm or the Vaganova, had she been confronted by this many different colors and textures at once. Blues, mauves, purples, silvers, golds, an electrifying shade of green she didn't even have a name for. Sequins, feathers, velvets, gauzes, and flesh, so much flesh, powdered and wrinkled and artificially tanned, suspiciously flawless and plump. Barbra Streisand looked half naked beneath her spangled jumpsuit, and Natasha felt embarrassed for her. Even the most humbly dressed person at the Oscars made actresses at Mosfilm premieres look like dowdy washerwomen.

Nor did this sensory exhaustion cease once everyone settled into the auditorium and the lights went out: every single audience member seemed to be wearing a different perfume, creating the olfactory equivalent of an elephant sitting on a pipe organ. By the time the ceremony began, all of these impressions had jumbled together and given her a terrible headache.

And yet, she was here. After all this time, after all the twists and turns the vagaries of life had lobbed at her, she'd made it to America. She was sitting in a crowd of some of the wealthiest, most successful people in the world—and some of them even knew who she was. The wide-faced man beside her turned to her just before the lights went out and revealed himself to be King Vidor, the director of the American *War and Peace*. "Audrey was wonderful, of course, but you were a marvelous Natasha—so youthful and free," he said.

Natasha blushed at the compliment. "Is she here?" she asked, feeling seventeen.

"Is who here? Oh! Ms. Hepburn? Of course!" He reached up and waved at a tall and reedy woman standing near the front rows. The woman waved back. There she was—Audrey Hepburn, older and bonier, yes, but almond-eyed and elegant as ever. Natasha wanted to get up and rush over and—what? Pledge her loyalty? Beg for a blessing? What do you ask of a goddess?—but the lights began to dim.

The ceremony was long and dull, as ceremonies are wont to be, and the Americans' plodding attempts at humor didn't survive

Natasha's rudimentary understanding of English. Badly jet-lagged, Natasha kept nodding off, and her head once rolled onto King Vidor's shoulder—who graciously let it stay. But when Jane Fonda swooped onto the stage in a jet-black gown and began to announce the Best Foreign Language Film nominees, Vidor shook Natasha awake. "It's your moment!" he whispered. "You're going to win—I'm certain of it!"

Vidor was right. *War and Peace, Russia*—they had trained her to listen for the title in English, not the familiar *Voyna i Mir*—that was what Jane Fonda pronounced after she opened the envelope, and the resulting adrenaline jolted Natasha from her drowsiness and sent her hurrying down the red-carpeted aisle. As she climbed the stairs to the stage, she cursed herself for choosing such a voluminous dress—if she tripped, her entire country would be humiliated. But she made it up the steps unscathed and, though she stumbled through her speech and felt foolish, afterward they applauded her like she'd done them all a tremendous favor, and this buoyed her spirits a little. King Vidor shook her hand when she returned to her seat. "Well done," he said. It was nice, after a year of motherhood's thankless labors, to be celebrated.

She didn't feel celebrated for long. Her excitement began to fade as the ceremony continued and the audience's attention turned elsewhere. When the lights went up a couple hours later, the handlers let her make an appearance at the after-party—after all, photos of the Russian triumphant needed to appear in American papers—but the handlers circled around her at all times, making conversation all but impossible. Sooner than Natasha wanted, they ushered her out and into the waiting limousine. Natasha settled into the cold leather seat, exhausted, and for the first time examined the golden statuette cradled in her arm like a child. When the car door closed, one of the handlers reached out and unceremoniously yanked the little gold statue from her arms, and it reminded her of Elizaveta, being carried away in the airport, and Natasha began to cry.

She cried quietly, wiping the tears as quickly as they came, wanting to avoid arousing her handlers' ire. She had never been away from her daughter, and this alone would have been difficult to bear. Before falling asleep the night before, she had thought of Elizaveta's impossibly tiny fingernails, and the particular way her hair curled at the nape of her neck, and she cried then too. But to be separated like this—halfway across the world, with her husband powerless to help—was unbearable. On the flight to America, Natasha had replayed that moment in her mind over and over like a nightmare, trying to understand how it had happened. If only she'd run faster. If only she'd given the Kremlin driver a better excuse. If only, if only. Now, watching the female handler cradle the Oscar instead of her, Natasha knew that nothing she could have said or done would have kept Elizaveta with her. She thought she'd learned to play the game, to exploit her situation to her own end. Now she understood that she was the one being exploited.

She was like a cosseted animal—one plied with all the food and drink and toys it could want, but kept in a cage. And Lev was too. She'd considered herself a respected artist, one whose loyalty had earned her the freedom to live as she pleased. Now she understood the truth: she, and Lev, and every artist in Russia were only puppets—bendable and, if necessary, dispensable.

Natasha still wished, with the usual unreasonableness people reserve for their spouses, that Lev had stood up to Furtseva. She wondered if the rest of her life was going to be like this, she and Lev tied together like a balloon and its string—her, reaching to get away, and Lev, pulling her down, urging her to be careful. After the scene at the airport, she might never be allowed out of Moscow again.

At this thought, Natasha's crying erupted into weeping, and one of the male handlers looked up at her with unexpected anxiety. He shifted in his seat and glanced at his female companion, hoping she would know how to deal with this sudden display of emotion. The female handler, who had a mole above her upper lip, reached over and handed Natasha a handkerchief. "Stop all this fussing," the woman said. "You'll need to pull yourself together by the time we reach the hotel."

Embarrassed, Natasha nodded like a little child, and she dabbed her eyes and calmed herself and hated herself for doing as she was told. How she wanted to wail like an infant, to kick and scream and rip the mole right from the handler's lip. She wanted to yank the car door off its hinges and run, anything to escape the limousine and its oppressive silence, to escape her life itself.

Natasha entertained these thoughts uncertainly, as one steps on an icy pond at the beginning of a thaw. She looked out the window and tried to catch a glimpse of Los Angeles as it rushed by in the dark, but she saw only streaked lights and formless shadows, as if some state entity had censored America itself. She had imagined herself here so many times: America, the place where you could buy anything you wanted, say anything you wanted, be anything you wanted. She'd never imagined she would be here like this, weeping and miserable. She thought how good it was that you couldn't see what lay ahead of you when you were young. How disappointed teenage Natasha would be to see her now—she'd made it to the West, and all she had to show for it was a headache.

She kept herself together as she exited the car and was escorted through a sea of waiting photographers, through the hotel lobby, up the elevator, down the hall. The female handler opened the door of Natasha's hotel room and made the same inspection she always did, in the name of "security." She looked behind curtains and in dresser drawers, beneath the bed, inside the closet. She even ran her hands through the many bouquets that had accumulated on Natasha's desk while they were away. "So many admirers," the woman said, and her hand lingered on an arrangement of garish salmon-colored roses. She turned to Natasha. "Sleep now," she said. "We have an early flight to New York, and you need your rest for the press conference there tomorrow. You'll be expected in the lobby at 6 a.m."

And then Natasha was alone, in her room that reeked of flowers like a funeral parlor. When the sound of the handler's footsteps drifted down from the hall, Natasha tore at the flowers and sent half of them flying to the floor. The vase of salmon roses broke at her feet and water soaked through her shoe.

This unexpected sensation—her stockings, wet inside her shoes, and her toes, wet inside her stockings—filled Natasha with remorse. Her handlers would be furious if an extra cleaning charge appeared on her hotel bill, and as Natasha bent to clear the salmon-colored roses from the floor, her fingertips brushed an envelope, one so tiny that the handler had missed it. She often got letters from admirers, and she'd learned never to read them: they were always dull or—worse—vulgar. But this one was so small that it aroused her curiosity. She opened it, and her English was just good enough to read what it said:

You were right. His name was Pinky. Forgive me? 8pm

Beneath was tomorrow's date and a New York City address. Maya was in New York, and she wanted to see her.

Natasha lay back on the bed and tried to ascertain, through her exhaustion, how she felt about this. She had dreamed of this reunion, but faced with the actual possibility—with being asked for forgiveness—Natasha wasn't sure what she wanted at all. Forgiving Maya wouldn't restore Natasha's spine, or give her a place in the Kirov, or return the years of life she'd lost—a life she could have even lived in America. Maya didn't deserve Natasha's forgiveness—if anything, she deserved to be ignored, for Natasha to return to her life in Russia and never speak to her again. Surely forgiveness only benefited the guilty.

"But then," Natasha thought, "I am guilty too." She'd betrayed her sister to Furtseva, gotten her blacklisted, ruined her chance at her own dream. When Furtseva dangled that opportunity in front of her, she hadn't even hesitated, and unlike Maya, she hadn't even done so hoping to take her place. All she'd wanted was for Maya to be unhappy. In a way, what she'd done was worse.

Natasha wondered what kinds of lives they would have lived if they'd been born someplace else. The state had saved them, yes, had provided classrooms and theaters and movie studios in which to learn and perform, had given them food and shelter and a place to belong, and then it pitted them against each other. It was as if they'd been born on a lifeboat, adrift at sea, and had spent their lives pushing each other off it.

Natasha traced her sister's words with her fingertip. She did not know what to do. She undressed and began the behemoth work of taking down her hair, piling hairpins into a nestlike stack on the counter. She undressed and bathed and then lay naked in bed all night, deliberating, and by the time the sun had risen she hadn't come up with an answer.

Nor had she decided by the time she boarded her plane to New York. Nor had she decided at takeoff, or by the time the stewardess came down the aisle with a gleaming cart of beverages. They hit turbulence over Arizona, and the cart was whisked away before Natasha had the chance to ask for anything. For half an hour the plane lurched into terrifying drops at unpredictable intervals. Natasha closed her eyes tight and wished she'd stayed home; this journey had brought no end of misery. The female handler, who in Los Angeles had made the unwise choice of trying oysters for the first time and had never been a hardy flier to begin with, disappeared into the bathroom and did not come out again, even when the skies finally cleared. The stewardess's voice crackled over the intercom, and she announced that they'd be in New York in four and a half hours.

New York—the city where she'd once planned to run away with Ilya and reinvent herself. The city where her sister was now making a new life—one that, by all accounts, did not include a child. Maya had never mentioned a child in her letters to Katusha. Perhaps she'd taken Natasha's advice and gotten rid of it after all. Perhaps she'd feared, as their own mother had, that being a mother would weigh her down.

If this was true, Natasha couldn't blame her sister for it. Motherhood did end your life, in a way—at least, a life solely of your own design. From the moment her daughter arrived, Natasha had been forced to filter every decision, every aspiration, every hope through Elizaveta's needs. She couldn't go out when she wanted or stay up like she wanted. Really, she couldn't want at all. She'd imagined, as the naive childless often do, that motherhood would be simple if you treated it like hosting a dinner party: you serve yourself first, so you know you won't go hungry, and you share the abundance left over. But Elizaveta was greedy, as all children are. She wasn't content with the crumbs from the table. She wanted everything for herself. Maybe Maya was the wiser one, running away—from having a child, and from Russia.

People fled the Soviet bloc all the time. Writers, composers, physicists, motorcycle racers—all people who had been in a plane, or a boat, or tramping through a field, like her, and decided to disappear. Even Stalin's daughter had fled to New Delhi and then America. Natasha wondered how it would feel to step out of your life. Would you feel crushable and small, like a snail without a shell, or someone who exited a chrysalis and sprouted wings?

If she wanted to, Natasha could leave her life behind. She could make a diversion, slip away just as Maya and Olaf and others had done—if they had managed it, surely she could too. She could run for her life and find a policeman. She could become an actress in America, perhaps with the help of King Vidor. She could be feted like all the spangled women who'd crowded the Oscars. Hadn't Ilya told her once that if she wanted something, she needed to reach out and take it?

Several thousand feet above the earth, Natasha realized, for the first time, that she was no better than her mother. She knew, with a certainty that surprised her, that like her mother, she was capable of leaving her family behind. Hadn't she made Elizaveta's fate the great lesson of her life—that life was only good if you got everything you wanted?

She could do it. Some would even celebrate her for it. But as much as she envied Maya, she couldn't imagine a life alone, coming home to an empty apartment, sleeping in an empty bed. She couldn't imagine leaving behind a motherless child, abandoning a husband who loved her. If she returned to Russia, to her family, she would have fewer choices, and her daughter would grow up with many of the limits and restraints that she had. But Elizaveta would have a mother and a father; she would be loved, and didn't that matter too?

Once, she'd thought that being bound to others was a kind of slavery. But a life lived in the sole pursuit of your own happiness was a life without love, and being free from love wasn't freedom at all—it was slavery to yourself. Natasha remembered sitting at the teahouse in Leningrad, dreading the burden of her sister's care. Now she understood that love could be an anchor.

This was why she couldn't desert her family—and why she couldn't ignore her sister, either. To love was to turn toward, not away. Their lives had been a tangled duet—Natasha pulling, Maya clinging, like that day so long ago at the Vaganova when they'd learned to waltz. But now they had the chance to be together one last time. Like a partner beginning a pas de deux, Maya had extended her hand. Natasha knew she had to take it.

Slipping away would not be easy. The handlers had been brought along for the sole purpose of preventing something like this. They would arrest her if she tried to find Maya, maybe worse. But this was her only chance. Watching the cornfields and lakes of America pass beneath her window, Natasha knew with an unexplainable certainty that she would never be in this country again.

Soon, the handler returned to her seat. "I'm sorry you're unwell," Natasha said, and though she meant it—the handler's face was a pitiable shade of green—she also wanted to get into her handler's good graces, in case mercy proved necessary.

But it was the first kind thing Natasha had said to her the entire trip, and the handler, who had spent half a lifetime in interrogation rooms and was a shrewd detector of insincerity, narrowed her eyes. "Don't pretend to be friendly now," she said. "Your charms aren't going to win you any favors." The handler looked over her shoulder and, satisfied that all of the passengers were either asleep or distracted, leaned in so close that Natasha smelled the vomit on her breath. "If you misbehave," she said, "your family will agonize over you," and she ran a bony hand up Natasha's skirt and pinched the flesh of her inner thigh so hard Natasha had to bite her tongue to keep from crying out.

CHAPTER TWENTY-FIVE

The next morning, Maya felt scattered and anxious all through her first class. Her young pupils, perhaps unconsciously absorbing their teacher's frame of mind, were equally distracted. Every day in the classroom had its share of foibles—any assemblage of eight-year-olds is bound to bring a little chaos—but this particular morning had been a true comedy of errors. A leotard strap had snapped, causing its owner to run from the room in embarrassment and tears. One girl kicked her classmate in the rear end during grand battement. Another, asking to use the bathroom, had been unable to make it in time, and though the custodian was promptly called, a sharp ammonia odor still lingered.

At first, Maya was unimpressed with the teaching life. She'd wanted a challenge, something that came with a little more prestige and felt less like babysitting. She worried that spending all her days on the building blocks of ballet would atrophy the muscle memory she needed to keep building dances of her own.

But then, after a few weeks, she began to fall in love with it, and with them, all these little children whose unmolded bodies and minds were entrusted to her care. She saw the hunger with which her pupils watched her—they were so open, so trusting, already smitten with ballet—and thought of her earliest days at the Vaganova. Once, like them, she'd arrived at ballet school for the first time, had consented to have her body and mind and very self shaped by the hands of strangers. She wondered what compelled a very young person to take on such a task. Why had she sacrificed everything and lived on so little, bunched her toes into shoes that made them blister and bleed? And why had she kept on doing it, year after year after year?

Eventually, watching these children learn to steady themselves at the barre, to bend deep into pliés, to take their first halting steps toward grace, she understood the answer to these questions. It was love. Love was the only thing that could sustain such voluntary discipline and sacrifice. Love told her which of the little girls in her class would go on studying ballet—not just next year, or the year after that, but in the years and decades to come. It wasn't just about the girls' range of motion or flexibility, but their determination—how many times they attempted a first pirouette, how closely they listened to her instructions. How deeply they were in love.

As Maya tucked her damp shoes into her practice bag, one little girl still stood in the classroom after all the others had gone, practicing a simple turn, trying to spot herself in the mirror as she did so. All of her classmates were in the hallway, pulling their tiny pink shoes off their feet, making jokes, chattering with their mothers. Only this girl remained, her concentration unbroken by the exclamations and laughter coming through the open door. Maya watched her and smiled. Only love could give you stubbornness like that.

Maya packed up the rest of her things and stood by the piano with her street shoes in hand, waiting for the little girl to finish. The world seemed so simple when you fixed yourself on one thing. Love one thing, and all it required of you was to become worthy of it. Maya envied the girl for the purity of her desire. Yes, she had once felt a love like that—it had become corrupted over the years by jealousy and ego, but these stains didn't render the surface beneath them any less noble. Perhaps, in this little classroom with the sun streaming down through a wall of windows, just like the classroom of her childhood, she could discover her first love again, this bodily language born in courts of kings.

The next teacher poked her head through the door, looked at her watch, and walked away. Maya knew they couldn't linger any longer. "Darina," she said, "it's time to go home," and Darina started as if she'd forgotten Maya was there and hurried toward the door.

Halfway there, Darina tripped, fell flat on her face and started to cry, more out of embarrassment than injury. Maya hurried toward her—oh, how good children were at hurting themselves—but Olaf, who had suddenly appeared in the doorway, got there first. "Ah, poor baby," he said, kneeling down, his thick accent charming even to Maya's ears. He set Darina on her feet and pulled a handkerchief from his pocket and dabbed the tears from her eyes.

Darina, who was too young to be afraid of strange young men with handkerchiefs, wrapped her little arms around Olaf's neck, her tears dissolved into hiccups. "There, there," Olaf said. "All better?" Darina pulled away and nodded, and then, with no less speed or vivacity than before, ran for the door.

Olaf stood and grinned at Maya. "They really gave you the littlest ones, didn't they?"

Maya, whose heart was feeling a cup too brimful, shrugged. "I don't mind." She walked over to the piano and flipped through the sheet music with no purpose at all except appearing busy. She'd been so grateful to him last night, when he'd found a solution to her problem, but she worried this gesture had been misconstrued. She swallowed and, though she didn't want to, said, "You would have been a good father." She didn't turn around—she didn't want to see his expression.

The air was still thick and warm from the girls' exertion. The parents' muffled chatter had faded away, and Maya could hear Olaf breathing. "I still could be," he said, quietly.

She heard him walking toward her and turned around. "Ah, no street shoes," she reminded him, wagging a finger, grateful for the diversion. Olaf pulled off his sneakers and walked over in his socks.

"I have bad news," Olaf said. "They've swapped out *Agon* for tonight—somebody got injured. Now they're doing something called *Serenade*."

"Ah, that's too bad," Maya said. "I've always wanted to see *Agon*. Remember when you showed me that magazine back at school? That time you first told me about Balanchine." She smiled to herself, remembering the cautious way he'd pulled the magazine from his practice bag, such strange contraband for a boy of seventeen.

"Yes, but you should still be excited," Olaf said. "It's to Tchaikovsky's Serenade for Strings."

"Serenade for Strings!" It was the very first music she'd set a dance to—with Olaf, all those years ago in the Vaganova practice room.

"You know," Olaf said, "I think I still remember the steps you made for us . . ." He set down his street shoes and came close to her and put his hands on her hips, and Maya did not pull away.

It was not an empty overture. Somehow, Olaf really did remember the steps she had made for them—the waltz's lilt, the turns en arabesque—and she remembered them too, and both of them remembered the sensation of being close to each other, not as they had been in London, fumbling, feigning lust, but as they had been in the Vaganova classroom, when they'd shared so much more than their bodies. They remembered what it was like to be young and unencumbered by regrets. They remembered what it was like to want something with the entirety of your being. They remembered what it was like to want each other—and Maya knew, as some unacknowledged part of her always had, that she'd wanted Olaf even then.

Toward the end of the sequence, Maya reached for Olaf's hand to guide her through a turn en arabesque and then pulled back—she'd misremembered the steps and moved a second too early.

But Olaf adjusted and took her hand. "It's all right—I'm not going anywhere," he said, and Maya believed him.

When they finished, Olaf came close, as if he wanted to kiss her, and Maya didn't know whether to lean in or pull away. Before she could decide, she saw the teacher of the next class poke her head through the classroom door again.

"I have to go," she said, breaking from him. "I have to change."

"Ah, of course," Olaf said, looking disappointed.

"But maybe you could meet me after the show tonight?" Maya didn't know why she was asking him for this, or what, exactly, she wanted, but the heart is such a fickle thing—who can know it? "Maybe we could get a drink at the hotel."

"Of course," he said. "Just knock on my door when you're ready. I'll be waiting for you."

"It might be late," Maya said.

Olaf smiled. "I'm used to waiting for you."

The most important moments in our lives like to sneak up on us when our attention is diverted elsewhere. Maya headed down the hallway, and now that her students were gone, and Olaf was too, her apprehension over seeing (or not seeing) her sister flooded back in, leaving no room for her usual preoccupations, like how she was going to slim down, what music she was going to use for her next ballet, and how she could finally meet Balanchine after all these years of anticipation.

On an ordinary morning, the last of these preoccupations would have been foremost in her mind. She always hoped, as she walked down the school hallways, that she would run into Balanchine. She thought that if she kept him in her mind, he might appear. But here she was mistaken: today, when she was at her most distracted, she would meet him.

It took her a moment to realize that the old man walking toward her was the same man whose picture Olaf had shown her in the Vaganova library, the one she'd kept tucked away in her dresser drawer. Anyone would have aged in the many years that had passed since then, but he was nearly unrecognizable. Even Natasha would not have recognized Balanchine from the man she'd met seven years ago. The nose was the same—yes, Maya would know that curved and beaky nose anywhere, the nose Olaf had once compared with her own—but he looked so much older than she'd pictured. His hair had gone white. His cheeks were hollow, and his jawline—his only feature Maya had once admired—now sagged.

These were not cruel observations, the vengeance of a punctured childhood dream, but the truth. Balanchine was looking more haggard than ever—the divorce he'd hastily obtained in Mexico had not achieved his desired aim of winning a young ballerina's love, and he was inflamed with sorrow and rage. He was hurrying down the hallway to find his assistant and instruct her to ban this ballerina and her new husband from the theater, and this accounted for his bitter expression, the grimness of his drooping jaw. When Balanchine got home that evening, he would look at himself in the mirror and see his craggy face and decide that this was why the young ballerina had rejected him: he looked like an old man. Soon after, he would chase after youth like a Russian Ponce de León, trying one treatment after another, including the injections of bulls' blood that may have infected his brain and ended his life too soon.

He noticed the soft young woman stopped in the hallway, her mouth open as if to speak, but he did not stop, and he scowled as he neared her in hope that she'd leave him alone. Maya saw herself reflected in his eyes: an aging, shapeless woman who could be neither lover nor muse, and thus had no use to him. She tried to say something, and he saw this, but he did not stop, did not even excuse himself as he brushed past her. Later, he would feel sorry for how abrupt he had been with this girl; he had disappointed her, as he had disappointed so many women in his life. Her face, which, for some reason, was familiar, would come to stand in his mind for all those disappointed women, and he would think of her face, without recalling whose it was, years later as he made his final confession from a hospital bed.

Maya stood frozen after he'd gone. She had hoped for this moment since she was a child, had hoped that seeing Balanchine would bestow some inestimably great wisdom or comfort upon her, would answer some question she'd carried all her life—a question about her worth as an artist, a dancer, a woman, a question her mother's death had laid upon her like a seal.

But she knew, as this weary old man passed her by, that no person could be this powerful, in her life or anyone else's, and she had been foolish to hope for it.

Even so, she felt lost. Her god had been toppled from his throne and there was no one to take his place. It felt easier, having seen Balanchine, to believe all the rumors she'd heard about him: everyone knew about his five wives, that he took his lovers—married and unmarried—from the ranks of the ballet, that he cast them aside when they grew too old for his purposes. Did it even matter if such a man was her father, or if he made astonishing ballets? Did it matter if what you made was beautiful, when you left suffering and destruction in your wake?

Maya was still thinking of this when she arrived back in her hotel room that evening, but the presence of her ticket on the table brought her attention back to what lay before her. She decided not to wallow. She dressed very slowly and deliberately, rolling her stockings up her legs, pulling her new chartreuse dress over her head, putting on tiny crystalline earrings that caught the light and scattered it. She picked up her jet-black eyeliner and then put it down again. Perhaps, if she arrived in her usual disguise, her sister would not recognize her.

That is, if she was coming at all. Maya had left Natasha's ticket at will-call with strict instructions for the clerk, and she was unsure, as she rushed out into the rain and indulged in a taxi, of what would be more difficult to face: seeing her sister for the last time, or knowing that Natasha never wanted to see her again.

The taxi pulled up to Lincoln Center, and Maya was struck anew by the beauty of this place—not the basement entrance she used as an employee, but its wide and opulent plaza, its shimmering fountain, the golden glow seeping out from each of the buildings on the square: the ballet theater, the orchestral hall, the opera house. Striding out onto the plaza, she felt like she was walking onto a stage, about to participate in some grand drama.

Her heartbeat tripled as she ascended the marble stairs to the theater lobby. She was not excited by the splendor of the throng of people around her, took no notice of their conversations, their perfumes, their chic dress. All her senses reached out for one face, once voice, one body she'd known before she was aware of her own existence. She looked around and saw couples drinking champagne, anxious parents checking their programs, vulgar young businessmen peering down from upper floors in an attempt to see down women's dresses, but she did not see Natasha.

She paced the length of the lobby. She lingered near an enormous marble sculpture of a woman with open legs, whose glad expression she did not notice. She went out onto the balcony and looked over the square, hoping to see her sister stepping out of a taxi or dashing in from the rain. But she did not, and when an usher walked around sounding a chime that signaled everyone to their seats, she obeyed him.

If Maya had been able to appreciate her surroundings, she would have noticed that the theater was like the inside of a jewel box, all bright golds and plush red. She would have seen that the theater's four tiers, golden and studded with white lights that sparkled like diamonds, resembled the Kirov's, where she and her sister had first sat with Katusha on that fateful night, where she had first fallen in love. She might even have perceived that she was being followed—not by flesh and blood, but by a presence, one that had lingered near her all her life and came especially close at the ballet. But she did not notice any of this, and as she took her seat—the second to last in a row, next to the empty seat where her sister would have been if she had come—she felt as alone as she ever had in her life. The theater was full of couples and families and people who were happy to be with one another, but her sister had not come.

The lights dimmed. It was certain now: Natasha didn't want to see her. The invisible string that had connected them all their lives was severed, once and for all. Maya resolved to resign herself to this; she settled into her seat and tried not to think about the rest of her life. The orchestra began to play Tchaikovsky's Serenade for Strings. The song was sweet and strong and pure. Though, because she had been born after Stalin slaughtered thousands of priests and rabbis and imams and bishops and monks and nuns and shuttered their places of worship, Maya did not have the language to express this, she felt there was a holiness to it.

The curtain rose, revealing women in long white tutus bathed in clear blue light, a light so blinding that the women stood with one hand raised against it. As the first stirring phrase of Serenade repeated, the women reached their raised hands past their faces and down into a port de bras—not as separate beings, not as seventeen women reaching seventeen arms, but as one organism that lived and breathed together—and in a single, seamless motion, the dancers' feet splayed out into first position.

It was such a simple thing—hands and feet changing from one position to another. An elemental thing, one Maya had taught her little dancers to do that very morning, and yet, it was a transformation. Here were women who had devoted themselves and their lives not to the mere imitation of beauty, but to becoming it. And this, this was what Maya wanted, what she had always wanted—a love so pure it could transform you into love itself.

It was wonderful, and it did not matter who had made it—or perhaps it did, perhaps bringing some sort of lasting beauty into the world could be a kind of repentance. Perhaps it could save you.

Maybe, maybe not. There would be time to sort through all this later—for now, for Maya, the world began and ended on that stage. She watched, and she knew so much about her life that was to come. She knew she would meet Olaf that night and welcome him back to their bed. She knew she would have another child—a girl, a girl who would grow up to be pure and strong like this song, an American girl who could become whatever she wanted—perhaps a dancer on this very stage, enacting steps her mother had set out for her. And Maya knew, without understanding why, that her mother had loved her, loved her still, was near her even now.

She was so engrossed that she did not notice anything around her—not the man on her right wiping a tear from his eye, not the woman coughing behind her, not the usher scolding a latecomer with angry whispers. All that Maya saw and felt and heard were these bodies bending time and space with their music, and she gave herself up to it. She vowed, as she had once vowed at the Kirov, as a little child with her twin sister beside her, that however and wherever she lived her life, it would be in pursuit of this.

As Maya made her vow, someone's foot slid towards hers. It pressed down on Maya's toes so slowly and so gently that Maya, still enraptured, didn't pay it any attention, assumed it was an accident; after all, it was dark and the theater was crowded.

And then, in the darkness, a hand reached out and took hers.

AUTHOR'S NOTE

For those of us enamored of the past, weaving fact into fiction is a thrilling and terrifying enterprise—one offering both a wealth of material and the weighty responsibility of representing actual events.

During the writing of this novel, I selectively quoted and interpreted historical figures and events to serve my story. Out of respect for these real people, who provided the most satisfying work of my life, as well as excellent—if imaginary—company in the pandemic's bleakest days, I'd like to explain how I did so.

Many of the historical events represented in this novel are factual. The Cuban Missile Crisis, though condensed, is represented as accurately as current records allow, including New York City Ballet staffers' panicked plans for evacuating Moscow, Kennedy watching *Roman Holiday*, and the accidental heroics of the Russian submarine officer Vasily Arkhipov. (Though I can't prove Kennedy fantasized about Marilyn Monroe during the Cuban Missile Crisis, I'd say the odds were good.) "Obscenity" in Russian art was tamped down after Khrushchev was horrified by a 1962 exhibition at the Moscow Manege—where, I'm delighted to report, he declared a painting only fit "for wallpapering a urinal."

Other events in history I altered or streamlined in the interest of my narrative. It was the Bolshoi, not the Kirov, that toured America in 1962, though *Spartacus* really was booed at the Metropolitan Opera, and members of the company met the Kennedys. The real-life Yekaterina Furtseva was closely involved in both the filming of *War and Peace* and the New York City Ballet's 1962 Soviet tour, but she was elected Minister of Culture in 1960, not 1959, and attempted suicide not long after.

The characters of Sergei and Irina Bondarchuk, Yekaterina Furtseva, Anatoly Petritsky, Leonid Yakobson, George Balanchine, and his New York City Ballet entourage (including Lincoln Kirstein, Jacques d'Amboise, Nora Kaye, Betty Cage, and Tanaquil Le Clerq), and, of course, Khrushchev and Kennedy, were all inspired by real-life namesakes. The characters of Natasha and Lev were inspired by the Soviet actors Lyudmila Savelyeva and Vyacheslav Tikhonov; Savelyeva had no twin sister, but she was born at the siege of Leningrad, studied at the Vaganova, and was cast as Natasha in Bondarchuk's *War and Peace*. Natasha's love triangle with Bondarchuk and Lev was fictional, though by all accounts Savelyeva and Bondarchuk deeply respected each other, and Savelyeva and Tikhonov were often photographed holding hands while promoting the film.

Other than his obsession with iced milk and cherries, much of what I've reported about Sergei Bondarchuk is true, including his remarkable vision for his film, his cruelty toward the actor who played Prince Andrei, and his hopping around during the filming of Natasha's waltz, waving fans and scarves in front of the camera (which, happily, can be witnessed in documentary footage). Sergei and Irina Bondarchuk were married until his death in 1994.

Most of my representations of the legendary choreographer George Balanchine are based on historical record. Balanchine accompanied his New York City Ballet abroad in 1962, and their stop in the Soviet Union really did overlap with the Cuban Missile Crisis. Balanchine's encounters with the fictional Maya and Natasha at City Ballet and the Vaganova were, of course, of my own invention, though I framed both these scenes with details of what Balanchine's life was like at that time. Though Balanchine was indeed in Russia during the filming of *War and Peace*, there is no evidence that he participated in its production, or ever had a child.

Maya's ballets, *Ballet School* and *Bolero*, were inspired by choreographic works of the same names by Asaf Messerer and Maurice Béjart. The Bolshoi performed *Ballet School* to great acclaim during its 1962 tour, and later, Bolshoi dancer Maya Plisetskaya became one of *Bolero*'s most brilliant interpreters. Balanchine's masterpieces *Serenade* and *Agon* need no introduction.

Finally, though the novelist writing across culture, language, and time strives for accuracy, accessibility is a chief concern as well. I chose to omit the Russian use of patronymics in the name of easing that accessibility.

ACKNOWLEDGMENTS

Every life contains some undeserved extravagance: mine is the abundance of teachers, mentors, editors, colleagues, and friends who loved this book into existence.

Thank you to the MFA faculty of Warren Wilson College, especially my advisors Peter Orner, T. Geronimo Johnson, Debra Spark, Hanna Pylväinen, and David Haynes, who helped shape *Maya & Natasha* in its infancy. Many thanks to my readers, Kirsten Lind, Hannah Markos, Annette Wong, and Joy Deng, and to my MFA cohort, whose camaraderie made all the difference.

Sincere gratitude to Andy Mozina, Gail Griffin, Bruce Mills, Bonnie Jo Campbell, Glenn Deutsch, Amy Rodgers, Lisa Cronkhite-Marks, Stephen Louisell, Michael Keller, Nicole Brennan, Meghan Florian, Diane Zinna, Ezekiel Jarvis, Natalie Bakopoulos, Stina Kielsmeier-Cook, Rebecca Randall, Sam Bartlett, Abby Ladin, Tim Reidy, Chris Castellani, Liam Callanan, Sarah Cypher, Juli Min, Jocelyn Mathewes, Leah Rumsey, and Lauren Carlson for their support and encouragement these many years.

My thanks to AWP's Writer to Writer, the Collegeville Institute, the Glen Arbor Arts Center, the Elizabeth George Foundation, Friends of Writers, The Mount (the home of Edith Wharton), the

Straw Dog Writers Guild, Lake Street Studios, and the Kalamazoo Artistic Development Initiative of the Arts Council of Greater Kalamazoo, for generously supporting my work.

Special thanks to the many scholars and historians whose abundant knowledge made this project possible, especially those who generously answered my many questions—questions about Cold War ballet and the Bolshoi's 1962 tour (Anne Searcy); about Sergei Bondarchuk and *War and Peace* (Denise Youngblood); and about the stilyagi and the world in which they lived (Bradley Gorski). Many thanks to Jennifer Homans, whose dance scholarship fed my initial interest in ballet and provided many crucial insights and details about Balanchine's life and work. Many thanks to the Icon Museum and Study Center in Clinton, Massachusetts, for piquing my curiosity about the Soviet Union, and the Detroit Film Theatre at the Detroit Institute of Arts for showing Sergei Bondarchuk's *War and Peace* in June 2019 and thus transforming this novel. Thank you to Yiyun Li, whose *Tolstoy Together* project inspired me to finally pick up *War and Peace* during the lockdown, and to Richard Pevear and Larissa Volokhonsky, whose translation of Tolstoy's masterwork is one of the great joys of life. Thank you to the Joffrey Ballet, for bringing Balanchine to the Midwest, and of course to New York City Ballet, for all the magical performances and rehearsals I've been privileged to witness these many years.

A special shout-out to the librarians and staff of the Jerome Robbins Dance Division of the New York Public Library for the Performing Arts, who were so gracious with their time and expertise and provided me so many film clips, theater programs, photography collections, and other ephemera that helped bring this world to life. My deep gratitude to the librarians and staff of the public libraries of Brookline, Massachusetts; Loveland, Colorado; Royal Oak, Michigan; Carmel, Indiana; and Kalamazoo, Michigan, for helping me continue my research no matter where life took me.

I'm so grateful also to Dorothy Giovannini, for providing an accompanist's perspective; Brook Sadler, for giving me a glimpse inside the mind of a dancer; Dr. Steve Kollias, for answering my questions about spinal injuries (and introducing me to the horrifying term "burst fracture"); and Jennifer Ward at The Station: Dancewear, for fitting me for pointe shoes and helping me understand dancers' heroic feet. Thank you to the ballet studios across the country where I experienced the joy of ballet in my own body. Thank you also to Seyong Kim at the Western Michigan University Department of Dance for allowing me to observe advanced dance instruction up close. Any shred of accuracy in this novel I owe to the many individuals and organizations listed above; any errors are solely my own.

To Allison Hunter, my fearless, tireless agent, for believing so strongly in this book and for providing crucial encouragement and editorial genius just when I needed them. (I am going to spend the rest of my life thanking you.) Many thanks to Natalie Edwards, Allison Malecha, all at Trellis, and Jemima Forrester in the UK. Many thanks to Molly Gendell for originally acquiring this novel, to Nicole Angeloro for her insightful and wise edits (and being a truly delightful person to work with), and to Kate Nintzel, Rachel Berquist, Eliza Rosenberry, and all at Mariner Books for giving my work such a wonderful home. And huge thanks to my publicist, Beth Parker, for working so hard for this book.

Much gratitude to my family, siblings, in-laws, friends, and community for all their patience and support during these last few mysterious years of writing a novel.

Thank you to Ryn, Katja, Kathleen, Kylie, Mini, Hannah, MS, BJ, and MK, whose care for my physical and spiritual health made it possible for me to work (and to live). Thank you to Fr. Gregory for his kindness to our family and for introducing me to Vasily Grossman.

Thank you to Sufjan Stevens and the choreographer Justin Peck, whose marvelous collaborations introduced me to one of the great loves of my life, and to Sue Boyle at The Studio: A Dance Center for Adults in Brookline, Massachusetts, for helping fan this love into an obsession (and for letting me wear a tiara during class).

And to Bryce, the real love of my life, the kindest and most patient man on earth, the one who makes everything (that is, writing and life itself) joyful. This book is yours, too. Σε αγαπώ, κούκλο.

ABOUT

MARINER BOOKS

MARINER BOOKS traces its beginnings to 1832 when William Ticknor cofounded the Old Corner Bookstore in Boston, from which he would run the legendary firm Ticknor and Fields, publisher of Ralph Waldo Emerson, Harriet Beecher Stowe, Nathaniel Hawthorne, and Henry David Thoreau. Following Ticknor's death, Henry Oscar Houghton acquired Ticknor and Fields and, in 1880, formed Houghton Mifflin, which later merged with venerable Harcourt Publishing to form Houghton Mifflin Harcourt. HarperCollins purchased HMH's trade publishing business in 2021 and reestablished their storied lists and editorial team under the name Mariner Books.

Uniting the legacies of Houghton Mifflin, Harcourt Brace, and Ticknor and Fields, Mariner Books continues one of the great traditions in American bookselling. Our imprints have introduced an incomparable roster of enduring classics, including Hawthorne's *The Scarlet Letter,* Thoreau's *Walden,* Willa Cather's *O Pioneers!,* Virginia Woolf's *To the Lighthouse,* W.E.B. Du Bois's *Black Reconstruction,* J.R.R. Tolkien's *The Lord of the Rings,* Carson McCullers's *The Heart Is a Lonely Hunter,* Ann Petry's *The Narrows,* George Orwell's *Animal Farm* and *Nineteen Eighty-Four,* Rachel Carson's *Silent Spring,* Margaret Walker's *Jubilee,* Italo Calvino's *Invisible Cities,* Alice Walker's *The Color Purple,* Margaret Atwood's *The Handmaid's Tale,* Tim O'Brien's *The Things They Carried,* Philip Roth's *The Plot Against America,* Jhumpa Lahiri's *Interpreter of Maladies,* and many others. Today Mariner Books remains proudly committed to the craft of fine publishing established nearly two centuries ago at the Old Corner Bookstore.